Also by Anne Wyn Clark:

Whisper Cottage

Ann Wyn Clark was born and raised in the Midlands, where she continues to live with her husband plus a chinchilla with attitude. She has three now grown-up children and six grandchildren. Much of her formative existence was spent with her head in a book, and from an early age, she grew to relish the sheer escapism afforded by both reading and writing fiction.

She has a love of antiquity and a penchant for visiting old graveyards, often speculating on the demise of those inhumed beneath.

The Last House on the Cliff is her second novel.

You can follow her on Twitter @EAClarkAuthor

The
Last House
on the Cliff

ANNE WYN CLARK

avon.

Published by AVON
A division of HarperCollins*Publishers* Ltd
1 London Bridge Street
London SE1 9GF

www.harpercollins.co.uk

HarperCollins*Publishers*
1st Floor, Watermarque Building, Ringsend Road
Dublin 4, Ireland

A Paperback Original 2022
1

First published in Great Britain by HarperCollins*Publishers* 2022

A catalogue copy of this book is available from the British Library.

ISBN: 978-0-00-846000-6

Typeset in Sabon by Palimpsest Book Production Ltd, Falkirk, Stirlingshire
Printed and Bound in the UK using 100% Renewable Electricity
at CPI Group (UK) Ltd

For Nain and Taid

Cartref yw lle mae'r calon xx

'Be sure to live your life.
Because you are a long time dead.'

Scottish proverb

∞

CHAPTER ONE

The first time I ever laid eyes on a dead person, I was six years old. And then it was never meant to happen.

Growing up, I was never fazed by death. For me, it had been a natural part of my not entirely conventional upbringing. My summers, and indeed every school holiday until the age of twelve, were spent in Anglesey, in North Wales, in the care and company of my slightly eccentric but kind-hearted Auntie Gwyn. And Auntie Gwyn owned a funeral home.

It did not occur to me at the time that it was an unusual thing for my parents to pack me off at every opportunity. Thinking back now, there was no earthly reason, other than the fact they didn't want me around, for them to send me away as they did. It dawned on me later that I was something of a burden to them, my mum in particular; my presence an unfortunate inconvenience. To feel unwanted as a child has a lasting effect and it has definitely moulded the person I am today.

Ty Coed Pinwydd was an imposing grey stone building, built, as far as I'm aware, at some point during the eighteenth century. It stood alone and somewhat aloof, the last house on the narrow road to the cliffs, the periphery to the rear teetering dangerously close to the crag and the sheer drop to the rocks beneath. The approach was set back from the main road behind low wrought-iron gates, which opened from the centre of a sturdy stone wall. The property itself was surrounded on three sides by a large lawn flanked by a copse of tall pines, a natural wind-break to shield it from the exposed grassy headland that stretched into the distance. From when I was tiny, I remember being warned time and again never to venture from the confines of the garden, and moreover the screen of pine trees, concealing the precipitous cliffs beyond. Often, I would play in the enclosed walled area to the rear of the house, entered via an old ivy-covered wooden gate beneath an arch. It was tucked into the right-hand corner and I always liked to think of it as a secret garden, like the one in the children's book. There was a tool shed, and herbs and vegetables grew in neatly tended rows, providing much of the food served at mealtimes. From here, the sound of waves breaking on the rocks could be heard on a still day, but the swaying sea of foliage visible above the wall provided an effective barrier much of the time, and it was easy to forget about the cliffs that lay on the other side.

On a marble pedestal in the centre of the immaculate turf of the main garden, a fountain surrounded the statue of a small angel, its head bowed in prayer. The gravel drive led to a turning circle before the large oak front door, which was accessed through a glass-fronted and rather incongruous twentieth-century veranda, a ferocious lion's head holding the brass doorknocker between its gaping jaws. The fanlight above was etched with the name of the property in gold capitals.

'The Deceased' that Auntie Gwyn and her workforce referred to with such reverence – I did not realise initially that they were, in fact, people who were no longer in the land of the living – would arrive, concealed from prying eyes by the blacked-out windows of a private ambulance, and be whisked through to the back of the house and into the mysterious 'preparation room', the large handwritten sign on its sliding doors declaring it 'Strictly out of bounds to anyone below the age of sixteen', installed no doubt for my benefit. Here, I would learn in time, the dead were washed and dressed, and made as presentable as they could be under the circumstances, before being put into refrigerators until grieving relatives came to pay them one final, emotional visit in the little chapel of rest at the back of the property. Or there were those poor unfortunates without family or friends to mourn them that were despatched post-haste to the local chapel for a quiet and lonely send-off. Taking her role very seriously, Auntie Gwyn always made a point of attending such services and would later impress upon me the importance of treating everyone in death with the respect and compassion they deserved, regardless of social standing or how they had lived their lives.

'God is our judge, Lowri,' she had told me. 'And in the eyes of the Lord we are all equal. *Even* Mr William

3

Probert.' Her eyes widened and she raised a greying eyebrow to emphasise the point.

I had seen Mr Probert only twice that I could recall; once when he entered the local post office, where I had been buying stamps with Elis, bringing with him an overpowering waft of stale urine, and on another occasion when he had staggered in a loudly inebriated state past the front of the house when I had been playing in the garden. He had lived alone on the edge of the village, shunned for the most part by the community amidst rumours of drunken wife-beating (his long-suffering spouse had passed away over a decade earlier), and the theft over time of several sheep belonging to a local farmer. He had lived like a recluse for the last few years of his life, toothless and wild-eyed, his beard long and matted, his clothes as filthy as the language he used to see off unwanted callers to his home. Years later, I learned that, after suffering a fatal heart attack, he had lain undiscovered, surrounded by rubbish on his kitchen floor for almost three weeks, his poor starving dog having chewed off half of his arm.

It was the smell which piqued my curiosity. You'd have thought such a repugnant odour would have deterred me from investigating further, but no; that was me all over. A nosy little girl. Too nosy for my own good.

Atop the trolley in the hallway lay a zipped-up black bag. I had heard a kerfuffle some minutes earlier, as the men who drove the ambulance brought something over the threshold and stopped to chat with Auntie Gwyn at the door before departing noisily.

The bag contained an unidentifiable long, undulating

mound. I was en route to the kitchen, having padded down the stairs in my nightie, looking for a drink and trying not to alert the adults in the house to my presence, since I should have been fast asleep several hours earlier. We had only arrived that Friday evening, the start of the long summer break. My parents were staying overnight before returning home to the Midlands (without me, of course) the following day. I could hear the hum of conversation from the living room which led off the hall to the left, the kitchen straight ahead of me and down a short flight of worn stone steps. Here the hallway forked to a dark, uninviting passageway on the right, leading ultimately to the preparation room. I didn't generally venture beyond the kitchen, more because it felt several degrees colder in that part of the house than for any other reason. On a breezy day the wind would whistle and moan eerily through the passage, never failing to send a shudder through me.

My mum and dad were essentially good people, just not ideal parents. They were devoted to one another and, while they were never cruel, I always felt like an intruder in their home. I say 'their' because it didn't feel like mine. My dad was warmer towards me, but perhaps too placid and easy-going, and I suspect he would just have gone along with whatever Mum wanted in order to keep the peace.

I was fed and clothed, and wanted for nothing materially, but I craved affection and attention, and neither were things my mother seemed able to offer. Thinking back now that I have a child of my own, her attitude towards me, finding fault aside, was generally one of shocking indifference. When I was small the only thing we ever really did together without my dad was go to church. Looking back now, I feel quite bitter about it – it was like a great outward demonstration of good character on her part. She would sing the hymns with such gusto. The meaning of the words meant little to me at the time, but thinking back to the lyrics '*slow to chide and swift to bless*' of one, nothing could have been further from the truth where my mum was concerned. She seemed particularly fond of the commandment '*Honour thy father and thy mother*' – with the unspoken '*or else*' as an addendum.

Without fail, as soon as school broke up for the holidays, I would be driven over a hundred and fifty miles to stay with Auntie Gwyn in that huge, rambling old pile. I never questioned this arrangement; I had never known anything else.

The house's remote, lonely setting seemed somehow accentuated on a grey, cloudy day; the screams of gulls and rush of the waves beyond amplified. But even on a bright day, my abiding memory is of being plunged into varying degrees of gloom wherever I wandered: the vast hallway and landing were permanently cold and dark, their walls painted burgundy; the sprawling living room, with its huge stone fireplace, heavy brocade drapes and Chesterfield settee, a sombre bottle green. The kitchen was tucked away below ground level, with scant illumination from a small single pane of glass above the sink. Even the sash window in the bathroom was of obscure amber-coloured glass, washing everything in a peculiar orange-tinted light. With hindsight, perhaps it was the nature of Auntie Gwyn's occupation which had influenced the décor and feel of the house. Which, on reflection, was austere and forbidding. But I never really dwelled on it; to me as a child, it felt like home.

One room at the far end of the landing was kept permanently locked and its contents a mystery. Of course, a locked door was a source of fascination to me. I would imagine the treasures it must conceal, and often tried to lift the little metal cover that swung over the keyhole and peep through. Frustratingly, curtains hanging at the huge windows on the other side were kept closed, the darkness masking whatever secrets lay within. I had asked Auntie Gwyn more than once why the room wasn't used but, thinking back, she had been evasive. One day she told me that the floorboards were rotten, and until she was in a position to pay for their repair, she intended to keep it locked for everyone's safety.

'We don't want you or anyone else crashing through the ceiling now, do we? There isn't anything interesting in there anyway – just a few old sticks of furniture. Nothing for little girls to play with.'

It had once been a family home: my father, Aron, had been one of five children and his paternal grandparents also shared the house when he was a boy. But sadly, two of his older siblings had met their maker as children; his much younger brother, Dafydd, whom I remembered only vaguely, had emigrated to Canada a couple of years earlier.

Auntie Gwyn would sometimes take out the old photograph album, introducing me to a family who were now a distant memory, with fading black and white pictures of a slight, smiling boy of around ten with tousled red hair (I knew this as Auntie Gwyn would always pat my own head and sigh, saying mine was the same shade), and a serious-looking girl of a similar height, with a mass of long, unruly curls like my own. *Hogan bach o'r coed* – that's what my dad teasingly called me when I was small. *The little girl from the woods*. I liked to look at the photographs. Having no siblings, I wondered what it would be like to be part of a large family, for them to have been my big brother and sister. Particularly as Carys, the girl, looked a lot like an older version of me.

I learned that the two were twins and their destinies had been equally tragic. Sionyn, the boy, had been caught in a rip tide and drowned while swimming in the dark waters beneath the cliffs at Llanbadrig church, and Carys had succumbed just two years later to viral meningitis at the age of thirteen. It was a curious thought to me that they had never grown up. Auntie Gwyn spoke of them often, Sionyn particularly. He was a sensitive, caring child and loved animals. He had rescued a young chaffinch with a broken wing and nursed it back to health. The bird refused to leave him even when given the opportunity to fly away, and would perch on his shoulder as he sketched in his room, and on his bedpost as he slept. When he died, the little bird pined and followed soon afterwards. Sionyn's bereft parents had the finch stuffed and mounted on a twig beneath a glass dome, lined with black velvet. Auntie Gwyn would take it out of the cupboard to show me sometimes, and I would lift the glass and carefully stroke its tiny head. The thought of how heartbroken it must have been would make me cry.

Carys and Sionyn had been very close, and would often be seen playing together in the garden, throwing a ball, or playing hide and seek in the copse. They somehow became immortalised in my imagination, as though they must still have been on some other plane of existence within the house, frozen in eternal youth, watching the comings and goings from beyond the grave. I understood little about death, only that it was supposed to be something that happened to old people. It didn't really occur to me at the time how sad their loss must have made Auntie Gwyn and the rest of the family.

My father had no interest in the funeral business and left home at eighteen to pursue a career in the motor manufacturing industry, taking him to the Midlands. It was here that he had met my mother some two years later. With their parents and grandparents long gone, only Auntie Gwyn and her two assistants were now left to rattle around in a property that could easily house twenty people.

The business had been in the family for decades, started by my great-great-grandfather, or hen hen Taid. Originally, the dead would have been transported by a horse-drawn hearse, a large sepia photograph of which hung in the entrance hall, with my hen hen Taid looking suitably sombre, holding the reins of one of two black horses wearing blinkers and black plumed bridles.

When she first took over the business, Auntie Gwyn had invested in a private ambulance – a large van with blacked-out windows, used to collect the bodies of the newly deceased. But only in recent years had she traded in the ancient Austin Princess black hearse, which had been her grandfather's pride and joy, for a second-hand 1980s Daimler model. Now in her fifties, she had never married and had devoted her entire adult life to serving the community in their hour of need. Various employees came and went over the years, but the two constants had long been Elis and Awel, a local brother and sister and distant cousins on my Nain's side. Both in their forties, they 'lived in', residing in two large bedrooms on the second floor, and helping with all aspects of the business. I was a little intimidated by the strange and hostile Awel, her straight, dark hair and unnaturally pallid skin reminding me of a witch in a book I had read. My presence seemed to be a source of perpetual irritation to her, and the door to any room she occupied would close abruptly as I passed by – not that I would have wanted to enter when she was on the other side. Elis, on the other hand, was warm and friendly, and would try to make me laugh by pulling funny faces. He was a huge bear of a man with wavy brown hair and hands like shovels, profoundly deaf since childhood as a result of the same outbreak of meningitis that had taken Carys, and as his diction and intonation had become harder for most people to understand over time, communicated usually by signing – something Auntie Gwyn had made it her business to learn and was keen to impart to me.

'Not everyone is like us, Lowri,' she had once informed me. 'Always make the effort to learn someone else's language, whatever its form. We are not the be-all-and-end-all.' I didn't fully comprehend the '*be-all-and-end-all*' she spoke of, but got the gist of what she wanted to convey.

On the other side of the door, the adults were clearly oblivious to my presence. I could hear muffled voices, my dad breaking into his mother tongue as he always did when we had travelled west of the border. Everyone generally spoke English for the benefit of my mum and, while I understood the rudiments of the Welsh language, I wasn't fluent myself. I did wonder later if not teaching me had been a deliberate ploy, so the adults could discuss sensitive issues without worrying I was listening in.

The terrazzo floor of the hallway was cold beneath my bare feet. I stood for a moment staring at the mound on the trolley, which was at shoulder height to me. I *had* to know what it was. Gingerly, I stood on my toes and reached out, my hand trembling in anticipation, and unzipped the bag. The rancid potency of the smell released almost knocked me back. Stringy grey hair, yellow from years of exposure to tobacco smoke and lack of shampoo, trailed from a roughly bearded human head, its transparent, blueish skin stretched taut over a wizened face. The angular cheeks were lined with blackened veins, the lips dark and bloodless. I suddenly realised something was moving – no, *crawling* – from the corner of the mouth yawning through the beard: minute, creamy-coloured vermicelli. Maggots.

I let out an involuntary shriek. Bizarrely, now I think back, it was the sight of the teeming maggots rather than the rotting corpse which startled me more. The living room door flung wide and Auntie Gwyn rushed out to see what had happened. My parents stood in the doorway, casting each other knowing grimaces. I jumped back guiltily, thinking Auntie Gwyn might be angry, but calmly she re-zipped the bag and took me by the hand.

'And what might you be doing down here, young lady? We'd better get you back to your bed.'

The need for a drink completely forgotten, I nodded mutely as she took me by the hand and led me back upstairs. My parents had retreated silently into the living room, the door closing behind them. I looked back over my shoulder at the lump that had been Mr Probert. One or two maggots had fallen to the ground and were writhing on the black and white tiles next to the trolley.

'Mr Probert has gone to sleep forever,' Auntie Gwyn explained as she tucked me back into bed. 'He was a very old man and it was his time to go. We all have to leave this earth one day, some of us sooner than others.' She hesitated. 'The body we leave behind is of no use any more, and it starts to decay very quickly after our soul leaves. While we live, we're like a lump of fresh meat, if you want to think of it that way. Have you ever seen – or smelled – a piece of meat when it has started to turn bad?'

I thought for a moment, screwing up my face at the memory. 'Mummy found some bacon she'd forgotten at the back of the fridge that had started to turn green. It was horrible and really smelly.'

'Exactly. It had gone off. And to be blunt, that is basically what happens to a person once their heart stops beating. Very quickly, their body starts to rot. And that is why we must bury them. Then they can return to the soil, where they came from, and feed the worms, who clean all the bad meat away and enrich the earth, so that vegetables can grow and feed the people who are still living, until one day it is their turn to go to sleep. And so it goes on. The circle of life.'

This was a lot of information to digest. 'So, one day

12

I will go to sleep forever and then the worms will eat me?' I felt suddenly panic-stricken at the thought.

'Not until you are an old, old lady. And when people are really old, they get very tired, and they've had enough of life anyway. It's the nature of things.'

'But what about Sionyn and Carys? They weren't old.'

She sighed. 'They were just very unlucky. But their souls are in a better place now.'

'What does a soul look like? Where do they go? Has Mr Probert's soul gone to the same place?'

'A soul can't be seen by the human eye. It's what makes us who we are, and it's a wonderful thing that it's freed once our bodies are worn out and useless. But how we behave during our lives will help God decide where the soul ends up once it has left us. And that's why we must always try to do good in this world.'

She patted me gently on the head. 'You go to sleep now, *cariad*. These are all things that you don't have to worry about, not for years and years.' She hovered briefly in the doorway as though about to say something else but thinking better of it.

'*Nosdawch*.' The light went out and the door closed behind her, leaving me in total darkness. I wriggled down beneath the covers, my mind whirring with what she had told me. When I think back now, I'm surprised I didn't have nightmares about Mr William Probert and his invisible soul, and the fact that one day a similar fate was waiting for us all.

And if our luck ran out, it might be sooner rather than later.

CHAPTER TWO

Present Day, July 2014

Ruby sat in the bath staring at the wall in front of her, wet auburn curls trailing down her back, her skinny little knees drawn to her chest. She looked utterly wretched, her pale, freckled face etched with misery. I felt overcome with guilt. Yet another occasion when I'd had to try to let her down gently; one more missed school trip that I'd never be able to pay for.

My heart plummeted as I looked at the tarnished taps, an unsightly blue-green dribble staining the area beneath the overflow of the chipped cast-iron bathtub; the patch of mould spreading from one corner of the ceiling that no amount of bleach seemed able to deter. The whole house was falling to rack and ruin and I had neither the means nor the energy to tackle any of it. Only that morning, the washing machine had given up the ghost;

thankfully, my saviour Nina had come to the rescue and taken the drumful of sopping wet sheets and towels home to rinse and spin. Something else to add to the ever-increasing 'to-deal-with-urgently' list. All thanks to my ex, Darren, or *That Bastard* as Nina preferred to refer to him, who had left me high and dry with bills coming out of my ears and a bruised ego.

In spite of the fact he'd finally left for the arms of another woman, I was actually glad to see the back of him. Whoever she was, the unfortunate soul was more than welcome to him. I wondered if she had any inkling of what she was letting herself in for. As the saying goes, marry in haste, repent at leisure. And believe me, I was extremely repentant. I should have listened to my gut instinct when I'd recognised his worrying fondness for alcohol, and blasé attitude to spending money he didn't have. My money, for the most part. But I had been so lonely after I lost my beloved Jonah, and desperate for a father figure for Ruby. Initially, Darren had seemed so good with her; so attentive to me. I persuaded myself the drinking wasn't really an issue, nor the late-night poker games. But almost as soon as the ink had dried on the marriage certificate, his true colours started to seep through. Naïve, stupid me.

Right from the start, he began systematically chipping away at my bank balance and my self-esteem. He would pick fights over nothing at all, seemingly to give him a legitimate excuse to go out for the night. At first, I tried hard to please him, but it became apparent that my efforts were futile. Eventually I would heave a sigh of relief each time the door closed behind him as he left the house for yet another late-night drinking session with his mates. I could do nothing right; he criticised the way I was bringing Ruby up; the food I prepared; the way I dressed and how I wore my hair. Shortly after we were married, I was undressing for bed one night and he had stared in disgust at my stretchmarks, the almost inevitable legacy of a pregnancy with twins.

'Can't you do something about those?' he had asked, screwing up his face. He made me feel unattractive and pathetic. Jonah by contrast had always done his utmost to bolster me, and even though they were undeniably unsightly, especially immediately after I'd given birth, told me he loved them because they were a part of me and our shared history. I soon realised too that Darren had no interest in replacing Jonah where Ruby was concerned, when he was quick to correct an old neighbour of his mother's that we bumped into in the street one afternoon.

'Never thought you'd settle down with a kiddie,' the elderly man had remarked with a wry smile, indicating Ruby.

'Oh no – nothing to do with me,' he had quipped. 'I'm just Uncle Darren.' He and the man had laughed, but I didn't find it funny. Especially since he had pulled Ruby up with a caustic remark when she called him 'Daddy' one day.

'I'm not your daddy. Don't call me that again.'

She looked utterly crestfallen. This thoughtless rebuke of my sweet little daughter hurt and incensed me more than anything he could have said or done to me. At that moment I totally despised him.

I got used to sleeping alone again, whether because he had stayed out all night or had chosen to sleep on the sofa rather than lie next to me. I'd begun to prefer it that way. Sex had quickly become purely functional, never an expression of love as it had been with Jonah. I felt like an object, there to fulfil an urge and nothing more. The marriage lasted a miserable eighteen months but, in all honesty, the blinkers had dropped from my eyes within weeks. All he made me feel now was anger – and much of that directed at myself, for entering into something so blithely when in truth my heart wasn't entirely in it. Maybe I just got what I deserved. After the divorce, I wasted no time in reverting to my previous married name – Morris – and tried to put all thoughts of him out of my mind.

If nothing else, it had taught me a valuable life lesson. I would be extremely cautious before getting involved with anyone in future. Ruby was my priority, and I was determined to love her enough for two parents. She had been so young when Jonah died that she barely remembered him, which was bittersweet – she could never miss him in the way that I did, but it was so sad, too, that she didn't have memories of her wonderful father, and would never have his steady, calming influence in her life. My heart ached for her; that I couldn't afford to buy her nice things or give her a more presentable home. She never complained, but some days it got to me more than others, knowing that her schoolfriends had the latest toys and pretty new clothes. She was a kind, thoughtful child, and it seemed so unfair.

I perched on the cork-topped stool next to the bath,

17

trying desperately to think of something that might cheer her up.

'We could go to the park on Sunday – take a picnic, feed the ducks. The weather's going to be really warm, according to the forecast.'

She turned to look at me with her huge green eyes and squeezed out a smile. 'Okay, I guess so. Can we take Mickey?'

Mickey was Nina's four-year-old retriever-cross, the sweetest-natured dog you could ever meet, and Ruby adored him. We regularly took him for walks, an arrangement which was mutually beneficial, as I couldn't commit currently to having the dog Ruby so badly wanted, and Nina was often exhausted after a long day on her feet at the little café she ran with her partner, Ronnie.

'Of course. I'll bake some brownies and you can choose the sandwich fillings. No peanut butter, though,' I added, mock sternly. When Ruby was still tiny, we had discovered quite by chance that she had a severe nut allergy, which meant she could easily go into anaphylactic shock even from being close to someone eating nuts. I remembered Auntie Gwyn once telling me that Elis had a similar issue, although maybe not to the same extent as Ruby, but Awel was still always very careful about what she gave him to eat. He was a fairly distant relative, but I did wonder if it was something that ran in families. Ruby's allergy was a constant source of worry to me, although she took it very much in her stride and had learned the importance of carrying her Junior EpiPen. That she was sensible about it was at least one consolation.

She nodded and rolled her eyes. 'I know. I'll remember my EpiPen. For emergencies.'

'Good girl.' I gave her what I hoped was an encouraging smile. 'It'll be lovely.'

She seemed to brighten a little and my spirits lifted momentarily. But I knew that as she got older, she was unlikely to be mollified by excursions to the park and home-made treats. I desperately needed a cash injection, and a turn for the better in my luck.

'Come on, let's get you out of there – that water must be getting cold.'

She rose and clambered from the tub, dripping onto the mat. I wrapped her in a towel, rubbing her angular shoulders. She was seven years old, but small in stature and as light as a feather, her limbs pitifully thin and delicate. I felt a stab of emotion as I watched her and wondered what her twin sister would look like now; even though they had not been identical, how much she would resemble this little dot who was the centre of my universe.

It would hit me like that sometimes, completely out of the blue. Amber had been the bigger of the two: *my* two beautiful babies. Ironically, she had seemed so much more robust. One tiny fist would punch the air defiantly, while the other arm wrapped protectively around her sister as they lay side by side in the incubator, Ruby curled into a passive, timid ball. No one could have predicted what happened. A tight knot formed in my throat and I pushed down the thought. I couldn't allow myself the luxury of wallowing, for Ruby's sake more than my own. Some things were just too painful to contemplate. The smallest spark of misery could lead to an inferno of grief which would engulf me; I knew that all too well. The last thing she needed was for me to become maudlin and get dragged back down, and there was always that danger if I began to reminisce.

'Right then, miss. It's getting late and you've got school in the morning. Hot chocolate and bed.'

'Can I have a story? *Please?*' she pleaded, pulling on her pyjamas.

'Just a quick one, then. Go and dry your hair and I'll bring you up a drink in a minute.'

Once dried, Ruby's wild auburn tresses made her look like Merida, the girl in the Disney animation. She'd been highly delighted when Nina pointed this out. The fact she was so slight only accentuated the mass of her curls. Her bedroom had become something of a shrine to her flame-haired heroine. She sat upright beneath her *Brave* duvet cover, sipping the hot chocolate with eyes like saucers as I read a chapter from Roald Dahl's *The Witches*.

'Are there really witches, Mummy?' she asked anxiously as I closed the book, reaching to switch off the bedside lamp.

'No, sweetheart, only in stories. Nothing for you to worry about.'

Clutching Benjy, her much loved floppy-eared, and now slightly saggy, stuffed rabbit, she snuggled down under the quilt, a look of relief on her face. 'That's good. I don't think I'd want to meet one.'

An image of Awel flashed through my mind, and I wondered what Ruby might have made of her. In spite of my general boldness as a child, the woman had certainly unnerved me. If I were to sum her up with one adjective, it would be *forbidding*, in every possible sense of the word. I hadn't thought of her for many years and my memories of her were generally negative. She had tried to put the fear of God into me once, when she caught me innocently helping myself to a freshly baked biscuit left to cool on a rack in the kitchen.

'Did anyone say you could have that?' she snapped.

I felt heat rising in my cheeks. 'Well, no – I . . .'

'That's stealing, you know. Taking something without asking.' She narrowed her eyes. 'Remember what happened to the thief at Llandyfrydog church.'

The story was one I knew well: Elis had taken me to the old church in the village once and showed me an unusual-shaped standing stone in a neighbouring field. Legend had it that a man had robbed the church of its silver one night, carrying it in a sack slung over his shoulder. God had apparently wreaked vengeance upon the culprit and turned him to stone as he fled the scene. Whatever the truth of it, the strange monolith served as a solemn deterrent to anyone of similar inclination and the church remained confidently unlocked thereafter.

I felt my lip begin to wobble as I replaced the biscuit and mumbled an apology, then ran from the kitchen in tears. Awel had a knack of making me feel bad and far smaller than I actually was.

She would be well on the way to old age now, her brother Elis, too; and Auntie Gwyn must be in her mid-seventies. I felt guilty that I hadn't kept in touch with my aunt, but events had conspired against me in a way and, as the years passed, I had become entrenched in my own problems; my own grief. But I'd lost my address book in the move to Dunswarton, and no longer had her telephone number. Maybe I should write her a letter, just to let her know I hadn't forgotten her completely.

I never found out what had gone on all those years ago, why my parents had stopped sending me to stay in Llanbadrig. There had been a major falling-out, that much I knew; Auntie Gwyn didn't even come to my dad's funeral. But nothing had ever been explained to me. It was as though a whole chapter of my life was closed without ceremony, with no thought as to how it might affect either me or my aunt, who had been more like a mother to me than my own ever was. It was never discussed. But I had been twelve and resilient, approaching the turmoil of adolescence and the irresistible appeal of boys, and soon I had moved on. I hoped now that Auntie Gwyn had been able to do the same.

*

Shortly after Ruby started at the little primary school in Dunswarton, I had begun working in the school kitchens as a dinner lady. It was here that I first met Nina. She was almost twenty years my senior, her own three children having grown up and flown the nest, and was bubbly and friendly. We'd hit it off immediately. When her husband Ronnie was made redundant, they ploughed his pay-off into setting up a little café, which stood along the main high street. Word quickly got round about Nina's mouth-watering breakfasts and afternoon teas, and business was soon booming. I was so glad for them both – they were such a decent, kind couple. With my finances being so tight, Nina often gave me the odd shift at the café (and the occasional free meal for Ruby and myself), and had been a real rock since the breakdown of my marriage to Darren.

Although we had never been close, it hit me hard when my parents died within months of one another. Losing Jonah had left me reeling, and although they'd never been especially supportive in the past, they did rally to my aid to an extent when they realised how much I was struggling mentally. Ruby was only two, and I think it was more her welfare which concerned them, if the truth be told. She was the most endearing, affectionate little soul and I think that, despite their relative indifference to me, she had captured their hearts, even though they had only seen her on a few occasions. On their last visit, shortly before Jonah's fateful accident, I had gone to make tea and came back into the room to find that Ruby had clambered unselfconsciously onto my mum's lap. She was gazing up at her, singing 'Row, Row, Row Your Boat' sweetly with a huge smile on her face. My mum looked up and I could see tears in her eyes. I felt choked. I was so glad that she had bonded with Ruby, but doubted that she'd ever looked at me like that when I was small. I wondered whether she felt a stab of remorse, or sorrow, even. I was an adult now, and had my own life, but still wished we could have been closer. Sadly it was never to be.

Newly widowed, I had become almost reclusive; obsessively fearful that something terrible might happen to

Ruby, and then terrified that something could happen to me, leaving her with no one to care for her. I was a mess.

Maybe my parents felt duty-bound after the lack of care they had shown me over the years. They encouraged me to move to be nearer to them – not *too* close, however – and found me a little terraced house to rent in Dunswarton village, only a couple of miles from their home in Warwick. They actually organised a removal van and did pretty much everything: arranging our belongings, even stocking the fridge and store cupboard for when we moved in.

To my shame, I didn't have the energy to feel grateful. Looking back, even when I eventually started to venture out a bit more, I had still been so depressed and apathetic, I just allowed them to take control. I was swept along with everything, leaving behind the home that Jonah and I had set up together. In my right mind I'd have resisted, but frankly I was just glad to relinquish responsibility at the time. I think that without their input and support, I'd have ended up being sectioned.

But within twelve months of Ruby and I moving to Dunswarton, tragedy struck when my mother was killed by a speeding driver running the red light at a pedestrian crossing. The stress of losing her so suddenly clearly took its toll on my dad, who collapsed one morning with a fatal heart attack and followed her to the grave, a mere four months afterwards. I found myself living in an area where I knew no one, a young widow with no job and no support network. I was desperately lonely and vulnerable.

And gullible with a capital 'G'. Darren must have seen me coming.

CHAPTER THREE

I came down the stairs, my head dull from yet another disturbed night, tossing and turning with the worry of my financial situation and what the future held for Ruby and me. Just as I reached the bottom, the post appeared through the letterbox and slapped onto the mat. My heart sank, wondering what further bills would greet me. I bent down to pick up the pile, shuffling through them as I made my way to the kitchen, and dropped them onto the table. Ruby was still sleeping, so I made myself a strong coffee and sat down to go through the bundle of letters. There was the obligatory dross: take-away leaflets and notification of special offers in the local supermarket; a glossy invitation to purchase one of the huge four-bedroomed detached houses on the exclusive new development at the outskirts of the village (in my dreams); two final demands for the gas and electricity respectively, and a letter for Darren, marked *Private and Confidential*. I had no forwarding address for him and was tempted to drop it back into the post box marked *Return to Sender*, but thought I'd better text him to let him know, in case it was anything important. I dropped the junk mail into the bin and set aside the bills and Darren's mail to deal with later.

At the bottom of the pile was an official-looking envelope, addressing me by my maiden name. I examined it for a moment, then ripped it open. Inside was a letter typed onto heavy cream paper, headed with the address of a solicitors' firm in North Wales.

'*Dear Miss Owen,*' it began.

I hope this finds you well. I regret to inform you of the passing of your aunt, Gwyneth Hughes Owen. Please accept my sincerest condolences at this distressing time. My company is representing Miss Owen and I would like to invite you to the reading of her last will and testament, which will take place at our office in Bangor the day following her funeral, which is scheduled for Friday 25th July at 12 p.m., in Llanbadrig church. Should you have any questions regarding the arrangements, please do not hesitate to contact me via email or on the telephone number beneath the letterhead. If you could please also confirm whether you will be in attendance, I should be most grateful.

Yours sincerely,
Meredith Williams

Stunned, I turned the piece of paper over in my hands. It was watermarked, and certainly looked genuine. And why would anyone lie about such a thing? I assumed that, as I had been notified about the will, there must be some mention of my name in there, but even if there was a small bequest coming my way, it would be bittersweet.

The stinging memory of Auntie Gwyn's words to me came flooding back. I'd have been about eight. We had been sitting on the veranda at Ty Coed Pinwydd one Saturday, eating cake and drinking tea, looking out into the garden. It was a beautiful summer's afternoon, the sun streaming through the shimmering trees and the flowers in full bloom.

She had turned to me suddenly and said, 'One day this will all be yours, my lovely. When I'm dead and gone, and grass is growing on my grave.' And I began to cry, flinging my arms round her neck; telling her I didn't want the stupid old house, I only wanted her and she must never leave me.

I felt overcome with guilt now. Auntie Gwyn really *was* gone, and I would never see her again; never be able to explain why I hadn't been in touch, or that she had so often been in my thoughts; that those long weeks spent with her had been the bright spots of a largely miserable childhood. My head began to spin. Without stopping to think, I picked up my phone and tapped out an email to Meredith Williams, asking if he had contact details for Awel. I had to speak to her, to find out what had happened to Auntie Gwyn. And even if I was too late, I felt an irresistible pull to return to the place I had once thought of as home.

After taking Ruby to school, I dropped Darren a text to let him know about his letter, then went straight round to see Nina at the café. I badly needed to talk to someone about Auntie Gwyn, and she was the only real friend I had. And I desperately needed a hug, something Nina was very good at. I suspected she thought of me as a surrogate daughter and I was only too glad to take on the mantle.

I helped her serve breakfasts to a group of workmen who came in regularly. They were generally pleasant enough, if a little rowdy, but I was in no mood for banter. My woes must have been etched onto my face as I placed pots of tea onto their table.

'Cheer up, love, it might never happen,' one remarked. I emitted a strangled sob and rushed through to the kitchen to compose myself. I heard another of the men make some quip about how that was the effect his mate always had on women and there was a roar of laughter. Nina told them to pipe down and came out to see if I was okay. By now, I was a blubbing mess. She gently relieved me of the tray I was still clutching and told me to stay put until they had gone.

When there was a lull, we sat at a table near the till and had coffee. It all came pouring out: how kind Auntie Gwyn had always been, and how bad I felt for not trying harder to contact her again. Too little, too late. It was the story of my life.

'It's very sad, I know,' Nina agreed. 'But you mustn't torture yourself with what might have been. You couldn't help losing touch. I mean, from everything you've said, she didn't try to contact you either. You were only a kid. And Christ knows you've had an awful lot to cope with these last few years. Give yourself a break.'

She plucked a bunch of tissues from a box on the counter behind her as I sat sniffing, clasping my hand as she passed them to me. 'Who knows – with a bit of luck, she might have left you a nice little sum. When's the funeral?'

'A week this Thursday. At least Ruby will have broken up for the holidays – school finishes on Wednesday. I need to contact my auntie's cousin, Awel, to find out if it's okay for us to stay at the house.'

Nina raised an eyebrow. 'And why wouldn't it be?'

'Oh, Awel was always a bit – well, she was never too friendly towards me, shall we say. Her brother was lovely though.'

'Well, if the house belonged to your auntie, I think you've got every right to stay there. If I were you, I'd just tell that old misery you're coming. End of. I'll speak to her if you want.'

Nina's forthright manner usually made me laugh but my heart was heavy. 'No, I'll ring her. But thank you, I appreciate it. I need to find out about the trains and everything. I was thinking of travelling up on Thursday or Friday this week.'

'Well, what are you waiting for? No time like the present. Go and use the laptop in the back. Ronnie's out there – he'll log you on.'

She got up and squeezed me against her ample chest as I rose from the table. 'You're a good person, Lowri. Time you had a bit of good luck.'

I managed a smile and kissed her cheek. 'What would I do without you?'

'I'm going nowhere! Go on, get that ticket booked.'

*

The rail journey seemed interminable. Our compartment was packed to capacity, and we had to perch on our suitcases in the gangway, squeezing to the side each time someone passed by to use the toilet or make their way to the buffet car. When we disembarked to change at Crewe, a message from Darren pinged through on my phone. Three words: Just bin it. That was it. No forwarding address. Not a hint of gratitude for letting him know about his letter, nor any sort of enquiry about Ruby. He really was a complete shit.

We had just enough time to nip to the loo, and then it was back on the train for the next leg. The carriage was mercifully emptier this time and we were able to find a seat, but the skies were still as heavy and bleak as my mood. Rain had poured unrelentingly most of the way, lending everything from the factory chimneys of the Midlands to the majestic mountains beyond the border country an air of foreboding. Thankfully, Ruby was excited enough for most of the way just to watch through the rain-lashed window, asking questions from time to time about the house we would be staying in, and all about Awel and Elis. I hadn't thought about them for so long and wondered how they had changed over the years.

My last visit to Ty Coed Pinwydd had been overshadowed by the huge row between my dad and Auntie Gwyn, and our departure had been abrupt. Nobody ever explained to me what had happened, and I was baffled and heartbroken for months afterwards. A whole chapter of my life had been brought to a close without anyone consulting me on my views, as though my feelings on the matter were completely insignificant. I'd barely had time to gather my belongings, let alone say a proper goodbye to my aunt or Elis. At the time I'd been hurt and confused, and cried most of the way home. I remember feeling completely emotionally wrung out by the time we arrived back in the Midlands. I often wondered if the argument had been something to do with the young girl who had gone missing in Llanbadrig that summer. Everything seemed to have gone wrong after that, and it was the only thing I could think of that might have sparked the falling-out. Although why, I had no idea. Maybe there was some concern for my own welfare, being of a similar age. But I dared not ask, as my parents weren't the type of people who were open to discussing such things with a child. I wasn't exactly seen and not heard, but their decisions were always final. And that was that.

I thought now of Auntie Gwyn, of how kind she had always been to me; the long holidays which had felt so carefree compared with life under my parents' roof and the constant stifling disapproval which had seemed to emanate from my mother. It filled me with sadness. My whole existence seemed to be full of regrets for one reason or another, about things I had done; things that I *hadn't* done or said, but wished I had. My heart was heavy. It seemed the only good thing to come from any of my actions or decisions over the years was Ruby.

We arrived finally at Bangor station. Thankfully the rain

had abated, although the air was cool for the time of year and the sky still white with cloud. I managed to haul the luggage onto the platform and looked around for a taxi. Ruby spotted a waiting black cab across the forecourt, and between us we dragged the bags over to the exit where a sullen driver, apparently disgruntled to be dragged away from his newspaper, reluctantly loaded them into the back of his vehicle and asked our destination.

It was quite the strangest feeling. Over two decades had passed since I last saw the house, but as the taxi turned the corner and our journey was almost at an end, I felt my heart quicken. It was as though the years had fallen away and I was twelve years old once more, excited for the long summer that stretched ahead, the freedom to explore the house and garden; the feeling of actually belonging somewhere.

But the reality was that Auntie Gwyn would not be there to greet me this time. Elis was an old man now, and many of the people I had got to know from the village might have moved away, or even be no longer living. The circumstances were far from happy and I was apprehensive, my stomach churning with nerves.

'Look, Mummy.' Excitedly, Ruby sat forward in her seat as the cab drew to a halt outside the gates. 'We're here!'

I felt suddenly choked. Tears flooded my eyes as I stared up at the building where I had spent so much of my childhood. Ty Coed Pinwydd appeared smaller and less grand than I remembered. It had an air of sadness and neglect. Its windows looked dull, the once pristine paintwork peeling; weeds poked in abundance through the gravel driveway and unidentifiable green shoots sprouted from the rusty guttering. The lawns were parched and overgrown; the surrounding pines seemed taller and almost threatening, as though they were closing in and nature was attempting somehow to reclaim the space.

I remembered arriving here as a twelve-year-old, full of eager anticipation as ever, that last visit. Christmas and Easter holidays were always good, but the long, halcyon summers were best of all. Maybe the passing of time has coloured my judgement, but the skies in July and August always seemed clear and cloudless, the sun blazing down from dawn until dusk. I would spend carefree days in and around the house, sometimes helping Auntie Gwyn or Elis with one thing or another, at others left to my own devices to while away the hours exploring or stretching out on the lawn or the bench in the walled garden with a book. The sunsets would always spill a glorious, crimson puddle of light into the rooms at the front of the building, lending everything a warm, rosy glow despite the overall sobriety of the house.

That day we'd had to wait for just over an hour for Auntie Gwyn to return from conducting a funeral, and I remember watching impatiently from the little sitting room at the front of the house, eager to see the hearse turning into the driveway. As they pulled in, Elis at the wheel and my aunt in the passenger seat, I had rushed out to greet them, relieved to be returned to my aunt's care and to see the back of my parents for the next few weeks.

I was just a child: maybe that's why I was so accepting of the nature of Auntie Gwyn's business; that in spite of everything, I never considered Ty Coed Pinwydd a dour or sombre place. For me it had always been associated with love and security and freedom. Until the shocking disappearance of a young local girl seemed to change everything in an instant, and nothing had ever been the same again.

*

'That'll be twenty, then.' I'd been so deep in thought that the driver's gruff voice startled me. He was holding the passenger door open, his callused palm outstretched impatiently.

'Sorry. I was miles away.'

I felt in my pocket for a tissue to dab my eyes, then rooted through my handbag for my purse.

'*Diolch yn fawr.*' I handed over a twenty-pound note. The man looked unimpressed, so I delved deeper and found him a handful of loose change. 'Sorry, I haven't got a lot of cash on me.'

Mumbling a begrudging acknowledgement of the payment, he deposited our bags on the drive unceremoniously and climbed back into the car, disappearing swiftly back down the road. We were left staring up at the house. The early evening air was chilly, but the sun had managed to break through the cloud and was visible through the trees, its dwindling rays casting long shadows over the grey stone walls. I breathed in the air; the familiar smell of pine and ferns and damp soil brought long-buried memories of my childhood flooding back. The sea was so close I could already taste the salt on my lips. I caught Ruby by the hand and crouched down to her level, pointing sternly at the copse encompassing the lawn.

34

'Listen to me now, you must *never* go through those trees.' She looked at me, her eyes wide, and nodded mutely.

'We're very close to the cliffs here and it's extremely dangerous.' The thought of what lay beyond made my heart turn over. 'I can't stress it enough. Do you understand?'

I used my most serious voice and was suddenly catapulted back in time to when Auntie Gwyn had told me the very same thing, so many times. I felt an ache deep inside, a yearning for what life had been like here all those years ago. I released her hand and straightened, swallowing the lump which had surfaced in my throat once more.

A sudden movement drew my eyes to an upstairs window, but who or whatever had made it quickly withdrew from sight.

'Well, miss, we'd better let them know we've arrived.' I heaved the large suitcase across the turning circle and opened the glass door into the veranda, then returned for the two holdalls. Ruby was still standing gaping up at the window.

'There was a lady looking down. She waved at me.'

'Oh, that's probably Awel. She'll be expecting us.'

An A4 piece of card had been pinned to the front door, typewritten in large, bold font: *CLOSED FOR BUSINESS UNTIL FURTHER NOTICE OWING TO FAMILY BEREAVEMENT*. Before I could knock, the huge door creaked open, its rusting hinges in dire need of oil. Awel stood before us, her once dark hair now steel grey, but still as thick and long as ever. Even now,

I found her demeanour intimidating. She forced a smile, which looked as if it was in danger of cracking her face, the lines that the years had imparted creasing into deep grooves around her eyes and lips. I remembered seeing her once coming out of the bathroom without her false teeth – she wore a plate at the front of her mouth – and it had rather shocked me. She had glared and asked me what the hell I was looking at. Auntie Gwyn later explained that it was a sensitive issue with her and I should never pass comment – something I would never have contemplated, anyway.

'Hello, Awel.' I was unsure how to greet her, but there was no hug forthcoming on her part and I felt disinclined to make the first move. I stood rooted to the spot, the air between us hanging awkwardly; a strange stalemate. When Meredith Williams, the solicitor, had forwarded Awel's telephone number, our subsequent conversation had been brief and her tone brittle, but I had hoped she might be a little friendlier when we met again in person.

'So, you're here at last. Better come in, then.'

It wasn't exactly a welcome. She held the door wide and stepped back.

'Ruby, come and say hello.'

Shyly, Ruby ventured forward and stood in my shadow. 'Hello,' she almost whispered.

'You must be Ruby. Your mother mentioned you over the phone. Hello Ruby, my name is Awel.' She extended a mottled hand, which Ruby shook tentatively.

Awel's expression seemed to soften a little. Maybe age had rounded off some of her sharper edges.

'I'll get Elis to come and help with the bags.' She

seemed to be looking me up and down, a little oddly. I was suddenly self-conscious of my scuffed shoes and the faded khaki combat jacket I'd picked up in a charity shop. My wardrobe hadn't been high on my list of priorities for some time.

'How was your journey?'

'Fine, thanks. The second train was fairly empty at least and we only had the one change. Glad to have finally arrived, though. It's been a long day.'

I lifted the huge case into the hall and looked around. The familiar smell of woodsmoke and beeswax that had always filled the air now had an undercurrent of mildew. The wallpaper was peeling and everything looked shabbier than I remembered. Above our heads, trembling cobwebs trailed along the coving and radiated from the tarnished brass lantern in the centre of the ceiling like Halloween decorations. The grandfather clock suddenly chimed in the hour, making Ruby jump.

From the gloom at the far end of the hall, the bulk of a tall man rose from the steps to the kitchen. Elis, hair peppered with grey, his powerful shoulders curved with the passing of time, lumbered towards us. Not for the first time that day, I struggled to contain my emotions. Hot tears spilled down my cheeks at the sight of the lovable giant. He grinned broadly, his tanned leathery face crinkling at the corners of his cobalt-blue eyes. He held out both enormous hands to me and shook my own with enthusiasm, then did the same to a bewildered Ruby. Embarrassed, I brushed my face with the back of my sleeve, and signed *Hello, how are you?* He grimaced, responding, *Getting old.* I hit back, *Don't be daft.*

'What did that mean, Mummy?' asked Ruby, looking from Elis back to me in fascination.

'Elis says he's getting old, sweetheart. We'll soon teach you to sign – it's fun.'

Ruby copied the *Hello* she'd seen us exchange, and Elis nodded, raising a thumb to signal his approval. He gestured to the bags and Awel signed to him to take them upstairs.

'Come to the kitchen, the kettle's not long boiled.'

We followed her down the passageway, Ruby clutching my hand, her eyes wide as she took in our surroundings. As we reached the kitchen doorway, I paused, knowing that Auntie Gwyn was lying in repose in the cold room a short distance down the dark corridor. I knew I would have to see her, but the thought filled my stomach with a hollow dread. Somehow, until that point there was still the possibility that there had been some terrible mistake: that she would breeze in as she always did, greet me with her effusive hug, wrapping me in those soft, kindly arms, smelling of talcum powder and lavender. Strange how the loss of just one presence could leave a house feeling so utterly desolate. I dug my nails into my palms and fought to remain composed.

'Mummy?' Ruby studied my face, her green eyes concerned.

'It's all right, sweetheart. I was just remembering something, that's all. It's been a long time . . . Come on, let's go and have a cup of tea.'

Although dingy, the kitchen was warm from the heat of the range, the only room in the house that didn't have a permanent chill in the air. As it always had, freshly washed laundry draped from an old-fashioned wooden airer suspended from the ceiling by a pulley. Almost instantly the huge copper kettle began to whistle, filling the air with steam as Awel heaved it from a trivet back onto the hob. I felt a pang as I saw the empty armchair beside the stove where Auntie Gwyn would always doze after supper, brown velvet covers threadbare over its sagging innards. We sat down at the old, heavy wooden table, disturbing a dainty tortoiseshell cat who was curled up on a battered fluff-coated cushion on one of the chairs. Arching her back, she rose to observe us for a moment, yawned, then stretched out languorously, closing her eyes once more.

'That's Pwtyn,' remarked Awel. 'She's missing your auntie, I think. Hardly been out of the house these last few days.' She sounded wistful and I realised that she too must be missing Auntie Gwyn a great deal. I felt suddenly guilty.

'What happened to her, Awel?' I ventured.

It felt almost unnatural talking to the woman. I couldn't remember a time when we'd actually had a proper conversation. Although I had intended to find out more about the cause of death when speaking to Awel on the phone, her hostile tone hadn't invited further questions. I had been given no details as to the nature of Auntie Gwyn's demise and there had been no one else to ask. She had been in poor health for some years, that much I knew. But how she had actually died hadn't been properly explained.

Awel sighed. She placed the teapot on a wooden trivet on the table, covering it with the old striped cosy knitted by my Nain.

'She'd been bad for months, if the truth be told. Her blood pressure was up and she'd been getting terrible headaches. But then she had a dizzy spell and took a bad fall; broke her leg. You know how she was, always on the go. I kept telling her she should slow down, but she never took any bloody notice of me. Her cholesterol was high anyway, but they think a clot developed as she wasn't mobile. It was very sudden.'

She fixed me with a cold, hard stare. 'You broke her heart, you know.'

Ruby's eyes widened. An unpleasant tight band prickled across my forehead and I felt as though I had been slapped. What could I say – I deserved it.

'I'm sorry. I feel so bad. Not that it's any excuse not to keep in touch, but a hell of a lot has happened to me these past few years. I suppose I've just been too wrapped up in what's been going on in my own life.'

'Yes, well we all have our problems, don't we?' Her manner was unapologetically harsh. 'It wouldn't have hurt you to drop her a line, or pick up the phone once in a while. But what's done is done, and there's nothing you can do about it now.'

Ruby and I sat in uncomfortable silence as, with gritted teeth, Awel buttered scones and plonked china cups and plates in front of us. I felt wretched.

Elis reappeared and joined us at the table. Sensing the atmosphere, he signed, *What's wrong?* as Awel, her face still stony, continued to busy herself and went to look for jam in the pantry.

She's angry with me, I responded. *But I'm angry with myself, too.*

He rolled his eyes and reached out, squeezing my hand reassuringly. *She'll come round. And you mustn't feel bad. Your auntie knew things had been hard for you. Your dad wrote and told her.*

This news surprised me. I was under the impression that all communication between them had long ceased. It had always made me sad, knowing how close they once were. I thought back to the last Christmas I had spent in Ty Coed Pinwydd and how well they had got on. School had broken up quite late for the festive period, on the 21st of December, and my mum was unwell with a virus. My dad seemed doubtful that I'd be able to go to Llanbadrig, but thankfully Mum had been most insistent that he take me. The plan was that he'd stay over for one night and then return to her the following day. I was hugely relieved, as I'd been looking forward to seeing Elis and Auntie Gwyn, and knew that a Christmas spent at home would have been dull and miserable.

We set off the day before Christmas Eve, mid-morning. As the journey progressed, snow began to fall unexpectedly. The traffic was moving painfully slowly, and the nearer we got to the Welsh border, the worse it became. But Dad was in good spirits. Without my mum, the mood seemed lighter and we'd chatted throughout the journey about this and that, stopping at a service station for hot drinks and cake to keep us going. He seemed different somehow; almost jovial.

It took nearly five hours to arrive in Llanbadrig. Snow gusted through the hallway as we entered the house, and Auntie Gwyn greeted us ebulliently, ushering us into the kitchen, where she plied us with hot leek and potato soup (or *cawl*, as she always called it) and crusty bread, beside the glowing heat of the range. That night I watched in wonder from my bedroom window as huge, feather-like flakes continued to fall relentlessly from the strangely pale sky, blanketing everything around the house and beyond in crystal white. By the following morning, we were snowed in at Ty Coed Pinwydd: something almost unheard of in Anglesey – being on an island, we rarely had heavy snow. But in the middle of nowhere as we were, there was no gritting of the roads or snowploughs, and conditions were treacherous. The wind howled through the house, battering the windows, and snow whorled across the lawn. My dad had been anxious to get home, but resigned himself to the fact he couldn't attempt the return journey until it was safe to do so. There was a lengthy phone conversation explaining his predicament to my mum, who was clearly not pleased but had little choice other than to accept the situation.

And so he spent Christmas Day with us all – Auntie Gwyn, Awel, Elis and me. While Auntie Gwyn and Awel prepared lunch, Elis and I built a snowman on the lawn and my dad actually came out to help, bringing an old scarf and hat that had belonged to my Taid, to add the finishing touch. It was the most relaxed I ever remember seeing him. We enjoyed Christmas dinner together in the kitchen and played card games in the sitting room, then all sat in front of the old TV to watch *Home Alone* for the umpteenth time, Auntie Gwyn and Elis falling asleep in their respective armchairs, and my dad getting merrier by the minute, cracking jokes about the appalling quality of the picture and helping himself to more whisky and mince pies. I remember him winking and smiling at me across the room and it gave me a lovely warm feeling, as though we had actually connected properly for once. It was the only time, too, I remember seeing Awel in a rather more human light as she laughed at something he said. I'd never really observed them in conversation before and they seemed to get along well, which surprised me. Whenever my mum had been with us, things always seemed strained, and Awel generally made herself scarce.

A few months after my dad died, I was going through his belongings and found a battered card I'd made for him at school when I was about six. *'To Daddy, Happy Father's Day, Lots of love from Lowri xxx'* and my attempt at a picture of him with wild, curly black hair and a big red smile. I was surprised and touched to find that he'd kept it. He hadn't been the best father, but definitely wasn't the worst. I think he'd have been a much more sympathetic parent with an alternative life partner, and felt sad that things could have been far better between us in different circumstances. There was so much that I wanted to understand about what I could perhaps have done differently; why I had always felt unwanted by my mother. What had really gone awry between him and Auntie Gwyn.

And now it was too late to ask either of them.

*

'Why is Awel so cross, Mummy?' Ruby asked anxiously, as we went up to unpack after an awkward half-hour of stilted conversation. We had been allocated a room

43

with twin beds at the side of the house overlooking the garden, the sweet angel in the fountain now a vaguely sinister silhouette against the darkening sky. The air in the bedroom was musty and stale and, despite the cool temperature, I released the catch and lifted the stiff sash window, desperate to let in some air. I stuck out my head and filled my lungs gratefully. A small bat darted past, startling me.

I turned to my daughter. 'Awel's just upset, that's all. She's missing Auntie Gwyn and lashing out at me because I hadn't been in touch with her for such a long time. People can be funny and touchy when they've lost someone they love. She'll be all right in a day or two, I'm sure. Don't you worry about it.'

I wasn't convinced myself, however, that Awel's mood would improve. I had long suspected that she had an inexplicable deep-rooted dislike of me, and my failure to contact Auntie Gwyn had only justified – and apparently intensified – her sentiments. All I could do was try to make amends; quite how, I didn't know. But Ruby needn't be burdened with any of this.

Her little face clouded over. 'I don't like it here. When can we go home?'

I cupped her chin in my hands and gave her my best shot at an encouraging grin.

'We've only just got here! Don't mind Awel – she's a bit cranky, I know, but she's got a lot to think about at the moment. Look, we'll have an early night after supper and go for a nice walk tomorrow. Hopefully the weather will have picked up a bit. I'll show you around. There's lots to see, and the beach isn't far at all. It's been a long day. You'll feel better after a good night's sleep.' I sat on one of the beds and bounced a little. 'See, the mattress is nice and comfy at least!'

She looked dubious but attempted a small smile. 'O-kay.' She eked out the word exaggeratedly, pausing for a moment. 'At least Elis is nice. You can teach me some signs so I can talk to him properly.'

'There you go. You'll learn a new skill in no time. Something to show your friends when we get home.'

Ruby plonked down next to me on the bed briefly, then got up again and gave an impromptu twirl. She stopped suddenly, looking thoughtful. 'Oh – where's that other lady? We didn't see her.'

'Which other lady?'

'You know – the one who waved at me from the window.'

'It must have been Awel. There isn't anyone else here.'

'But she looked, well, different from Awel.'

An unpleasantly cold sensation passed through me. 'What did she look like, this lady?'

She considered for a moment. 'I couldn't see her properly. She was wearing a scarf or something on her head.'

'Ah – there you go. She must have taken it off before she answered the door.'

Ruby shrugged. 'Maybe.'

That had to be it. This was the most likely explanation. There were only a couple of regular staff that worked alongside Awel and Elis, and they had been given leave. No one else lived in, not now Auntie Gwyn was gone. The thought of the funeral that faced us entered my head suddenly and once more my stomach churned. I felt bile hit the back of my throat. The prospect of it filled me with dread.

I texted Nina to let her know we had arrived safely.

Hope all goes well, she responded. Keep us posted with how ur getting on x

I smiled to myself. I knew Nina was itching to know if I had been left anything in the will. Judging by the state of the house, it might just be more trouble than it was worth.

I replied, Will do. Speak soon x

I began to put away our belongings, hanging my old black Next trouser suit and Ruby's only smart navy-blue dress, bought in the sale from TK Maxx, in the ancient wardrobe. I winced, realising we would now probably reek of mothballs, of which Auntie Gwyn had been such a proponent.

I folded Ruby's pyjamas and placed them on the bed nearest the door, along with Benjy the rabbit, who had been her bedtime companion ever since she was tiny. Ruby perched on the stool in front of the dark kidney-shaped dressing table, casting a critical eye over the three reflections of herself glaring back, and frowned even more. She examined the various dusty ornaments and the old tortoiseshell brush-and-comb set, still tangled with grey hair which had probably belonged to Auntie Gwyn. She sniffed at it tentatively and pulled a face.

'Everything is really old. And it smells funny. *And* it's cold. I wish we weren't staying here.'

I sighed, pulling down the sash once more. The odour was the lesser of the two evils: neither of us needed to catch a chill, Ruby least of all. Replacing the hairbrush,

46

she stood to look out into the garden, cupping her hands against the pane like binoculars. She gave a sudden gasp and stepped back sharply, her eyes wide with fright. 'There's someone on the grass looking up at me, Mummy.'

Catching my breath, I darted over to the window, shielding my eyes from the reflection in the glass. I shrank back in alarm at the sight of a dark, hooded figure gliding swiftly across the lawn. My heart racing, I watched from behind the curtain as it paused and looked back briefly at the house, its featureless face tilted upwards, before melting into the trees. It was only a fleeting glimpse and I couldn't be sure if it was male or female.

Unnerved, I closed the curtains hurriedly.

'I expect it was just one of the kids from the village messing about,' I told her, trying to keep my voice steady. I remembered how sometimes they would dare one another to come up to the house after dark and try to peer in through the windows, half-hoping for, half-dreading the ghoulish sight of a corpse. Of course, they never did. Auntie Gwyn would usually see them off with a flea in their ear, or send Elis out to do the same.

But I knew in my heart that there had been no morbidly curious children prowling outside that evening. I felt a prickle of foreboding as I remembered the mysterious disappearance of little Beca Bennion all those years ago, and felt compelled to clutch Ruby to me in a protective hug.

Because whatever the gender, our intruder was an adult. And it had been watching my daughter.

CHAPTER FOUR

Not wanting to worry Ruby, I decided to wait until she was safely in bed before mentioning the prowler in the trees to anyone. It had left me feeling uneasy and I was finding it hard to settle. But as we sat round the kitchen table, I began to relax a little.

Maybe Elis had given Awel a talking-to, as thankfully she was more civil over supper. She had made a hearty root vegetable stew, which was welcomely warming, since the evening air felt chilly and damp after the earlier showers. Ruby tucked in with gusto and Elis laughed, gesturing that she had a healthy appetite for one so small. After a decent portion of sticky toffee pudding and cream, she was pink in the cheeks and ready for bed.

Elis found extra blankets and I took Ruby back to our room and tucked her up for the night with Benjy. She was too tired to have a wash and I didn't want to take her into the cold bathroom, anyway – I was hoping to find a heater the next day to warm it through so that she didn't finish up with a chest infection, or worse. Her premature birth had left her susceptible to bronchitis, which always made her quite ill. I'd forgotten how cold the house could get – or maybe I just hadn't noticed it in the same way as a child.

Being an imaginative little girl, Ruby had always been frightened of the dark. She loved to listen to stories and watch films, but even things most people would consider innocuous seemed to trigger anxiety in her. The 'Child Catcher' in *Chitty Chitty Bang Bang* had put the fear of God into her, and she would check under her bed every night, terrified of someone waiting to snatch her. At home, she would ask me to wait outside the bathroom at night sometimes and always peeped behind the shower curtain to make sure nothing (or no one) nasty was lurking in the bath.

Now we were in a strange house, all these unfounded fears were amplified. Even with the door ajar and the landing light seeping into the room, she was anxious that I stayed with her, so I sat holding her hand until she drifted off. Eventually confident that she was unlikely to stir, I crept out of the bedroom and back downstairs. I was still worrying about the figure we had seen in the garden, and took a cursory look across the lawn from the window in the small sitting room at the front of the house. I could see very little through the darkness, but all seemed quiet – almost *too* quiet.

Even though we lived in a village, Dunswarton was a fairly lively place; I was used to the constant background noise of passing cars and the steady footfall of chattering people heading to the local shops or pub as they ambled past our house. I found it comforting, particularly as I was on my own with Ruby.

The silence here was an unsettling reminder of how isolated we really were.

Satisfied that the front door was securely locked and the chain on, I made my way back to the kitchen, where Awel had cleared the table and was already laying it for breakfast.

'Is there anything I can do to help?' I offered. 'You look worn out.'

She lifted her face to look at me and I saw that her eyes were swollen and raw. A lump rose in my throat.

'I need to be busy, keep my mind occupied. If I sit, I just think – and it's no good.'

She cleared her throat. Her tone was earnest, with no evidence of the earlier animosity. She just sounded desperately sad. 'This has all been a terrible shock, you know – for me and for Elis, too. I keep expecting to see her sitting there –' she nodded towards the human-shaped dent moulded into the seat-pad of the old armchair. 'Ironic, really. We deal with death here all the time, and I just get on with it; always have. But when it's someone you've known all your life . . .' She shook her head miserably and dropped her gaze. 'I can't believe she's gone forever. It's just too . . . final.'

Her voice cracked with sudden emotion. I lifted a hand to reach out to her, but dropped it just as quickly. I felt awkward – and useless.

It was so strange too, seeing Awel displaying such human sentiment. To me as a child, she had always seemed incredibly frosty, unfeeling. Clearly there *was* a heart beating in there, after all. I was finding it hard to equate this softer side with the person I had always believed her to be.

Maybe this was an opportune moment for a distraction. 'I saw someone outside earlier – looking up at the house. It's put the wind up me a bit.'

Awel continued to lay out the cutlery as if I hadn't spoken.

'Any idea who it could've been?'

She sighed wearily. 'There's a new campsite opened down the road – we often get people from there walking through the woods these days. I'm sure some of them think they can trample where they like when they're on holiday. They're not doing any real harm, I suppose.'

'Oh.' I wasn't completely reassured, but it could be one explanation.

'A bit annoying maybe, but nothing to concern yourself about.'

I nodded. There had been another purpose in my coming back downstairs and, although the timing may not have been ideal, I'd been building up to the request. 'Can I . . . is it possible to see her?'

Awel's jaw tensed visibly. She set the sugar bowl on the table and raised her eyes to meet mine, her expression grave.

'Are you sure you want to? She's not quite ready yet.'

'Yes. It's something I need to do, I think.'

She inclined her head silently and, with the rolling gait of one stiff with arthritis, led the way jadedly up the steps and down the dimly lit corridor. Even in the height of summer, there was an appropriately unearthly chill in the passageway, and it had been an unseasonably cool day. I shivered, wrapping my arms across my chest as we approached the double doors leading into the preparation room. At once the smell hit me: so familiar and yet indefinable. Chemical, with a sickly-sweet undertone.

The smell of death.

I stood tentatively just inside the doorway as Awel wheeled a hydraulic trolley across the floor and carefully slid one of the trays from the mortuary refrigerator onto it. My heart hammering and trembling with nerves, I approached the trolley. I don't know why I felt so apprehensive; maybe it was the stark reality of being confronted with my aunt after so many years but in a completely altered state. I knew I was being ridiculous, but couldn't help myself.

Awel peeled back the dark green sheet and I caught my breath, grabbing the metal side of the trolley to steady myself. Auntie Gwyn's hair had been combed neatly to one side; her face was pale and smooth as alabaster, her closed lips unsmiling. I could find no remnant of the person she had been betrayed in that blank expression. It was like looking at a marionette. I knew now I would never see those kindly eyes again, tightly closed as they were. There was no evidence of the caps beneath their lids, though I knew they were there. I had witnessed enough bodies prepared in the past to know the process.

Awel usually did most of the embalming and laying out of the deceased, although Auntie Gwyn would step in to lend a hand from time to time. One day, when I was about ten, she had been preparing an elderly lady from Carreglefn who had been brought in a couple of days beforehand. I had never been squeamish, and after I had begged her repeatedly to let me see how things were done, she had eventually given in and shown me how a running stitch inserted with a long, curved needle, under the top lip and through the nose and back again, would keep the mouth from gaping open.

'The eyes won't close properly after death without a little help; the jaw, too,' she had explained as deftly she slipped spiked plastic caps beneath the old woman's eyelids. 'People want to see their loved ones looking peaceful, as though they're sleeping, not with the pain of their passing etched on their faces. No one wants to remember someone looking like that.'

I had watched in fascination. 'So does it hurt when people die?'

'Not always, no. But sometimes it can – or at least, the moment before their death. And however anyone has died, whatever thoughts and feelings that made them the person they were have left them, and their face changes, loses its natural expression. We want them to look as much like they did in life as possible.'

I thought of her words now, remembering the warmth of the smile that usually lifted her soft, rounded cheeks, the way her eyes had twinkled with mischief. I wondered suddenly whether her own passing had been painless, and something twisted in my gut. Bending forward, I planted a kiss on her forehead. It felt cold and firm beneath my lips.

I pulled the sheet back over her face, tears pricking my eyes.

'*Nosdawch*, Auntie Gwyn,' I whispered.

*

Despite, or perhaps because of, the raw emotion churning inside me, I quickly fell into a deep sleep. My dreams were filled with Auntie Gwyn, my own small hand wrapped in hers as we had both been years ago, then the image of her lifeless form lying on the table in the preparation room. I don't know whether it was the sight of her bloodshot eyes snapping open and turning to stare at me reproachfully, or the sudden sharp cry from Ruby, which shocked me into wakefulness.

'*Ow!* Stop it!'

Disorientated, my heart pounding, I reached for the bedside lamp on the small table beside me, cursing as I knocked over the glass of water I'd brought up to bed. A low shadow seemed to be moving along the opposite wall. It may have been that my eyes were still adjusting to the gloom. Rubbing them with closed fists, I sat up. I couldn't be sure, but thought I heard the door to the room click slowly shut.

I was fully awake now, rigid with fear.

'Ruby? What's the matter?'

'Why were you brushing my hair? You woke me up.'

'I wasn't – I was fast asleep. You must have been dreaming.' My eyes darted nervously round the room. I forced myself out of my own bed and went to sit at the edge of Ruby's, every one of my senses on high alert. She had hauled herself up to a sitting position, the blankets yanked past her chin.

'You pulled my hair – it hurt,' she said accusingly, her lower lip trembling with indignation.

'I didn't, sweetheart. Maybe it caught on something and it felt like it was being brushed. You *were* fast asleep, after all.' From the corner of my eye, I saw what at first glance appeared to be a spider on the edge of Ruby's bed. As I went to brush it away with my quivering hand, I realised that a knotted clump of her red locks lay atop the fringed cream counterpane. My stomach turned over. Following my gaze, Ruby's eyes widened in alarm.

'Look! There's a great big ball of it.'

'Aww, it's nothing to worry about. It probably got tangled with the edge of the bedspread and, when you turned over, it tugged at it and some came out.' I wasn't convinced by my own explanation, but could think of nothing else that might sound plausible. I was conscious that I needed to present a calm veneer, despite my mounting anxiety.

Ruby looked a little dubious but seemed reluctantly to accept what I had told her, and flopped back down. I stroked her hair and hummed softly to her, the tune to 'Suo Gân', an old Welsh lullaby that Auntie Gwyn would sing to me as a child. This was something which had never failed to soothe her since she was tiny. Soon she was breathing deeply and sleeping once more. I crept back across the threadbare rug and into bed, easing myself beneath the covers. But by now I was beyond sleep, my eyes having grown accustomed to the meagre level of light cast by the lamp's low wattage bulb. I hardly dared close them. I sat, propped against my pillows, gaze fixed on the door, convinced it would reopen at any moment. Every creak and groan as the house settled for the night set my pulse racing.

No real harm appeared to have been done. But a shiver ran through me with the sure realisation that someone had been in our room.

And whoever they had been, their focus was clearly on Ruby.

CHAPTER FIVE

The noise of the front door slamming pulled me sharply from my slumber. Muffled voices carried from the hallway. Reaching for my watch, I groaned, seeing that it was almost 9.45 a.m. I felt exhausted, after having lain awake until daybreak, certain that someone was lurking, waiting for me to slip into unconsciousness and creep back into the room.

'Look, Mummy!'

Groggily, I turned over to see Ruby hopping from one foot to the other at the window. 'What is it, sweetheart?'

I eased myself stiffly from the bed and plodded heavily to stand behind her, to be greeted with the endearing sight of two red squirrels scampering playfully across the lawn, their creamy-white bellies flashing as they flipped and leaped about.

'I've never seen one before. Aren't they sweet!' Her eyes shone. It lifted my spirits to see her looking so delighted and I wrapped my arms around her shoulders.

Her hair felt warm and soft as gossamer against my skin. Breathing in the scent of her strawberry conditioner, I dropped a kiss onto her head. The morning had brought sunshine and unbroken blue skies, and already the temperature in the room felt warmer and more welcoming.

Ruby was such a caring, sensitive child. It had been obvious from when she was quite tiny that she had incredible empathy with animals. She loved to watch wildlife programmes on TV, and would get very upset if she heard news of an animal being injured or mistreated in any way. Even if she spotted a worm or snail on the path in front of her, she would pick it up gently and put it to the side so it wouldn't fall victim to someone's heavy feet.

One day when I'd gone to collect her from school, it was clear from her face as she came out of the classroom door that something was wrong. I think she must have held it all in until she saw me. She had come rushing across the playground and wrapped her arms around my waist, sobbing as if her heart would break. I asked her what was the matter, but she was crying so much I couldn't make sense of what she was saying. I led her back to the building to ask her teacher what had happened. She smiled weakly, patting Ruby on the head.

'We've had a bit of an upset this afternoon, haven't we Ruby?'

Ruby nodded through her tears. The teacher proceeded to explain that Ruby had earlier witnessed a much bigger boy from another class tormenting an injured pigeon in the playground. I learned that she had bravely pushed her way past him, carefully wrapping the bird in her

58

coat, and carried it indoors to safety. Sadly the bird had died shortly afterwards, probably from shock, and Ruby was distraught. She couldn't bear to see any creature suffering and it made me so proud of her.

'I want to be a vet when I grow up,' she had announced one day. 'Then I can help sick animals get better.' Despite her being so young, I firmly believed she would work hard enough to achieve her ambition, too. I knew in my heart that she was destined to take care of people or animals in some way. It was just in her nature.

'Ooh – is that another one?' She pointed excitedly at the trees. 'Quick – take a photo, Mummy!'

I grabbed my mobile from the bedside cabinet and snapped a few times in the hope of getting a decent shot, but the creatures were impossibly quick and I lost sight of them. I lowered the phone, raising a hand to shield my eyes from the glare winking through the gaps in the foliage, and followed Ruby's outstretched arm, registering a flicker of movement weaving amongst the dense border of pines. It vanished almost instantly. I felt suddenly cold. Whatever it had been, it was no squirrel.

'Come on, madam, let's get downstairs for breakfast.' Hastily, I steered her away from the window, glancing back over my shoulder into the garden. All was apparently still, but I had a prickling sense of unease. There had been someone watching the house once again; I was sure of it.

We washed and dressed, and headed down to the kitchen. Awel had long been up, and greeted us with a smile as we entered. She shooed a reluctant Pwtyn from her chair so Ruby could sit down, and brought us porridge with honey and a steaming pot of tea. We had just begun to tuck in, when a deep voice called through from the hall. A tall, broad-shouldered man dressed in scruffy jeans and a faded Oasis T-shirt, appeared in the doorway, ducking down beneath the lintel as he entered. He looked surprised to find us there. His eyes seemed to be scanning my face with – with what? Interest? It was a little unsettling.

'Lewis, this is Lowri, Gwyn's niece, and her daughter, Ruby.'

Lewis nodded and smiled warmly. '*Su'mae*,' he said.

Ruby turned her head sharply towards me. 'What does that mean?' she whispered behind her hand.

'Just "How are you", that's all.'

I nodded back, trying to appear composed. 'We're fine, thank you.'

I could feel his eyes on me again and the sudden heat in my cheeks made me self-conscious. I took a gulp of tea, wincing as I burned my tongue.

'Lewis is my stepbrother,' Awel explained, apparently oblivious to this unspoken exchange. 'He helps us out with odd jobs from time to time.'

I was taken aback. I knew very little of Awel and Elis's background, only that their mother had been related to my Nain. Lewis had a pleasant, rugged face. I would have said he was in his late thirties; possibly early forties. A few years older than me, anyway. His clear blue eyes peered in my direction from beneath a thick tawny fringe, which he kept pushing back with the heel of his hand.

'I'm all done, now. It's patched up pretty well for the minute, but if we have another heavy downpour, I think

60

the whole lot will need replacing.' Seeing my perplexed expression, he grinned. 'The guttering. Coming away from the roof at the back. It's seen better days.'

Awel sighed. 'More expense. And the coffers aren't looking too healthy just now – business has been so slow these last months. Hasn't helped with Gwyn, well, you know . . .' Her lips tightened.

'I think that new place in Cemaes has taken a lot of our trade.' She chewed her lip, clearly contemplating the future implications of competitors, then inhaled resolutely, flaring her nostrils.

'Anyhow, I've decided to shut up shop until Gwyn's funeral is done and dusted, whether things are tight or not. We just did the one last Friday, but I can't think straight at the moment. I don't want to go making any stupid mistakes.'

'I've told you what I think,' said Lewis, glancing at me again as he tapped a finger on the table. 'Sell. It's too much for you now. Even the house itself is a money pit, never mind the hassle that goes with the business. You could buy a nice little retirement bungalow nearer the town, start to wind down a bit. You're not getting any younger.'

'Thank you for the reminder,' Awel responded tersely, shooting him a warning glare. 'You forget that neither the house or the business is necessarily mine to sell. But come what may, this is our home – Gwyn always promised we'd never have to leave. They'll have to carry me out in a box.'

Lewis raised an eyebrow and threw me a sideways look but said nothing.

'Well, I'll be off, then,' he announced after an awkward pause. 'If not before, I'll see you Thursday. At the funeral,' he added, grimacing.

He inclined his head in my direction and held my gaze for a moment, his eyes wide and unblinking. I felt a warm flush somewhere in my chest.

'Nice to meet you both. See you again. Ta-ra.'

We watched him leave. He left a strange silence in his wake, as though a whirlwind had passed through.

'He's a bugger, that one. Means well, but always thinks he knows best.' Awel shook her head. 'Heart of gold, though. He's got a lot on – he took on a job looking after the maintenance of the new caravan site, but he still always finds time to do jobs for us. He's a real grafter, you know – bought a wreck of an old cottage on the road the other side of the church a couple of years back and did it up a treat. Handy chap to have around.'

'He seems nice,' I agreed. 'I never knew you had a stepbrother.' And he did. Seem nice – and was undeniably good-looking with it. I felt a tingle of excitement at the prospect of seeing him again.

'Our father, Iolo Morgan, married his mother, after Lewis's own dad died. Poor woman had a dog's life with him, just like our mam before her. I'd tried to warn her what he was like, but she thought it was just sour grapes. Took her own life when Lewis was just a lad and he went to live with his mam's sister in Caernarfon for years. It was my dad that drove her to it, of course. Terrible business.' She shook her head. 'Yes, the day that old bastard went missing, there were a lot of happy people round here, believe me.'

I glanced uncomfortably at Ruby, who was agog, and motioned surreptitiously to Awel to change the subject, but she was oblivious. I had a vague recollection of Elis and Awel's father coming to the house once or twice when I was small. My impression of him had been of someone scruffy, bearded and loud, and I would always be hurriedly shooed out of the way. I had been astute enough to realise that he wasn't popular, particularly after overhearing a conversation Awel was having with Auntie Gwyn on one occasion when she had referred to him as a 'filthy old sod'. It had stuck in my mind ever since.

'Almost twenty years it's been, now.' She seemed distracted, her voice becoming increasingly high-pitched. 'They never found any trace of him. Probably fell down a ditch somewhere in a drunken stupor, or he's lying at the bottom of Llyn Alaw. Waste of space, he was. Good riddance to bad rubbish; that's what your Auntie Gwyn always said.'

She began to clear the table, her brow furrowed and mouth pinched into a thin line as though the memory of her errant father had left a disagreeable taste. In fairness, he did sound pretty vile. Poor Lewis. It sounded as though he'd had a rough time.

'Ruby, can you run and get my mobile for me please, sweetheart? I left it upstairs.'

Ruby looked hesitant for a moment, but nodded and trotted out of the room. I seized my chance.

'Awel, I didn't want to worry Ruby, but I think there was someone in our room last night. No one else has a key to the house, do they?'

She looked taken aback. 'Well, only a couple of the

casuals. But I'm sure they've all handed them back in at the moment, seeing as we won't need them for a while. Are you sure?'

'Pretty sure. I . . .'

'Maybe Elis popped his head in to check on you. He's very fond of you, you know.'

Ruby reappeared, and handed over my phone breathlessly. 'I ran all the way up the stairs and back down,' she announced.

'Thank you, darling – but you didn't need to rush.'

She shook her head. 'I wanted to get back down quickly. I don't like it up there on my own.' She looked up at me with anxious eyes, slipping her hand into mine. I gave it a small squeeze.

'Oh, you are a silly. There's nothing to be scared of.' I glanced at Awel, who gave me a tight smile.

'No, nothing to be frightened of in this house.'

'I thought I might take Ruby for a walk up to the church as it's such a nice morning,' I ventured. 'Is that okay?'

'Hmm? Oh yes, get her some fresh air. Good idea. I need to have a proper chat to you later, though, about the – *arrangements*.' The word was said with emphasis. She cocked her head, swivelling her eyes meaningfully towards the door that led to the preparation room. 'Lunch will be at one o'clock.'

*

Lewis pulled up outside his cottage and took a deep breath before climbing out of the van. He felt he was constantly treading on eggshells these days and was weary of confrontation.

Catrin had supposedly been sifting through her belongings, but it was proving an apparently arduous task and taking far longer than it should have. She'd assured him that once she had managed to pack everything up, she would put most of it into storage and then find a flat nearer the hotel where she worked. But Lewis wasn't hopeful of anything happening in the near future. She was obviously dragging her heels and it was beginning to wear thin.

'Oh. You're back.' Catrin was sitting in the living room, her knees drawn up beside her on the armchair, leafing through an interior design magazine. She didn't look particularly thrilled to see him.

'Just come to grab a bite to eat and a *panad* and then I've got a few things to catch up with on the site. D'you want anything?'

'Hmm? I'll have a cup of tea if you're making one – not really hungry at the moment.'

'Erm – any progress with the sorting out?' he ventured, sticking his head round the kitchen door as he waited for the kettle to boil.

'A bit,' she responded frostily. 'It's a long job – I've got a lot of stuff here. You know that. I wasn't expecting to be moving out quite so soon.' She glowered at him and went back to the magazine.

Lewis rolled his eyes and retreated into the kitchen. He'd have to grin and bear it for the time being. In the meantime, he would just give her a wide berth as much as possible. At least she had a job to go to and it gave him some respite.

His thoughts turned suddenly to Lowri and, without

really knowing why, he found himself smiling. Pretty girl. He'd always wondered what she looked like. She'd seemed nice, too. It was a long time since he'd looked at anyone else and although he had no real intention of pursuing anything, it gave him a warm feeling to have a pleasant distraction for a change.

And God knew he needed one.

*

Ruby and I began our walk from the front of the house, up the narrow lane towards the little church, said to be the oldest in Wales. The unadopted path from the back of Ty Coed Pinwydd, which overlooked the cliffs, would have brought us out at the opposite entrance to the graveyard; the route was much quicker but infinitely dicier, and I was anxious to instil good habits in Ruby, as Auntie Gwyn had always done with me.

It felt strange now, to think that Auntie Gwyn used to make this pilgrimage regularly, to lay flowers on the graves of her parents and siblings, knowing that one day this would be her own final resting place. It was the most peaceful spot imaginable. The spongy, undulating turf of the cemetery was bordered by an old stone wall, beyond which was no more than a narrow strip of unfenced land between the coastal path and a sheer drop to the sea below. As a child, I would explore the graveyard while Auntie Gwyn tidied the family plots, trying to read the faded inscriptions on the ancient headstones and wondering about the people interred beneath. Now I wanted to find the graves of my grandparents, in the knowledge that Auntie Gwyn was to be laid to rest near them.

The ascent from the main road to the headland was gentle initially, but the narrow, single track grew steeper as we climbed. Some things had changed since I was last there – the rough stone walls of the rundown old cottage some two hundred yards from Ty Coed Pinwydd had been rendered and painted cream, its roof retiled in smart mauve slates. The low wall which shielded it from the road had been repaired and painted the same colour, and a new varnished wooden gate now hung between the once redundant gateposts. A blonde-haired woman standing in one window looked a little startled by our presence, and raised a hand, waving hesitantly as we passed by, and we waved back.

As there was no pavement, we stayed close to the verge and in single file as we followed the curve of the lane, the hedgerows of hawthorn and gorse filled with twittering birds towering above us to left and right, beyond which rolling fields stretched as far as the eye could see. The rain of the previous day had made way for a glorious morning; already the growing warmth of the sun meant we could abandon our jackets, mine slung over my shoulder and Ruby's tied round her waist. It made a welcome change from the temperatures which had met us on our arrival. A new holiday park had been established in one field, presumably the one where Lewis worked, and as we passed the entrance, a small group of children kicking a ball outside a large tent stopped to observe us for a moment, before continuing their game.

Soon the church came into view, its bell tower rising against the backdrop of clear skies meeting sea, surrounded by headstones, jutting from the green turf like dominoes, waiting to be knocked down. I paused for a moment to catch my breath and then we continued the last few yards to the grey stone arch that led into the graveyard. It created the perfect frame for the view beyond, a snapshot of coarse grass and slate and endless water, the colour of jade. Ruby skipped through excitedly, and up the path winding between the tombstones that ran past the church itself.

'Where are your Nain and Taid's graves, Mummy?'

I frowned as I looked round. It had been so long since I'd been there that I couldn't remember the exact spot. The oldest graves, some dating back to the eighteenth century, seemed to be on our left, so we climbed to the higher ground on the opposite side behind the church and began to scour the inscriptions. I took a moment to drink in the view. I could better appreciate now just how breathtaking it was. Gulls wheeled above us; the teal waters, rippling with lines of white foam, stretched for miles to the distant horizon, beyond the rocky outcrop of the headland. I caught Ruby by the hand and pointed to the coastal path which ran along the cliff.

'You must be very careful up here,' I warned, remembering again to voice what Auntie Gwyn had instilled in me. 'That's the path that comes in from the back of the house. If we go for a walk out there, don't *ever* go too near the edge. The land can crumble without warning and there is nothing but rocks beneath us. I know I've told you before, but the cliffs are very dangerous. Always stick to the beaten track and stay near me, d'you understand?'

She peered out at the sea and nodded vigorously, her

eyes fearful. 'I don't want to fall down there. It looks scary.'

I looked below and felt suddenly cold as I remembered what had happened to young Sionyn. He may not have fallen but, the rocks aside, the waters beyond were undoubtedly treacherous. The thought of Ruby succumbing to such a fate made my stomach drop. I gripped her hand so tightly she let out a squeal.

'Mummy, you're *hurting* me.'

I led her nearer the church and kept one nervous eye on her as I scanned the graves. It soon became obvious we had a near-impossible task. It was like hunting for a needle in a haystack.

'We're going to be here all day at this rate. Come on, let's see if we can get into the church. With a bit of luck, they may keep records in there of where people are buried.'

I turned the iron ring at the centre of the heavy door to the building. As it creaked open, we found ourselves in an entrance porch, with old wooden benches at either side. The familiar incipient chill and smell of damp earth I had always associated with old places of worship hit us at once. Beyond this, a curtain of metal chains hung from the next doorway. We passed through them, and then through another hefty door which had been propped open, into the main body of the structure. I felt as if we ought to be whispering, even though there was no one in evidence to disturb.

'Good morning.'

Startled, I turned to see a small, silver-haired woman arranging a vase of white flowers on the altar, bathed in a shaft of sunlight which streamed through the glorious blue stained-glass window at the far end of the church. She had been so quiet that we hadn't noticed her. She put down the vase and approached us. Ruby stood shyly at my side, pressing against my hip.

'Good morning.'

The woman smiled. 'Can I help you at all? Or are you just browsing?' Her accent was local, the tone soft. She looked about sixty and wore a royal-blue short-sleeved nylon overall over her clothes and sensible lace-up shoes.

'Actually, my aunt is being buried here next week.' My heart plummeted as I said the words. It still felt like a bad dream.

'Oh, I'm sorry.' She tilted her head to one side sympathetically. 'Forgive me, but you're not from the island, are you?'

I shook my head. 'My dad was. I spent a lot of my childhood here, staying with my aunt, but I was brought up in the Midlands.'

'Ah, I see.'

'Silly question probably, but do you work here?'

'I'm the verger. Just having a bit of a tidy-up and then I'll be locking up again until later this afternoon, so you caught me at just the right time.'

'I'm actually looking for my grandparents' graves. It's been so long since I was last here and I'm afraid I've forgotten where they are.'

'Well, I may be able to help, then. We have a register of all the plots. Let's have a look, shall we?'

Just inside the door and behind the oak pews was the worn limestone font, covered with a carved oak lid.

Against the opposite wall stood a heavy, dark wood dresser. The verger bent down and opened one of its drawers. She took out a huge, ancient-looking ledger and placed it on the small wooden table in the centre of the floor, which held the visitors' book.

'Now then, what were your Nain and Taid's names?'

'Mair and Idwal Hughes Owen. They died over thirty years ago. My dad's brother and sister are buried here, too. They were called Sionyn and Carys, and they both died as children – about 1970, I think.'

'Hughes Owen?' She looked taken aback. 'Oh, then you'll be Gwyneth's niece.' She cocked her head, reaching out to press my hand gently. Her fingers felt cool against my skin. 'I'm Hannah Pugh. I moved here from Holyhead in 2010, when my husband passed away. I came to know your aunt well these last few years – such a lovely woman. I'm so sorry for your loss. She devoted most of her life to serving this community, as you know. She'll be sorely missed by a lot of people round here.'

I attempted a smile and nodded. It still felt so strange, hearing Auntie Gwyn referred to in the past tense.

'I'm Lowri – this is my daughter, Ruby.'

'Pleased to meet you both.' From the pocket of her overall, Hannah produced a pair of half-moon gold-rimmed glasses, perching them on the bridge of her nose. She opened the book carefully, peeling back the yellowing parchment pages. Running a fingertip gently over the words, she leaned forward, squinting a little, then tentatively turned a few pages at once and pointed.

'Here we are. Idwal Hughes Owen. *A fu farw Ionawr 15ef 1988 yn 81 mlwydd oed.*'

71

Ruby, who had been silent until this point, looked up at her questioningly. 'What does all that mean?'

'Your great-grandfather – or hen Taid – died on the fifteenth of January 1988, aged seventy-one,' explained Hannah. 'And *this* is where he is buried.' She indicated the number in the margin of the ledger. 'Come on, I'll show you.'

We followed her from the building and back out into the graveyard, blinking in the sun as we climbed the mossy bank to the far right of the cemetery. Three graves stood side by side, two with heavy, dark grey marble headstones; the third and evidently much older one marked with slate. I peered at the wording etched into each.

'The inscriptions tend to fade more quickly here – it's all the salt in the air,' Hannah told us. 'But these are still quite legible.'

My grandparents shared one grave, my Nain having followed her husband two years later. A small bunch of wild flowers had been clumsily arranged in the metal holder beneath the headstone. To the one side of their plot was an older grave; again, a married couple with the same surname. My Taid's parents, perhaps? But to the other, a John Hughes Owen had been laid to rest, the date being 1970. A long, freshly made daisy chain had been draped over the headstone.

'Ah, someone's been here recently,' remarked Hannah. 'This must be the Sionyn that you mentioned – it's how we often refer to people called John round here.'

I looked around, but there appeared to be no plot nearby for Carys. I had assumed that she and Sionyn would have been buried together. I hadn't really paid attention as a child when visiting here with Auntie Gwyn, but now it felt somehow important that I knew. With the exception of my Uncle Dafydd, I had lost all of my immediate family. As stipulated in their will, my parents had both been cremated, their ashes scattered in the Garden of Remembrance back in the Midlands, and I had never known my maternal grandparents. It was comforting to think that most of my dad's family had eventually been reunited, here in this beautiful, tranquil place.

'Would the family have all been buried in the same area? My aunt died as a child too, but she doesn't seem to be here.'

'I would've thought so. But it's possible she's somewhere else. Would you like me to check the register again?'

'Thank you. It'd be nice to know where they all are – and exactly where Auntie Gwyn will be buried.' I felt a sudden pang of misery as the reality of it all hit me. The idea of her being sealed in a box and put into the cold ground forever was something I didn't want to think about. Not my lovely Auntie Gwyn.

Ruby and I waited as Hannah went back into the church. I looked around at all the graves and tears sprang to my eyes. At that moment, the thought that at some point every one of us would end up in such a place was almost too much to bear.

My daughter looked up at me anxiously, clutching my arm. 'Don't be sad, Mummy.'

I forced a smile. 'Oh, take no notice of me. I'm fine.'

I ran the back of one hand over my cheek. 'What was it Auntie Gwyn used to say? *This too shall pass.*'

She looked at me quizzically and started to say something when Hannah reappeared, looking puzzled.

'Are you sure your Aunt Carys was buried here? I can find no mention of her.'

I frowned. 'Oh. I'd always thought she was. That's odd.'

'I suppose it's possible that she could be in Llanbabo churchyard – several people from the parish have been interred there over the years.'

'I'll see if Awel knows. Thank you for checking, anyway.'

'I've just had a look at the funeral arrangements for next week and your Aunt Gwyneth is going to be laid to rest with her brother, apparently. Nice that they will be together again after all these years.'

'Yes. Thank you.' I glanced back at Sionyn's grave, which Auntie Gwyn had tended so well all these years, and felt something tighten in my chest. I cleared my throat. 'Well, I suppose we'd better be getting back for lunch. Nice to meet you, Hannah – and I appreciate your help.'

'Likewise. And you're very welcome – it's what I'm here for.' She smiled.

We walked from the church with Hannah and said our goodbyes at the gate. Footsteps from behind us made me turn my head, in time to see a figure disappearing hurriedly round the back of the church. Hannah, who was heading in the opposite direction and a few feet ahead of us, stopped to look over her shoulder.

'Oh, that'll probably be Alun, the church gardener. He always comes up the other way, over the coastal path. I'll see him later – need to get home to feed the cats now – they'll be wondering where I am! See you soon.'

We made our way back down the lane. I made a mental note to ask Awel where Carys was buried so that perhaps we could visit to lay flowers. I intended to order a wreath for Auntie Gwyn from the local florist, and some smaller bunches for the other family members. I wondered fleetingly who might have left the wildflowers on my grandparents' grave and the daisy chain for Sionyn. It was touching that someone still cared enough to acknowledge their existence.

CHAPTER SIX

After lunch, Awel suggested that Ruby might like to assist Elis in the garden.

'He's finding it all much harder these days with his back – I'm sure he'd appreciate a little helper,' she said, casting a brief wink in my direction. 'Your mam and I have a few things to discuss.'

Ruby seemed quite excited at the prospect of being useful and went without complaint.

We sat on the old bamboo-framed settee in the veranda, sipping tea and looking out onto the lawn. The delicious smell of ripe tomatoes rising from the numerous plants along the full width of the window sill was almost intoxicating.

'She's a nice little girl,' remarked Awel to my surprise, as we watched Ruby following Elis eagerly across the grass, armed with a small trowel held gingerly in gloves so big that they went past her elbows.

'Things haven't been easy for her.' I clasped my arms

across my chest, feeling a surge of love for my daughter, who looked tinier than ever in the shadow of Elis's huge frame. 'Her dad died when she was only two, and my second marriage was a disaster. Money's always been an issue and I'd love to be able to give her a few more treats but it just hasn't been possible.' I bit back tears. 'She deserves more.'

'She has your love and she knows it,' Awel said quietly. 'That's a lot more than you ever had from your own mam.'

I stared at her. This seemed a little too direct. 'Well – I . . .' I squirmed. 'We were never close, no.'

I didn't like to dwell on my relationship with my mother, particularly as she was no longer with us and there would now never be an opportunity to confront her about certain things she'd said and done over the years. What was past was past, and I saw no point in attempting to analyse her attitude towards me. The truth was that it hurt – and I had always tried to rationalise her coldness by telling myself that she just wasn't the maternal type. But I knew nothing of her upbringing and often wondered if there was more to it.

As I grew up, things between us became increasingly strained. When I reached my teens, I began to rebel, and kicked against what I felt were her unfair restrictions. My dad was always a bit more relaxed about things, but she seemed determined to make my life a misery – or at least, that was how it felt. I remember one ridiculously irrational outburst she'd had when I wanted to go to a house party, thrown by a boy in my class, with some friends. When she had told me I couldn't go, I argued with her and it had escalated into a major row.

'You're only fifteen!' she had yelled, grasping me by the shoulders. 'God only knows what goes on at these things – everyone gets carried away, people get their drinks spiked, and before you know it there's a baby on the way. How would that make you feel, carrying a baby that had been forced upon you? And can you imagine how that child would feel, born under such circumstances? Not to mention how people would look at *us* as your parents, allowing such a thing to happen. Selfish, that's what you are. Selfish.'

I remembered the wild look in her eyes as she'd shouted the words into my face. I knew she'd had a convent education: I could only assume that the nuns' indoctrination had damaged her in some way. She was almost deranged, as though on the verge of some sort of breakdown. It felt to me not as if she actually cared about *my* welfare, but more that she was making some point. About how *I* was impacting on the way people thought of *her* as a parent, as if I was some sort of delinquent – which I really wasn't. My dad had reasoned with her and calmed her down, but the extreme way in which she'd reacted actually made me not want to go to the party at all. It left me feeling horrible at the time, and the memory of it made me shudder now.

Awel tipped her head a fraction and looked at me almost pityingly. 'We knew things were never great for you at home. Gwyn always worried about you. Your dad did write now and again – I don't know if you were ever aware.'

'No, I wasn't – not until yesterday. Elis mentioned it. I thought they'd lost touch completely after that falling-out. I'm glad, even if I didn't get to speak to her myself, that she had been told something about my life. I hope she knew that I thought of her often.'

'It's just a shame you couldn't have seen her again, or at least spoken to her. She thought the world of you, you know.'

She sighed, staring straight ahead unseeingly.

'Anyway, that's what I need to talk to you about.'

'Oh?'

She inhaled deeply, then paused for a moment, shuffling her feet against the floor. The tendons in her neck tensed, as though she was building up to something momentous.

'I don't know exactly what your position at home is these days – whether you're settled, or what plans you may have for the future. I don't know if you were hoping that, as you've been contacted directly by the executors, you might be in for some sort of windfall. What I *do* know is there might be a few surprises in store when this will is read after the funeral. Just so you don't get too much of a shock.'

'Surprises?' I felt my stomach dip, wondering where this was all leading.

She set down her cup and saucer on the small bamboo table in front of us and turned to face me. 'Well, now. Years ago, your Auntie Gwyn had high hopes that you might run the business one day. We discussed it at length – she wanted it to stay in the family. The only possible fly in the ointment might have been your Uncle Dafydd, but he has no interest in coming back from Canada. He can't even make the funeral.' She rolled her eyes. 'He's done very nicely for himself out there, thank you, so bugger the rest of us. He always was self-centred.'

'Charming. But surely Auntie Gwyn wouldn't have expected *me* to take it over – I mean, I know nothing about the business really.' My mind was whirring. Would I even *want* to run a funeral home, if that's what Awel was implying?

'No, no. That's not what I'm saying. Look, I don't know the exact terms. That Meredith Williams chap is playing his cards close to his chest, but I'm pretty sure since you haven't been here for such a long time, Gwyn may well have made changes to her original plans. She always was practical – she may have thought she'd need to have an alternative arrangement in place. I'm not saying you'll have been completely overlooked – far from it,' she added hastily. 'But it seems more likely that the company will have been left to Elis and myself, to do with as we see fit. Even though business has tailed off in recent years, we've kept things afloat to be honest, and I'm fairly sure that's what Gwyn will have requested.'

I looked out at Ruby and my heart sank. I hadn't considered that Auntie Gwyn might leave me the whole business; not really. But now the idea had been planted, I began to think how much better life could be for us if we moved to Llanbadrig permanently. Ruby was young enough to adapt quite easily. Apart from Nina, there was really nothing to keep us in the Midlands. The school certainly wouldn't struggle to find another eager mother to fill my job in their kitchens. I could learn the ropes – my maths had always been strong, and even if it took me a while to get to grips with the actual funerary side of things, I felt fairly confident that I could deal with the financial aspect of the company.

'But we don't know for sure yet what Auntie Gwyn has said; it's all a bit hypothetical. I mean, at the moment, I'd have no idea where to start with any of it. But given the opportunity, if she *hadn't* changed her mind, I'd really like the idea of helping people in their hour of need. God knows I've been in the same position myself and I was so grateful to the undertakers. It's such a worthwhile job.'

Awel looked solemn. She chewed her lip, twisting the fabric of her apron in her hands, her voice suddenly soft. 'It's more of a vocation, actually. I couldn't imagine doing anything else with my life, but it's definitely not for everyone.'

I felt deflated. Seeing my face, she went on, 'Of course, we would guide you if it *has* been left to you. But do you really think you could cope with dealing with distraught people all the time? It can take its toll on you.'

I thought for a moment. 'I'd be prepared to try. Anyway, I'll cross that bridge when I come to it.'

Awel shrugged. 'Well, time will tell. I wanted to pre-warn you before we sit down with Meredith Williams next week. I know it's not the ideal job for everyone. As I say, I don't know for certain what your auntie decided in the end, but I've a pretty good idea. The business her Taid worked so hard to build up would always have come first with Gwyn.'

The gloves discarded, Ruby came rushing to the open door, a sheen of sweat across her forehead, her eyes shining. 'Elis says I can have my own patch of garden round the back – to grow strawberries, or anything I like!'

'That'll be nice. I see you're picking up the signing quickly. Is he teaching you how to weed too, though?' I couldn't help but smile at her enthusiasm. She ran straight back to re-join Elis, who waved from the far side of the lawn. I waved back, but my attention was caught suddenly by a slight movement behind him. My eyes travelled beyond his outline to what appeared to be a human shape standing close to the foot of one tree.

Watching.

I leaped to my feet, my heart racing.

'There's someone over there – look!'

Awel wasn't quick enough to rise from her seat, and whoever it was seemed to melt into the bushes before she could join me. She frowned.

'I can't see anyone.'

'They've gone. I did tell you, there was someone out there last night, too – Ruby saw them looking up from the lawn. It's given me the creeps a bit.'

Awel sniffed dismissively, pursing her lips. 'Like I said, it's probably just a holidaymaker out for a walk – it's a free country, after all.'

I didn't share her confidence. I stared into the trees and a shiver ran through me. Something about the figure didn't feel right and it had left me uneasy. I decided I needed to keep a closer eye on Ruby.

'I'll go and see if they want any help,' I told Awel. 'I could do with some fresh air.'

'Carry on. I have things I need to be getting on with, anyway. Just have a think; you know, about what I told you.'

She collected the teacups and went back into the house.

Studying the pines anxiously for any further sign of movement, I caught up with Ruby, who was still watching Elis, and took her firmly by the hand.

'Are you going to help us, Mummy?' Before I could respond, something caught her eye. 'Ooh, what's that?'

She broke free suddenly and sprinted towards the fountain.

Elis was kneeling on an old mat, engrossed in weeding the border and clearly unaware of Ruby's burst of excitement. I turned to see what she was looking at. Before I could protest, she had plunged an arm into the murky water. At once, she pulled out something and waved it aloft.

Elis, noticing the activity, lifted his head. He paled visibly. Dangling limply from Ruby's closed hand was a sopping, old-fashioned rag doll, dripping pondweed from its spindly limbs.

'Where did the dolly come from, Mummy?'

I signed to Elis. *Do you know anything about this?*

He responded with a shrug, shaking his head slightly. But the troubled expression that clouded his face told a different story. It was very odd. I approached to look at the doll more closely. The wild orange woollen hair was sparse, the triangular felt nose coming loose. Dirty candy-striped red and white legs dangled beneath an equally grimy sky-blue floral dress. But there was something strangely familiar about it.

'*Doli glwt.*' The name came to me from nowhere. It wasn't my doll: I was sure of that. But I *knew* it; and a long-buried memory flashed through my mind. I shuddered.

'Put it down, Ruby, it's filthy.'

Ruby dropped the thing onto the grass and stared down at it longingly. 'Can't we wash her? She'll be fine then. How did she get there?'

'I've no idea.' I glanced back at Elis, who seemed preoccupied with an apparently tenacious thistle. 'I don't think it's a good idea. She'll be covered in germs. Probably best if she doesn't come into the house.'

Her face fell. 'But we could put some disinfectant on her – the germs would be all gone then,' she protested.

Silently, Elis hauled himself to his feet and plodded over to where the doll lay. He stooped to pick it up, then hurled it into the trees. Without looking at either of us, he returned to his weeding. Ruby's eyes welled with tears and she ran back indoors, sobbing.

I stared at Elis, baffled and furious that he'd been so tactless. I marched over and tapped him on the shoulder.

What was all that about? I signed angrily. *There are ways of doing things, you know. You should have let me deal with it.*

The thing was filthy. Gone now.

I threw up my hands. *But you needn't have been so obvious about it. Ruby's really upset now.*

He shrugged as though it was nothing. It was most unlike him. His face seemed to close and he resumed his gardening, avoiding my eyes. It was clearly not open to discussion. Exasperated, I followed Ruby back into the house, where I found her with her face buried in Awel's apron as she hugged her close. I had never seen the woman showing affection to anyone before. The

84

transformation in her since we had last met was astonishing. To be truthful, it made me slightly uneasy.

I did my best to placate Ruby. 'Don't cry, sweetheart. We can get you another doll – we don't even know where that one came from. Elis was just worried, that's all. It really wouldn't be a good idea, bringing something like that inside. All sorts of organisms live in the water – it could be carrying some sort of horrible disease.'

Ruby stopped sniffing and wiped her eyes. She looked up at me reproachfully. 'But she looked sort of sad. I could have made her better.'

'I'm sure we can find another one that needs your love just as much. Come on, let's go down to the shop. They have a proper ice-cream counter there.' I looked at Awel. 'They do still sell them, don't they?'

She nodded, smiling down at Ruby, who brightened a little. She rubbed her nose with the back of her hand.

'Can I have a Flake?'

'I think we can probably stretch to that, yes.'

If only life were always that simple; misery erased instantly by the promise of sweet treats.

I thought back to when I was small. Auntie Gwyn would always have a large paper bag of goodies waiting for me whenever I arrived for the holidays: chocolate bars of one sort or another, mainly. It would be sitting on my bedside table and I would make the contents last, taking one bar out every couple of days and having the occasional nibble as I pored over whichever book I had my nose in at the time. One morning, during the Easter holidays when I was about seven, I remember being quite upset, as I'd wanted to accompany my aunt to see a distant relative that she visited regularly, but wasn't allowed to go. It was more the fact I was being left under the sole supervision of Awel, since Elis was driving Auntie Gwyn on this occasion, and I really didn't feel comfortable with the woman.

Auntie Gwyn had been kind but firm. 'My poor cousin is in a hospital for people with mental illness,' she had explained. 'They won't allow children inside, I'm afraid – and I really don't think you'd like it in there, anyway. We'll only be gone a couple of hours. We're calling at the shop on the way home and I'll bring you something back, so you'll have that to look forward to. Is there anything in particular that you'd like?'

I'd thought about it and asked for a big bar of chocolate filled with caramel. The prospect of this had made me feel much better, and I settled down with my book in the sitting room, waiting eagerly for their return.

After about an hour, Awel came to call me into the kitchen for lunch. I remember telling her in a small voice that I wasn't very hungry. More than anything, I didn't want to spend time alone in her company.

'You have to eat, child,' she'd said sharply.

'Auntie Gwyn's bringing me chocolate back. I can have that later,' I attempted weakly.

Awel glared at me from above her glasses. 'Can't miss proper meals then fill up on sweets. Your aunt wouldn't hear of it.'

Reluctantly, I had followed her to the kitchen and sat down to a plate of egg and cress granary bread sandwiches, which were actually very good. She perched opposite me, watching me eat with a critical eye.

I nibbled self-consciously, swinging my legs beneath the table as I ate. 'When will Auntie Gwyn be home?' I ventured.

'As soon as she's able. She doesn't usually stay there that long.'

I had never really questioned my aunt's visits and wasn't entirely sure where it was that she was going. 'What's mental illness?'

She raised an eyebrow. 'Where did you hear that?'

'Auntie Gwyn says that the people in the hospital all have mental illness and that's why they don't let children in.'

Awel took another bite of her sandwich and nodded slowly. I waited while she finished chewing.

'If someone has a mental illness, it means that they're not quite well in the head. So sometimes they can act a bit strangely and do things that no one is expecting all of a sudden. I suppose it could be a bit frightening for a child.'

I considered this for a moment. 'So Auntie Gwyn has a cousin who is strange?'

'A little; yes. But harmless – she wouldn't hurt anyone. At least, I don't think she would.'

I was filled with sudden panic. 'She wouldn't hurt Auntie Gwyn, would she?'

Awel gave a peculiar laugh. 'No, no. Your aunt is quite safe.'

'Why don't you go to see the strange lady? Are *you* frightened of her?'

She looked taken aback. 'No, definitely not. And I do go sometimes. But she's not really a relative of mine.

She's a distant cousin on your aunt's father's side. And Elis just goes along to keep your Auntie Gwyn company.'

I thought about all of this and it made sense. I finished my sandwiches in silence, then asked to be excused to return to my book. Soon the sound of tyres crunching over the gravel had me flying to the door to greet Auntie Gwyn and relieve her of the huge bar of chocolate she was waving at me.

Everything else was quickly forgotten.

*

The nearest shop was a good thirty minutes' walk away, but the route was pleasant and a good opportunity for Ruby to forget about the doll. She chatted happily, eagerly anticipating the ice cream which awaited her. For a while, it was almost easy to forget why we were in Llanbadrig. Spending time in Ruby's company was always a delight. I knew only too well that childhood was such a brief time and these moments were precious. In a few years, she would be an adult and would make a life for herself in which I might not even play a large part, for all I knew. The thought made me sad and was something I didn't want to dwell on. I looked down at her and squeezed her hand as she made observations at every turn. Her innocent enthusiasm was infectious.

'Look, Mummy. That's a swallow, isn't it?' A small blue and white bird, with a distinctive forked tail and pointed wings, dipped and soared erratically ahead of us. 'They make neat little nests – Miss Rodriguez brought an old one into school for our nature table. She says they build them every year under her roof.' She giggled.

'She's got a tattoo of one on her shoulder – she showed us!'

'What – a nest?' I teased.

'No, silly. A swallow.' We watched as the bird disappeared over the hedge. 'I think *I'll* have a tattoo when I'm grown up.'

'Oh? And what will you have?'

'I'll have one of Merida, on my arm – right here.' She pointed. 'I might have two. One of a cat, as well.'

I smiled wistfully to myself, questioning the likelihood of Merida still being her heroine even in twelve months' time. I wished she could stay seven forever.

As we rounded a bend, an old silver Mercedes convertible screeched without warning towards us, then veered to the opposite side of the road before straightening. We had been walking on the grass verge anyway, but I yanked Ruby almost into the hedge as the driver passed by, gesticulating aggressively in his rear-view mirror. Both Ruby and I were shaken.

'You okay? Stupid man – he was driving far too quickly.' I stared after the car which was disappearing into the distance and wondered if the driver was local. Whoever he was, he shouldn't be allowed behind the wheel.

*

The shopkeeper who served us, now quite elderly, seemed to recognise me at once from when I was a child and greeted me with a huge smile. Once I'd checked that there was no danger of any contamination with nuts, he gave us each a huge cone of vanilla ice-cream, with a flake for Ruby, and waved a hand when I went to pay. He told us how sorry he had been to hear about Auntie Gwyn.

'The end of an era, it is. She looked after my parents and my wife when – you know. Always knew they were in safe hands with Gwyn and her team. I thought she'd take care of me, too, when the time came. I know just what to ask for – something a bit special. I've got it all written down.'

I nodded and thanked him but was thankfully spared hearing the details of his alternative funeral plans when another customer entered. We wished him a good afternoon and made our exit.

The round trip to the shop took us over an hour but cheered Ruby up considerably, so it had been worth it.

I was surprised to see a silver car parked in the turning circle in front of Ty Coed Pinwydd as we arrived back, and then recognised it as the same vehicle we'd had a near miss with earlier. As we approached, the door to the veranda opened, and a tall, smartly dressed man with cropped greying hair stepped out. There was a swagger about him, an annoying air of smug self-importance. Noticing us, his demeanour changed abruptly. He seemed oddly startled.

My hackles rose. 'You nearly crushed us earlier, I hope you realise,' I said angrily.

He opened his mouth to speak, but was interrupted by the appearance of Awel in the doorway. She appeared ruffled and was twiddling with her apron again.

'Lowri, this is Dr Price. He called by to bring the forms – for the death certificate.'

The man stepped forward and extended a limp, well-manicured hand, which I shook half-heartedly. His thin smile didn't reach the deep-set green eyes which were scrutinising my face unnervingly. I had a vague recollection of seeing him once before, somewhere in the dim and distant past.

'You really need to keep tucked well in on these roads, you know – especially with a child in tow.' His voice was syrupy, with the merest trace of a Welsh accent, his expression bland and patronising.

I gritted my teeth. 'We *were* tucked well in. You were driving on the wrong side of the road.'

'No harm done though, eh? Just be more careful in future.' He looked from me to Ruby. 'And who's this young lady?'

'This is my daughter. The one you almost flattened.'

He ignored my comment, his eyes lingering on Ruby a fraction too long, and I drew her closer.

'Yes. Yes, the resemblance is unmistakable.' He paused, his eyes fixing me with a stare, then turned back to Awel. 'Well, must press on. Just call me if you have any queries. Good day to you all.'

He climbed into his car, studying us for a moment in the wing mirror, then pulled away sharply.

I shuddered. 'Moron – he could have bloody killed us! The way he spoke, anyone would've thought it was all *our* fault.'

'He owns the local surgery, unfortunately, so we can't really afford to upset him.' Awel looked uncomfortable. 'He confirms causes of death and signs all the paperwork we need to proceed, so he could make things awkward if he wanted to. Can't say I've ever been wild about him myself.'

'He's no spring chicken – what'll happen when he retires? He must be in his sixties.'

'There's a son, Rhodri. He's been working abroad somewhere for a couple of years but came home recently. Just started at the practice. Much more agreeable than his father. They don't get on too well, apparently.' She arched an eyebrow. 'Poor Mrs Price has Alzheimer's – she's been in a home in Holyhead for the last four years, so they have a housekeeper, Eluned. I know her well. She's overheard a few *humdingers* of rows between father and son in the past. Anyway, I can't see Dr Iwan Price hanging up his hat just yet. He likes to do the rounds – lots of rumours about his antics with some of the women in the area over the years.' She gave an exaggerated wink.

'Eugh. Rather them than me.'

Awel laughed. 'I think you'll be safe. He's definitely got his eye on the more well-heeled ladies. Angling for a mention in a lot of wills, I shouldn't wonder.'

She beamed at Ruby. 'All better after the ice cream, *cariad*?'

I wasn't sure how to take this new, smiley version of Awel. Maybe she'd been replaced by a clone. It was a bit disconcerting.

Ruby nodded. I inspected her shiny chin. 'Hmm – and very sticky. Come on, you'd better go up and wash your face and hands.'

Ruby looked worried. 'Will you come with me? I don't like it up there – it's always dark.'

92

I sighed. 'Come on, then.'

The house felt welcomely cool after the heat of the sun. While Ruby was getting cleaned up, I went to replace my purse in the bedroom. As I pushed the door, something didn't feel quite right; almost as though someone had recently breezed through. The hint of an unfamiliar, musky odour hung in the air; like perfume that had been opened too long.

I stopped in my tracks and stared down at Ruby's bed. Benjy the rabbit and her pyjamas had been tossed onto the floor. There, sitting squarely in the middle of the pillow, still sodden and filthy, was the rag doll. An awful coldness radiated through me. I couldn't let Ruby see the thing. Quickly, I hoisted up the sash and, gingerly picking the doll up by one foot, lobbed it out of the window, staring down to where it had landed, face up, on the ground below. Gooseflesh prickled my arms. I could see Elis, who had just returned from replacing his tools in the shed round the back of the house. He was plodding wearily across the lawn, his hands supporting his lower back and clearly stiff from his exertions. He hadn't noticed me.

Ruby appeared in the doorway to find me hurriedly peeling off the pillow slip, a damp, dirty patch spreading from its centre like a tie-dye.

'What happened, Mummy?'

Scrunching the pillowcase up in my hands, my eyes darted round for inspiration.

'Clumsy me – I just came to collect my glass and spilled some of the water. Not to worry – we'll find you a fresh one.' I shepherded her towards the stairs, glancing back at the half-opened window. 'Let's go and have a cup of tea.'

I found myself looking about us as we passed down the hallway, half expecting to see an intruder. Surely neither Awel nor Elis would have put the doll there? It felt like some sort of sick joke and I didn't appreciate the humour. If it hadn't been for the fact I'd seen him drive away, it wouldn't have surprised me if the smarmy doctor had been the culprit.

'I'm just making a *panad*,' said Awel, as we entered the kitchen. 'There's juice if you'd prefer, Ruby.' Noticing my face, she placed the kettle on the stove, her eyes narrowing. 'Is anything wrong?'

Pwtyn began to rub round Ruby's legs. She crouched to fuss the cat, which was a useful distraction.

I crossed the kitchen and gestured with a thumb. 'That doll is back,' I mouthed to Awel.

Her brow knitted into a frown. She spoke in a low voice. 'Where?'

'On Ruby's bed.'

Ruby lifted her head. 'What's that about my bed?'

'Just that I spilled the water – Awel is going to look for a clean pillowcase for you.'

Awel began to lay the table. 'Ruby, would you mind going to ask Elis if he'd come in for some tea, please?'

Ruby hesitated briefly, then skipped out through the door and I turned back to Awel.

'Someone left it on the pillow. It's soaked through. But who the hell would have put it there? Are you sure no one could have let themselves in?'

The colour had drained from Awel's face. She seemed

to be avoiding my eyes. 'I – I don't know. I really can't explain it.'

I felt suddenly annoyed. 'It couldn't have just got there by itself, could it!'

'Believe me, I've no idea. I'm sure it wouldn't be any of the casual staff. There have been some strange things going on since your auntie passed. Stuff being moved; things going missing. Almost as though someone's trying to tell us something.'

'Oh, come on; surely you're not implying we have a ghost? And *please* don't go saying anything like that in front of Ruby – you'll scare the life out of her.'

'I'm not implying *anything*. I'm just saying, that's all. It always pays to keep an open mind.'

I would have laughed if I hadn't felt so rattled. The idea that the doll could have been moved by the hand of some phantom was ludicrous and I found it hard to believe that Awel could genuinely think such a thing.

I remembered talking to Auntie Gwyn once about whether she believed in the supernatural. I was about nine; she had come to tuck me in one night, but far from being ready for sleep, I was going through a phase of reading ghost stories and, while they didn't usually spook me, one of the *Goosebumps* books had sent my imagination into overdrive. Even though I was only a child, she had always considered her answers to my questions carefully; she was never dismissive of anything without having reasoned it through.

'I've never seen one, but I'd never scoff at anyone who had claimed to,' she had said on reflection. 'There's so much on this earth we don't really understand. You

95

would think that in my line of business, I might've had the odd encounter – but I never have. But even if they *do* exist, I don't think we have anything to fear from them, so you have nothing to worry about. There is far more to fear from the living than the dead, *cariad*. Always remember that.'

Her words had satisfied me at the time and stayed with me ever since. And nothing would convince me now that any unexplained happenings in the house could be attributed to anything other than a very solid and worryingly twisted human hand.

Ruby and Elis joined us and we sat round the table, eating warm *crempog* with butter and drinking tea from china cups. Tea at four o'clock had always been sacrosanct in Ty Coed Pinwydd and it was one ritual I had dearly missed.

I signed at Elis. *I thought you'd got rid of that rag doll?*

He pulled in his neck and puckered his lips, looking confused. *I did.*

Well, someone left it in our room.

He shot a look at Awel and shrugged. *It wasn't me. Could the little girl have brought it in?*

In a word, no. She's been with me all afternoon.

We seemed to be going round in circles. If either Awel or Elis knew anything about the doll's reappearance, they clearly weren't prepared to share it.

Awel was intent on changing the subject.

'I'd like to show you the proposed order of service for the funeral. We've been looking through some photographs – see if you like the ones we've picked out.'

We went through into the living room. This was the first time I'd entered the room since our arrival and it was obviously not occupied much. The weighty curtains were partially drawn, letting in only a narrow shaft of light. Awel pushed them aside, releasing a swirl of dust motes. I looked around: everything was as I remembered, but with an edge of decay. Lacy cobwebs hung from the corners of the old stone fireplace and the air smelled fusty.

'Sit, sit.' She waved us towards the Chesterfield settee, large patches of its green leather worn and dull. On the low mahogany coffee table sat a neat pile of photographs, next to which was a battered, bulging cardboard folder.

'These are the ones we've chosen. We just need to whittle them down,' she told us, handing me the pile. Ruby squashed herself close to me on the chair and together we looked through the various pictures of Auntie Gwyn, from babyhood through to the present day. Some of the images were familiar, but others were new to me. She had never been a beautiful woman, even in her youth; handsome would have been a better word. But in the more recent pictures, there was a sadness in her eyes and her increasing frailty was evident. I swallowed down the tears which were threatening, feeling the constriction in my chest.

'We can have up to five in the pamphlet if we want,' Awel explained. 'What do you think?'

I cleared my throat. 'Maybe four – one as a baby, a child, a young adult and how she would be recognised today.' I shuffled through once more and handed back the pictures I thought showed my aunt to her best advantage. She had never been vain, far from it; her physical appearance was never high on her list of priorities. But there were one or two photos that really didn't do her justice at all.

It was ironic really: Auntie Gwyn had always been so concerned that the deceased handed over to her care should be primped and preened to look their best, and yet while she ensured that she was always tidy and well turned out, she never wore make-up or bodily adornments herself. She favoured function over fashion: trousers over skirts; brogues over stilettos. Her hair was clean and combed, but never styled or coloured; she would attack it with the scissors periodically if it started to annoy her. I don't think she ever went to a hairdresser in her life. A complete absence of vanity.

When I was about eleven, I remember watching in fascination as she carefully applied powder and lipstick to an elderly lady, then a slick of red varnish to the woman's carefully trimmed and filed nails, before folding the hands neatly across the chest.

'Do people's nails get longer after they've died, then?' I'd asked, staring curiously at the gnarled fingers, and the clippings which she had collected in a kidney-shaped steel receptacle.

'Oh, no,' she'd explained. 'It's just that the skin starts to shrink back, making it look as if the hair and nails are still growing. That's why they need a bit of a tidy, just to make them look presentable.'

The next time she needed to perform a manicure, she had called me in and asked if I would like to help. I became quite adept at shaping and polishing the nails, and it made me feel useful. I was always a bit blasé about it: it didn't occur to me that it was an unusual thing to be doing.

Some three years later, I remember watching my mum getting ready for a party one evening and, keen to show off my skills, offered to do her nails. She had hesitated initially, but my dad encouraged her to let me help. I chose a pearlescent peach shade to complement her apricot blouse, and made quite a decent job of it, even if I say so myself.

She had actually praised my handiwork and seemed pleased. 'Where did you learn to do that?' she'd asked, flexing her hands before her to admire them.

But when she discovered that it had been through helping Auntie Gwyn, the colour drained from her face.

'You mean – you practised on *corpses*?' The corners of her lips curled downwards in revulsion. She turned to my dad, where he sat in his armchair reading the newspaper, accusingly. 'Did you know about this? That your sister allowed her to . . . to *touch* them?'

His cheeks flushed. He looked from me to my mum and opened his mouth, but no words came out. She shook her head, disgusted by his complicity, and turned back to me.

'I suppose you thought it would be funny to use me as your first living guinea pig, huh?'

'No! I just . . .'

But she had stomped from the room and slammed the door behind her, leaving me bewildered and hurt. Later, as she put on her coat to leave the house, I saw that she had removed the varnish. It seemed that whatever I did, it was never right in her eyes. I was destined to be a lifelong disappointment to her.

Ruby had picked up the old folder and started to pull out the photographs it contained. Some were ancient, sepia pictures of Ty Coed Pinwydd as it had been when my hen hen Taid had first set up the business, the whole family standing solemnly in their Sunday best in the foreground; the boys in knee breeches and slicked-down hair, the girls' high-collared, tight-waisted dresses reaching to their ankles. Dates had been written on the backs of most of the pictures in faded blue ink. They had been filed roughly in date order, if a little randomly, according to subject, and I was concerned that Ruby was muddling them all.

'Careful, sweetheart. Don't mix them up – the old ones should all be at the bottom.'

She gasped. 'Who's this, Mummy?' She was staring at a black and white snap and flipped it over to reveal the date – 1968. 'The girl looks just like me!'

I picked up the photograph. It was of Sionyn and Carys, playing near the fountain in the garden. They'd obviously been throwing a ball to one another and had paused to pose for the camera. And Carys was, without doubt, the image of Ruby. The likeness was astonishing and I felt the hairs on my arms prickle.

'Well, I never. I haven't seen that one before. Yes, you look very similar.'

'Is she the one whose grave we were trying to find in the church?'

The image drew my eyes like a magnet. 'That's right. Awel – I meant to ask you – d'you know where Carys is buried? We couldn't find the grave at Llanbadrig. Hannah, the lady working there, told us she might be in Llanbabo churchyard instead.'

'Hmm? Oh, I'm sure your aunt must have told me at some point, but I'm afraid I don't remember. Carys died long before we came here. Yes, I suppose she could be in Llanbabo. Your hen hen Nain and Taid are buried there, I believe.' She began to tidy away the pictures that Ruby had strewn all over the table with a sudden inexplicable urgency. I watched her curiously.

'Let me help.' One by one, I began to examine the pictures to ensure they were being replaced in the correct order. There were many I hadn't seen before and I would have liked to look at them all properly, but Awel seemed anxious to put everything back now we'd made our selection for the order of service.

'Ooh – is that me?' I pulled out a glossy print of a chubby, laughing baby, held aloft in outstretched, freckled arms by a woman with her back to the camera. A scarf covered her head, long titian curls protruding from beneath it. 'Who's that I'm with?'

Awel glanced at the image. 'Oh, I think that's probably Gwyn's cousin. She used to visit quite regularly when you were small. I forget her name now . . .'

'Look!' Ruby, who had been watching sulkily as we put the photos away, gave a sudden squeal. She was indicating a colour snapshot which had fallen to the floor. As I picked it up, my stomach lurched.

I turned the picture over in my hands. It was dated December 1962 and showed a little red-haired girl wearing a tinsel crown, her face lit by a beaming smile, standing before a huge Christmas tree in the entrance hall of Ty Coed Pinwydd. Against her chest, she was proudly clasping what was clearly a Christmas gift. A pristine rag doll, with a mop of bright orange hair and a triangular red nose, dressed in a blue floral smock.

'*Doli glwt.*' My voice was barely more than a croak. Somehow I had known the doll – but had no real recollection of having seen it years ago. 'That's the one Ruby found in the fountain – or one identical.'

'Ah, so *that's* Doli glwt.' Awel took the picture from me, her eyes focused firmly on the image. Something resembling discomfort flickered across her face. 'I remember Gwyn talking about that doll – Carys loved it apparently; took it everywhere with her.'

'Maybe she'd told me, too.' *Someone* must have described it once; the doll seemed familiar to me, but I felt certain I'd never laid eyes on it before. It had triggered something in the depths of my subconscious that I couldn't place, but found strangely unsettling. If I retrieved the thing, perhaps it would help me to remember.

I thought for a moment. 'Maybe we *should* wash her and place her on Carys's grave, if we can find it. What d'you think, Ruby?'

She threw up her hands in dismay. 'But she's gone! Elis chucked her into the trees.'

'Oh, I'm sure we can find her.' I held Awel's gaze for a moment. 'I'll go and have a look.'

*

After breakfast the following day, Elis said that he would drive Ruby and me to Llanbabo, which was some seven miles away. I had a real bee in my bonnet now about finding Carys's grave, especially since her treasured doll had turned up like that. I couldn't get it out of my head. I had difficulty sleeping yet again; not because I held any store by Awel's suggestion of spooky goings-on, but owing to a genuine concern that someone must have been in our room. It was a disturbing thought.

By mid-morning, the heat was already oppressive. Even with the windows open, the air in the car had felt stifling. It was oddly reminiscent of that day all those years ago – the awful day that the police knocked on the door to tell us that a young local girl had gone missing. We had waved my parents off only the previous afternoon, and I had the whole summer break before me. Or so I thought.

I can still recall that morning with such clarity. I had accompanied Elis to the supermarket in Holyhead and, amongst other things, we'd bought a big bag of ice-pops to freeze when we got back. I remember it as if it were yesterday: my hair blowing in the warm breeze as I stuck my face out of the car window, wishing I hadn't worn shorts as I shifted uncomfortably to stop the backs of my bare legs sticking to the hot leatherette seat. Upon our return, we were greeted with the sight of a police car in the drive. Flustered and red-faced, Auntie Gwyn had rushed out to meet us, explaining what had happened. It was completely shocking.

For days, the whole area was a hive of activity as the police conducted their search, and the local people came out in force to help – all to no avail. Posters with pictures of Beca appeared as if by magic, nailed to every telegraph pole and in every shop window; the same school photograph that smiled out from every newspaper and the television news bulletins. That face would be forever engraved on my memory: the long, dark hair swept into a ponytail, the snub nose sprinkled with freckles, the dimpled cheeks. The atmosphere over the whole area was oppressive, one of foreboding and eventual resignation. The freedom to roam and play outside unhindered was suddenly snatched from me and every other child in the area. At Ty Coed Pinwydd there seemed to be a lot of anguished exchanges between the adults and much whispering behind closed doors. And within the week, my parents had returned and the terrible disagreement between Auntie Gwyn and my dad ensued. I had never seen him so angry.

Thinking back now, the girl's disappearance seemed to be the catalyst for me being whisked away from Llanbadrig, never to return. I suppose I wasn't old enough then to fully appreciate the gravity of the situation. If anything, it probably felt a bit exciting at the time. But I certainly understood the impact it seemed to have had on my own existence.

She was never found – that much I gleaned because of the occasional update on the national news delivered by a grave-faced reporter. The incident was never discussed at home, which, thinking back, was a little odd. I often wondered over the years what had become of the poor girl, especially whenever there was a report of another missing child in the headlines. As I got older, I realised how worrying it was that something of such magnitude had happened so close to where I had been living. And it occurred to me then that the girl could just as easily have been me.

*

The old church at Llanbabo stood on an awkward bend in the road, which was mercifully quiet. We parked opposite the graveyard where the track was widest, next to a rough stone wall, over which spilled a hedge composed largely of brambles and nettles. I scrambled across the seat from the passenger's side to get out of the car, to avoid being cut to ribbons. An abundance of butterflies skittered in and out of the hedgerows, and swifts rose and swooped around us. It was a glorious day.

Elis led the way, creaking open the low wrought-iron gate, from which a path meandered between the graves. The grounds were unkempt and overgrown, and the majority of headstones looked fairly ancient. Ruby and I lagged behind to look around, while Elis strode purposefully ahead, then stopped in front of a cluster of graves to the left of the church. He waved us over.

These are your great-great-grandparents' graves, he signed. *I suppose she must be here somewhere.*

Elis seemed a little impatient, I thought. Maybe it was the heat.

The inscriptions were even fainter than those on the family plots in Llanbadrig, but the names just about legible.

Ruby moved in and out of the headstones, reading the words aloud as best she could. These were my hen Taid's parents, his father, like my Taid, also called Idwal; his mother, Eleri.

105

'Here she is!' announced Ruby triumphantly, pointing to a low slab of slate in the row immediately behind. Much of the inscription was obscured by the long grass around the base and yellow lichen which crept over the surface, but the name, Carys Hughes Owen, was clear enough. I placed a hand on the warm stone, my eyes filling with tears. Why had they buried her here and not with Sionyn? It was as though they'd forgotten about her, putting her so far away amongst all these much older graves. It made no sense.

So you know where the grave is now, Elis declared, dusting off his hands as if that was an end to it. *Mystery solved*.

But for me the mystery had only deepened.

*

We washed the doll and left it to drip in the sun so we could take it to Llanbabo at some point. I found some polythene in which to wrap it, but Elis dug out an old curio cabinet, which was even better. When the doll was almost dry, I took it in and pegged it to the airer in the kitchen. Even more of the woollen hair had dropped out in the process, but at least it was clean. Knowing now where Carys had been laid to rest, it seemed all the more poignant, and important to take something that had been dear to her in life to commemorate her existence. I was on an emotional knife-edge anyway, but finding that she had been separated from the rest of her immediate family in death had really upset me. It seemed callous, somehow. I was baffled as to what the reasons behind it all were.

CHAPTER SEVEN

Awel had received a phone call from Meredith Williams, the solicitor dealing with Auntie Gwyn's financial affairs. He was terribly apologetic, but wondered if it would be possible to reschedule the reading of the will for the day before, rather than after, the funeral. Apparently, his elderly mother had already been waiting for an operation for months, and a late cancellation, meaning that the opportunity to bring her surgery forward to the day we had been due to meet, was too good a chance to miss. We agreed that it would be fine. The contents of the will would be the same whenever it took place; the date of the reading seemed, at the time, irrelevant.

The original plan had been to meet Mr Williams at his office in Bangor, but he was happy to come to Ty Coed Pinwydd under the circumstances. I was worried about what Ruby would do while we all assembled for the meeting, but Awel's friend Eluned kindly offered to take her to the Sea Zoo for the afternoon, as she had arranged to take her own granddaughter, who was just a little younger than Ruby. Ruby seemed quite enthused and I was grateful. At least she would have company of her own age for a while.

Just before noon on the day of the will reading, Eluned came to collect her. Ruby climbed shyly into the back of Eluned's red Fiesta and we waved them off, Ruby sitting slightly awkwardly next to Eluned's sulky-looking granddaughter, Nerys. I had hoped they'd hit it off, but it wasn't looking too hopeful.

After a lunch of mushroom omelette (of which I had eaten very little), Awel and I went to sit on the old, slightly lumpy sofa in the cosy sitting room at the front of the house. After the heat of the previous couple of days, the temperature had plummeted again and we had a log fire burning. Awel felt the living room was too large and the kitchen too informal for such an occasion, and decided we should assemble in this other, smaller reception room. The same ancient television I remembered watching as a child stood in one corner, its age suggesting it was rarely watched any more, an antique brass art-deco-style standard lamp in another.

We heard the crunch of tyres on gravel and I turned to look out of the window. The solicitor stepped out of a large, shiny black BMW as though making a grand entrance, pulling a brown leather briefcase from the back seat.

Awel went to let him in. He was a stocky, dark-haired man in his forties, dressed impeccably and clean-shaven. A waft of expensive-smelling aftershave preceded his entry into the room.

'Mrs Morris, pleased to meet you.' His handshake was firm and reassuring, his smile genuine. 'I'm Meredith. I really must apologise, I believe I addressed you incorrectly in the letter I sent.'

'It's fine.'

'I'm sorry for having to rearrange at such short notice. My mother has to go in for a small op – there was a cancellation so they've squeezed her in; nothing serious, thankfully. But well, you know . . .' He looked awkward. 'Erm – do you have a table where I can lay out my paperwork, please?'

Awel wheeled across an old, green baize card table that had been pushed against the wall and positioned it in front of the wing chair.

'Is this big enough?'

'Perfect. May I?'

He proceeded to remove a sheaf of papers from a folder in his briefcase, then waved a hand at the chair. 'Should I sit here?'

'Of course.' Awel glanced at me, the hint of a smile playing on her lips as Meredith carefully opened out the back of his suit jacket before lowering himself onto the seat.

'Now then, shall we begin?' Opening his spectacles case, he took out a pair of designer steel-rimmed glasses and peered at the front page of his notes. 'Oh. Is Mr Elis Morgan joining us?' He looked round as if expecting to see Elis lurking in a corner somewhere.

'I'll go and get him. I think he's still resting after lunch – he's not getting any younger. None of us are, unfortunately.' Awel gave a wry smile.

She left the room, leaving an uneasy silence hanging between Meredith and me. I realised now that this had been a mistake – with the funeral looming, I really wasn't in any fit state to concentrate on anything he might have to say.

'Are all the funeral plans going well? Must be strange, Miss Hughes Owen having been in the business herself, I suppose,' he ventured, then checked himself, his cheeks tinging pink.

Awel reappeared with a bleary-eyed Elis in tow. Meredith rose to shake his hand, then went through the ritual of smoothing out his blazer once more as he sat. This was all so wrong. Auntie Gwyn wasn't even in her grave, and here we were, discussing her money. It seemed almost mercenary. I felt suddenly sick and wasn't sure I could sit for much longer.

'I don't know whether you have any inkling of the contents of Miss Hughes Owen's last will and testament,' he began, 'but I'd like to read it out verbatim, and then you can put any questions you may have to me. Is that all right?'

Awel signed to Elis, who appeared slightly bemused, but we all nodded our assent.

'Please, I don't mean to be rude, but if you could just get on with it.' I sat on the edge of my seat, wringing my hands.

Meredith looked uncomfortable. 'Of course, of course.' His eyes scanned the document on the table before him. He began to read, mumbling as though digesting the content as he went.

This is the last will and testament of me, Gwyneth Hughes Owen, of Ty Coed Pinwydd, Llanbadrig, Anglesey, whereby I revoke all former wills and testamentary dispositions heretofore made by me and declare this to be my last will. I appoint my solicitors, Rowland and Williams, to be the executors of my will.

His words faded in and out as I stared into space. I could feel tears threatening, thinking all the time about Auntie Gwyn and how I had made no effort to contact her in her old age, when she had shown me nothing but kindness. I felt ashamed.

And then:

With addendums to follow, I give, devise and bequeath my estate both real and personal of whatsoever nature and wheresoever situate unto my niece, Lowri Hughes Owen, conditional upon retaining Ty Coed Pinwydd as an operational business and providing a lifelong home in their retirement for my cousins and loyal friends, Awel and Elis Morgan.

Awel sat bolt upright. She shot me a strangely stony look, but rearranged her face quickly into a thin smile.

She signed frantically to Elis, who raised his eyebrows, grinning at me reassuringly.

The room began to sway. I excused myself and went out into the hallway, clutching the frame as I opened the front door and gulping in the cool air as it rushed in. So Awel had got it all wrong: Auntie Gwyn had changed nothing. I could hardly take it in.

Meredith stuck his head out of the sitting room door as I stood shakily just inside the veranda. He appeared anxious, his brow furrowed in concern. 'I'm terribly sorry if this is causing you distress. Do you think it might be best if we call a halt to the proceedings for today? I realise this probably isn't the most auspicious occasion. Perhaps we should rearrange until after the . . .'

'No.' I wiped my eyes with a sleeve and drew myself up. 'It's been a bit of a surprise, that's all. No, let's just get it all out of the way. One thing less to worry about once the funeral is behind us.'

'Very well; if you're sure.' He looked unconvinced.

We resumed our places in the sitting room, my eyes fixed distractedly on the window, not focusing fully on Meredith's words as my thoughts drifted constantly to poor Auntie Gwyn. There seemed to be a lot of waffle and convoluted language; he paused frequently to allow Awel to convey exactly what was being said to Elis. But the gist of it all was that I was the main beneficiary, with a few provisos – mainly that Awel and Elis would be well taken care of until the end of their days but that their input with the business should be phased out, and that I was expected to follow in Auntie Gwyn's footsteps. I felt as if I was over a barrel in one way; but *what* a

112

drastic change in my circumstances. From dinner lady to business owner, in one fell swoop. It was mind-blowing.

'Well, that concludes Miss Hughes Owen's final wishes.' Meredith took off his glasses, wiping them with a square of cloth from their case. 'Does anyone have any questions? From my end, it does all seem fairly straight-forward. And as Mr Lewis Bevan was otherwise engaged today, he'll be informed of his bequest in writing.'

I jerked my head round, suddenly aware that I must have missed something fairly significant.

'I'm sorry – did you say Lewis?'

'Yes. Your aunt had taken him under her wing some years ago and he repaid her kindness by assisting with various aspects of the business and general maintenance, free of charge.'

'Can you repeat that last bit you read out, please? I think I must have switched off for a moment.'

Meredith glanced at Awel, whose face looked pinched and drained of any vestige of colour. Her hands were folded tightly in her lap, the knuckles white. I couldn't decide if she was building up to some sort of outburst.

The solicitor appeared flustered. He scratched his head and pored over his notes once more, retracing the lines with a finger to find his place before continuing falteringly.

'There is a . . . erm . . . a pecuniary bequest of twenty thousand pounds – the fruition of a life insurance policy, to Lewis Bevan. For services rendered over the years.'

My mouth fell open. '*Twenty thousand?* That seems quite a lot.'

'He *has* been very helpful,' interjected Awel defensively. Her breathing sounded laboured now; suppressed, even.

I turned to her. 'It's just that I was under the impression things were in a sorry state financially. Not that I'm going to quibble,' I added hastily, 'if that was what Auntie Gwyn wanted.'

Awel glowered at me. Her voice was shrill. 'The business isn't in great shape, no. But without Lewis's input, it would be a damned sight worse. And Gwyn had set a certain amount of money aside – for this and that.'

I wasn't sure exactly how Lewis had helped, but had to trust my aunt's judgement. After all, I hadn't seen her for so long – a great deal must have happened over the last two decades. My lengthy absence precluded me from questioning any decision she may have made. And at that moment, I felt that he was probably more worthy of the whole lot than I was.

I stood up, feeling suddenly exhausted. 'If that's all, Mr Williams—'

'Meredith; please.'

'If that's all, Meredith, I'm very sorry, but this has been a lot to digest. I really can't think clearly at the moment. Thank you for taking the time to come here today.'

He rose to his feet and extended a hand. 'Maybe we can chat again if there's anything you'd like me to clarify. I appreciate this hasn't been the ideal time for you all. I do hope that everything goes smoothly with the funeral. I had the pleasure of meeting Miss Hughes Owen on a few occasions and she was an admirable lady.'

I nodded mutely, the words I intended to utter sticking firmly in my throat as tears spilled down my cheeks. I stumbled from the room and up the stairs. In spite of everything, Auntie Gwyn had never forgotten me. She had put me first, even above the unwaveringly loyal Awel and Elis, and I had never done anything for her. I felt terrible about it all. Flinging myself face down onto my bed, I wept into the pillow until eventually falling asleep from sheer exhaustion.

*

When I awoke the room was dim. The trickle of light passing through the partially opened curtains cast long shadows across the bed and I felt frozen, pulling the covers around me. I glanced at the bedside clock, seeing from the illuminated dial that it was half past nine. Ruby was already sleeping, tucked into her bed with Benjy at her side, red curls fanned out beneath her on her pillow. I felt guilty that I'd slept through her evening and hoped she was okay. I would have to ask her how she got on in the morning.

I sat up, rubbing my eyes, my stomach dropping as the memory of the will resurged. I had such mixed feelings about it all, guilt being the overriding emotion.

I hauled myself to my feet and stepped lightly across the floor, then made my way shakily down to the kitchen.

Muffled discourse from the other side of the closed door made me pause before entering. The conversation had begun in Welsh, lapsing into English. It seemed as though Awel and Lewis were discussing the will. His voice sounded edgy.

'All the same though, I'm not sure . . .' There was a pause. Then, 'How did she take it, anyway?'

115

'Okay, I think – she just seemed surprised, more than anything.'

'I can see why – I'm pretty stunned myself. Hadn't realised the old girl felt quite so indebted to me.'

'Well, God knows she had good reason to. We all have. After . . .' Her voice faded. I strained to hear, but the room had fallen silent. I pushed the door in time to see Lewis with a finger pressed to his lips, as though warning her to keep quiet. Their heads whipped round as I stood in the doorway. They both looked at me guiltily.

'Sorry – am I interrupting something?'

Lewis's cheeks reddened and he seemed to squirm. He looked almost apologetic.

Awel stiffened. She flashed me a broad smile, which failed to conceal her discomfort.

'No, not at all.' She patted the back of the chair she was standing behind. 'Come and sit, and I'll make you something to eat – you must be starving. You slept through supper – I thought it best not to wake you.'

I smiled weakly. I knew I should probably eat something, but food was the last thing on my mind. My stomach was still in knots after the reading of the will and I knew that *I* was the one who should be feeling sheepish.

'I missed Ruby. How did she get on this afternoon?'

Awel pulled a face. 'I think the Sea Zoo was a hit, but let's say I don't reckon she'll be asking to play with Nerys again any time soon. Eluned says she's a bit spoiled – Nerys was miffed that it wasn't just the two of them. Her face was tripping her all afternoon, apparently.'

'Oh dear. Never mind – at least she liked the zoo. Did she eat all her tea?'

'Every mouthful. She's very easy to please.'

In spite of myself, I grinned. Ruby definitely took after Jonah in that respect. A noise from behind made me turn my head to see Elis appearing from the passageway, sleeves rolled up, his hands caked in soil. He clutched a carrier bag in one fist.

Awel signed to him briskly. *Did you actually pick some more* tatws *in the end? I want to make something for Lowri's supper.* She seemed impatient.

What the hell d'you think I've been doing? he responded, waving the bag aloft irritably. *Had to use the bloody torch.* He glared at her, then turned to me, attempting an encouraging smile, but his eyes were filled with anguish. There had obviously been some sort of disagreement while I was still in bed. I hoped Ruby hadn't heard them arguing.

'I'll make you a warm potato salad, Lowri – some lovely new spuds we've got at the moment.'

'Thank you, but I'm really not hungry.'

The atmosphere had become unbearably tense.

Lewis looked from Awel to Elis uneasily. He stood up and stretched, glancing at me from the corner of his eye. 'Well, that's me, then. Better get back – we've got a lot to do in the morning.' His face fell. 'See you all tomorrow. *Nosdawch.*'

I followed him to the front door, my arms wrapped across my chest. I felt I needed to at least mention the money he'd been left and clear the air.

He beat me to it.

'I'm not a gold digger, Lowri.' His blue eyes locked earnestly with mine and, in spite of everything, I felt something flutter in my stomach.

'No, no. I know that.'

'I thought a lot of your auntie. She – she was one of the good ones, you know?'

'Yes, she certainly was. And I understand you've done a lot to help here these last few years. Much more than I ever have. I really don't deserve any of it.' I felt tears threaten once more.

He ran a hand gently from my shoulder to the elbow, where it lingered for a moment.

'Don't beat yourself up. Awel's filled me in – you've had more than your fair share of crap to deal with. The best advice I can give you is just do what your auntie would have wanted with this place and make her proud. She would ask for no more than that.'

'I'll try.' I clutched my head with both hands. 'Oh God, it's all so much to take in. And I'm *dreading* tomorrow. I'll never sleep tonight with all this going round my mind.'

He looked at me sympathetically, his head tipped to one side. 'Why don't you take a sleeping pill? Awel always has some. You'll feel better about it all once the funeral's over and done with.' He glanced anxiously at his watch. 'Sorry. I really must go. Hope you get a decent night.'

He leaned forwards and brushed my cheek with his lips. I was slightly stunned but not unreceptive. I managed a small smile and wished him goodnight.

I put a hand to my face as I watched him drive away.

118

Was he just being friendly, or was there more to it? I rather hoped it was the latter. I went back to the kitchen, in time to witness a heated exchange between Awel and Elis.

She had her back to me and was signing something frantically, jabbing a finger towards him, the muscles in her cheeks pulsing.

But it's just not . . . he turned, dropping his hands as he saw me coming through the door.

What's going on? I looked from one to the other. The air prickled with animosity.

Elis looked pained. He shrugged and let out a sigh. *I can't do anything right. I'm going to lock up.* He left the room abruptly, leaving me puzzled and Awel simmering.

'Has something happened?'

'No, no.' Almost aggressively, she began to take potatoes out of the bag, dropping them one by one into the washing-up bowl, then fished a peeler from the utensil drawer, slamming it shut.

'Is there anything I should know?' I blurted out. 'You could cut the atmosphere in here with a knife.'

Her eyes didn't meet mine. She was focused firmly on peeling the potatoes. 'Of course not.' She stopped for a moment, clutching the edge of the sink. 'I'm sorry. I suppose I'm just tired and irritable, that's all. It's been such a strain lately. I really need to put tomorrow behind us, move on with things. It's hanging over me, all this.'

I understood only too well. She must be feeling pretty devastated, but I couldn't bring myself to discuss the will with her, not before the funeral. It would have to wait until everything was behind us. Then maybe I could come up with a solution that would please everyone.

'Awel – Lewis says you usually have sleeping tablets – can I have one, please?'

She hesitated, then nodded. She put down the peeler and wiped her hands on her apron. Opening the corner cupboard, she revealed a whole shelf full of medications of one sort or another, all neatly stacked.

'Good grief, it looks like a chemist's dispensary in there!' I remarked. I wondered why there were so many different pills and potions in the house. Maybe a lot of them had been poor Auntie Gwyn's.

Awel smiled wryly. She rifled through and removed a blister pack from one box. Popping out a pill, she handed it to me.

'Have your supper first, then take it right away when you're ready for bed – it should take about half an hour to kick in.'

*

Lewis closed the door into the cottage behind him quietly in the hope of not disturbing Catrin, but movement from the darkness at the far end of the room told him she was still up. His heart sank. A stony face peered round the side of the wing chair, the features distorted eerily by the shadows of low flames which still danced in the grate.

'Where the hell have you been?'

'Sorry, I was trying not to wake you.'

'Well, that's pretty obvious. I thought you'd have been back hours ago.'

He froze in the doorway. 'I've just been up to Ty Coed Pinwydd. They're all in a bit of a bad way, you know, with the funeral looming. And Lowri's feeling pretty cut up that she hadn't seen her auntie for so long.'

Catrin snorted. 'Well, so she should be. And what's it to you, anyway? You don't even know the girl properly.'

He chewed the inside of his cheek. 'I feel sorry for her, that's all. She's got a lot on her plate, on her own with the little kid and everything.'

'I hope you aren't feeling *too* sorry.' She glared at him accusingly.

Lewis stiffened. 'Oh, come on. I'm not looking for another relationship yet – we've been through this.'

She narrowed her eyes. 'It's funny how you come over all concerned when there's a pretty face in the mix.'

He frowned. 'How do you . . .?'

Catrin gave a scornful little laugh. 'I saw her. Walking down the lane, the other day. Not exactly Godzilla, is she?'

He ground his teeth. He was in no mood for a row. 'Think I'll turn in. I've got an early start tomorrow and I'm bushed.'

'Well, that's nice,' she huffed. 'I've waited up for you and now you're just going to bugger off to bed. Can't you even spare me a few minutes for a chat these days?'

He sighed. 'Sorry. Look, what d'you say to going for a late lunch the day after the funeral – my treat. I can knock off early. The café in Church Bay is always a safe bet.'

She wrinkled her nose and pulled a face. 'Can't you stretch to something a bit more . . . upmarket?'

Lewis's heart sank. Despite his recent inheritance, he

121

had just intended something along the lines of decent pub grub as a gesture of goodwill, but realised he would have to bite the bullet to shake her out of her mood. Even if they were no longer officially an item, he still had to share a house with her for the time being, and he hated an atmosphere. 'There's always Melin Llynon, I suppose.'

Catrin managed a smile. 'Ooh, posh! Okay then. What time?'

'I'll ring ahead – I'm thinking about two o'clock. That all right with you?'

She nodded and for the moment peace was restored. Lewis edged towards the door.

'See you in the morning, then. *Nosdawch.*'

'I'll be going up in a minute myself. I'm just having a *panad* – d'you want me to bring you one up?'

'Sure – why not. Not too much milk in mine, please.'

Once in the bedroom, Lewis sank onto the bed and rubbed at his eyes with the heels of his hands. A tense ridge had set in across his shoulders. He'd done his best to keep things amicable. The situation between Catrin and himself was becoming increasingly strained, but she knew so much he felt beholden to her. Lewis had tentatively suggested she just move back in with her parents in the interim, but she wouldn't hear of it. It would have been an admission of failure on her part: they'd always said the relationship wouldn't last. He'd felt he should cut her some slack until she could find a suitable rental. And now he'd been backed into an even tighter corner.

The money was one thing.

But now *this* . . .

What a mess. What an almighty fucking mess.

122

CHAPTER EIGHT

The morning of the funeral had finally arrived. I woke with a sick, hollow feeling in the pit of my stomach, the dread having almost built to a crescendo over the last few days. I wanted to put it all behind me now; to start looking to the future. All those services over the years that had been overseen by Auntie Gwyn, that had all been part of a day's work to her. And now here we were, saying our final goodbyes without the input and support of the one person we'd always relied upon to carry it off with such aplomb. Everything felt askew.

I thought back to one particular funeral that Auntie Gwyn had conducted for a local man in his late thirties, who had died suddenly and very unexpectedly of a brain haemorrhage. I had been about nine at the time, and it was oddly fascinating to me that someone could be apparently healthy and alive one minute, then gone forever without warning the next. He was relatively young, but to me at that age, all adults seemed old; some more so than others, of course. The man's wife and two children, a boy and a girl, had come to view the body the day before the burial. The boy was only about six and perhaps too young to fully grasp what was happening, but the daughter was just a little younger than me, and very upset. I had been sitting reading *Harriet the Spy* in the little sitting room, but, hearing them enter, peeped round the door into the hallway to watch as the family cautiously followed Auntie Gwyn in the direction of the little chapel of rest. Being the nosy child I was, I tiptoed after them.

Auntie Gwyn had been so professional. She spoke quietly and calmly, choosing her words carefully as she addressed the confused children, taking them each by the hand while their distraught mother stood sobbing as she gazed down into the open coffin.

I heard Auntie Gwyn explaining to the children that their daddy was safely in heaven now, but he would always be watching over them, and that he would be very proud of them both for being so brave and taking such good care of their mummy.

'And you can still talk to him, you know,' she'd said in a soothing voice. 'He will hear you. My own daddy died a long time ago, but I talk to him even now. He's always with me – in here.' She tapped her chest and smiled, winking reassuringly.

Along with a pile of magazines, there was always a sketch pad and coloured pencils kept on the low table in the waiting area, and while the mother spent time alone with her husband, Auntie Gwyn led the children back into the lobby where she encouraged them both to write a few words and draw pictures that they could leave with their daddy.

For a while, I went back to the book I'd been reading, but, hearing voices, leaped up to watch through the crack in the door as the family came back into the hallway. The woman's eyes were red and puffy; she looked slightly unsteady and Auntie Gwyn was holding her gently by the arm. As they reached the front door, I saw the little girl reach up and give Auntie Gwyn a grateful hug, handing over an extra picture she had drawn for her. My aunt's head dropped, her shoulders sagging as she closed the door behind them; then taking a deep breath, she composed herself, straightening as she came back inside, a smile pasted on and ready to greet a middle-aged man who had come to make inquiries about her taking on his grandmother's funeral.

It may have been her job – but it suited her so well. She was a true people person. That was why she was so highly thought of in the community. She always put her clients and their families first. Her own happiness had been secondary; she had effectively devoted her whole life to her work. I wondered if she had ever been in love; ever had the desire for a family of her own, and her chosen career path had prevented it. I realised now how hard it must have been for her sometimes. She had always put a brave face on things, no matter how she had been feeling underneath. I hoped, if it came to it, that I could step up to the mark and keep her memory alive. I owed it to her.

The four of us, Awel, Elis, Ruby and me, sat in the back of the funeral car, which Lewis had elected to drive.

One of the company's regular casual workers, a burly farmhand named Curig, had offered to drive the hearse. After days of clear skies and sun, these last two days, the weather had finally broken. It felt appropriate somehow. Huge grey clouds hung ominously above the church and a chill blast of air hit us as we climbed from our vehicle. The sea beyond the headland was choppy, its steely surface reflecting the dour colour of the heavens.

The wooden gate to the church had been propped open in preparation for our arrival. Elis and Lewis stepped forward, along with Curig and three other men from the village. Between them, they carefully lifted the coffin from the hearse and carried it at waist height under the stone arch, hoisting it to their shoulders as they made their way slowly up the path. The bell began to toll, its timbre slow and solemn. Awel looked as pale as death herself. She stumbled a little and I caught her by the arm as we followed them, heading the procession of mourners to the door of the building. Ruby's uncertain little hand found mine and, three abreast, we entered the church.

Hannah was standing inside the doorway, giving out the orders of service. As she passed me one, she squeezed my hand, smiling sadly. I felt dazed and slightly nauseous. We positioned ourselves in the front row, staring straight ahead to where the casket, adorned with the spray of pink roses that Ruby and I had chosen, rested on the catafalque. People continued to file in and soon the church was packed to capacity. An elderly man played a mournful entrance piece on the organ and then for a moment all was quiet, save for the shuffling of the pamphlets as everyone looked to see what hymns had been chosen and the occasional sigh or whisper as they saw the photographs of Auntie Gwyn.

The service was a blur. Reverend Parry, the earnest but pleasant middle-aged minister, read out the eulogy which Awel and I had written between us, and everyone joined in singing a muted rendition of Auntie Gwyn's favourite hymn, '*Calon Lân*'. The organist played us out to the tune of '*Bugeilio'r Gwenith Gwyn*' ('Watching the White Wheat'), a piece of music which she had always loved and seemed fitting.

A harsh wind whipped round us as we left the building and followed the bearers as they shouldered the coffin towards the freshly dug grave. Although the rain had kept off, fine salt spray blew in from the sea, enough to dampen our clothes and hair. Ruby clung onto my hand like a limpet.

'What's happening now, Mummy?' she whispered.

'They're going to say prayers, then Auntie Gwyn will be buried.' I felt a sob rise in my chest and clenched my jaw.

The mourners assembled at the graveside as Reverend Parry said prayers and delivered the committal. There was a lot of sniffling and people mopping at their eyes. I watched Awel, who wept silently as the huge oak box was lowered into the ground. She glanced upwards briefly and gave me a strange, distant look. Her face was unreadable.

Everyone's attention seemed to be focused on the grave. It all suddenly felt quite surreal – as though none of this was really happening. A waking dream. I was a bystander, encased in a bubble, observing from afar. Something drew my attention to the higher ground towards the coastal path. A solitary figure, dressed in a dark hooded coat, stood watching the proceedings. The shoulders seemed to be moving rhythmically, as though shaken by sobs. It was hard to say whether the person was male or female, but seeing me looking, it froze for a moment, then turned swiftly and headed towards the stone arch that led back to the cliffs in the direction of Bull Bay and the road away from Ty Coed Pinwydd, disappearing over the headland.

*

The buzz of muted conversation filled the living room. Awel and I had spring-cleaned and made everything as presentable as possible the previous day, before the mourners began to arrive in their droves for the wake. People stood in huddles, the odd few perched awkwardly on the settee or the dining chairs that we had positioned around the periphery of the room. Elis, assisted by an eager Ruby offering milk and sugar, was standing behind a trestle table on tea and coffee duty. I proffered a tray bearing schooners of sherry – not my preferred tipple, but something Awel thought appropriate, as Auntie Gwyn had always loved it. Everyone wanted to offer their condolences and share anecdotes about Auntie Gwyn. I had never been particularly good at talking to strangers and was finding it a strain.

Reverend Parry collared me as I was heading back to the kitchen to replenish the drinks.

'I hope you were pleased with the service, Lowri?'

'It was lovely. Thank you. So good to see how many

people turned out – Auntie Gwyn was obviously well-loved in the community.'

'Oh, definitely. She dealt with my dear mam's funeral, shortly after we moved into the area a couple of years ago – did a wonderful job.' He paused to take a sip of tea. 'So do you plan to stay on now, or are you leaving us again?'

I chewed my lip. I'd thought of little else ever since the reading of the will. On the face of things, it was a no-brainer; I should grab the opportunity with both hands and rejoice that Auntie Gwyn had put me in this position. But there was still a lot to weigh up. The business clearly needed an overhaul and I wasn't sure I had the confidence, let alone the know-how, to tackle it. Even with Awel and Elis in the picture, neither of them were getting any younger and I still had Ruby to consider. I'd be sad to leave Nina, and Ruby would miss Mickey and her schoolfriends. But then there was the reality of clean sea air, wide open spaces; no more worries about rent. The opportunity to build on an existing business which was all about helping others. I kept flitting between excitement and despair over it all. Maybe I'd feel better and more rational after a day or two, having put the funeral behind me.

'I'm in two minds, to be honest. I do love Anglesey, though.' And I did: being back in Llanbadrig reminded me just what I had been missing. Maybe now I was that bit older it meant even more to me, that sense of connection; belonging. It was hard to explain.

'Well, as your roots are here, it would be good for young Ruby to be brought up on the island – speaking from personal experience, I can highly recommend living here. It's good for the soul.'

'Oh, I know. I used to stay with Auntie Gwyn all the time, years ago. But my roots are actually divided, as my mum came from the Midlands.'

He looked puzzled. 'But – I thought your mam was from Llanbadrig.'

'No, no; that was Dad. My mum was English – she came from Warwickshire.'

'Oh. Right. My mistake.' He seemed suddenly distracted, tipping the cup and saucer in his hand to one side.

'Careful, you're spilling your tea!'

'Oh dear.' He fumbled in his jacket pocket for a tissue and mopped at his sleeve. His eyes began to scan the room. 'If you'll excuse me, I ought to mingle a little as I'll have to leave soon – another service at two o'clock.'

'Yes, of course. Thanks so much for everything.'

He nodded and smiled hesitantly before moving off to speak to Awel. I watched him for a moment, puzzled by his apparent change in mood.

Lewis caught my eye from across the room as I returned from the kitchen with more drinks. He smiled and my stomach gave a little flip as he made his way over. He looked handsome in his suit, if a little uncomfortable.

He studied my face for a moment. 'How are you doing?'

'I'm okay, thanks. A bit knackered now, though.'

'It's been an emotional day.' He cocked his head sympathetically. 'Here, go and get yourself a seat and give me that tray. I'll see if I can offload them for you.'

I handed over the sherries willingly and a tingle passed through me as his hand brushed against my own briefly. I thanked him and watched for a moment as he began to move through the crowd playing host, then sought a chair near the window, content to people-watch and rest my feet for a while. The rain had begun to fall with a vengeance immediately after the burial and was now sheeting against the window, distorting my view of the garden. I took out my phone and began to text Nina. She'd asked me to let her know how things had gone.

But from the corner of my eye, fleeting movement between the trees told me that someone was observing the house from a distance. I suddenly remembered the hooded figure from the graveyard.

I needed to know who this person was; why they felt unable to join a gathering where all were welcome. Dropping my phone mid-text and ignoring the deluge, I hurried from the room and ran out through the front door, stupidly not even stopping to put on a raincoat.

'Hello?' I called out. 'Can I help you?'

The figure seemed startled. It hesitated for a moment as if unsure where to go, then turned and retreated quickly behind the dense green curtain of foliage. I rushed across the lawn, my shoes sinking into the sodden turf, mud splashing my trousers. Cold droplets trickled down my face and neck.

'Hello? Would you like to come in?'

I looked from one side to the other, but could see no one. Exasperated and soaked to the skin, eventually I returned to the house where Awel was waiting anxiously on the veranda.

She looked aghast. 'Good grief girl, you'll catch your death! Whatever were you doing?'

'There was someone out there. But when I went to look for them, they vanished. It's really weird.'

She cast a look at the thicket and wrinkled her nose. 'A lost holidaymaker, perhaps. Come on, let's get you a towel. And you'd better change.'

'But I've nothing else suitable to wear . . .'

'We'll find you something. No shortage of black clothing in this house.'

*

Damp-haired and dressed now in one of Auntie Gwyn's rather frumpy white high-necked blouses and a black knee-length skirt of Awel's pulled in with a belt, I returned to the gathering, feeling self-conscious. Lewis arched an eyebrow and smirked playfully. He offered me a sherry, which I declined.

'What happened to you?'

'I thought I saw someone outside in the trees, so I went to investigate.'

His eyes widened. 'You're kidding. In *this*?' He gestured to the window.

'Look, I'm sure I've seen somebody watching us on a few occasions now. Any ideas who they might be?'

He shook his head and put down the tray on the sideboard, running a finger under his collar and loosening his tie. His eyes slanted towards the fireplace.

'Could be anyone. Might not even have been the same person every time. They get all sorts coming for a nosy at the house – death holds a strange fascination for some people, doesn't it? Plenty of weirdos out there – most of 'em harmless, thankfully.'

'But I'm sure this same person was at the church today. They looked – upset.'

'Well, your Auntie Gwyn was a popular lady. Helped a lot of people round here through a rough patch, myself included.'

'Why would they have stayed away from the service, though?'

'Search me. Maybe they were having a bad hair day.' He grinned. 'Don't let it worry you.'

Someone across the room had caught his attention. He mouthed something in Welsh and waved.

'Sorry.' He turned back to me sheepishly. 'I'm being summoned. My . . . erm . . . friend has to leave to go to work – got to give her a lift. I'll try to pop back later.'

I looked over my shoulder to see a petite girl of about thirty, pouting glossy red lips in Lewis's direction from near the doorway. I had noticed her earlier in the church, sitting near the back. She tossed her long, bleached blonde hair and scowled at me as our eyes met. I felt deflated, slightly upset even, to learn that he was apparently spoken for. I had thought there was a bit of a spark between us. Maybe it was wishful thinking.

Elis was looking flustered as people continued to queue for hot drinks. I looked around for Ruby, but she was nowhere to be seen. I made my way round the table to offer my assistance.

Where's your little helper? I signed.

Elis shrugged. *Went to the toilet a while ago. Not back yet.*

133

I stood serving tea and exchanging pleasantries for a few minutes, but began to feel a prickle of concern that Ruby hadn't reappeared.

Elis, can you manage without me for a bit? I'm going to look for Ruby.

He waved a hand towards the door. *Yes; go, go. Everything's under control.*

Awel was coming in from the hallway as I left the room.

'D'you know if Ruby is still upstairs?'

She frowned. 'No; she was helping Elis, last time I saw her.'

'She's been gone ages – she said she was going to the bathroom. I'll go and check if she's okay.'

A line of around seven people had formed along the landing, waiting to use the toilet. I glanced to the end to see if Ruby was amongst them, but they were all adults.

'Excuse me – has anyone seen my daughter? The little girl with the wild red curls?'

They looked from one to the other, shaking their heads.

'There's a lady in there at the moment. Been in there a while, too,' one man informed me, rolling his eyes.

I sighed. Maybe Ruby was in the bedroom. I went to look but the room was empty. As I came back down the landing, the bathroom door opened and a plump, sheepish-looking middle-aged woman came out.

'You'll need more paper, I'm afraid,' she told the man at the front of the queue.

I went straight to the cupboard at the far end of the landing and took out a packet of loo rolls. Glancing to

134

my left, I noticed the door that was usually kept locked was ajar. I took the toilet rolls and deposited them outside the bathroom, then hurried back to look into the room.

Bizarrely, the door was now closed. I tried the handle but it was locked once more. I sniffed the air. There was a trace of that smell again – the musky, slightly off perfume that I had noticed when the doll had been left on the bed. Pressing an ear to the door, I strained to hear if there was any movement on the other side. Silence.

Maybe I'd been mistaken. I squeezed past the line of people and made my way back downstairs.

I wondered then if Ruby had gone to see Pwtyn in the kitchen. Animals drew her like a magnet. The cat was curled up asleep in her usual place, but there was no one else about. I was beginning to feel anxious. Frantically, I searched the other rooms downstairs, but there was nothing to suggest that Ruby, or anyone else, had been in any of them – and why would she, anyway? She had been wary of even going to the bathroom unaccompanied ever since we arrived, let alone exploring the rest of the house. I glanced down the corridor towards the preparation room but quickly dismissed the thought that she would have strayed down there, especially not on such a dismal day. It felt eerier than ever.

'You're not lost, are you?' A deep voice from the gloom of the passageway made my heart turn over. I spun round to find the doctor, Iwan Price, emerging from the direction of the mortuary, dripping a trail of water across the flagstones. He gave me a sickly smile.

'Just came in the back way.' He pointed over his shoulder with a thumb.

I must have looked disbelieving.

'Nearer to my car – I'd have got even more drenched, otherwise,' he explained.

I was taken aback. My whole body stiffened. 'Have you seen my little girl?'

'No. As I said, I've just arrived – couldn't make the service earlier, unfortunately, but I wanted to pay my respects.'

His eyes seemed to bore into me. It was unnerving. I had a sudden recollection of when I had first seen him. I must have been five or six years old, and was playing in the garden at the front of Ty Coed Pinwydd. A tall, dark-haired man had come out of the house and stopped in his tracks as he saw me. He stood watching for a moment, then called across, 'What's your name, then?'

I hesitated, unsure whether I should answer. Auntie Gwyn had always impressed upon me that I shouldn't talk to strangers. Sensing my caution, he smiled broadly. His narrowed eyes said something else entirely.

'It's all right, young lady. I'm your auntie's doctor.'

Reassured by this, I told him. He studied me a little strangely. 'Ah. Yes. Of course.'

And then he had climbed into a large black car and driven away.

I dropped my gaze now, noticing that his shoes and the bottom of his trousers were wet and mud-spattered.

'The wake's being held in the living room,' I told him abruptly. 'If you do see Ruby, can you tell her I'm looking for her, please.'

He inclined his head a fraction, then proceeded towards the hallway, glancing back at me briefly. I shuddered and went back upstairs, on the off chance that Ruby might have gone up to the bathroom again. It was most unlike her to wander off.

The queue for the toilet was shorter now, but still no one had seen anything of Ruby. Trying to think rationally, I went quickly back to the living room. People were still sipping tea and sherry, gathered in small, civilised huddles. The subdued hum of voices bounced from the walls. Frantically, I scanned the room for the familiar flash of bright auburn hair, but most heads were dark or grey, or even shinily bald. And none of them belonged to a small child.

I felt as if everything were playing out in slow motion. A cold, mounting sense of dread was building inside me. We were in a house full of people, most of them strangers, and not one of them had admitted to having seen my daughter. I was hit with the sudden realisation that something was very, very wrong.

My gaze sought Awel. I spotted her at the far side of the room in conversation with an elderly, white-haired woman propped up on an aluminium walking frame.

'Awel!' My trembling voice caught in my throat.

Her eyes met mine and narrowed as I approached, as if unsure of what I was about to say. I could feel the panic bubbling in my chest, the sound of my heart thudding through my head.

'I think . . . I think that someone's taken Ruby.'

*

Everyone present at the wake joined in the search for Ruby, going through the whole house and even into the

137

woods and beyond. But after almost two hours, it was quite apparent that she was gone. I was beside myself, every awful, unthinkable possibility turning through my head.

Eventually, Awel told people to go home and they gradually dispersed, all with requests to be kept informed if Ruby should show up.

'Don't worry, *cariad*,' one apple-cheeked old lady said kindly, squeezing my hand as she slipped on her coat. 'I'm sure she'll turn up soon. Probably playing hide and seek, eh.' Her smile couldn't disguise the troubled look in her eyes and it did nothing to allay my fears.

With the last of the mourners gone, the house felt colder and emptier than ever. It was as though, as they departed, every vestige of hope had trickled away with them. I knew now that the police needed to be brought in. Contacting them felt like an admission of how potentially serious the situation really was. I began to tremble with cold fear as one name kept resurging in my mind.

Beca Bennion.

*

'Can you give me the address once more please, miss?'

I could hear the subdued sigh of exasperation and shuffling of paperwork at the other end of the line. No doubt the policewoman thought me just another neurotic mother. More than four hours had elapsed, and by now I was frantic.

'Someone must have snatched her,' I sobbed. 'She would never go off by herself – she's scared of her own shadow. And she doesn't know anyone here.' The bitter tang of bile rose in my throat as I remembered what had happened all those years ago. This wouldn't be the first time a young girl had gone missing in Llanbadrig – and on the previous occasion, she had never been seen again.

'We're looking into it. Officers will be round within the hour to take a full statement from you. Please try to stay calm. Children often go exploring and have no idea of the worry it can cause their parents. She'll probably turn up very soon.'

I sat at the kitchen table, staring skyward. I was shivering now, more from shock than cold. Every minute felt like an eternity. Awel pressed a glass of brandy into my quivering hand. 'Drink this. It will help to settle your nerves.'

I swigged, then spluttered as the pungent liquid hit the back of my throat. My mind was darting to every possible, appalling scenario and I was bordering on hysteria.

'Think, now. When did you last see her?'

'I've already told you. She was still helping Elis when I went out into the garden. It must have been about two-ish.'

Awel turned to Elis, her face ashen. *Elis, did you notice Ruby talking to anyone in particular?*

He shook his head forcefully. *Too busy serving the guests. I'm sorry I can't be more help.*

His shoulders slumped despondently. He sat back in the chair, staring at the floor between his feet.

Despite the disagreeable taste, I knocked back more of the brandy, shivering as it slid down my throat. The glass shook in my hands, and I gripped it so tightly I thought it might shatter.

Within minutes, there was a loud rap at the front door. Awel went out into the hallway and returned accompanied by two police officers, a tall man of around forty with receding hair, and a young uniformed woman with a sleek dark bob peeping from beneath her cap, who smiled at me nervously.

'I'm Detective Sergeant Evans – acting Detective Inspector for Amlwch rural police,' announced the man, his chest thrust forward, 'and this is WPC Roberts.'

Prompted by an irritable nod of her colleague's head, the girl hurriedly produced a notebook and pen from her jacket pocket.

'Please, have a seat. I'll make some tea,' announced Awel, busying herself as the officers joined me at the table.

'Mrs Morris, you reported that Ruby disappeared from the living room here earlier this afternoon? Can you repeat her description and what she was wearing, please?'

Something contracted in my chest as I described Ruby from earlier that day, atypically neat and tidy in the little navy-blue dress, black T-bar shoes with white ankle socks; her hair clipped back into her new butterfly hair-slides.

'No coat?'

I recalled the bright pink cagoule, which had been hurriedly thrown over her that afternoon as we left the church and the rain began its assault. We always joked it clashed with her hair. I had realised it was missing from the hall stand after she disappeared.

'And there was a wake in progress?'

I took a deep breath. 'Yes, that's right. She'd been helping Elis here –' I indicated the downcast figure sitting

140

in Auntie Gwyn's armchair chewing his nails '– with the drinks, and she left the room to go to the toilet. She hasn't been seen since.' I felt a sob rising in my throat, clapping a hand to my mouth.

'So, Elis.' DS Evans turned to him, somewhat officiously. 'What time was this?'

Awel tapped Elis on the arm. He looked up blankly, his face a picture of misery.

'Elis is deaf,' I explained.

DS Evans seemed impatient. 'Can he communicate?'

'He's not stupid,' I snapped. 'He just can't hear.'

Can you run through it again please, Elis? I signed. *What time you last saw Ruby.*

Elis looked from me to the officers. *About two thirty, I think.*

He dropped his eyes again, as if not wanting to engage further. I relayed his response.

The policeman grimaced. 'He *thinks*? Can't he be more specific?'

His tone made me bristle. 'The whole afternoon is a bit of a blur for all of us. It's been an exhausting and upsetting day. All I know is that Ruby was in the living room when I went outside at about two p.m., and by the time I came back she had gone.'

His eyes widened. He frowned, folding his arms and pulling in his chin, his mouth turned downwards. 'You went *outside*? But it's been absolutely *pouring* with rain this afternoon. Why on earth would you go out in such weather?'

'I thought – I thought I saw someone out there, in the trees. I may have been mistaken.'

I shot a glance at Awel, who was looking increasingly agitated.

'And this person you *thought* you saw – can you describe them?'

'No. They were wearing a hooded coat. Could've been a man or a woman.'

DS Evans pushed back his chair, gesturing irritably to the young WPC, who blushed slightly and began scribbling copious notes. 'And they were alone?'

'As far as I could tell; yes.'

'Did anyone else *think* they saw someone out there?'

The emphasis on the word irked me. 'I've no idea. It was only because I was looking out of the window – I wouldn't have noticed otherwise.' I remembered the doll. 'I did suspect that someone had been in the house the other day, too – an old doll we found in the garden turned up on Ruby's bed.'

Awel pulled a face. 'I do wonder if that wasn't Ruby herself, you know . . .'

I turned to her in exasperation. 'It *couldn't* have been her, I told you. Why aren't you taking it seriously?'

She looked at me pityingly. I balled up my fists and cast my eyes skywards. At that moment I wanted to throw something at her.

DS Evans cleared his throat and puffed out his cheeks, exhaling deeply. 'So you believe it's possible that someone was watching her before, then?' He thought for a moment. 'If you could forward us a recent picture of Ruby – I assume you'll have some in your phone? I'll leave you my contact details. And we'll need a list of the people who attended the wake. Most unfortunate that they all left – it would've been easier to question everyone in one place.'

Awel's face flushed. 'We – I didn't think. They'd all been here for hours – some of the people were quite elderly, and I thought they needed to go home.' She scratched her head. 'Everyone had been helping to search for Ruby – we turned the whole house upside down earlier, so she's definitely not hiding anywhere in here. We were all out in the gardens and the woods, too. Weren't we?' She seemed flustered, turning anxiously to me to corroborate this, and I nodded.

'Virtually the whole community and even some from further afield called in at some point during the afternoon. The house was heaving.'

'Well, we're going to have a fair bit of legwork to do, then.' The muscles twitched in Evans's cheeks. He rose from the table. 'I'll check the house again myself – just to be on the safe side. What about the child's father – is he on the scene?'

'Ruby's dad passed away when she was tiny. She's all I've got.' The enormity of it all suddenly hit me. I buried my face in my hands and a howl escaped from my throat. This couldn't be happening. Any minute, I would wake and realise I'd been having a bad dream.

His tone softened. 'I'm sorry, Mrs Morris. Rest assured we will do everything possible to find your daughter. We already have officers combing the area. Please try not to distress yourself.' He turned to Awel. 'Maybe the doctor could prescribe something for her – settle her nerves?'

'I'll give him a ring.'

'No! I don't want anything. I need to be awake when

143

she gets back.' I turned to Evans in desperation. 'You will find her, won't you?'

'We'll certainly do everything possible. It's only been a few hours – hopefully she will be safely home by the morning.'

The almost imperceptible glance exchanged between Evans and the young WPC didn't escape my notice. My stomach clenched. I wondered what the statistics were for missing children being found unharmed after several hours. It was unbearable.

DS Evans and WPC Roberts went through every room in the house a second time. I followed them like a small anxious dog, hovering outside each room they entered. I watched from the landing as they went into the bedrooms and stopped outside the locked door.

'What's in this one?' Evans inquired, twisting the handle impatiently.

'Not much, as far as I know. But I don't know where the key's kept.'

He looked at me pointedly, so I hurried down to speak to Awel, who was frantically pacing the kitchen. She shook her head when I asked about accessing the room.

'I've no idea, I'm afraid. Gwyn tucked it away somewhere and I've never come across it. There's never been any need to go in there, to be honest.'

I relayed this to the police officers and DS Evans shrugged, turning to his colleague. 'We'll have to rely on the tried and tested, then.'

WPC Roberts looked slightly irritated but smiled obligingly, then went back downstairs and outside to their patrol car. She returned within minutes, handing him something, and stepped back. I saw that he now held a large paper clip, which he opened out and bent into an L-shape. After a few minutes of fiddling with the lock, the door clicked open.

'Works like a charm every time.' He smiled smugly.

'Be careful,' I warned. 'Auntie Gwyn always said some of the floorboards were rotten.'

I peered through the door as the officers entered, flicking on the light just inside the door. There appeared to be nothing within but various items of furniture, covered in dust sheets. The pair spent a couple of minutes searching and returned from the room, shaking their heads. My heart sank.

'Well, I think we can safely say she's not hiding anywhere in here.' Evans looked grim. 'We'll leave you in peace for now, Mrs Morris. But if you should hear anything in the meantime, please do keep us informed, as we will you. Otherwise we'll see you first thing in the morning.'

*

After the police officers had left, we sat in uncomfortable silence. I felt rooted to the spot. It was completely surreal: as though I was an observer trapped in a bubble, looking on as a nightmarish soap opera played out around me. It had nothing to do with me; nothing to do with Ruby. Not my precious little girl. Once again I thought back to that final summer I'd spent with Auntie Gwyn, and the smiling face of the dark-haired girl from the village who had disappeared, staring out from every local shop window. Surely this couldn't be happening.

I swiped through the images stored in my phone to find a clear picture of Ruby. I remembered one I'd snapped in the park, that glorious Sunday shortly before we came to Llanbadrig. We had taken Mickey with us and found a shady spot under a tree near the duck pond. Clutching a small carton of apple juice with a straw, she was sitting cross-legged on the picnic blanket, the dog lying at her side. I'd caught her unawares, turning to beam up at me, the sun glinting on her curls.

The face of an angel.

A feeling of abject terror rose in me. What if there would be no more photos? What if I never saw that beautiful smile again? Never held her little hand as we crossed the road, or waved her off at the school gate with her *Brave* lunchbox; never buried my face in that hair as I folded her in a hug at half past three, listening to her excited chatter about all she had done that day in class; never went to the park to feed the ducks or cuddled up on the sofa with a huge bag of popcorn to watch a movie together.

I reflected on my own childhood, realising how my relationship with Ruby and that of mine and my mother were poles apart. Maybe I was being unfair, but I couldn't imagine my mum being particularly upset if I'd gone missing. In fact, I wondered if it might even have been a relief to her.

During Year Five of primary school, I'd formed a brief but happy friendship with a girl named Aaliyah. I didn't make friends easily, possibly because I was never around in the school holidays, and it was nice to have someone who wanted to share my company at break times and sit next to me during class. Unfortunately, her family were only passing through for a few months while her dad, an IT consultant, was on a work placement at a local company. Inevitably – and regrettably – we had lost touch when they eventually returned to the States. I went to the impressively large house her parents were renting on a few occasions for tea after school; my mum reciprocated by inviting her to ours once or twice, but I always felt slightly embarrassed; not by the humbler surroundings, but by the lack of atmosphere and warmth in our home. Aaliyah had two older sisters and a baby brother, and the hustle and bustle of her family life was a stark contrast to the formality and solitude of my own.

One glorious afternoon in May, we'd been playing in Aaliyah's sprawling back garden. Her parents were sitting on wicker chairs on the patio under a parasol, keeping a watchful eye on the baby who was intent on escaping the blanket laid out for him on the lawn, to eat soil, or anything else he could lay his hands on.

'He's a pain,' Aaliyah had said grumpily, as her mother called for her to prise a pebble from the baby's chubby fist for the tenth time. 'You're so lucky that there's only you.'

'Oh no, I think you're the lucky one. I wish I had a little brother or sister. It can be really boring and lonely sometimes.'

Aaliyah looked at me and smiled. 'I do love him really. I shouldn't moan, I know. It's a shame for you – and for your mum, that she can't have another baby.'

I remember looking at her curiously, wondering what she meant.

'I heard my mum talking to my dad about it,' she explained. 'Your mum told her she can't have babies. That's why there's only you.'

This was news to me and actually quite upsetting. I was baffled as to why my parents had never sat me down to tell me, but couldn't bring myself to ask them. I recall looking at my mum years later and wondering if she really couldn't have more children or just didn't want them, since she didn't seem all that keen on me. Maybe she had been reluctant to repeat the experience.

I missed Aaliyah terribly for a while after she and her family moved on; but it was shortly before the summer holiday and, once in Anglesey again, everything was soon forgotten as I slipped back into life at Ty Coed Pinwydd. Looking back, how transient things really are in childhood.

I never forgot Aaliyah's words. After my mum died, I did try to ask my dad about what she'd told me, but he was dismissive and said that there must have been some misunderstanding. I suspected there was more to it than that, but didn't push it as he was so grief-stricken. From my perspective, at least, my mother had been a complex human being. Maybe this would have explained some of her behaviour. But now I would probably never know for sure – not unless Awel or Elis could shed some light. It was all very unsatisfactory.

It was so different for me. I was defined by my daughter: without her, my existence was meaningless. The sheer desperation and helplessness I felt was overwhelming. I forwarded the image to the number DS Evans had given me and put my phone into my bag. I wept silently, staring into space. Ruby was missing and I was floundering in an ocean of blackness. How could I go on if she never came back?

'Can I get you something to eat?' Awel asked eventually. Before I could respond, my mobile began to buzz in my cardigan pocket. I whipped it out and hurried into the hallway to take the call. A deep male voice came down the line.

'Mrs Morris?'

'Speaking.'

'This is DS Evans. I just wanted to update you.'

My heart leaped, praying for some good news. 'What's happened? Have you found her?'

There was a brief silence. 'I'm afraid not. But it seems a lady in a passing car believes she saw a figure with a child a short way along the road from the house – it was the pink jacket that made her look twice, she said – making their way towards the church at about the time it's believed Ruby disappeared. Our officers are focusing their attention on the area now.'

The church. All I could think about was that coastal path, the sheer drop. What if she'd fallen? And who on earth would she have been with? Feeling suddenly light-headed, I felt the phone slip from my hand, clattering onto the tiled floor, and reached for the corner of the wall to steady myself.

'Is everything all right?' Awel appeared in the kitchen doorway, her face drawn and anxious. She dragged a wooden chair from further down the hall and guided me into it.

'That sergeant thinks Ruby might have been seen

149

heading for the church. Oh, Christ – where the hell is she?' I could contain myself no longer. The chair rattled against the tiled floor with the sobs that tore through me.

Awel placed a tentative hand on my arm, her brow furrowed. 'The police are doing their best. I'm sure she'll turn up.'

'But what if something terrible's happened to her? I *knew* she wouldn't have wandered off on her own, and now there's been this sighting, it's obvious she's with someone. I just can't understand why she'd have gone with anyone she doesn't know – she's usually so timid. I can't get my head round it.'

'Hello? *HELLO?*'

Awel bent down stiffly and picked up the phone. DS Evans was still on the line, asking what was happening. I heard him tell Awel he'd be round first thing in the morning and then he hung up.

Awel helped me back into the kitchen. I sat, hunched over the table, my mind darting. I *had* to remain positive. *No news is good news*; one of Auntie Gwyn's favourite expressions. I whispered it to myself, desperately trying to hang onto that thought. But all the time, the memory of the news bulletins from that terrible summer kept flashing into my mind and a sick feeling wallowed in the pit of my stomach. Little Beca Bennion had vanished from the face of the earth, never to be seen again – and only a short distance outside Llanbadrig.

The same place from where my Ruby had been taken.

*

After a phone call from Awel telling him what had happened, Lewis had hurried back to see if there was anything he could do to help. Of course, there really wasn't, but I was grateful that he had offered. There was something very solid and reassuring about his presence.

Elis sat in front of the range, eyes cast perpetually downwards as though hoping to find some clue on the ground. He blew his nose noisily from time to time and looked disconsolate, seemingly unable to make eye contact with me. I thought briefly that maybe I should put an arm around his shoulder, reassure him that none of this was his fault, but couldn't summon the impetus. I felt strangely numb. Awel fussed round making endless cups of tea for us all, most of which were left to turn cold. Lewis tried to lighten the tone by talking about the annual Anglesey Show, which was being held the following month, but I took in nothing that was being said.

My stomach began to grind once more. I could feel panic welling inside me: with the possible exception of Elis, was I the only one really taking the situation seriously?

Eventually I jumped to my feet. 'Look, I'm sorry but I can't think about shows or the bloody weather, or anything else right now.' My voice echoed through my head, loud and high-pitched. 'Has no one got *any* idea who could have taken Ruby? Someone at the funeral must have seen *something*. Are there any known weirdos in the area? I feel completely helpless just waiting around – we're wasting precious time.'

Lewis glanced at Awel. He sounded shaky. 'Look, I'm

sure the cops will find her. And to my knowledge there aren't any . . . you know, sex offenders round here.' He looked uncomfortable. 'We're a small community – someone's bound to know *something*. Just sit tight and try not to worry.' He smiled weakly and reached for my hand. 'It'll all be okay. She's a kid – she's probably having an adventure somewhere.'

I couldn't believe he was being so flippant and shook off his grip. My words tumbled out angrily. 'Well, I'm glad *you're* not concerned. I hope you never find yourself in the same situation. But I don't suppose you'd get it, would you, not having kids of your own yet. This is every parent's worst nightmare I'm going through; do you realise that?'

He looked hurt, his eyes appealing to Awel for support. She gave a small shrug which seemed to say, *You're on your own.*

Lewis puffed out a long breath. 'I *am* concerned; of course I am. Just trying to look at it from all angles. And to make you feel a bit better – if that's possible.' He pressed his palms together in supplication. 'Foot-in-mouth syndrome.'

I felt bad then. I sank back onto my chair, folding my arms on the table and staring at the wall unseeingly. 'Sorry – I'm beside myself.'

'That's understandable.' Awel pulled up a chair beside me, her gaze shifting from me to Lewis as though happy to step in now. 'But he's right. The police are doing all they can and they have the expertise and resources to do it. Best thing we can do is sit tight and let them do their job. Hopefully we'll hear something very soon.'

Despite her reassurances, the uncertainty in Awel's voice was ill-disguised. Nothing anyone could say was making me feel any better. I actually wanted to curl up and die.

*

At Awel's insistence, I went up to bed at half past one. Lewis had stayed for a short while after I'd gone upstairs. As I was undressing, I could make out some sort of conflab from below which went on for several minutes, then heard footsteps stamping along the hallway and an angry clunk, which I assumed was Lewis letting himself out of the front door.

I messaged Nina to tell her what had happened. I should probably have phoned earlier, but had been in too much of a state. I would try to ring her the next day, hopefully with some good news. The alternative wasn't something I wanted to consider.

In spite of myself, I managed a couple of hours' sleep, but the second I awoke and remembered what had happened, the tears flowed once more. It was as though some malevolent creature was gnawing at the centre of my stomach, gorging on the thought of my constant torment. I got out of bed and reached for Ruby's pyjama top, pressing it to my face and breathing in her sweet scent. Where *was* she? I was going out of my mind. I felt impotent and wracked with guilt. I had failed in the one fundamental requirement of motherhood: to protect my child.

I pulled on a cardigan, then made my way downstairs. I unlocked the front door and went out into the garden, gazing into the darkness. Ruby must be out there somewhere, but I had no clue where to even begin looking. She could have been bundled into a car and driven miles away by now. Through the trees, I could hear the ominous rush of waves dashing the rocks, a grim reminder of the cliffs and the potential threat they posed. My heart felt like a lead weight.

I went back into the house feeling completely helpless. Awel had fallen asleep in the armchair in the kitchen, a blanket slipped over her by Elis, who had retreated to his room. The air was cool, the range having long gone out. I tiptoed in and went to pour a glass of water from the tap. She stirred, sitting up and blearily running a finger under each eye.

'Oh, I must have dropped off. What time is it?'

'Sorry – I didn't mean to disturb you. It's almost four.'

'No news?'

I shook my head. 'I just don't understand. How could she have just vanished like that? She'd never go anywhere with a stranger, I'm sure of it. God knows I've drummed it into her enough times. Maybe it was someone else that the woman saw – there must be other children who own pink jackets.'

'Then we must hope and pray that she's safe somewhere – that maybe she went out and fell and couldn't walk home, and the police will find her with a sprained ankle.'

Even as she said it, I could see the doubt in her eyes. The thought that my darling Ruby could be out there in the dark, cold and terrified, was destroying me.

'I *have* to go and look for her. I feel so useless just

waiting around like this. At least if I start searching, I'll be doing something constructive.' I kept wondering about the woman who thought she may have seen her. Who was she? Should I try to find out, speak to her myself? Maybe she would remember something else that she hadn't thought of at the time. I needed to do *something*.

'Lowri, the police are searching. Don't you think a group of trained officers has the best chance of finding Ruby? I even heard their helicopter earlier. I'm sure they're doing all they can.'

My mind began to fly. 'But she might be scared witless – hiding somewhere. She doesn't like the dark. She's such a nervy little thing.'

'Not like you.' Awel's mouth curved into a half-smile. 'You were a feisty young madam, as I recall.'

'I was still frightened of you. I thought – well, I thought you hated me.' I felt the heat of blood rising in my cheeks as I said it.

She looked taken aback. 'Never! I was just – lacking patience, I suppose. Maybe I've mellowed a bit in my old age.'

I nodded. I had definitely discovered a warmer side to Awel that I hadn't realised existed. Although even now, there was still something – an occasional edge, a strange expression that seemed to surface from time to time. Almost as though the bitter memory of some past misdemeanour had resurfaced, and the resentment for me with it. I couldn't think what I might have done to upset her.

I felt queasy from worry and lack of sleep; as though my eyes were filled with grit.

Awel seemed to read my mind. She eased herself from the chair and stretched. 'Let's have a *panad*. I need something to perk me up.'

I raked out the ashes from the stove, a task always allocated to me as a child by Auntie Gwyn, and fetched a scuttle of smokeless coal from the bunker outside. Awel coaxed a fire and soon the kitchen was warming through, the kettle boiling on the hob.

Every time I thought of Ruby, my stomach contracted painfully. It was like someone twisting a tourniquet deep within my core. I was on pins, nervous energy coursing through me.

'I'll put the washing away while the tea's brewing,' I told her. 'I've got to be doing something – I'll go mad if I just sit here brooding.'

I unwound the cord from the wooden airer suspended above the range, and lowered it to collect the dry laundry, folding it all into a pile and placing it on the back of the chair. I stopped suddenly.

'Where's Doli glwt? Did you get her down?'

Awel turned to look at me. 'She was pegged to the frame, last time I looked.'

'Well, she's not there now.'

It felt as if ice was being dripped slowly down my spine. My daughter had vanished without trace and the doll with her.

*

The whole of the next day seemed to pass in a fog. DS Evans called round briefly at first light to say that his officers were now widening their search towards Cemaes and in the opposite direction of Bull Bay. They had already scoured the area around the Old Porcelain Works nestling in the valley at Llanlleiana, a ghostly ruin abandoned after being destroyed by fire several years earlier, around a mile from Llanbadrig church. They had found nothing of note, he said.

I felt exhausted after the previous night and tried to catch up on some sleep later in the morning, but it was hopeless. Being in the house felt claustrophobic. I went out alone and spent the entire afternoon combing the gardens and the spinney, then up to the church via the cliff path. I was expecting to see police officers out in force, but they were conspicuous by their absence. I doubled back and headed once more for the church along the main route, slowly picking my way along the lanes, eyes to the ground, looking under hedges for signs of anything that might give some indication Ruby had passed by. Eventually I admitted defeat and returned to Ty Coed Pinwydd, hoping that the police might have had better luck elsewhere.

DS Evans didn't return in person but touched base with me once more later in the evening over the phone, basically to say there was nothing new to share as yet and to try not to worry. As if.

He told me that, unless there was anything of importance to report in the meantime, he would see me again the following morning. I did mention the missing doll, but got the impression he didn't think it especially significant. It was all so frustrating.

I was kicking myself now for not letting Ruby have a phone; she'd asked me for a mobile several times as a few of the children in her class owned one. I thought initially it was ridiculous to give such young children their own phones and irresponsible of their parents. But after a conversation at the school gate with some of the other mums, I thought more about it and considered it might actually be useful if she ever needed to contact me. I decided eventually it would probably have to wait until she was older. It was an expense I could do without. If only she'd had one with her, she could have called for help. Money might not be the answer to all our woes, but it certainly has its uses.

I tried to ring Nina but was cut off immediately for some reason. Deflated, I left her a brief voicemail asking her to call me and decided to turn in for the night, praying that the next day would bring something positive.

That this catastrophe would be over for me, and more importantly, for my darling Ruby.

CHAPTER NINE

I didn't want to make a habit of taking the things, but the one I'd taken previously had helped, so I reluctantly accepted the sleeping pill Awel offered me. I drifted off surprisingly quickly. I awoke to darkness, still feeling groggy. In that weird limbo between sleep and wakefulness, disjointed thoughts meandered in and out of my mind; mainly about Ruby and when we would be reunited. Scenarios that I wasn't sure were real or imaginary played out in my head.

But suddenly I was wide awake and sitting bolt upright. At first, I thought it was my imagination, but the noise grew gradually louder. Music was being played somewhere in the house. I stumbled from my bed and strained to listen. It was definitely coming from upstairs – what sounded like a slow and clumsy attempt to play the harp.

I froze, remembering the maudlin little song, 'The Ash Grove', from infant school:

She sleeps 'neath the green turf

Down by the ash grove . . .

When I was small, Auntie Gwyn used to have a huge, ancient harp in the living room, that had belonged to her Nain, and I would often try to pluck a tune from it, but it was beyond my capability. And it had long gone.

Or so I thought.

I eased open the bedroom door and stood, listening. The sound was muffled but had grown louder since I stepped onto the landing. I moved slowly towards the room from where the notes seemed to emanate. There was a sudden bang, followed by the reverberation of a dissonant chord; as though the strings had been strummed in a fit of pique. I rushed to try the door but frustratingly the handle just rattled as it had previously. It was possible that there was a dead lock and once shut, the key was needed to open it once more.

My heart pounding now, I made my way downstairs. DS Evans may have had the knack with an improvised lock-pick, but I'd tried to open doors myself in the past when I'd locked myself out and found it impossible. There had to be a key somewhere in the house – but where to even start looking? I went from room to room, through all the drawers and cupboards in the kitchen, the sideboard in the living room; the old dresser in the small sitting room. It was futile.

Eventually I gave up and returned to the kitchen to put the kettle on. There was no way I'd be able to sleep now. It was completely bizarre.

I wondered if I'd had anything through from Nina. She was generally so quick at responding to me. While waiting for the water to boil, I went back upstairs to get my phone. Annoyingly, the screen had cracked when I dropped it, even more so because I hadn't had it very long. I'd recently signed up to a better deal with a cheap tariff and now I would need a new handset. Great.

A message notification flashed up and I tapped to read it. As I did so, I almost dropped the thing again.

Blinking back at me was one capitalised line from an unknown number.

I KNOW WHERE SHE IS

In a blind panic, I tried to ring Nina again. It was only just gone 5 a.m., I knew, but she was usually an early riser and I was praying she'd already be awake and that she'd answer this time. I was surprised and quite upset that she hadn't called after receiving either of my messages. I desperately needed to hear her comforting, rational voice, and to share my fears with someone who knew and cared about Ruby almost as much as I did.

The second she picked up, I began to bawl.

'Lowri? What on earth's wrong? Calm down, love, I can't understand what you're saying. What message? No, I haven't seen it. Bloody phone's been playing up – I think it's on its way out.'

Between sobs, I managed to tell her what had happened.

'Oh, Lowri.' There was a lengthy pause, and I wondered for a moment if we'd been cut off.

'Okay. Okay, let's think. Ruby's a smart cookie; she wouldn't go off with a stranger, would she?'

'That's exactly what I thought. But I can't see any

161

other explanation. A local woman told the police she was sure she'd seen her with an adult.'

'Right. But it's a small community, yes? Someone must know something. Everyone usually knows everyone else's business in those places.'

'But no-one seems to know anything. And the police don't appear to be doing a fat lot, as far as I can tell. I just don't know what to do.'

'You don't have to *do* anything, flower. Sit tight and let them do their job – that's what they're paid for.'

'It's the waiting around – it's driving me insane.'

'I know it must be a complete nightmare for you. But try to get yourself some rest and eat properly to keep your strength up. Look, I'll see what I can sort here. If I can get cover for the café, I'll . . .' She broke off for a moment and a muffled interchange from her end told me she was covering the handset. 'I'll ring you back later, darling. Get yourself back to bed for a bit and hopefully there might be an update from the cops by the time you get up. Try to keep calm – I'm sure she'll turn up soon.'

CHAPTER TEN

True to his word, DS Evans knocked the door at nine o'clock sharp, along with the young WPC, who looked more uncomfortable than ever. They were accompanied by a short-haired, middle-aged woman wearing a tatty fleece and trainers, whom Evans introduced as Nansi. The morning air was cool, but sunlight flooded the hallway as I let them in and I screwed up my eyes against the glare.

I learned that Nansi was the family liaison officer assigned to the case, which worried me all the more as it appeared to imply they weren't hopeful of finding Ruby imminently. She was very smiley, to the point of seeming patronising, but everything she asked me I'd already explained to DS Evans and WPC Roberts the previous night. Had Ruby ever wandered off before, had she made friends since we arrived that she might have gone off somewhere with, was she homesick? No, no and no.

The woman seemed to be contributing little to the

proceedings as far as I could tell, and it irritated me. In spite of Nina's advice, I hadn't gone back to bed and had been awake for hours, pacing the kitchen. I felt incredibly anxious and agitated. My head was pounding. All I wanted was for them to find my daughter; from my perspective, it was as though they were going through the motions and very little was actually happening. Nansi must have read my mind.

'Obviously we want to keep you informed every step of the way, Mrs Morris. We followed up a prospective lead last night, after a gentleman in Bull Bay called to say he thought he'd seen a little girl fitting Ruby's description walking along the main road, although unfortunately it turned out to be a case of mistaken identity. But please let me reassure you, we're a bit like the proverbial ducks – all serene on the surface but paddling madly underneath the water. There's plenty of investigative work going on behind the scenes. We're taking this very seriously indeed.'

As she'd said the words 'fitting Ruby's description', my pulse began to race briefly, but deflation kicked in just as quickly. I wondered how common false leads were in such cases.

Hoping that they might be able to act on it in some way, I was still itching to show them the message I'd received.

'I've been wanting to speak to you, too – I got a strange text last night.'

The police officers' eyes swivelled collectively towards one another. 'Oh?'

Pulling my phone from my pocket, I opened the text

message and held it up. DS Evans leaned forward to read it and stood back, eyebrows arched. He shot a strange look at Nansi, who avoided his eyes as she stared down at her trainers, rocking gently on the balls of her feet, and looking as though she'd rather be somewhere else.

'Do you have any idea who sent it?' she asked eventually.

'None – nor how they got my number. Unless –' I flipped the phone over, and groaned. As I had only recently been assigned a new mobile number, I'd taped it to the back to remind me. Someone at the wake could easily have seen it when I left it in the living room to go outside.

'Our officers have also made a discovery.' DS Evans took out his phone and scrolled through to a photo which he enlarged, turning the screen to face me. 'Is this at all familiar to you, Mrs Morris?'

I peered at the image. A torn scrap of blue floral fabric and a few strands of orange wool in a clear plastic evidence bag had been laid against a piece of white paper to show them clearly. My stomach turned over.

'Doli glwt.'

'I'm sorry?'

'It's an old doll – belonged to one of my aunts as a child. We found it recently and I washed it – it's the one that was placed on her bed – remember, I told you about it? And that I'd realised it was missing just after Ruby . . .' I looked up at him and wondered if he'd actually been paying attention. 'Where did they find these?'

'Caught in a hedge, on the road up to Llanbadrig church.'

'Did they – was there anything else?' My hands began to tremble. I was desperate for news but, at the same time, dreading that it might not be what I wanted to hear.

'Not yet, I'm afraid – but they're still searching.'

Evans pursed his lips. 'Well, unless it's some sort of prank, it's possible the text message might provide us with a lead.'

My pulse quickened. 'D'you mean – you might actually be able to trace the caller?'

He sucked in air through his teeth. 'Of course, we do have telecommunications experts who can find these things out . . .'

Nansi glanced at the young WPC who rolled her eyes and grimaced. Evans didn't appear to have noticed.

'I know you see it all the time on the telly, but it's not as straightforward as they make it sound,' she explained. 'It *can* be done, but it won't be a five-minute job, I'm afraid. And we don't have anyone who can do it locally. May we take your phone with us, though?'

'Of course.' I paused. 'Let me just drop my friend a quick text.'

I clicked on Nina's number. Police need my phone so will be off-radar for a bit. May have a lead x

A response pinged back almost immediately. What's ur postcode? X

*

The second the officers had left, I pulled on a jacket and went straight out, heading purposefully towards the church once more. If they'd found the piece of material

166

in the lane, this must be a sure indication that Ruby or whoever had taken her had trodden the same path very recently. Despite Nansi's assurances about her team's efforts, I couldn't just sit around waiting: time was of the essence and I was all too aware that every minute Ruby was missing, hope of finding her safe and well was diminishing.

I was covering the same ground over and over; up and down the coastal path, every inch of the graveyard. The wind coming in from the sea was cool, despite the morning sunshine, and I zipped up my jacket against its force. In desperation, I decided to walk across the headland to Llanlleiana, hoping that the police might have overlooked something that would strike a chord with me. I blundered my way downwards towards the secluded pebble beach, tucked in the dip just beneath the ruin of the Old Porcelain Works. A low curved wall separated the building from the bay. The whole place felt eerie and abandoned, and I climbed the grey stone steps that led into the crumbling edifice with some trepidation. I scanned the ground – looking for what, I didn't know. It was less than inviting. A handful of rusting beer cans and a few dog ends had been discarded in one corner, among the rubble and coarse overgrown grass. Ferns insinuated their way between what had once been the windows. The sea breeze whipped round my face and I had to keep pushing back my hair to see where I was putting my feet for fear of tripping on the uneven ground.

'Su'mae.'

Startled, I spun round. Curig, one of the regular casual

workers from Ty Coed Pinwydd, was standing watching me from between the pillars where the door had once been. I hadn't heard anyone approaching and caught my breath. I remembered him from Auntie Gwyn's funeral. He was as broad as he was tall, and filled most of the entrance. Looking beyond his huge frame, I could see a black and white border collie darting across the beach.

'Oh, hello. You made me jump.'

'Just walking Sam.' He gestured behind him with a thumb. 'You shouldn't be down here on your own, you know. Dicey if you were to have a fall or something. No bugger would hear you and you can't get no signal on a mobile, neither.' He was staring at me a little too intently and I felt suddenly uncomfortable. I didn't know the man really, and here I was, all alone with him and apparently not another soul for miles.

'Any news – about the little girl?'

I shook my head.

'Bad business, all that. Hope she turns up. You must be worried sick.' He continued to hold me in his gaze for a moment, then turned and whistled to the dog through his teeth. 'Ah well, better be off. *Pob lwc* with it all.' He tipped his head towards me a fraction, then plodded back towards the beach. I watched as he skimmed a pebble into the water, glanced back to throw me a salute, then carried on in the direction of Bull Bay with the dog bounding ahead of him.

My pulse began to slow once more. Curig was probably harmless but I was relieved he had gone. As he'd said, coming here alone had probably not been a sensible move. And, aside from being ill-judged, my solo efforts had been futile. If a whole team of police officers had failed to find anything meaningful, the likelihood of my landing on something was pretty slim. Despondently, I made the arduous ascent back up the steps cut into the hillside to the cliffs, and trudged back towards Llanbadrig, hardly caring if I stumbled and fell to my death. Everything seemed hopeless.

*

The wind had dropped, giving way to a bright and temperate afternoon, but the hours passed painfully slowly. A constant empty ache throbbed within my chest. I wandered around the house aimlessly, feeling an increasing sense of despair. After the distraction of the anonymous text message, I had almost forgotten the strange harp music from the previous night. Neither Elis or Awel had any idea where the key to the locked room down the landing had been put and, try as I might, frustratingly I could see nothing through the keyhole of the room from where I'd heard the melody.

Awel seemed to think I might have dreamed it after taking the sleeping tablet.

'*I* certainly didn't hear anything,' she had said dismissively. 'They can play games with your mind, those things, if you're not used to them.'

Realising she thought it was all in my head, I dropped the subject eventually. Perhaps I *had* imagined it. By the evening, I was starting to feel quite unwell. Maybe it had been as a result of the soaking I'd got after the funeral, but my throat was sore and I felt unnaturally cold. I was getting stabbing pains in my chest and back sporadically, but did my best to ignore them. I had too much else to worry about.

Darkness had begun to fall, a mellow evening to follow the eventually warm afternoon. Facing west meant later and often breathtaking sunsets, but I'd been in no mood to admire the pink-and-gold-streaked sky. I felt unable to face the fish pie which Awel had prepared and sat shivering in the armchair in front of the range. Elis watched me with some concern and gestured to Awel, who placed a hand on my forehead and frowned. She made honey and lemon, gave me two paracetamol and insisted I went to bed. I felt wrung out and knew I needed to rest. Reluctantly, I climbed the stairs. No sooner had I gone into the bedroom and undressed, there was a loud rap at the front door. I pulled on my pyjamas and dressing gown and went back out onto the landing, only to hear a familiarly assertive voice carrying from below.

'I'm looking for Lowri – is she here?'

My heart soared briefly. 'Nina? Is that you?' Slightly unsteadily, I went down to the hallway, to find Awel regarding my friend with suspicion and not a little curiosity. Nina was standing in the open doorway, framed by the halo of the porch light. She had plaited her greying afro hair into coloured beads and was wearing a boldly striped hooded poncho, pompoms swinging from its hem, and biker boots. Beating his tail frantically between her sturdy leg and the doorpost was Mickey, who could barely contain his excitement as I approached. At the sight of them both, I promptly burst into tears and ran into Nina's open embrace.

'Thank you *so* much for coming. This is a complete nightmare.'

Nina hugged me hard. 'Couldn't leave you to face all this on your own, now could I?' She shot a look at Awel, who bristled. Elis appeared from the kitchen and looked questioningly from Nina to Awel.

'Lowri *isn't* on her own. *We* are here for her.'

'Well, the more support she has, the better; I'm sure you'll agree. And if anyone can find Ruby, it's our Mickey.'

Awel peered down at the animal with some distaste. 'You'll have to keep him away from the cat. She's terrified of dogs.'

'Mickey's a big softy. Wouldn't hurt a fly. I'm sure they'll get on like a house on fire.'

She glanced back at her van parked on the gravel and then turned pointedly to Awel. 'I could murder a cup of tea. The M6 has been hell this afternoon.'

Awel looked taken aback. 'Of course. Come on in.'

Elis gave Nina a broad smile and led the way, with Awel close behind. Nina winked at me as we followed them down to the kitchen, Mickey close at my side, nuzzling my hand. Pwtyn hissed and leaped from the chair as we entered, her tail fluffed up like a feather duster. She bolted out of the kitchen and straight up the stairs. The dog stared after her, bemused.

At once, Elis sat down in the armchair and beckoned eagerly to Mickey, who went straight across to him for a fuss. Elis looked up at me, then nodded towards Awel ruefully.

I'd love a dog, he signed. *She's never wanted one.*

171

We sat at the table while a disgruntled-looking Awel made tea and sandwiches, begrudgingly placing a bowl of water under the table for Mickey. The kitchen was cosy, and I felt less shivery snuggled into my dressing gown. Maybe the honey and lemon and tablets had helped. But Nina's presence was undeniably comforting.

'So, tell me everything.'

Nina sat in silence as she sipped her tea and nibbled the cheese and tomato sandwich Awel had made, nodding from time to time, then shaking her head as I relayed the sequence of events: the doll; the unidentified figure outside; the odd text message.

'Did the police say how long it'd take to trace the phone that sent the text?'

'No. I don't think there's anyone who can do it in the area.'

Nina looked around. 'That figures. I mean, I suppose it's just a small rural force, isn't it? Even more out in the sticks than we are at home.'

I noticed Awel's mouth twitching. 'There's not much crime round here as a rule,' she said brusquely.

'Maybe not – but when something *does* happen, you'd like to think they're on the ball. Now that we've got technology to help us solve things, we should be making the most of it, don't you think?'

She turned back to me. 'And you say they're focusing on the area around that old church?'

'Yes.' My stomach turned over once more as I thought of the cliffs.

'Can we take a walk up there?'

'What – now? But it's dark . . .'

'No time like the present. Besides, I could do with stretching my legs after being cooped up in that van all afternoon – and I'm sure Mickey would love a walk. We can use the torch on my phone if you haven't got one . . .'

'Elis has a decent flashlight,' chipped in Awel. 'You can take that if you really can't wait until tomorrow. But d'you feel up to it, Lowri?'

I still didn't feel brilliant, but was bolstered by the thought of Mickey picking up on something. The renewed possibility of finding Ruby overruled everything else.

'I'll be fine if I wrap up. At least it's not raining.'

Awel fetched the torch from the shed and nudged Elis, who rose reluctantly from his seat to accompany us.

I took an old peacoat of Auntie Gwyn's from the hall stand, pulled on my boots and wrapped a scarf round my throat. Brandishing the flashlight, Elis led the way. The air was cool and damp, but so fresh; the moon a silver-white crescent reclining against the inky-blue backdrop of the star-littered sky. That was another thing I had missed about Llanbadrig: the clear, unpolluted night skies, the lack of synthetic neon glow to remind us we were living in the twenty-first century. I remembered once as a child watching a seemingly endless meteor shower in awe, something I have never seen since. The unspoiled beauty of the place was quite breathtaking.

Held by Nina, Mickey, now wearing an LED collar, strained eagerly at his lead. I hooked my arm into Nina's and we headed up the lane, the swaying beam of the torch illuminating the path ahead. Remembering our encounter with Dr Price's car, I warned Nina to keep in to the hedge and dropped into single file behind her at the first bend in the road.

As we reached the caravan park, Mickey began to get excited. He tugged Nina through the entrance. I hurried to catch up with Elis and indicated that we should head after them onto the site.

Where are we going? He looked disorientated.

I pointed at the luminescent green light around Mickey's neck.

Following the dog's nose.

Most of the caravans were well-lit, and traditional-style solar lamps glowed along the path that wound between them. The owners clearly took the maintenance of their individual plots seriously and many had created little gardens and had even built verandas and decked areas around their vans.

Mickey had pulled up sharply outside one small, rusting static caravan with no such adornments, surrounded by overgrown turf. He seemed agitated, whimpering and turning to Nina then back towards the door. There was total darkness within; no car or any other sign of habitation outside. We all looked at one another. My heart in my mouth, I took the torch from Elis and played the beam through the open curtains nearest the door. I could see no one, but rapped on the glass. No response. I knocked again and waited a moment before trying the handle. The door creaked open.

'Hello?' I called tentatively. I could feel the rapid thud of my heart inside my chest. Though fuelled with adrenaline, I was equally terrified of what we might discover inside. Before Nina could stop the dog, he bounded over the step and ran frantically from one end of the van to the other, sniffing in every corner, his tail slicing the air. His frenzied movement caused the whole structure to shake. Pausing at one flimsy-looking door to the right of the entrance, he began to paw it with urgency, whining pitifully.

Elis moved me aside gently and entered. He flipped the switch just inside the door. Nina and I followed. The strip-lighting in the kitchenette area flickered into action. It was dim but sufficient to see by. The interior was old-fashioned and had seen better days. Next to a half-empty packet of digestive biscuits, two dirty mugs sat on a small table under the kitchen window, flanked by benches upholstered in grubby floral fabric. On the wall opposite, a small stainless-steel sink was piled with unwashed plates and cutlery. At the far end, two further longer benches formed an L-shape around a small carpeted area, beneath a window stretching the full width of the van. The air smelled damp, with an unmistakeable hint of urine.

Mickey was still pawing anxiously at the interior door just inside the entrance. Holding him by the collar, Elis pulled the handle and felt inside for the light.

Nina gripped my arm protectively, as though to hold me back.

There, in a crumpled heap on the bed, lay Ruby's pink cagoule. In desperation, I wriggled free of Nina's grasp and pushed past Elis to retrieve it, to hold something that had been in contact with Ruby.

'No! Don't touch it,' yelled Nina. 'There may be – I don't know, traces of forensic stuff or something on it. We need to call the police.'

We stood staring down at the little jacket. There was nothing else in evidence. But I knew now that my daughter must have been here, and accompanied by someone. I felt suddenly nauseous and stumbled outside, gulping in mouthfuls of the night air.

Nina took out her phone and dialled for the emergency services. We stood in a little clutch on the grass outside, Nina's arm around my shoulder, Elis hovering anxiously, and waited for the police's arrival.

*

The caravan was cordoned off as the forensic officers did a sweep of the interior and bagged up, among other things, the cagoule and coffee cups. DS Evans and WPC Roberts arrived shortly after them, this time without Nansi in tow. Evans looked flustered.

'So you say the dog led you here?'

Nina bristled. 'Yes. Ruby and Mickey are great pals. I had a strong feeling he'd give us a lead.'

I could tell immediately from her expression that Nina hadn't warmed to the sergeant. 'I'm surprised your officers didn't search the site. It seems an obvious place to look, to me.'

'They're covering the whole area. They've actually been knocking doors and questioning the holidaymakers staying in the caravan park. They would certainly have come to this one in due course.'

She looked unimpressed. Releasing me from the reassuring pressure of her arm, her head at an angle, she looked pointedly at DS Evans. 'Can I have a word?'

I looked on as they walked a few yards away from

176

where we'd been standing. WPC Roberts smiled at me awkwardly. I wondered what all this meant; whether it was a good or bad sign, finding the coat but no Ruby. Despite Elis's presence, I felt suddenly very alone. I reached for Mickey, who obliged by sitting at my feet, gazing up at me. I ran my fingers through his soft auburn fur, tears pricking my eyes. Ruby must have been so close – but how long ago? Had she shared a meal with her captor? Even with her healthy appetite, I couldn't believe she would have accepted food willingly from someone she was frightened of. She could be very cautious. Nina had treated her to an outing to Cadbury World for her sixth birthday and she had steadfastly refused to eat any chocolate, thinking she might turn into a blueberry like the awful Violet Beauregarde in *Charlie and the Chocolate Factory*. I had laughed at the time. It didn't seem even remotely amusing now.

Nina turned her back and addressed the sergeant in a lowered voice. His face hardened perceptibly. He straightened, standing with both hands clasped behind his back, rocking a little on his heels. His eyes dropped, evidently uncomfortable as he responded. She nodded solemnly, made some remark and returned to us, her face unreadable.

'What is it, Nina? What did you say to him?'

She hesitated, then pasted on a smile. 'Oh, just asking how many officers they have working on this, you know. The usual.'

'No, I *don't* know. There's nothing usual about *any* of this. The longer it goes on, the less hope I have of her ever being found.' I felt a sob rise in my throat. I was shaking now, as though a tremor had begun some-where deep within myself and was beginning to reverberate throughout my whole body.

Nina clasped my hand firmly. 'Try to stay positive, Lowri. Think of Ruby – she always looks on the bright side. Let's take a leaf out of her book. I don't know why – I have a strong feeling a breakthrough is just around the corner.'

She smiled encouragingly and I tried to cling onto her optimism. Nina was very much a glass-half-full-type of person – she often seemed to have positive 'strong feel-ings' about situations. Besides, the alternative was just too much to bear.

*

I felt increasingly unwell, but sleep evaded me once more as I lay staring at the ceiling, worrying about Ruby. I sobbed silently as salty tears trickled down my face, wetting my ears and the pillow beneath my head. Clutching Benjy to my chest, I kept revisiting the last time I had seen her at the wake, standing beside Elis. Did she seem happy? Had anything – or anyone – appeared suspicious at the time? I tried to picture the other people who had been close by, but it was a blur. I'd been so focused on the figure in the garden that, to my shame, I had paid my daughter little attention at that moment. And now I was paying the price.

How very careless I had been.

CHAPTER ELEVEN

The Girl's Story

The little girl rubbed her eyes and sat up. Despite her best efforts to stay awake, she had eventually dropped off. The room was dim, but the residue of light from the extinguished bars of an electric fire left a soft glow and, as she became accustomed to the gloom, she could discern the old woman's fidgeting outline, observing her from the opposite bench. A scratchy, musty-smelling blanket had been draped over her and she shrugged it off.

Realising she had stirred, the woman jumped to her feet and flicked the light switch, making the child squint with the initial glare. She stepped forward, eagerly thrusting a slightly squashed bar of chocolate into the girl's hands, and sat down beside her.

'*Wyt ti eisiau bwyd?*' she asked brightly.

The girl shook her head in alarm. 'I didn't understand. What did you say?'

'Are you hungry?'

'A bit. Thank you.' She peeled off the wrapper and took a cautious nibble. The woman had clearly been holding the chocolate and it was stickily unappetising. 'When can I go home? My mum will be worried.'

The woman's eyes began to dart. 'Oh, I'll let her know all about it. It's all right. Best if we stay out of the way for now.'

'But why? Who *is* this bad man you were telling me about?'

The old woman seemed twitchy. She looked down at her rough, mottled hands and began picking at a hang-nail on her thumb, her fingers in constant motion. The girl stared in ill-disguised horror, noticing for the first time that the middle and third finger of her left hand were no more than misshapen stumps, the first three digits on her right hand truncated and without nails.

'Someone told me – he takes little girls. You need to stay hidden – you'll be safe here.'

'But no one else mentioned him. Are you sure?'

The woman's head seemed to wobble. 'They don't know about him. Not like my friend. I've heard what he can do. He's wicked.'

She got up and began to pace, wringing her hands. She exuded a strange manic energy, making the child shrink back into the bench nervously. The apparently hollow floor vibrated unnervingly with the woman's foot-steps.

'Why did we move from where we were?' the girl

ventured. 'It was much nicer in the other place.' She was beginning to feel frightened. Having spent the past few hours in the company of this strange elderly woman, she bitterly regretted having listened to her apparently anguished pleas to help her find her dog. The woman had seemed terribly upset and pleaded with the girl so hard that she'd felt unable to refuse. It was obvious now that it had all been a ruse to lure her away. The child remembered how she had always been warned, both at home and school, not to speak to people she didn't know. She wished she had paid heed.

'Too close, too close,' the woman muttered.

'Too close to what?'

'Not what; *who*,' she snapped. The girl recoiled slightly and the woman's tone softened. '*Paid â phoeni*; I'll look after you.' She sat beside her, suddenly smiling again and revealing crooked, discoloured teeth, the lines deepening in her sallow skin. Her wild hair, as wide as it was long, was almost wheaten; a blend of grey with faded copper, with an odd darker band at the ends. She wore an eccentric ensemble of trainers, jogging bottoms and a knee-length floral dress, which hung from her as though borrowed from someone at least two sizes bigger.

'I want to go home,' said the girl in a small voice. She could feel tears welling in her eyes. 'When can I go home?'

'Soon, soon. When he's gone.'

'But when will that be? I want to go . . .'

'You'll see your mammy again soon enough,' snapped the woman impatiently. 'Just one more night.'

'Do you promise?'

181

The woman nodded. With her thumb, she traced a cross on her chest. '*Addo . . . cris, croes, tân poeth.*' Seeing the child's baffled expression, she added. 'Cross my heart.'

A noise outside sent her rushing for the light switch. She peered round the curtain. The child got up to see what it was, but was quickly pushed back into her seat.

The woman flapped her hands anxiously. 'Stay down,' she instructed in a stern whisper. 'He might be out there.'

She ducked down and peeped from the corner of the window frame. The girl watched, frightened but equally fascinated by her captor's exaggerated, almost melodramatic gestures.

The woman's tone became suddenly frantic. 'We'd better move again. *Brysia.*'

'What?'

'Hurry!'

The girl began to cry. 'I don't like this. Please take me home.'

'Not yet. Soon, soon. *Shwsh* now.'

Grabbing the startled child by the hand, the woman yanked her from her seat. She opened the door a fraction and looked from left to right, then pulled her outside, pushing it closed behind them. The night air was cool and the grass wet beneath their feet.

'This way, come on.'

'But my coat . . .'

'There's no time.'

They made their way towards the main road, the woman all the while dragging the reluctant child behind parked cars and beneath window level, dodging the lights from within. When they reached the road, she hesitated for a moment before turning right.

'Keep in to the side,' she hissed. Despite her advancing years, the woman was remarkably sprightly. The girl had to trot to keep up with her. Although growing accustomed to the feel of her own hand against the hardened skin of the woman's palm, she still felt slightly repulsed by the deformed fingers. She wondered what had happened to them, but didn't dare ask. The child was shivering now. She quelled her tears with the worry that she would make the old woman angry. She really was very odd and the girl wondered what she might be capable of.

The woman veered suddenly into a field. Treading gingerly in her wake, the girl tried to focus on where she was placing her feet in the darkness. They appeared to be heading back down the road, rather than in the direction of the church. The child could only hope that the woman had relented and was going to take her back home. The whole situation had turned into a nightmare.

CHAPTER TWELVE

Present Day

Lewis had been scrolling through his phone while waiting for Catrin to finish her shift at the hotel, and was startled when the van's interior light flashed on as the door finally swung open. She slumped into the passenger seat beside him without a word of explanation or apology, tossing her handbag into the footwell.

He glanced at the digital display on the dashboard. 'You took your time. I thought you were supposed to finish at half past.'

'Oh, you know how it is. Something always comes up at the last minute.' She smoothed down her hair with one hand, her gaze focused on the road ahead with the trace of a smile twitching at the corners of her mouth. He regarded her curiously for a moment, then rolled his eyes and started up the engine. Catrin leaned back in her seat, singing along to the strains of 'Titanium' which pulsed from the radio. There was something different, secretive, about her lately; Lewis couldn't put his finger on it. Maybe she'd found someone else. He rather hoped so.

She wound down the window as they passed the caravan park. 'What's going on there, d'you think?'

Uniformed police were milling around the site entrance, the beams of their flashlights bobbing and weaving through the hedge.

'Search me. Maybe one of the vans has been broken into. Kids, probably. They've got bugger all better to do.'

'Hmm. Maybe. Ooh – or *maybe* they've found something. Exciting!' She rubbed her hands together. 'I'm sure Awel will be on the blower right away if they have.' She sniggered. 'Oh, what a tangled web . . .'

'Shut up, will you.'

'*Ewww!* A bit touchy, aren't we?'

'It's not funny, Catrin. You've got a warped sense of humour.'

'Well, pardon me for breathing. You've turned into a right miserable sod, do you know that?' She closed the window once more. 'Anyway, I've found a flat and I'll be out of your hair in the next couple of weeks. You won't have to put up with me for much longer – and *I* won't have to listen to *you* moaning at me all the fucking time.'

She turned up the radio and folded her arms huffily, staring pointedly to her left. They continued the rest of the journey in chilly silence.

For Lewis, her departure from the cottage couldn't come a moment too soon.

Lewis tossed and turned for the best part of the night. As part of his daily routine, he had checked the empty caravans earlier that evening but there had been no sign of anything untoward. Maybe she hadn't been there after all. He would need to look again. He could only hope that nothing bad had happened. He felt torn between a sense of loyalty and his conscience. Gwyn had been so good to him; but this was a step too far. He couldn't go to the police without implicating himself, but he knew in his gut that he ought to come forward if the child wasn't found soon. It just wasn't fair – not on her, nor on Lowri.

He had to come up with something. Fast.

CHAPTER THIRTEEN

DS Evans returned my mobile early the following morning. He looked sheepish as I answered the door in my dressing gown, and stood shifting awkwardly from one foot to the other. He glanced back over his shoulder and I looked beyond him to notice several cars parked on the road outside the gate. It was apparent from the men and women hovering with photographic equipment that the press had descended upon us. As soon as I appeared, an excited shout went up, and I could see a wall of cameras being pointed in the direction of the house. I was past caring about how I would look in a newspaper with my unkempt hair and bags under my eyes, but wondered if such attention would be a help or a hindrance in the search for Ruby.

'Mrs Morris – a few words please?' 'Mrs Morris – how are you bearing up?' 'Mrs Morris – would you like to tell us what you think may have happened to your daughter?'

I felt suddenly sickened. This was blatantly intrusive and really not what I needed at all.

I could see WPC Roberts sitting behind the wheel. She and Nansi had remained in the police car, which was parked on the gravel just outside the front door. Nansi waved from the back seat and smiled a little shakily, and my heart sank. Sunlight winked through the trees but did nothing to lift my spirits. I knew from their faces that the police had nothing positive to share.

I ushered DS Evans into the house and closed the door.

'I'm afraid there's little we can do about that lot.' He gestured with a thumb towards the door. 'Hopefully they'll get bored and clear off soon. If they become a nuisance, we'll get some officers to guard the entrance for you.'

He went on to explain that attempts to locate the device which had sent the text had unfortunately been fruitless.

'The telecoms officer explained that if the battery's dead – or if it's been removed – it's not possible to get any data. Looks like your mystery caller knows what they're doing. But if you should receive something else, please let us know immediately.'

I stared at the phone in my hand, almost willing another message to appear; anything that might give some clue as to my daughter's whereabouts. I felt completely deflated, and now quite unwell. The sore throat was back with a vengeance and I was achy and shivery. My chest felt constricted and it hurt to breathe in; but all I could think about was Ruby. The thought of who she might be with and what kind of ordeal she was going through haunted me constantly. It was torture.

'What about Ruby's cagoule? Haven't the forensics people been able to get anything useful from that?'

'Oh no – that'll take a few days. But rest assured, the moment we learn anything, you'll be informed.'

'A few *days*?' All I wanted was to have Ruby home safe and well. Finding that she had been held by God knows who in a grubby old caravan had only inflamed my anxiety.

Evans looked uncomfortable. 'I'm afraid we're also having to deal with a serious situation in Amlwch at the moment and are managing things as best we can until we get reinforcements. Things are generally pretty quiet here as a rule, but . . .'

He stopped abruptly.

Hearing footsteps on the tiled floor, I looked over my shoulder. Nina had appeared behind me, already dressed and apparently ready for action. We had shared a room, she in Ruby's bed, with Mickey sprawled at its foot. He swished past her now, and stood expectantly in the doorway, his tongue lolling.

'Go on then, fella.' Nina shooed him outside.

'Whoa.' She recoiled slightly at the sight of the cameras poised for action along the lane. Mickey bounded onto the lawn, where he promptly raised a leg to relieve himself. Nina laughed. 'Well, they'll have had an eyeful there anyway! That'll teach 'em.'

The policeman glanced over at the dog and then back at Nina. He nodded slightly, but his face looked pinched. He forced a small cough. 'Good morning.'

'Morning.' Her eyes scanned him from head to foot. She appeared vaguely amused by his obvious discomfiture. 'Have there been any developments?'

'Not as yet, I'm afraid. But the minute we do hear . . .'

'You'll be sure to let us know.' Nina rolled her eyes. 'Can you tell us what you're actually doing to find Ruby, Officer? Only the fact that it was *us* that discovered that caravan hasn't exactly filled me with confidence, to be honest.'

Evans was immediately defensive. 'There are procedures to follow. We've conducted a thorough door-to-door . . .'

Nina snorted. 'Not that bloody thorough from where I'm standing. Listen; a little girl has been missing well over forty-eight hours now. Do you have *any* leads at all?'

Evans opened and closed his mouth like a goldfish. His cheeks burned.

'I'm not being funny, but wouldn't a case like this normally be handled by a more senior officer? I mean, do you have enough experience of this sort of thing?'

Evans looked furious now. 'I am acting DI while our inspector is away on long-term sickness absence. I have all the relevant OSPRE qualifications.' He cleared his throat and ran a hand over his hair, the tendons in his neck bulging. 'We're pursuing various lines of enquiry. After the possible sighting by one local woman, we're focusing on the area around the church. And the caravan park, of course,' he added hastily.

'I think that ship's sailed,' muttered Nina under her breath.

I remembered the photograph he'd shown me of the

scrap of material from Doli glwt's dress. 'What about the fabric you found from the doll? Did you get anything from that?'

'As I said, it takes a few days to get the forensic team's test results back from the lab.'

Nina's voice quavered with anger. 'I'm sorry – I just feel that not enough's being done. I don't know too much about these things, but I *do* have the common sense to understand that the sooner a missing child is found, the better. There seems to be a lot of fannying around, as far as I can tell.'

Evans drew himself to his full height, towering above both of us. His lower lip jutted in indignation. 'We're conducting our investigation by the book. My officers have already scoured the area but the people in the community have organised another search later today, too, if you'd like to join them. They're gathering up by the church at around midday. In the meantime, I'm afraid you'll just have to trust us to do the best job we can, under the circumstances.'

Nina spluttered. '*What* bloody circumstances?'

Evans looked flustered. He seemed momentarily at a loss for words. Nina raised her hands in exasperation.

'What concerns me is that your best job might not be good enough. It's wonderful that the locals are doing their bit, but I'd have hoped for a bit more from your lot. I appreciate you're a small rural force, but I'd still expect a hundred per cent effort.'

He opened his mouth to respond but Nina bluntly raised a palm. 'Talk's cheap. Let's just see some evidence of action.'

She turned and flounced back into the house. Evans looked rattled but I was grateful she had spoken out. Things seemed to be moving painfully slowly and the longer Ruby was missing, the more I was beginning to despair of ever seeing her again.

Evans glared after her. 'Your friend seems very hostile, Mrs Morris.'

'We're worried sick here, DS Evans. Please – if you think there's anything that could be done to help from our end – the waiting around's unbearable.'

'The best thing you can do is to sit tight and let us do our job. I was trying to explain our predicament to you when we were—' he looked pointedly past me down the hallway '—interrupted. A local drug dealer we've had under surveillance has barricaded himself into his neighbour's house and taken a woman and her small son hostage at gunpoint. We've had armed officers watching the property day and night for the last three days. I know it's no excuse, but the timing couldn't be worse. We have several members of staff currently off sick and two senior officers on sabbatical. Once we have more resources at our disposal, we'll be able to step up the investigation further. Although please believe me when I say we are doing our utmost to find Ruby,' he added hastily, 'and even now, everyone is working overtime to ensure no stone is left unturned.'

My heart plummeted. So the investigation into Ruby's disappearance was playing second fiddle to catching some lowlife with a gun before he ran amok. It was unbelievable.

Evans was scrutinising me anxiously.

'Forgive me for saying so, but I think you could do with some proper rest. You don't look at all well.'

He was right. My chest was becoming tighter and I felt lousy.

Mickey gave a sudden bark, startling me. I looked out to see him streaking across the lawn in pursuit of a red squirrel, which shot straight up the trunk of the nearest pine, then nimbly jumped from one long branch to another, disappearing into the foliage.

I caught my breath. How had I not remembered before?

'Oh my God! I've just thought – I tried to get some photos the other day of a couple of squirrels – I'm sure there was someone out there at the time, moving in the trees. I might have a picture of them on my phone.'

DS Evans was turning to leave. He stopped in his tracks, his eyes registering a glimmer of interest. 'May I see?'

I was still clutching the handset. Clumsily, I opened the images folder and with unsteady fingers began to flick through slowly. I was terrible at deleting unwanted images and stored far too many pictures, so that it was hard to know exactly where to look.

What had the date been? About July 20th . . .

There they were. My pulse quickened.

I clicked on the first picture, a blur of orange against green as the squirrels darted across the grass. I should have taken video footage instead. Typical of me not to think of it at the time. I'd taken eight photos in all, but infuriatingly each shot was much the same. I wasn't a natural photographer anyway, and they moved so quickly, it was hard to capture a decent image. My heart sank.

I went back through each one carefully, scrutinising the landscape of the garden. *There*. A definite shape between two trees. I pinched the image wider, but was disappointed to see that it was really not much more than a shadow, and in profile at that. Deflated, I held it up to show DS Evans, who had been tapping a foot on the tiles as he waited.

He screwed up his eyes and peered closer. 'Hmm. Well, I'd say there *is* someone there, but it's very poor quality, I'm afraid. Forward it to me – forward them all, in fact, and we'll take a closer look at the station. I'll ask our technician if she can enhance the image. I'm not too hopeful though, to be honest.'

Seeing my face, he added, 'But it's worth a go, I suppose.'

Another hope dashed. I felt sickened – if I had only taken more care, taken a bit of time to learn how to take better photos with the phone. I selected all the useless images and forwarded them to DS Evans. He acknowledged that they had all come through and headed back to his vehicle, telling me he'd be in touch again soon. Nansi and WPC Roberts waved as they pulled away.

I watched as the assembled press officers parted and the patrol car drove away, then hurried back into the house to avoid the cameras, Mickey close behind me. Nina was sitting in the kitchen with Awel, her expression thunderous. She drummed her fingers on the table.

'That copper's really getting up my nose. He's too wishy-washy by half. We need someone with a bit of "oomph" on the case, not a friggin' wet lettuce.'

'I think you've sent him into a flat spin.' I attempted a smile, but my stomach was in knots. 'I've just forwarded him some pictures I took of the garden a while ago. I'd hoped that I'd caught a shot of someone out there, but as usual my crap photography skills have let me down.' I shook my head in frustration.

'Don't worry about it, love. How were you meant to know what was going to happen?'

'Oh, and the icing on the cake – they're dealing with a bloody siege somewhere in Amlwch and haven't enough officers on the case at the moment. No wonder they've seemed so half-soaked about everything.' I felt tears brimming and put a hand to my mouth. Everything felt totally hopeless.

'You're kidding! For God's sake.'

Nina stared at me suddenly, her brow knitting into a frown. 'You need to get yourself back to bed pronto. You look bloody awful.'

I opened my mouth to protest, but Awel was quick to back her up. 'Go on, up the wooden hills.' She placed a cup of tea in front of Nina, glowering down at poor Mickey who had dropped at her feet, his chin on his paws. Pwtyn had made herself scarce.

'I'll bring you up some more honey and lemon. Can't have you poorly when Ruby gets back, can we?'

'But the search – I wanted to help.'

'Don't you worry about that. There'll be more than enough people. You need rest or you're going to end up seriously ill, take it from me.'

*

I must have needed the sleep. The sun had begun to wane by the time I opened my eyes. I fumbled blearily on the bedside table for my phone as a message pinged through.

But at once I was wide awake as I stared at the words on the screen.

I clambered from the bed and down the stairs, two at a time, calling out for Nina. Awel appeared from the small sitting room, where she had been watching TV.

'Is everything all right?' she asked anxiously.

'Where's Nina?' I felt light-headed, my heart racing. 'I've had another text message.'

'She came back from the search around the headland and then went out again some time ago with the dog. A wonderful turn-out, there was – I reckon half the island showed up to help. No news yet though, I'm afraid.' She looked away and gave a small cough.

'Sorry – you say you've had another message? My head's all over the place – all those journalists out there waving cameras – so unnecessary. It's not like they're even doing anything to help. Shouting stupid questions, cluttering up the lane. Bloody parasites.' Something like anger flashed across her face, but she tightened her lips. 'Come, come and sit in here and let me see.'

I sat beside Awel and showed her the screen. Her throat rose and fell and she looked paler than ever as her eyes turned back to mine. She seemed to be struggling to digest the message.

As I reread it myself, I felt nauseous. 'What does it mean? Who the hell could be sending these things?'

Her voice had an odd edge. 'This sounds to me like someone's playing games with you.'

'I'd better let DS Evans know. He did ask me to contact him or Nansi if I got any more messages.'

She nodded mutely. I was about to dial when Nina's voice called through the letterbox. There was an urgency to her tone that sent a chill through me. I rushed out into the hallway to let her in. Clamped between Mickey's jaws was what looked at first glance like a filthy bundle of rags. Upon closer inspection, I let out a gasp.

'Where did you find this?'

She waved a hand. 'Out there – in those trees. He just came running back with the thing – won't let it go.'

I kneeled to stroke Mickey's head and spoke as calmly as my pounding heart would allow. 'Good boy. Drop it.'

His teeth remained stubbornly closed.

Without a word, Awel breezed past us into the kitchen, returning moments later with a handful of cat treats. She dropped them on the floor next to the dog.

'Here, boy.' To our surprise, Mickey released his find and began to wolf down the crunchy morsels.

'Never known a dog turn their nose up at anything. They're all the same: born greedy,' she said with a smirk.

Gingerly, I picked up Doli glwt by its straggly hair, now slimy with saliva to add to the grime. Tucked into the neckline of its dress was a small scrap of folded paper. I winkled it out between forefinger and thumb. Every nerve in my body began to prickle.

It was a picture of Merida, Ruby's heroine; a sticker peeled from the pages of a comic. A comic that I'd bought for her myself.

*

DS Evans and Nansi arrived soon after the call, along with a flustered-looking WPC Roberts. We stood in the hallway staring down at the bedraggled doll, which I'd placed on top of a plastic bag on the floor. No one spoke for a few moments and time seemed to stand still as the offending article took centre stage. The WPC eventually picked it up with a vinyl-gloved hand, placing it carefully in a clear evidence bag, which she then sealed up.

'That picture is Ruby's, no question. I'm sure she must have put it there to leave us a clue.' My heart fluttered, suddenly feeling a connection to my daughter; a small ray of hope.

'And you say you found this in the copse over there?' He waved a hand behind him.

Nina nodded. 'Well, strictly speaking, the dog did. I hope this means you'll be conducting a thorough search of the area.'

Evans frowned. He sniffed officiously, standing with his hands clasped behind his back. 'Our officers have already been through there once; but yes, we'll be carrying out a fingertip search. I'll get onto it right away.'

He was about to return to his patrol car when I remembered the text.

'Wait! There's something else.'

I fished the phone from my dressing gown pocket and handed it over, anxious for his reaction, almost as if he might be able to glean some vital clue from these words and solve everything in one fell swoop.

Evans just stared at the message. His face blanched. He flashed the screen towards Nansi, casting his eyes as he did so beyond me and down the passageway, as though expecting to see someone emerging from the gloom.

'We'll look into this as soon as possible. In the meantime, I need to initiate the search of the woods. It looks as though the doll has been dropped there very recently. There may be other crucial evidence that might lead us to Ruby.'

He excused himself and left abruptly with WPC Roberts, leaving Nansi hovering awkwardly in the doorway. She gave me a thin-lipped smile. 'A TV appeal to help find Ruby has been organised – it'll be going out on the local news later this evening. I realise you're unwell, so we'll handle everything – you don't need to attend. The more information we have to share, the better. It may just jog someone's memory.'

My head was spinning with all of this. Things suddenly seemed to be escalating and I felt as though I was losing control completely. Ruby was no longer just my little girl – it was as if overnight she had become public property. One of those victims' names that became forever synonymous with the monsters responsible for their demise. A wave of indescribable horror washed over me. What if this new search turned up what I had been dreading from the minute she vanished?

Seeing my face, Nina grabbed me by the hand.

'Come on – let's go and sit in there. It's getting chilly and I'm sure we could all do with a – what is it they call it here? A nice hot *panad*.'

She led me into the sitting room, with Nansi and Awel close behind. It was going to be a painfully long evening.

*

We watched from the window of the small sitting room as vehicles drew up outside. Several uniformed police officers moved the disgruntled journalists back and erected a metal barrier outside the gate, meaning that they had a less clear view of the house. The garden was soon filled with yet more officers brandishing sticks and flashlights. Mickey let out an excited bark and bounded eagerly to the window, seeing the dogs accompanying some of them.

'Calm down,' instructed Nina sternly. He dropped to the ground and looked up at her shame-facedly.

The whirring of helicopter blades grew louder and a bright white searchlight strobed from the sky across the tops of the trees.

Apart from the heavy police presence, there wasn't much evidence of anything happening, until a shout went up and one officer began to signal with a torch. Several others swarmed towards the waving light, disappearing into the depths of the wooded area.

Anxiously, I paced the room. The TV was blaring an episode of *Panorama*, but no one was paying its grainy picture any attention. Infuriatingly, despite several efforts from each of us, we had been unable to tune into the channel airing the appeal for Ruby's safe return earlier in the evening. Owing to Auntie Gwyn's apparent aversion to modern technology, there was no wifi at the house either. I could only hope it had triggered some public response, if nothing else. Nansi told us there was a reconstruction of Ruby's last known movements planned for the following afternoon, at the same time of day she'd disappeared. It felt to me like pissing in the wind.

The weather had been so bad, it seemed unlikely anyone other than the woman driver who had spotted her going down the lane would have seen anything, but I had to cling onto the hope that maybe someone who'd been passing through might hear about it and it would prompt some subconscious observation.

Nansi tried to keep the conversation light, but no one was in the mood for small talk. Nina was keen to grill her about the investigation so far and didn't hold back with expressing her opinion of DS Evans.

'Correct me if I'm wrong but, from where I'm standing, he strikes me as a bit of a chocolate teapot. What's he like to work with?'

Nansi puffed out her cheeks. 'Look, he might seem a bit anal and his manner's sometimes – a bit off, shall we say – but he's actually a very good copper. I know this must be intolerable for you all; Lowri especially. But he's doing everything he can with the resources available to him. It may not feel like it, but I know all this will be keeping him up at night.'

Nina nodded but didn't look entirely convinced. She went over to the window, watching the officers moving in and out of the trees. 'These TV appeals – do they often get results?'

'We can get sent down a lot of blind alleys. But once in a while they reach the right person and we get a breakthrough. Hopefully someone else will have spotted Ruby's jacket – it's very distinctive.'

I remembered buying the cagoule in Debenhams. I'd wanted a more subtle shade for her – pale blue or cream – but Ruby loved the bright pink and had pleaded with me. I gave in eventually and she was highly delighted. I thought now of her wearing it for what might have been the last time and instinctively cradled my head with both hands in despair.

I noticed Elis watching me, his face anguished. Awel had made us all yet more tea, but I had let mine go cold for the third time. I was still shivering but, so intent now on watching the activity outside, I hardly noticed.

Elis fetched a heavy, coarse blanket, which I wrapped absently round my shoulders, my gaze constantly straying through the opened curtains. The waiting was intolerable. The area the police team were covering was probably a couple of hundred yards wide and equally deep; it wasn't possible to tell from the house exactly where they were focusing their efforts.

At least half an hour had passed before an officer emerged from the trees. As he approached the house, I saw it was DS Evans, his face grave. The feeling of cold, sickening dread began to seep from my stomach through my whole body. My heart hammering against my ribcage, I rushed to the front door, Nina anxiously trying her best to hold me back. I turned to her, tears coursing down my cheeks, my mind flying to every terrible possibility.

'They've got something, I know they have.'

'Let's just see what he has to say. Deep breaths.'

Nansi came out into the hallway, her face chalk white. Everything seemed to be playing out in slow motion.

I flung open the door. 'What is it? What have they found?'

DS Evans exhaled, his eyes not meeting mine. 'One of the dogs has uncovered what appears to be human remains. We have no way of knowing at this stage exactly how long they've been there, not until the forensic team perform a thorough analysis of the discovery and the soil surrounding it.'

I felt my legs buckle and Nina grabbed me, holding me firmly to her. A terrible image of Ruby's lifeless body flashed through my mind; face down, her clothes torn. Everything began to swim.

Evans hastily stepped forward, clasping my arm. His voice was steady.

'Mrs Morris, we don't believe the remains are in any way connected to Ruby. They are in a state of decomposition consistent with someone who has been dead for a very long time – possibly decades. As I said, we'll know more once the pathologist has conducted an autopsy.'

Awel appeared suddenly in the doorway of the sitting room. From her deathly pallor and the way her face was contorted, I thought she was about to be sick.

'So you say there's been some poor soul buried in those woods for years? Do you have any idea who they could be?'

He turned to her. 'Naturally we can't say conclusively at this stage. Look, I shouldn't really speculate and I probably oughtn't to say anything. But we suspect from items accompanying the . . . the body, that it could be a young girl who went missing not far from here over twenty years ago. It was all over the news at the time. You may recall the name . . .'

'Beca Bennion,' finished Awel. 'Oh yes. I remember it well.'

*

My relief was such that I began to sob uncontrollably. I felt so weak now, drained of any reserves of strength, either physical or mental. My legs were wobbling like those of a new-born calf. Nina led me gently back into the sitting room, Awel and Evans close behind us. I sank into the chair next to Elis, who patted my hand and offered a sad but reassuring smile as Awel conveyed to him what the police had found.

Not Ruby. *Not Ruby*. But where on earth *was* she? And what, if indeed it *was* Beca Bennion, had actually happened to the poor girl all those years ago? It was of little comfort to know that someone, even if not recently, had disposed of a child so close to home. And my own was still missing.

CHAPTER FOURTEEN

Exhausted but beyond the ability to sleep, we remained in the sitting room until daylight had started to creep through. We watched the police forensic team dressed in white hooded overalls to-ing and fro-ing between their vehicles and the now cordoned-off area surrounding the woods. A few die-hard journalists had remained in the lane, but the police were keeping them at a safe distance and divulging nothing, much to their obvious annoyance.

Nansi left us at about eight o'clock – she had no partner but there was a cat to feed, she told us.

'I'll get my head down for a couple of hours, but I'll be back later after the reconstruction. Hopefully the appeal will have generated a few calls – the minute anything comes through, I'll let you know.' She looked exhausted and I felt quite sorry for her, actually. I'd learned that she was divorced, with one adult daughter who had moved to Edinburgh with her family, and she rarely saw them. I suspected the job was something to fill the lonely hours rather than a passion.

Eventually, two officers emerged, carrying a stretcher covered with a black bag. They loaded it into the back of a van with blacked-out windows parked at the far side of the driveway. My stomach twisted, knowing what it concealed. I reflected on the horror of it all and clapped a hand over my mouth, stifling a sob. Awel, sitting almost apologetically on the edge of her seat, hands in her lap, had filled Nina and me in about the whole tragic tale of Beca Bennion.

The identity of her father a mystery, Beca had been raised by her maternal grandmother after her wayward teenage mother, Rhian, had died as a result of complications shortly after her birth. Beca was a naïve, sweet girl. One day shortly after her twelfth birthday, she had gone to the shop on an errand for her Nain and disappeared from the face of the earth. Apparently, she'd been talking for days about meeting her father. She'd seemed excited, and had told her Nain that she thought she'd guessed who he was and intended to reveal her identity to him – quite how she'd found out, she wouldn't say, although she'd been searching through an old box she'd discovered, containing her mother's photos and letters, only the week before. Beca wouldn't tell her grandmother the man's identity until she had confirmed her suspicions, but sadly she never got the opportunity. Whatever clue she had found in the box she must have taken with her, as there was nothing useful in there when the police went through it. Just the usual: zany photo-booth snaps of Rhian and some friends pulling faces, Take That concert tickets, a Valentine's card, a pink silicone wristband for a charity fun run. Poignant mementos of a simpler time before drugs overshadowed her existence.

'The whole village was out in force looking for Beca for days. The police thought it possible that she'd arranged to meet the man she believed to be her father and then something terrible had happened as a result of coming face to face with him. I mean, Rhian had fallen in with a bad lot. Whoever the child's father was, he was no good; that's for sure. The police had to call time on the investigation eventually. The grief killed her poor Nain. Beca had become her world since Rhian died – the girl actually called her "Mam", since she'd never known her real one.'

Awel shook her head sadly. 'She blamed herself – she thought Beca was just being fanciful and making up stories, as she'd always wanted to find her father, so hadn't taken much notice. She was only in her late forties, poor woman. Stepped out in front of a bus in Cemaes a couple of months later. She'd been taking medication – for the upset, you know. No one was ever sure whether she did it on purpose or she was just in a daze. Terrible, whatever the reason.'

Although their circumstances were quite different, the parallels with Ruby's disappearance were all too similar. I felt sick with worry. Seeing my expression, Nina squeezed my hand.

'They haven't confirmed that it's Beca yet. And in any case, whoever it is, there's no reason to assume that this awful business is in any way linked to Ruby, you know.'

But from the look on her face, I could see that she was beginning to think that it just might be.

*

Although still awaiting the results of forensic tests, later that afternoon, DS Evans rang to confirm that they were ninety-nine per cent sure the remains were those of Beca Bennion. Shoes and a necklace found with the body, or what was left of it, matched the description given all those years ago by the girl's grandmother. He asked if we could refrain from discussing the discovery with anyone else for the time being, until the police had made a formal public statement.

'Everyone's going to see the cordon, I know. We'll make up something to keep the press off the trail for a bit, but they'll have to be informed sooner or later. Mrs Morris, I appreciate how distressing this must be for you, but please try to keep calm.'

I felt anything but. My gut was churning like a washing machine and I had a persistent empty, aching sensation between my ribs. I had begun to lose all hope of ever seeing Ruby alive again.

Seemingly oblivious to my distress, DS Evans went on. 'The Bennion girl went missing over two decades ago. It's highly unlikely that Ruby has fallen into the hands of the person or persons responsible for this. There have been no other such cases in the area since.'

'I wish I shared your confidence. All I know is, my daughter's out there somewhere and the thought of what might be happening to her is sheer agony.' I could feel panic bubbling inside me once more. 'And then there's the texts – either someone actually knows something or they're just a sadist enjoying seeing me suffer – and you can't even locate the sender.'

The weighted pause from the other end of the line told me I'd hit a nerve.

'I can't talk to you now. I have to go.'

'Mrs Morris . . .'

I disconnected the call. If the police couldn't find my lovely Ruby, what hope was there? Blood rushed in my ears and my head felt as if it might actually explode.

I thought back to one occasion when Ruby was about three and we'd been shopping in the supermarket. I had released my grip on her hand – only for a split second as I bent to put something in my basket – and when I turned round, she had disappeared. I was beside myself, convinced someone must have snatched her, rushing up and down the aisles calling her name. And there she was, oblivious to the anxiety she had caused; in her own little world, looking at the toys.

'Look, Mummy! Peppa!' She was beaming from ear to ear, clutching a cuddly Peppa Pig toy to her chest, her delight evident. I didn't know whether to laugh or cry. I grabbed and squeezed her so hard that she protested loudly and tried to wriggle away. I had never known fear like it – only minutes had passed but it felt like hours, as though everything was happening in slow motion. Still trembling, I abandoned the basket, scooped her up and carried her out of the shop. All I wanted to do was get her home, lock the door on the outside world; wrap her up in cotton wool forever. And now here I was, actually living the nightmare I had played out so often in my mind. I was struggling to keep a grip on reality.

I'd managed only a couple of hours' fitful sleep and felt increasingly short of breath, but knew I needed to get out there and look for myself. The waiting, the not knowing, was worse than anything I'd ever experienced.

I checked my phone again in case I'd missed anything from the mystery texter. Nothing new had come through, but I kept rereading that last cryptic, disturbing message:

THINK YOU REALLY KNOW WHO YOUR FRIENDS ARE?

Should I be watching my back? Or was someone just playing cruel mind games with me?

*

Nansi returned later that evening. She seemed uncomfortable and it put me on edge immediately. I wondered what she could have learned. Awel, Nina and I were still gathered in the kitchen after supper; Elis had gone to walk Mickey down the lane. Nina was doing her best to keep my spirits up but, yet again, I had been unable to eat with everything going through my head. I was existing on the odd cup of tea and intermittent burst of adrenaline. In between, I felt completely drained. Earlier I had caught sight of my reflection in the bathroom mirror. I seemed to have aged ten years almost overnight, my face gaunt and grey, eyes sunken. The hours were dragging, and with every ring of the house phone or rap of the front door I was bracing myself for the worst news. It really was a living nightmare.

'Well, the TV appeal generated a lot of phone calls,'

Nansi told us as she pulled up a chair. 'Most of them not very helpful, I have to say.'

'But?' Nina raised her eyebrows questioningly.

'I'm sorry?'

'From your face, it looks as though there's a *but* coming.'

Nansi ran her tongue across her lips and laid her palms flat on the table. I saw that her nails were short and blunt; no nonsense. Her expression was grim.

'A couple who were staying in one of the caravans last week with their two children have come forward. They're back home in Liverpool now, but they said that a man in his forties from one of the other vans seemed to have been watching the kids with a bit too much interest. They thought he looked – well, *creepy* – that was how they put it. Anyway, to cut a long story short, just to rule him out, we looked into his background – and it looks like he has form.'

I felt my stomach drop and gripped the table edge. Nina stiffened, clutching my hand so tightly it hurt.

'Who is he, this man?'

'He lives in Stockport. He's been done in the past for flashing kids in his local park; one attempted abduction of a ten-year-old girl. So we've been in touch with his local force and they paid him a visit earlier this afternoon.' Nansi's shoulders fell as she exhaled. 'He wasn't in, but the officers spoke to his neighbour.' Her eyes flicked anxiously from Nina's to mine.

'And?' Nina was on her feet now, her fists curled into tight balls, almost as though preparing to go and confront the undesirable herself.

211

'The old girl next door said she heard a noise outside after she'd gone up to bed last night, and looked through her window to see him digging a hole in his garden. They're sending officers in to excavate the area. We're just waiting for them to report back.'

It was as if the walls were closing in on me. Everything became suddenly blurred and, barely aware of my surroundings, I stumbled from my chair and out of the kitchen. I could hear the echo of concerned voices behind me, but the words were unintelligible. I needed to get outside; to breathe clean air. I was suffocating. I'd just made it into the cold passageway leading to the preparation room when I was violently sick. I had eaten so little, there was only bitter liquid to bring up. My stomach heaved painfully as I retched. I dropped to my knees, my head throbbing, and let out a scream; an awful, primitive sound coming from somewhere deep within me over which I seemed to have no control. The realisation that the police were now definitely looking for a body was like a stab to the heart.

My Ruby must be dead.

CHAPTER FIFTEEN

The Girl's Story

They had waited, concealed in the trees outside, until the building was in darkness. The girl could barely keep her eyes open and was trembling with the cold. Her hands and feet were numb. The prospect of actually getting inside and into the warm was keeping her going. The woman moved in a peculiar, jerky fashion, almost like a bird. She seemed to be fidgeting perpetually; as though she found it impossible to keep still.

'Come on,' she said eventually, once everything was still and quiet. She tugged the child by the hand and they emerged onto the sodden lawn, then hurried across to the back of the building. Everything looked very different in the dark and the girl wasn't entirely sure where they were.

There appeared to be several large containers of some

sort towards the edge of the turf. Puffing and blowing, the woman manoeuvred one, clearly a weighty thing, to one side. She tapped her foot on something solid. From her pocket, she took out a small torch and flashed it on the ground. It revealed a rusting manhole cover, overgrown with grass, a large ring in its centre. Grasping the ring with both hands, she heaved the cover back and turned to her young companion, who was staring in horror at the gaping blackness of the aperture below.

'Go on, then.'

The girl was paralysed with fear. In spite of herself, she began to sob.

'*Shwsh, hogan!* Be quiet,' the woman growled angrily. She looked around, then gestured frantically for the girl to step into the hole. Shakily, the child climbed down onto the metal ladder concealed beneath the ground. The woman followed, reaching up to slide the manhole cover back into place. They began to make their way into the cold, eerie depths, each footfall clanging against the rungs as they descended. The only light was from the weak stream of the woman's flashlight. Still sniffing back tears, the girl tried not to imagine what lay at the bottom.

At the foot of the ladder, beyond a small square area of flattened soil, they were faced with a heavy, solid wooden door. Producing an old-fashioned key from her capacious trouser pocket, the woman clicked it open. They entered a gloomy, frigid corridor, cold flagstones beneath their feet. The door closed slowly behind them. The girl felt more frightened than she had ever been in her life. She thought of home and tried to summon every ounce of courage she could. Soon she would be back there again – the woman had promised. She *had* to hold onto that thought.

The woman guided her to the left, which felt counterintuitive. The girl was sure the opposite direction would lead into the main house, which had been visible, if only in silhouette, from the lawn. It was so dark and unwelcoming, as though they were entering the very bowels of the building. At the end of the passageway, they were met with another door. The woman felt on top of the frame and lifted down a substantial-looking metal key. She unlocked the door, revealing a narrow wooden staircase, again leading downwards. The stairs were shallow and steep and the child followed cautiously, feeling her way in the dim along the stiff rope banister attached by rusting iron hooks to the wall, every step creaking beneath the woman's weight as she descended ahead of her. At the foot of the stairs, yet another door opened onto a cold, dark room. The woman pressed a light switch, pulling the door shut behind them. The girl blinked as she grew accustomed to the meagre glow flickering from the filament of the bare bulb suspended from the centre of the ceiling. She looked around and gasped in horror. They were in a windowless cellar room, around twenty feet square, with bare stone walls and a concrete floor painted dark green. In one corner was a small, grimy handbasin and a bucket. On the floor next to these, a mattress was pushed up against the wall, over which was slung a crocheted blanket and one dirty, striped pillow. To the other side of the mattress, the girl was puzzled to see a heavy, full-length green brocade curtain draped across the wall.

But on the walls either side of the makeshift bed, piles of long wooden cases were stacked, one atop the other. The girl counted four in each pile – eight against each wall. The sight filled her with a sudden cold dread. She recognised them for what they were: she had seen one only recently.

They were surrounded by coffins.

CHAPTER SIXTEEN

Present Day

Awel and Nina had been amazing. They cleaned me up and helped me into the sitting room. Awel wrapped me in an old shawl of Auntie Gwyn's, and brought me her cure-all brandy with warm water and a little sugar, in a bid to settle my nerves. Between sips of the concoction she guided patiently to my mouth, I could feel my teeth rattling together as I sat staring straight ahead of me unseeingly.

How had it come to this? A sad, but not entirely untimely goodbye to my beloved aunt, a nostalgic visit to my childhood home. What could have heralded a new beginning for my daughter and me now ripped from under us in the cruellest way. I felt as if I had unwittingly lured her to her death.

Poor, poor Ruby.

Nina watched me anxiously for signs of a relapse, squatting beside me and gently rubbing my back; talking in her best calming voice.

'Could be nothing,' she said, smoothing the curtain of hair from my face as my head fell forward. 'I'm sure there are loads of false alarms in these situations.' She exchanged glances with Nansi, her eyes encouraging some signal of reassurance. 'Isn't that right?'

Nansi, pale and clearly worried, mumbled an unconvincing affirmation and left shortly afterwards, with the promise of updating us the second any news came through. I was still distraught and beyond consolation. The thought of my beautiful, sweet daughter being snatched and used by some pervert then dumped like rubbish was so painful I thought I might implode. I actually *wanted* to. I had to be with her. It was more than I could bear.

Elis returned with the dog and Awel took him into the hall to tell him what was happening. He loomed in the doorway briefly and didn't seem to know what to do, other than to offer me a feeble smile, then disappeared once more with Mickey at his heels.

When DS Evans finally pulled up alone in his car, I was anticipating the worst. My breath coming in rapid, shallow gasps, I watched from the window as he approached the house, unable to glean anything from his closed body language. Awel went to let him in as I sat, shaking from head to foot and almost wetting myself in fright. Nina wrapped a protective arm around me as he walked into the room.

'I wanted to let you know in person, Mrs Morris. The

218

excavation of the garden in Stockport has uncovered the body of an old chocolate Labrador. It seems that the dog passed away yesterday afternoon and its owner waited until after dark to bury it. A thorough search of the house was also undertaken and there's no evidence to suggest that the individual has any connection to Ruby's disappearance.'

I began to cry with relief, clinging onto Nina for dear life. *Thank God*. But the feeling was short-lived: even if this particular lead had amounted to nothing, Ruby was still out there, and it concerned me now that focusing on the wrong suspect, even for a few hours, may have diverted the police's efforts and given her real abductor momentary reprieve – and further opportunity to do Christ knows what. The briefly suppressed panic began to build inside me once more.

'I must – I need to go and look for her.' I tried to stand, but my legs were weak and uncoordinated. Now that the shock was wearing off, I felt completely wiped out and increasingly unwell.

Nina guided me back into my seat and persuaded me I'd do better to get a proper night's rest before embarking on another search. Reluctantly, I swallowed more paracetamol, then took myself off to bed in the hope of shaking off the annoying bug and feeling stronger, both mentally and physically. It had been a particularly gruelling day, in more ways than one.

The following morning, I was woken by the jangling ringtone of Nina's mobile from the landing. My throat felt as if it had closed completely and my head throbbed. Every intake of breath triggered a sharp pain in my back.

Wearily, I sat up and peered at the clock. It was only twenty to eight. Nina was already dressed and had been downstairs to let Mickey outside. I could see from her face that she was upset as she came back into the bedroom. She glanced at me anxiously as she went across to open the curtains, revealing a bleak expanse of grey sky.

'Morning, lovely. This is such crap timing and I hate to leave you in the lurch, but I've just heard that Ronnie's mum's been taken into hospital after a nasty fall. He's beside himself and I want to be with him. I'll make sure everything's okay at home, and come back as soon as I can.' She stood looking out of the window, keeping an eye on the dog, who was busily exploring the garden, ignoring the handful of bored-looking press officers who were still hovering by the gate.

My heart sank. Nina's strong presence had been comforting. But I understood that she really needed to support Ronnie. I tried to smile, but felt my lip quiver. Turning and seeing my face, she looked torn.

'Oh, sweetheart! Listen, would you like me to leave Mickey with you? He might be able to help – his nose is the best guide we've had so far in all this.'

'Thank you.' My voice was hoarse. 'Yes, I'd be glad to have him. And Ruby will love him being here when . . .' I fought back tears. She sat down on the bed and gave me a squeeze. I pressed my face into her shoulder, breathing in the familiar floral scent of her perfume. She released me and cupped my face in her solid hands, her expression stern.

'You stay strong now, you hear. She'll turn up, I'm sure of it. Just keep positive. No news is good news.'

'That's just what Auntie Gwyn always used to say.' I managed a weak smile.

Nina grinned. 'Well, she sounds like a wise old bird, your auntie. Make that thought your mantra.'

*

After breakfast, I waved Nina off with a heavy heart. Two police officers stood guarding the gate and moved the barrier aside for her to pass. I watched as she drove through the gap between the assembled photographers and heard her shout through the opened car window, 'Why don't you lot just piss off? Haven't you got anything better to do?'

They stared after her as she disappeared down the lane. It was so typical of Nina and ordinarily I would have laughed. But in spite of Elis and Awel, it was as if I was facing everything alone once again. With Nina gone, I felt suddenly overwhelmingly isolated and desperate. We were in the middle of nowhere: the bus service was erratic, the nearest stop a good mile away on the main road. And what if I'd had my own transport; where would I go? Not that I wanted anything, but even the local corner shop was a good half an hour away on foot. I felt cut off from civilisation and slightly panicked by the thought.

Above all else, I ached for Ruby. I didn't know which way to turn or what to do next. The constant effort of trying to remain positive was exhausting. I felt I was hanging on by a thread that was becoming thinner and nearer breaking point by the hour.

There was still a definite atmosphere between Awel

and her brother. Elis had become increasingly withdrawn and morose ever since Ruby had gone missing and seemed to be avoiding being alone with me. I felt bad that he must feel culpable, but was puzzled as to the cause of the obvious rift with Awel. Surely she wasn't blaming him, too? That would be really unfair. Apart from whoever had taken her, the only other person at fault in all this was me. I was Ruby's mum; she had been in a strange place and I had dropped my guard. Elis had been preoccupied with serving the guests – and in any case, Ruby had only gone to the bathroom in the house; it wasn't as if he'd allowed her to wander off in the middle of nowhere. I should have been keeping a closer eye on her; she was my responsibility, no one else's. It made it all the harder to bear.

Awel had sent Elis to the supermarket to buy dog food, amongst other things, and said she had some paperwork to go through. I felt rougher than ever, the breathlessness and stabbing pains in my back having got progressively worse, but decided to drag myself out and walk the dog up to the church, in the vain hope that we might find something the police had missed. I pulled up my hood, kept my head down and steadfastly ignored the intrusive stream of questions shouted by the journalists, eager for a scoop, as Mickey and I walked briskly past them.

The police cordon was still around the copse, its purpose clearly tantalising to the press. The sight of it sent an unpleasant tingle up my spine. I wondered about poor little Beca. She would have been almost my age now, had she lived. It made me shudder to think that she had been lying there in the woods for all those years, so close to the house. Even more that she had been killed and disposed of during my last summer with Auntie Gwyn. What if whoever had put her there was still in the area? Despite DS Evans's assurances, I wasn't convinced this had no connection to Ruby. The thought made me feel quite sick.

It was a cool morning and there was a fine mizzle in the air. With Mickey leading the way, I trudged up the lane, finally reaching the stone archway of the churchyard. Through it I could see where we had laid Auntie Gwyn, the flowers still fresh around the mound of soil. It had been only three days since the funeral but felt like weeks. I was as if I was enveloped in a thick fog, clouding everything around me, the days merging into one another. I walked towards the periphery of the graveyard and stood precariously close to the cliff edge, staring down at the white-tipped waves rolling in. My chest felt hollow and empty. Gulls soared above us, their melancholic cries filling the air. I would usually gain a sense of peace from this place, but today it felt lonely and utterly desolate.

Mickey gave a small bark and began to strain at his lead suddenly, as though he was onto something. I soon realised that he had spotted a man with a small dog walking towards us across the cliff path. I steered Mickey back towards the church, pausing to look at Auntie Gwyn's floral tributes.

The grave was marked by a wooden cross, put in place until the ground had settled once more. Draped around it was a long daisy chain, like the one left previously on Sionyn's headstone, which had been removed temporarily to have Auntie Gwyn's name added. I stooped to examine it, then glanced around, half expecting to see someone watching me. But there was no one; the dog walker had disappeared over the headland and I was quite alone. I felt suddenly uneasy and, clutching Mickey's lead, hurried for the refuge of the church.

I was hugely relieved to find Hannah inside, removing the dead flowers from the altar and putting them into a plastic bag. Seeing me, she stopped at once and came towards us, her usually serene expression replaced with genuine anguish.

'Oh, Lowri. I've been thinking about you. What a shocking business this all is. Have you . . . has there been any news?'

I shook my head. I could feel the omnipresent knot rising in my throat and swallowed it down.

'The other day, someone thought they saw Ruby with an adult, heading this way. But the police don't seem to be having much luck.'

'I see they've been looking in the woods.' She hesitated. 'They were here again yesterday, searching the area with the really old graves where the ground's begun to subside. It's getting worse – lots of rabbit holes around the plots and the turf's really unstable – one young officer twisted his ankle. I did warn them. We've had the press poking around too – I keep meeting them in the lane. They're itching to get a story – I don't know what they think they're going to find out from me.'

I thought again of the black bag being carried from the spinney on the stretcher and my stomach keeled. 'I keep hoping Mickey here will pick up on something. The other day, he led us to one of the caravans – you know, on that new site down the road – and Ruby's cagoule was inside, but there was no sign of her . . .'

The tears flowed now. I buried my face in my hands. Saying it aloud, everything felt even more hopeless. Hannah put an arm around my shoulder and led me to a pew. She simply sat next to me, holding my hand, and waited patiently for me to stop sobbing.

'Listen, I'm about finished here. Why don't you come and have a *panad* with me? I only live a couple of hundred yards down the road.' She glanced down at Mickey, who was lying at my feet, and grimaced. 'Ooh – how is he with cats?'

I smiled weakly. 'He's fine. He's my friend's dog – very good-natured.'

She seemed reassured by this, stooping to scruff the fur behind his ears as he gazed up at her, his tail twitching against the stone floor. I waited while she locked up and we made our way back down the lane. The air was still misty and damp, and cool for July. As we turned the corner, we were met with the sight of Lewis in his van. His face lit up; he raised a hand to wave, and we returned the gesture.

'Oh, he'll have finished my tap then, hopefully.'

'Sorry?'

'Lewis. He was calling round to put a new washer in my kitchen tap – it's been dripping for weeks. I left the back door key under the mat for him. He's so helpful – built some really sturdy shelves in my cellar last year, ever so cheap. Such a nice young man and he can turn his hand to anything.' She paused, dropping her chin, and looked at me from beneath feathery silver eyebrows. 'He split up with that Catrin recently, you know. She didn't know when she was well off, if you ask me.'

Her eyes seemed to say, *You could do worse*. I managed a weak smile.

I realised I was shivering and was glad when we reached Hannah's little stone cottage. It was set back from the road behind a clipped box hedge, with a neat front garden, the path leading to the wooden portico lined with mauve hydrangeas. The house exuded what I'd describe as an air of calm. It was small and beautifully maintained, and seemed to reflect Hannah's personality perfectly. The white-painted front door opened straight into a small sitting room, carpeted in cream and furnished simply but comfortably, with a pot-bellied wood-burner sitting in the rugged hearth, and two small teal-blue chenille settees, one of which was occupied by a fluffy black and white cat, who, in spite of Mickey, seemed unruffled by our presence and simply squeezed her eyes more tightly shut as we entered. I noticed movement in the doorway at the far side of the room and looked up to see a stripey ginger tail disappearing through it.

'We used to have a dog,' explained Hannah. 'Swti's generally not too bothered by them. My other cat, Tomos, isn't so keen, mind you. He'll make himself scarce until you've gone.' She laughed, then noticing my face, looked suddenly worried.

'Oh dear. You don't look at all well.' She felt my hands and frowned. '*Duw anwyl dad*, you're so cold! Get out of that damp coat and have a seat, and I'll fetch you a

226

blanket. I'll put a drop of whisky in your tea – my mam used to swear by it.'

Hannah put some logs on to burn and hung up my jacket to dry. Mickey made himself at home, sprawled out sleepily in front of the flickering flames. Soon I was cosy, wrapped in a fleecy blue throw and hugging a steaming mug of tea. I had protested about adding the whisky, but she was most insistent.

'Medicinal purposes only. Trust me; it'll help.' She sat opposite me, running a hand along the purring cat's back. 'Oh, I meant to tell you. I was thinking about what you said; about your Aunt Carys not being buried in Llanbadrig with her family. I asked Reverend Parry about the possibility of her being buried in Llanbabo. He spoke to the minister there and asked him to check the parish records – there's no mention of her there, either. Very strange.'

I sat up. 'But Elis took me there, to Llanbabo. We found the grave – I was going to take Carys's doll and put it . . .'

She shook her head adamantly. 'The only record of the burial of any Carys Hughes Owen in either church-yard is from about ninety years ago. A sister of your hen hen Taid, I believe. It must have been her grave that you saw.'

Goosebumps prickled along my arms. I pulled the blanket around me more tightly. 'Then where *is* she? It makes no sense.'

'I really don't know. But I agree – it's a bit odd. You would've thought she'd have been laid to rest with her brother, or her parents. All long before my time here,

I'm afraid, and neither of our ministers are from the island originally, so their knowledge of local family history is limited. Don't Awel or Elis know anything?'

'Apparently not. Or if they do, they're not telling me.'

She sat back, eyeing me curiously. 'Is everything – all right between you all?'

'Yes. Yes, of course – I'm just very emotional and tired, and everything's getting on top of me. This whole thing has upset us all so much – and then there was the shock with the will, too. Things feel a bit, well, strained at the house.' I thought better of mentioning Beca Bennion, remembering that DS Evans had asked us not to tell anyone about the discovery for the time being.

'What happened with the will, if you don't mind my asking?'

I sighed. 'I think Awel expected the house and business to be left between her and Elis, but it turns out it's all been left to me. I feel quite guilty about it. I've been away for so long, I don't think I've any real right. But I've also got to think of Ruby, of our future . . .' Hot tears sprang to my eyes. 'And now I can't even be sure that we'll have one.'

'Now don't you get thinking that way.' Her voice was firm but kind. 'There may be a breakthrough just around the corner.'

'The longer this goes on, the more I'm beginning to lose hope.'

'Well, you mustn't. We're all praying for you. I'm sure Ruby will turn up soon.'

I bit my lip. Hannah meant well, but no amount of bargaining with the Almighty was going to return my daughter to me. I didn't share her faith, but she had been so kind and I didn't want to offend her.

A sudden scrabbling noise and plaintive mewling came from the kitchen. Hannah rolled her eyes. 'Tomos wants to go out. Excuse me a minute.'

As she left the room briefly, I leaned back in my seat, gazing absently into the tangerine glow of the crackling fire. One log shifted slightly, and Mickey's ears lifted and swivelled like periscopes. He emitted a whimper and turned his head towards me. A soft thud from above, followed by slow creaking, made me sit up sharply. I had thought we were alone in the cottage and it was slightly jarring.

Hannah came back through the doorway, beaming. 'That cat, honestly. He'll be back scratching to come in again in a second. Doesn't know what to do with himself half the time.' Seeing my face, her smile faded.

'Is anything wrong?'

'No. I just – well, I thought I heard someone moving around upstairs.'

'Ah – that'll be my sister, Leisa. She's staying with me for a few days. She hasn't been too well, unfortunately.' She glanced over her shoulder as though expecting Leisa to appear suddenly, but there was no sign of her. 'I'll take her up some lunch shortly. She was supposed to be going back to Aberystwyth tomorrow but I don't think she's up to the journey just yet. Maybe she's got the same bug you seem to have caught.'

I nodded and smiled half-heartedly. It seemed strange that she hadn't mentioned her house guest earlier. I felt a little discomfited and finished my tea in silence, then

229

thanked Hannah and made my excuses to leave. It was gone eleven o'clock, and another day seemed to be ebbing away with no progress on any front. I didn't know what to do, where to even begin looking. It felt like wading through treacle.

Hannah showed me to the door. From upstairs, we could hear the faint warbling rendition of a familiar tune. She smiled.

'Leisa must be feeling a bit better. I'll go up and see her now. Poor soul's been here almost a week and she's been stuck in bed for most of it.'

It was the song, though, that made me catch my breath. The same haunting tune I'd thought I heard from behind the locked door at Ty Coed Pinwydd. As I started down the lane, I threw a backward glance at the cottage and noticed the curtain twitching in one of the windows upstairs. Maybe Leisa had heard me leaving. I lifted a hand to wave, but could see no one. I shrugged my coat more tightly around me and hurried on my way.

I had hoped that Mickey might have picked up a trail or had some sort of intuition – or *something*. But all he seemed to want to do was lead me back to Ty Coed Pinwydd. I supposed that Ruby's scent must have been everywhere in and around the house, since she had spent so much time there since our arrival. Or maybe he was looking for Nina. Either way, he wasn't proving much help. He was a lovely dog and I was glad of his company, but that was about it.

The walk back down the hill was a real slog. I was feeling increasingly shivery and ill and the effort left me exhausted. I could have gone the long way round and come in at the back of the house to dodge the press officers, but really didn't have the energy. There was still a tenacious handful just outside the gateway, but their numbers had dwindled. The remaining few looked damp and downcast as I walked past them, and their enthusiasm seemed to be waning.

'Can you tell us anything about what's behind the cordon, Mrs Morris?' one enquired half-heartedly. I ignored him and strode forwards as purposefully as I could, given my feelings of malaise. They would find out soon enough what the police had discovered; I wasn't about to be the one to give them another story to latch onto.

Lewis's van was parked on the drive as we arrived back at the house. I was completely exhausted now and in no mood for conversation: my intention was to feed Mickey and then go straight back to bed.

As we entered, I could hear raised voices coming from the kitchen. Lewis emerged, red-faced and agitated. Seeing me, he tried to compose himself.

'What's happened?'

'Oh, just a difference of opinion about the business, that's all. Awel and I don't always see eye to eye. I'm sure you know how she can be.' He grimaced. 'Nothing for you to worry about, anyway.' He stared at me, his brow suddenly creased with concern. 'Hey, you don't look at all well. Are you sure you're . . .'

His words faded into the background. It was as though I was going into a tunnel. I felt myself sliding; falling. And then I knew no more.

For the first time in my life, I had fainted.

*

I awoke in bed, Awel leaning over me and Elis hovering anxiously in the doorway. My head was banging; I was wringing with sweat and felt nauseous. As I attempted to sit up, the stabbing sensation in my back almost took my breath away.

'Oh, thank God you're back with us. You frightened the life out of me! I've called the doctor.'

I opened my mouth to protest but she raised a hand. 'Don't worry, Dr Price is out of town today. It'll be his son, Rhodri, coming to see you.'

'I don't need a doctor. I just want to sleep, then I'll be fine.'

'You're obviously very poorly. People don't pass out for no reason – and you're burning up. He can just check you over; see if you need medication or something.'

I heard Lewis's voice, calling to ask Awel if I was okay. I looked up to see he had appeared beside Elis. He offered me a small wave and a feeble smile.

I raised one arm to return the gesture and attempted to sit up, but my head and back hurt too much. Tentatively I put a hand to the base of my skull and found a huge, painful lump. I must have hit it when I fell. I groaned and slid back onto the pillow, closing my eyes.

I was vaguely aware of a brief conversation between Lewis and Awel. The gist of it was that he needed to go home, but would she please update him about my welfare. I think I heard him call goodbye to me, but hadn't the energy to respond.

I drifted off again. I don't know how long I'd been sleeping for, when a man's distant voice called me back to consciousness.

'Mrs Morris?'

My eyelids felt impossibly heavy.

'Mrs Morris, I'm Dr Price.'

Gradually he came into focus. Rhodri Price was standing next to the bed. He was a similar build to his father, Iwan; tall with dark, swept-back hair. But his face was kindly and concerned, with none of the conceit or synthetic niceties that I disliked about Dr Price the elder. He had wide, grey eyes, which seemed to be appraising my own.

'Do you think you can sit up for me?'

With a little help, I managed to wriggle up against the pillow, self-consciously pulling down my T-shirt, which had ridden up over my midriff. He looked vaguely amused.

'I hear you've had a bit of a turn. You're very flushed – I'm just going to check your temperature.' Producing a digital thermometer from his case, he inserted it into my ear while I lay passively waiting for the verdict.

He looked at the reading and winced. 'Yep, you're definitely warm. I want to take your blood pressure and pulse too, if that's okay.'

I let my arm flop onto the bedcover as he wrapped a cuff around my bicep and I felt the squeeze as it tightened.

'Hmm – a bit on the high side, but nothing to be too concerned about.'

He held my wrist for a few seconds, his grip firm and cool, then listened to my chest with a stethoscope. He frowned and asked me to sit forward, then placed it on my back. He smelled nice, I noticed, recognising a waft of sandalwood as he leaned forwards.

'Sounds a little . . . congested. Have you had a cough?'

I shook my head. 'Not really. Just a bit of a head cold.'

He raised an eyebrow sceptically. 'Pain in your chest, or shoulder and back?'

'A bit, I suppose,' I conceded.

'I think we both know you have more than a head cold. Do you tend to suffer with bronchial complaints?'

I shook my head. This much at least was true.

'I'll take some bloods and check things out thoroughly, just to be on the safe side. Bed rest and plenty of fluids in the meantime.'

'But . . .'

He looked apologetic. 'I know you're having a terrible time of things, Mrs Morris. But you still need to look after yourself, make sure you don't become seriously ill. I imagine you'd prefer not to be hospitalised. I think you're probably very rundown and with the rubbing noise going on in your lungs, I'm pretty sure you have pleurisy. The bloods will tell us whether it's viral or bacterial – if it's the latter, you'll need antibiotics. I'll prescribe an NSAID for the discomfort for now and a tonic to help build you up. Hopefully we'll soon have you back on your feet.'

I slumped back down despondently. This was really not what I needed; not now. But Dr Price was right: I would be of no use to anyone if I became really poorly, least of all Ruby. I had to resign myself to the fact I needed to rest in order to get better if I was to continue looking for her and bring her home. And time was not on my side.

*

Lewis sat slumped in his van outside Ty Coed Pinwydd collecting his thoughts, his forehead resting on the steering wheel. He hadn't signed up for this. Lowri was a nice girl, and now, on top of everything, she was clearly seriously ill – all as a direct result of this . . . this *fiasco*. She had nothing else in her life as far as he could tell – the little kid was the centre of her universe. It was tantamount to torture. The whole appalling situation was all so *wrong*.

Reflexively, he raised an arm against the shock of a sudden flash, realising a photographer had snapped him from just beyond the gateway. *Fuck*. Gritting his teeth, he switched on the ignition, revved the engine and stepped on the accelerator, scattering the small cluster of journalists still gathered in the lane. He turned the corner and put his foot down, his heart sinking further as he thought of Catrin, waiting at home ready to greet him with yet more sarcasm and vitriol. He'd had enough for one day.

In fact, he'd just about had enough of everything altogether.

CHAPTER SEVENTEEN

Things got worse before they started to improve. The blood tests confirmed viral pleurisy, that, although not as severe as the bacterial variety, wasn't responsive to antibiotics and therefore had to run its course. Possibly because of my fragile mental state, it had hit me hard. Dr Price the younger gave me strict instructions to rest and a seemingly endless supply of ibuprofen, which I took reluctantly, since it made me feel queasy. The fever was making me confused, and I was drifting constantly in and out of a fitful sleep for the next twenty-four hours. Even getting to the bathroom and back was exhausting.

Elis needed no prompting to take charge of looking after Mickey, while Awel fussed round me constantly with hot and cold drinks, trying to ply me with soups and stewed fruit, for which I had no appetite. I had no real awareness of what was going on around me. All I wanted to do was sleep. I tossed and turned, my thoughts a jumble of present and past events, which kept wandering to my lovely Jonah and our early days together. Recollections of happy times that I usually kept locked away somewhere deep inside me, with all the other memories that were just too devastating, too painful to confront.

I was seventeen when I'd met Ruby's father and he was almost twenty-one. I hated school with a passion and left as soon as I was able. I had begun working as a receptionist-cum-general-dogsbody for a local building company and Jonah, one of the firm's contractors, would often call into the 'office' (more of a prefabricated hut, really) to collect or drop off paperwork. He was well-built and tall, with the tan typical of one who worked outdoors all year round. His dark hair was styled into a Morrissey-esque quiff and he had huge brown eyes, which I caught glancing my way whenever he came through the door. The first few times he said nothing, but would grin – a little shyly, which I found endearing.

I started to look out for him and would feel my heart quicken whenever he appeared. I found myself making more of an effort with my appearance on the off chance he might call by. I'd been out with several lads in my teens, but had never had any serious boyfriends. I hadn't really been looking for a relationship up to that point, to be honest. But we started to exchange bashful smiles, and after a few visits, he actually introduced himself and asked my name, after which he would always greet me with a cheery, 'Hi, Lowri.' His presence always brightened my otherwise dull working day. Eventually, he plucked up the courage to strike up more of a conversation.

'Do you live round here?' he asked one day, blushing a little.

I smiled. 'Yes, about ten minutes' walk away. Dead handy – I don't even need to catch the bus.'

'Cool.' He coloured again, raising a hand awkwardly to the back of his head. 'Erm – I was just wondering, would you like to go for a drink one night? Or something?'

I laughed. 'Sounds interesting. What sort of something did you have in mind?'

He seemed flustered; I felt bad then, as it had clearly taken him some time to muster the courage to ask me out.

'I'm joking. Yeah, that'd be nice. I'm free tomorrow evening, if you've got nothing else on?'

He looked taken aback, as though he hadn't really expected me to accept. 'Um, yeah, great. I can pick you up, if you like.'

I hesitated. I didn't really want my parents peering out of the window to see who I was going out with. It was doubtful that they would be particularly interested – I just felt it was none of their business.

'No, it's okay. I can meet you somewhere, as long as it's not too far from here. What about The Slug – it's a nice little pub.'

He nodded enthusiastically. 'Great. Say about seven thirty?'

'Yeah, that's fine. See you tomorrow, then!'

Grinning from ear to ear, he walked straight out of the office, returning moments later. 'Sorry, I forgot to say, "Bye"! See you tomorrow.'

We started seeing one another regularly after that and Jonah gradually came out of his shell. I discovered that he lived alone with his dad, his mum having died when he was small. It sounded rather as though he had become something of a carer from a young age, his father having developed a debilitating dependency on drink after losing his wife. I quickly realised that, in spite of everything, my own upbringing had been a breeze compared with Jonah's: his dad had lost his job and even when sober, which wasn't often, he had become withdrawn and uncommunicative. Jonah was clearly intelligent, but had left school at sixteen to find work and bring in some money. He was funny and kind and I found myself falling hard for him.

When we'd been dating for about six months, Jonah's dad was hospitalised after collapsing one night outside the local pub. It became apparent that his liver failure had passed the point of no return and, within a fortnight, he was dead. Despite the fact he had hardly been a model father, Jonah was completely shell-shocked. I went to stay with him and helped to sort out his dad's messy finances, dealing with the taxman and the DSS. I had always had a head for figures and liked getting things in order, so tackled the task with enthusiasm. Their home was council-owned, and deemed too large for a single occupant. Since his dad's was the name on the rental agreement, Jonah had no rights as a tenant and was expected to vacate the property as soon as possible. It was disgraceful.

'Guess I'll have to find a bloody bedsit.' He sat with his head in his hands the morning his eviction notice arrived. My heart went out to him.

'What if we get a place together?' I blurted out. 'We're both earning – not much, I know, but with two wages we might find a reasonable private rental somewhere.'

He looked up at me, his eyes wide.

'Really?'

'Sure, why not? It's not like my parents would miss me – I don't think they know I'm there half the time.'

We scoured the local newspaper and estate agents' windows for rental properties, listing those that looked promising. We viewed six terraced houses in the area, none of which were really up to much. But the seventh, a mid-terraced cottage a short walk from work, was cosy and clean and we both agreed it was just what we were looking for.

My parents raised no objections to my moving out. I think they'd long given up on any earlier aspirations they may have had for me, to be honest. They even donated their old settee, which wasn't brilliant but in a considerably better state than the one from Jonah's place. My mother seemed to have abandoned her idea of moulding me into the perfect Christian as soon as I reached adolescence. I wondered if they were actually glad to see the back of me.

Jonah and I were as poor as church mice but it was the happiest time I can ever remember. I didn't have any really close friends anyway, and had lost touch with those I used to socialise with as, inevitably I suppose, we all gradually went our separate ways. Jonah became my whole world. We were together a full nine years before I fell pregnant; I had been in no rush to start a family, as we'd been trying hard to save and get on an even keel financially. The pregnancy, although not unwelcome, came as something of a surprise. Jonah was incredibly protective of me; keen to provide for me and the baby when he or she arrived. When we found out I was expecting twins, he was so excited that he rushed out and bought a double buggy. I had arrived home from work to find it sitting in our living room, along with a bouquet of yellow roses and two identical cuddly toy rabbits, one for each of our precious babies.

We had been told that we were having two girls. Excitedly, we discussed at length what we would call our twins, he teasing me that I'd want something Welsh and unpronounceable. He used to drive me mad, deliberately stuttering over any word containing a double L. 'How can it be Clan? There's no C!' He would laugh, and I would roll my eyes in exasperation and say that it wasn't *Clan*, it would never be Clan; it was *Llan* and how hard was it to say it properly?

'What about naming them after us? Hmm. Lowri and Joan. It has a nice ring to it.' I had thrown a cushion at him and declared adamantly that neither was an option as far as I was concerned. And so it went on.

It was only when our babies were born and we saw their glorious shocks of red hair that the names were pretty much decided for us. For both of us, our love for them had been instant, instinctive and fierce, and had taken us both by surprise.

And God, I loved *him*. *So* much.

How could I have known then the way things would turn out? The shared grief of losing baby Amber at only one week old had brought us even closer together. With time, I was coming to terms with what had happened and learning to be happy once more. And yet within two years, I was going through it all again, when a freak accident at the building site where Jonah was working brought the police to my door with the worst news imaginable.

*

I kept reliving the terrible moment when I'd had to identify Jonah's bloodied body, the memory of his ashen face in death overshadowing all the beautiful memories I had of him and the times we'd shared. And then Ruby's little face would flash into my consciousness and I would wake, my face wet with tears. What if she really was with her daddy now? What if I had lost both of them forever?

Between the torment of my dreams, night and day, the melody of 'The Ash Grove' kept echoing through my head; an unwelcome earworm. I heard it as the off-key notes plucked from the old harp, and then Hannah's sister's distant, lilting voice; the haunting lyrics I remembered from school niggling at me. The tragic story of a lost love.

She sleeps 'neath the green turf . . .

It was as though someone was trying to tell me something, and it wasn't something I wanted to hear. Once the tune had started it seemed to continue on repeat. It felt interminable.

The fever broke on the third day. Deep into the night, I woke, cool and damp with sweat, feeling slightly more lucid. The room was dark, a tiny sliver of light seeping through the gap between the curtains.

I became aware of a figure at my bedside. My first irrational thought was that Jonah had somehow materialised and was waiting for me to join him. I quickly realised, however, that this was a solid human presence, not some other-worldly being, and froze at the sudden touch of roughened skin tentatively stroking my forehead. I wondered in slight discomfort if Awel had been keeping a vigil over me. But as my eyes grew accustomed to the gloom, it became apparent that this was not Awel. It wasn't anyone I recognised at all; a small, slight frame with what appeared to be an abundance of wild, pale hair.

I screamed – rather pathetically. Plainly startled, the figure made hastily for the door, pausing briefly to look back at me.

And then it was gone.

For a moment, I had a retained image of the outline that seemed to hover briefly, observing me from the doorway. I lay, my heart pummelling my ribcage, wondering who or what on earth I had just encountered. As I gradually regained control of my breathing, I tried to rationalise. Maybe it was the fever. I'd definitely been delirious. It was quite possible my mind was still playing tricks on me.

I pulled myself up to a sitting position and swung my legs over the side of the bed, peering at my phone on the table next to me. The screen was blank, the battery clearly dead. I groaned and shakily tried to stand, gripping the edge of the bed for support. My legs felt weak beneath me, as though in danger of giving way. I switched on the bedside lamp and looked round for my handbag, where I always kept my charger. It was on the opposite side of the room, beneath the dressing table stool.

But as I crossed the floor, I saw that it was on its side and open, the contents spilling out around it. My one lipstick was opened and twisted upwards, the lid from a tube of hand lotion cast aside; the few coins that had been in my purse tipped out.

At first, I felt angry, thinking how disrespectfully my belongings had been treated. But then a cold feeling washed over me. Why would anyone be going through my bag – and was it possible then that there actually *had* been someone in the room and they'd been searching for something?

I rifled through the scattered objects, trying to remember exactly what else I'd been carrying around with me. The mobile charger, paracetamol, wet wipes, tissues, tampons. They were all there. Even the bank-notes in my purse and my cashpoint card. All present and correct.

And then I had the most awful thought. Ruby's Junior EpiPen . . .

Frantically, I felt inside the handbag in case it had slipped into the lining, checking and rechecking every compartment with trembling fingers. I groped around on the floor, just to make sure it hadn't rolled behind the dressing table.

Nothing. It was definitely missing. I could feel the pressure of my pulse, throbbing in my head. I was panic-stricken. I'd completely forgotten until now that I'd been keeping it safe for her – it had been in my bag since the day of the funeral.

Nothing else had been taken – so why would someone want the EpiPen? Would they even know what it was? And more importantly, what if Ruby needed it? My mind began to race, yet another worry to compound my concerns for my little girl's welfare. What a useless, negligent mother I was. I couldn't believe my own stupidity.

Who should I tell? And what could anyone do, anyway – no one knew where she was, so the fact she wouldn't have her EpiPen if it was called for made no difference to anything. Except that it did; *of course* it did. If she had an allergic reaction, it could save her life.

Fuck.

Did someone else know that? Is that why it had been taken? With the exception of the elderly shopkeeper who gave us the ice-creams, I couldn't remember telling anyone about it. I hadn't even thought to mention it to Awel – I had no concerns about Ruby eating her food, since I knew she'd always been in the habit of preparing things to accommodate Elis's allergy. It was just something we'd always lived with, Ruby and I; an accepted part of our routine. This was a bizarre development. I couldn't think straight.

I should call the police, let them know what had happened.

I plugged in the phone and switched it on at once. It was so flat that it took several minutes for anything to happen, but eventually it vibrated, buzzing into life. The icons lit up and I waited anxiously to see if any messages had come through, clutching the handset like a lifeline. I stared hopefully at the screen, willing it to bring me something positive.

245

There were five missed calls and three brief voicemails from Nina, just saying she was checking in with me and would call back. Two flat-sounding voice messages from DS Evans, basically telling me that there was nothing new to report as yet.

Shakily, I jabbed at the buttons with the number he had given me and waited hopefully for a ringtone. It went straight to voicemail. I tried Nansi's number, but again was met with an answer message. Frustrated, I tried Evans once more. Still not picking up.

I sank onto the bed, staring down at the contents of my bag strewn across the floor. I took deep breaths, trying to rationalise what might have happened. Was it possible I'd done this myself – looking for something in my previously delirious state – and now had no memory of it? It was very odd that no money or anything else was missing. It wasn't beyond the realms of possibility, either, that the EpiPen could have been lost at some earlier point – maybe at the church, even – and I just hadn't noticed. Perhaps I was making something out of nothing.

The sudden bleep made me jump. I quickly swiped at the message to see who it was from.

There were just two taunting words, again from an unknown sender.

GETTING WARMER

CHAPTER EIGHTEEN

The Girl's Story

'We can go upstairs later. It'll be safe then. But we'll hide in here for now.'

The girl wasn't sure which was worse – the fear of being discovered by the bad man of whom the woman had spoken, or being stuck with her peculiar, jittery companion in this chilly, damp space filled with reminders of death. She was frozen and tired and longed for the comfort and safety of her own home.

'Where are we? And what – what's in those . . . boxes?' she ventured. The thought that they might actually be occupied terrified her. She remembered peering, fearful but equally fascinated, into the gap created where the shifting ground and headstone had parted company, as she stood next to one of the ancient graves outside

Llanbadrig church. She had wondered if she might be able to catch a glimpse of what lay beneath. She had been told it was impossible; that there were several feet of earth piled on top of the caskets. But the girl remained unconvinced and had looked around determinedly for other plots in a similar state. Here now without anyone she trusted to protect her, she had no desire to see any coffins at all.

'They're all empty. They store spares down here for when they're needed.'

'Oh.' She felt momentary relief. Then, 'How do you know for sure?'

The woman threw back her head and laughed. 'I'll show you if you don't believe me.'

'No!' the girl squealed. 'No, I believe you.' She glanced anxiously at the coffin lids. 'How long do we have to stay down here? I really don't like it.'

'It's fine – I come down here all the time. No one ever bothers me.'

'But – where do you actually live?'

The old woman looked surprised. 'I live here, of course, *twpsyn.*'

The girl frowned. 'Here? Is this your house, then?'

She seemed suddenly irritated by this line of questioning. Despite her advancing years, her reactions were more like those of a child.

'You're being silly now. And you're too nosy by half.'

Wary of upsetting her, the child bit her lip. 'Sorry,' she mumbled. 'I just wondered, that's all.' She was shivering; both from the chill air and the discomfiting situation.

Noticing, the woman thrust her the blanket from the mattress.

'You must keep warm. You don't want to get ill,' she warned. It wasn't very thick and smelled damp, but the girl wrapped it around herself anyway. She sniffed back tears.

Her companion seemed to soften. 'We'll go upstairs soon. It's not so cold up there and we can have a hot drink.'

They sat in silence for a few minutes on the mattress. The woman seemed less agitated now and had begun to hum tunelessly. The girl's curiosity got the better of her.

'You didn't actually say what your name is.'

'Ah, well that would be telling.'

She tapped her nose with the stump of one finger and grinned, revealing her stained teeth once again. The girl shuddered. She drew the blanket tighter around herself and huddled against the wall. Her eyelids grew heavy and soon she was asleep, dreaming of being safely back in her own cosy room and bed.

And away from this creepy old house and the creepy old woman.

CHAPTER NINETEEN

Present Day

Catrin was watching from the kitchen window of the cottage when Lewis pulled up that afternoon. As he climbed from the van, she scowled and walked away. His heart sank. She was becoming increasingly awkward and unpleasant about his visits to Ty Coed Pinwydd, and no amount of insistence on his part that there was nothing between himself and Lowri would persuade her otherwise. He tried his best to ignore her remarks and had continued to visit the house regardless since Lowri had fallen ill, just to check how things were going. Thankfully she was a little better, but he'd been quite worried about her for a couple of days. He felt partially responsible.

Lewis was beginning to feel suffocated at home. Even though it was really none of Catrin's business any more, she couldn't resist needling him about things. Their relationship was well and truly over, but she seemed reluctant to relinquish her claim on him. When he asked her to move in with him two years ago, he'd had no inkling of how materialistic she could be; nor of her potential for jealousy and what she was capable of when riled. Only months ago, after they arrived home from the pub one night, she had actually tipped a pint of iced water over him as he lay in bed, accusing him of giving the barmaid the eye all evening. Later she apologised profusely, but when he found worms wriggling in his lunchbox the following day, he suspected she wasn't as sorry as she'd made out. He had realised too late that you never truly know someone until you have lived with them. And that secrets are best not shared, whatever the circumstances.

In a weak, drunken moment, feeling the need to unburden himself, he had blurted everything out one night shortly after Catrin had moved in with him. He couldn't trust her now not to open her mouth about everything she knew out of sheer spite. From bitter past experience, he had learned that she was not one to let a grudge slide. It was keeping him awake at night – that, and the worry of what would happen when it all came out. Which, he knew with sickening resignation, it was sure to do.

He took off his muddy shoes in the hallway and, bracing himself for another row, walked through to the living room. Catrin was sitting in Lewis's preferred armchair, smoking; something she only did when she needed to calm down. Rolling his eyes, he flopped down in the chair opposite.

'How's your little damsel in distress today?' Her tone was acerbic, her doll-like, heavily made-up face twisted into a snarl.

He bristled. 'Look, Lowri's not *my* anything. And she's still not too good – pleurisy, the doctor reckons.'

'Aww, *bechod*.' She glowered and took another drag of her cigarette, blowing the smoke from the corner of her mouth. 'All tucked up in bed then, is she?'

'Yes. Not that I've seen her,' he added. 'I needed to speak to Awel – about – you know . . .'

'Your little "situation"?' She laughed scornfully. 'Oh, the shit's really going to hit the fan soon.'

'I wish you didn't sound so bloody gleeful about it all. I'm praying it can be resolved without too much aggro. I've been dragged into something I wanted no part in, and now it's out of control.'

'Maybe you should've thought of that before you made yourself so useful.' She leaned forward and stubbed out the cigarette in the ashtray at her feet. 'You've made a rod for your own back.'

'I've made several,' Lewis muttered under his breath.

'Huh? What was that?'

'Nothing.'

There was a beat of hostile silence. Catrin looked up at the mantel clock and pulled a face. 'Time I wasn't here.' She rose from her seat, twisting her long blonde hair into a bun with the band she'd had wrapped round her wrist. She glanced briefly in the mirror, frowning at her heavily made-up reflection. Lewis noticed her roots needed retouching.

'D'you want a lift?'

'Nah. I need some fresh air. Clear my head.'

Lewis watched as she went out into the hall to put on her shoes and rain mac. A moment later, the door slammed. He got up and went through to the kitchen, in time to see her disappearing at an angry speed down the lane. He let out a long, slow breath. The atmosphere was suddenly much lighter without her presence.

He made himself a coffee, then went back into the living room and sat in what he'd always thought of as *his* chair. He was sure she did it just to wind him up. The remote control was resting on the arm, so he flicked on the TV and scrolled through to see if there was anything worth viewing. As he leaned back in the seat to watch the snooker, something dug into his leg. He wriggled forward to see what he had sat on.

Shit. Catrin had left her phone. Now he would need to drop it off – she always took it to work to let him know what time to collect her. He knew he should probably let her make other arrangements but, in spite of everything, still didn't like the idea of her walking back in the dark if she couldn't cadge a lift. He'd take it in a bit – there was no rush. He just wanted some peace and quiet; time to think properly. Something had to be done, but he really didn't know what.

*

Lewis leaned against the slightly tatty reception desk of the small family-run hotel in Cemaes where Catrin worked as a waitress. He wondered if her younger brother, Bryn, was still on the premises. They'd always had a mutual dislike for one another, which had reached

253

a new level since his falling-out with Catrin, and he would prefer to avoid him.

'Catrin? I haven't seen her today, love. Her dad rang – said she wouldn't be in as she wasn't feeling too well. Lot of bugs going round at the moment, I know.'

'Her *dad*?'

Menna, the pleasant middle-aged receptionist, pushed her glasses back onto the top of her head and put down her iPad. She seemed puzzled. 'Yes. I did think it was a bit odd. Did you try her phone?'

'That's just it, I came to bring it to her – she left it at home. She said she was coming into work.' Lewis's mind began to fly. Maybe she'd gone running home to her parents – it wouldn't be the first time.

Menna studied him for a moment. 'You two had a few words?'

'Hmm? Not really, no more than usual.'

'Just wondered. Maybe she was upset and couldn't face coming in today.' She winked. 'Oh well, kiss and make up later, eh!'

He gave a half-hearted smile. Clearly neither Catrin or her brother had said anything, and he wasn't about to explain their domestic arrangements to Menna. Once Catrin had moved out, everyone would know soon enough that they were no longer an item.

'Don't worry. Her Bryn will probably run her back once she's calmed down. He's not long finished his shift in the kitchens and he often nips in to see their mam and dad on his way home. I bet she'll be back in the house before you.'

Lewis nodded. 'You're probably right. Oh well, at

least I won't have to come out again later. See you tomorrow then, maybe.'

'Hope you two sort it all out. See you, love.'

*

It was gone eight o'clock and a dismal evening. The lights should have been on, but the cottage was in total darkness when he got back. Where the hell was she? Lewis was starting to feel uneasy. For Catrin to have gone out with no way of contacting him, or anyone else come to that, if there was a problem, was most unlike her. Although she had stormed out in a huff, she would have realised her phone was missing pretty quickly and called him from someone else's. And she'd normally be keen to inform him if she intended to go to her mam's – just to let him know he was well and truly in the dog house.

He didn't have Marian's – her mam's – number in his own phone, so switched on Catrin's mobile and waited. Nothing happened. The screen was completely blank.

He went upstairs and rummaged in the top bedside drawer in the spare room where Catrin had been sleeping for the charger. He gritted his teeth. Good God, she was untidy. How could one person accumulate so much junk? Exasperated, he decided to lift the whole thing out and tipped the contents onto the bed. A couple of paperback books, an old Arctic Monkeys CD, pamphlets from a designer outlet, a bundle of receipts, a half-empty blister pack of pills, make-up, hand cream, a small jewellery box, odd fragments of broken ornaments, hair bobbles. Two redundant chargers that she had failed to dispose of. But thankfully, there was the one he actually needed. He plugged in the phone and started replacing everything carefully as he waited for it to spring into life. But as he picked up the CD case, it fell open and something dropped to the floor. He looked down to see what it was.

Wrapped in a clear plastic sandwich bag was a phone battery and SIM card. Lewis felt slightly sick. He took the battery and card out of the bag and stared at them. The pay-as-you-go SIM was for Giffgaff, but he knew that Catrin's mobile contract was, and always had been, with O2.

His stomach dropped. He sat on the bed and began sifting through the contents of the drawer, more thoroughly this time. He looked at the receipts, paperclipped together. His jaw dropped at the cost of her new Michael Kors handbag, paid for in cash.

Three hundred fucking quid!

There was an invoice for their fridge; a till receipt for the flashy retro kettle which she'd recently bought to replace the old knackered one. A pair of boots from L.K. Bennett, a cashmere sweater, Crème de la Mer moisturiser – again, all eye-wateringly more expensive than he'd realised. All bought instore, cash payment. But in the middle of the bits of paper was a receipt from Tesco for a mobile phone – bought six months ago. And cheap – only twenty-two pounds – definitely not the sort of thing Catrin would want to be seen toting around.

But where was it? He looked apprehensively at the silk-covered jewellery box sitting in the drawer and picked it up once more, prising open the metal clasp. There was the phone. Not quite a brick, but a very basic thing. He stared for a moment in disbelief, then lifted it out, turning the handset over, and levered off the back.

The battery and SIM were missing.

Once Catrin's regular mobile had charged, Lewis entered the PIN (predictably her date of birth) and called Marian. As usual, her tone was brusque. No; neither she nor Catrin's dad had spoken to their daughter since Tuesday. And he *certainly* hadn't phoned in to tell her colleagues that she was ill.

Lewis promised to let her know as soon as Catrin showed up, and ended the call. He felt a rising sense of panic. Something was very wrong. Unless . . . He searched through Catrin's contacts and pressed her best friend Brenda's number.

'Nope – haven't heard from her today at all. Is everything okay?'

'I don't know. She didn't turn up for work and they said her dad had called in sick for her. I was sort of hoping it might've been someone *you* know – y' know, getting someone to cover for her.'

There was an ominous silence from the other end of the line.

Then: 'I think you need to call the cops. She wouldn't just go AWOL. You've got me worried now.'

It was properly dark now, more so where they lived because of the complete lack of street lighting. Lewis sat shivering on the settee, staring at the empty chair where Catrin had been sitting earlier. He knew in his heart that something bad must have happened and that, despite his reluctance to involve them, he really needed to alert the police.

He had a terrible, hollow feeling in his gut as he dialled the number. It felt like the beginning of the end.

CHAPTER TWENTY

Present Day

I felt weakened and exhausted but, in spite of this, considerably better than I had done for days. I'd left a message with DS Evans about the latest text, but wasn't hopeful after the previous occasions that the police would be able to learn anything from it. It seemed that whoever was sending me the messages knew exactly what they were doing.

I rang Nina back later the following morning. Apparently, she had called Awel a few times to ask how I was doing. Nina's mother-in-law still wasn't in a good way, and understandably she was reluctant to leave poor Ronnie, who was worried sick.

'By the way, there were two dodgy-looking blokes at your door the other day when I walked past, looking for that bloody ex of yours. Looks like he's in hot water.'

'Darren?' My stomach dropped. 'Christ, what's he done now?'

'Well, I stopped just to tell them you were away and they asked if I knew where they could find him. When I told them you two had split up ages ago and he'd buggered off somewhere, they didn't look best pleased. Sounded like they'd come to call in a debt – and a substantial one at that.'

'And he'd given *my* address. What an arsehole.' Normally, such news would have sent me into a flat spin, but compared with everything else that was going on, a couple of heavies calling on me seemed a minor inconvenience.

'Don't worry, love. It's him they want. They'll catch up with him eventually. I'd like to be a fly on the wall when they do. Couldn't happen to a nicer fella.' She laughed throatily. 'What goes around, comes around.'

Maybe it wasn't very charitable of me, but the thought of Darren receiving a pasting after everything he'd put us through didn't trouble me in the slightest at that moment. In fact, if I'd known his latest address, I'd probably have passed it on. I wasn't feeling anything like sympathy towards him at all. I'd actually texted to tell him about Ruby, on the off chance that he might have been concerned. The message had been delivered and read, that much I knew; but he hadn't even bothered to respond. He was a callous bastard. Perhaps he needed to learn that actions ultimately have consequences.

'So, you say DS Whatshisname hasn't come up with anything useful, then. No great surprise there.' I could hear the huff of exasperation in her voice.

'I had another text yesterday. I think someone's enjoying winding me up. But they've been unable to trace the sender so far.'

'What did this one say?'

I told her and she harrumphed. 'I think you're probably right. Just wish we knew who the bugger was. Why anyone would get a kick out of tormenting you is beyond me. There are some real dickheads out there.'

'It's freaking me out, thinking someone round here's got it in for me. I mean, what the hell could I have done to upset anyone? I've only been here five minutes.'

'I doubt you've done anything, darling. Some people are just twisted – you know, like those social media trolls or whatever they call them. Got nothing going on in their own lives and it gives them a bit of a buzz. Don't let it get to you.'

'But what if they actually *do* know something? There's been other weird stuff going on – Ruby's EpiPen's missing. I was wondering if someone had been through my bag while I was asleep – or if I could have tipped it all out myself and forgotten. I *have* been a bit away with the fairies. I really thought there was somebody standing by my bed last night, but now I don't know if I dreamed it. I feel like I'm losing the plot.'

'But who could've been in your room? There's only Awel and Elis in the house – surely it wouldn't have been either of them?' She sounded dubious.

Discussing it with Nina, everything seemed less sinister somehow and more likely to have been my imagination. I felt a bit foolish.

'No; no of course not. It's just . . . bizarre.'

'Ask them – there might be a perfectly innocent explan-ation. Or as you say, it could have been your own mind playing tricks. It really wouldn't surprise me. Awel was saying you've been seriously out of it for days, but even without being so ill, you've been under a massive strain.' There was a pause. 'Hang in there, kidder. Fingers crossed some light'll be shed on it all soon. I feel awful for deserting you, but Ronnie's in a bad way. He's always been really close to his mum. Just hoping the old dear pulls through.'

*

It was almost lunchtime when I eventually surfaced. The weather was grey and miserable, and so cold it felt more like November. Rain battered the windows, making everything darker and gloomier than ever. Awel was standing at the kitchen worktop, chopping vegetables to make soup. Seeing me, she hurriedly dropped everything and guided me into a chair like an invalid. Mickey greeted me enthusiastically, then returned with his head held low, as though he wasn't sure where his loyalties should lie, to sit in front of the range beside the beaming Elis, who put down the bowl he was eating from to give me a huge welcoming wave.

'How are you feeling?' Awel pressed a mug of tea into my hands, as I sat, slightly spaced out, at the table. I managed a feeble nod and smile.

'Would you like some *stwnsh menyn*?' She indicated Elis, evidently relishing the mushy contents of his dish, a revolting combination of potato and broad beans, mashed up with buttermilk. It was something Auntie Gwyn used to make now and then, and I loathed it.

The very thought of it made me want to retch. I put a hand over my mouth. 'No. Thank you.'

She gave me a wry grin. 'Not everybody's favourite, I know.'

It became apparent that things had been happening while I'd been ill. I learned that Awel was anxious to resume business as, the longer we remained closed, there was the concern that the newly opened funeral company in Cemaes would start taking all our potential future customers. She had been going through the accounts and things weren't in brilliant shape.

The siege at the house in Amlwch had thankfully come to an end. It sounded as though the man holding the woman and child hostage eventually realised the futility of it all and gave himself up. It was good to hear that one situation at least had had a positive outcome.

Forensic analysis of the bones found in the woods had confirmed, as suspected, that they were definitely those of Beca Bennion. It seemed that there was a significant crack in the skull, consistent with her either having fallen and hit her head, or someone delivering it a vicious blow. Either way, since the body had been buried, there was no question that a third party had been involved, although the police seemed to have no leads currently as to who it could have been. It was all deeply disturbing.

Our financial position aside, Awel was keen that we should step up and offer to conduct Beca's funeral.

'The least we can do is give the poor girl a decent burial. I didn't know her Nain well, but she was a good woman. Losing both her daughter and granddaughter like that must have completely destroyed her.' She shook her head sadly. 'Bereavement is a terrible thing, especially when there's a child involved.'

Awel resumed preparation of the soup, adding a generous knob of butter to a huge saucepan, which she heaved onto the stove. She tipped in diced onions, carrots and celery. I watched as she added chunks of potato and leeks, then seasoning. The aroma as everything began to sizzle should have whetted my appetite, but I felt the stirrings of nausea in my gut.

I recalled a funeral that Auntie Gwyn had arranged when I was about nine. A toddler from a local farm had died as the result of a tragic accident involving a huge bale of hay, which had somehow become dislodged and rolled from the barn loft, crushing him. The little boy, Sami, was an only child. His parents, deathly pale and hollow-eyed, came to visit him in the chapel of rest. I had covered my ears to block out the anguished howls, like those of an injured animal, that came from the mother as she entered the room. The evidence of her agony echoed through the whole house; even now, the thought of that gut-wrenching sound sends a chill through me. Although Auntie Gwyn always tried to remain detached and was ever professional and respectful of those in her care, this particular incident seemed to cast a shadow over her and everyone else in Ty Coed Pinwydd that lasted for weeks. I found her crying more than once, something I'd never witnessed before, and it upset and confused me. The poignant sight of the tiny casket as it was finally carried from the house that day and the raw grief of the mourners gathered outside to follow the hearse will remain with me forever. When we laid Amber,

Ruby's twin, to rest, the memory of it all came flooding back, and I understood all too painfully some of what Sami's mother had gone through. The loss of any child is the cruellest, most horrendous thing imaginable. It was something I had done my best to forget and I tried to shake the thought.

'Have the police said when they're releasing Beca's remains?'

'No. They're still trying to see if they can get anything from them, but I think it's pretty unlikely after all this time, don't you?'

I shrugged. 'I really don't know. I mean, people have been convicted of really ancient crimes with the help of all the tests they do these days. It scares me to death thinking there's someone still living round here that could've been responsible.'

Awel stood stirring the vegetables. She threw in a large bunch of fresh parsley and poured over boiling water from the kettle, releasing a cloud of fragrant steam. She glanced over at Elis, slumped forward in Auntie Gwyn's old chair and apparently oblivious to our conversation. He was making a fuss of his new best friend Mickey, whose front paws lay across his slippered feet. Pwtyn seemed begrudgingly to have accepted the dog's presence. Curled like a loaf, paws tucked beneath her, she sat on the dining chair next to mine, looking down at him suspiciously through half-opened eyes.

'We can't know that for sure – that it was someone local. Might've been a holidaymaker or someone passing through.'

'I suppose.' I paused, my stomach roiling as all the

possible scenarios ran through my mind. I couldn't cope with the idea of Beca's funeral being taken on with Ruby still missing. It seemed completely inappropriate and I was surprised and upset that Awel had suggested it.

Elis looked up, suddenly aware Awel's eyes were on him. He placed his bowl in his lap and raised an index finger.

Did I miss something?

She grimaced. *Young Beca – I was saying, we ought to do the funeral.*

He raised an eyebrow, his lower lip jutting. *Not just yet, surely?*

We'll ask DS Evans how soon it can take place, next time he calls.

'When was the last time you spoke to him?' I wondered if he'd received my voicemail about the text yet.

'He rang yesterday – nothing to report but he was asking after you. That Nansi has been taken ill apparently, so she won't be around for a while. Maybe give him a bell, if you feel up to it.'

'I did try to ring him last night. I'll try again in a bit. Erm – has Lewis been here much, while I've been ill?' I hoped my voice sounded casual.

'Not really. He's been busy at the site all week. Always lots of stuff to do in the school holidays, you know. Why d'you ask?'

'No reason. Just wondered. And . . . we haven't had any other visitors?'

Awel shook her head. 'Only Hannah Pugh – you know, from the church. Pleasant woman. She seemed quite worried about you.'

'That was kind of her.' I suddenly remembered about Hannah's sister, Leisa. It did seem odd that she hadn't mentioned her. I wondered if she had returned home yet.

'And Rhodri – Dr Price, of course. Oh, he's such a *nice* young man. Who'd have thought a father and son could be so different . . .'

'Well, from everything you've told me, Elis isn't much like his dad either. And nor are you.'

'True, true.' Her face clouded. 'Least said about *him* the better.'

I was about to mention my bag being emptied out when something stopped me. The more I thought about it, the more I wondered if maybe I *had* done it myself. I *was* still feeling pretty woolly. Besides, so far, Awel had seemed fairly dismissive of anything else I'd brought up: the harp music; the doll appearing on the bed; the figure in the trees. On this occasion, she might have good reason to doubt my judgement: my head was all over the place.

I got up, grabbing at the edge of the table for a moment to steady myself. I felt light-headed and quite wobbly. 'I think I'll have a bath – try to liven myself up a bit.'

'You do that. Take your time.' She smiled warmly. 'It's good to see you up and about. The *cawl* should be ready when you come back down.'

*

I didn't actually make it back downstairs. The effort of taking a bath drained what little energy I had, and, once dried and in clean clothes, I flopped back onto the bed and fell asleep once more. The hall clock, chiming in the hour, woke me. It was three in the afternoon. Apart from the noise of the wind and incessant rainfall, the house seemed unnervingly still and quiet, as though everyone else was out. I groaned, remembering I hadn't called DS Evans. Wriggling into a sitting position, I reached for my phone to ring the mobile number he'd given me, but it went straight to the voicemail service. I hung up.

For the first time in days, I was actually beginning to feel a little hungry, so decided to go down and help myself to some soup. The air was cool, so I slipped on a cardigan over my T-shirt. The landing seemed darker than ever owing to the dour slate-grey skies. Summer appeared to have deserted us completely.

Awel had left a note on the kitchen table. *Popped out for groceries. Dog gone with Elis to* . . .

I couldn't make out the last word, but suffice to say I was all alone. The house really did feel eerily empty. I switched on the lights to make it feel less threatening, then heated a bowlful of soup and buttered some bread.

Sitting at the table, beyond the door I could hear the wind whistling through the corridor which led to the preparation room. I thought of all the poor dead souls who had passed through the house over the years and shuddered. As a child I had never really let it bother me. But here now on my own, I began to feel ridiculously nervous. I gave myself a mental shake, washed the bowl and cutlery and hurriedly made my way back upstairs, deliberately not looking down the passageway as I left the kitchen.

But as I reached the top, the creak of a door to my right sent a shiver of fear rippling through me. I froze, my hand gripping the banister. It sounded like the slow click of a key turning in a lock. I could have sworn I glimpsed a shadow pass beneath the locked door at the far end of the landing. How I wished Elis had left Mickey behind! My heart racing, I flew back down the stairs and into the little sitting room, where I switched on the TV for some background noise and watched anxiously for Awel and Elis's return. My breathing gradually slowing, I wondered if I'd imagined the noise – or at least blown it out of proportion. Maybe the wind had caused the door to rattle, could even have wafted some-thing in the draughty old room to create movement – it was certainly fierce enough. I sank into the armchair and stared at the TV set. The picture quality really was appalling, but it was a welcome distraction.

I was beginning to feel a little calmer when I heard the familiar but distant ringtone of my mobile. My stomach dropped as I realised I'd left it upstairs. Steeling myself, I went back up to the bedroom, averting my eyes from the threatening recesses of the dingy landing. Typically, just as I reached it, the ringing stopped.

I swiped at the screen to see the call was from a with-held number. As I made my way back downstairs, the handset pinged. I had a voicemail.

'Mrs Morris; DS Evans here. Just wanting to update you with an interesting development. If you could ring me back at your earliest convenience on . . . *blah blah blah*.'

I cut off the message and went into the sitting room, then with quivering fingers tapped in his number. I knew there were things I needed to discuss with him. But what was it he wanted to share with me?

*

'Ah, Mrs Morris! I hope you're feeling better.'

'Much; thank you. I was sorry to hear Nansi's not well. Please give her my best wishes.'

'Yes, yes. She's slipped a disc in her back – again.' The words were weighted with exasperation.

'Erm – I wondered what you wanted to tell me?'

There was an ominous pause from the other end of the line and my stomach turned over. Surely if it was really bad news, he'd have called to the house – the police didn't usually do things like that over the phone. Did they?

I detected a long inhalation of breath. 'I'm sure you're aware now that the remains we found *were* those of young Beca Bennion. Unfortunately, we're no further forward with identifying the person or persons responsible for her death. However, our forensics team have made an interesting discovery.'

Another pause.

'Yes?'

His procrastination was painful.

'Well . . . erm . . . the forensic analysis of Ruby's cagoule threw up some hairs belonging to your daughter. But the DNA from those hairs has been further tested, and cross-checked after one of the technicians noticed something. To cut a long story short, the DNA was found to be very similar to that extracted from Beca's skeleton. Mrs Morris, it looks a certainty that you were quite closely related to this poor dead girl.'

I sank into the chair, staring straight at the wall in front of me but seeing nothing. From the hallway, the steady, echoing tick of the grandfather clock seemed suddenly amplified. I was expecting the hour to chime, like a death knell.

'What – how can that be possible?'

'Well, I don't want to be insensitive, but the identity of Beca's father was never known. If you could cooperate by providing us with a saliva swab, it would help to prove what the forensics team believe. It seems feasible that you two were half-siblings.'

No no no! My whole head pulsed with an unpleasant burning sensation. Every muscle in my throat tightened.

I heard my words come out as a croak. 'My dad would never . . . no, there must be some mistake. He was a good man, a decent man.'

The room began to swim. I clapped a hand to my mouth, honestly believing I might throw up.

His response was quiet but firm. 'We never really know anyone one hundred per cent, I'm afraid. As a police officer, I learned that pretty quickly. You may have to accept that your father sowed his wild oats at some point; after all . . .'

Anger stirred within me now. '*No*. I don't have to accept anything of the sort. It's rubbish. There must have been something wrong with the sample – maybe the hair they checked wasn't Ruby's . . .'

'It was a perfect match for the strands of hair you provided from Ruby's hairbrush.' His voice sounded harsh. 'I'm sorry; I know it's not what you want to hear, but unless Ruby is *not* your biological daughter, you and Beca were definitely close relatives.'

The implications of this news filled me with deepening dread. If indeed I *was* related to Beca, the likelihood that my daughter's disappearance was connected to hers was increasingly probable. I kept casting my mind back to that summer when Beca had gone missing: conversations halting whenever I entered the room, the row with Auntie Gwyn, me being dragged away with no explanation. Surely my dad couldn't have had some connection with all of this? No. It was unthinkable. I couldn't let myself even contemplate such a thing.

'I'm sorry; I can't think straight. I need to get my head round this. Of course – of course I'll do a swab test. Anything to help. This is just a terrible shock, you understand.'

I ended the call without even remembering to ask if he'd received my message about the latest text. This unwelcome news had thrown me into turmoil. I wanted to cry but felt numb. I was being sucked into the vortex of a worsening nightmare, spiralling downwards. God only knew what lay at the bottom.

I thought back to my miserable little house in Dunswarton, the grind of daily life, the bills. Right now, I'd have swapped my current situation for a lifetime of penny-pinching and drudgery in a heartbeat, if only I could have Ruby safely back with me. It had put everything into perspective.

How I wished I'd never come back to Llanbadrig. It had brought me nothing but pain.

CHAPTER TWENTY-ONE

Catrin's body was found early the following morning by an elderly dog walker taking his spaniel through the graveyard at Llanbadrig church. She had been strangled with the belt from her mac, her body dumped against the wall facing the sea. The poor man was being treated for shock.

Lewis was reeling from the news. As soon as DS Evans and the young WPC knocked on the door, he had known. Naturally, there was a barrage of questions: how had she seemed when she left the house; had they argued; could he think of anyone who might have wanted to harm her? His head was spinning. Who could have done this? Poor Catrin. He'd long since admitted it to himself, but now he had to tell the police that he didn't love her any more. But he would never have wished this on her. He wouldn't have wished it on anyone.

They left with a promise of returning should they have any further information. Lewis felt sure that he was probably top of their list of suspects. That was what they always thought, wasn't it – the partner or someone close to the victim had to be the most likely perpetrator.

He kept thinking about the phone. He wondered whether he ought to tell the police. Maybe he should take a look at it himself first.

Just in case.

*

One of the chargers in Catrin's drawer that Lewis had thought defunct was, of course, a perfect match for the other mobile. As the tinny jingle announced it had woken, he waited for a moment and then shakily jabbed at the keys with her regular PIN code. Nothing. He tried his own birthday, then Marian's, Catrin's mother.

INCORRECT PIN

His heart sank. What else could she have used? He thought for a moment and then tapped in the date they had started seeing one another. He felt a stab of guilt as the icons appeared at once on the screen.

Quickly he opened the phone book, but was baffled to find only two contacts, neither of which he recognised. One was just a number; the messages were one-sided and had a worryingly sinister tone. The other contact was simply saved as two initials: *S.D.*

Who the fuck was that? It meant nothing to him. He began to scroll through the texts with an increasingly nauseous feeling. Hoping to find some sort of clue, he rifled frantically through the other drawers, all in a predictable state of disarray. Nightdresses, underwear, leggings, tights. Something was bulging inside a pair of

274

fleecy pink bed-socks that were balled up together. Stuffing a hand inside, he pulled out the contents, his mouth dropping open. It was a huge wad of fifty-pound notes.

What the hell had Catrin been up to? He realised now that there had been far more going on with her than he could ever have dreamed possible. He would sleep on it, but maybe it really *was* time to inform the *heddlu*.

*

The police were quick to respond to Lewis's request to call round the next day. The rain had been falling steadily through the night, and the bruised, smoky skies did nothing to lift his mood. Lewis handed over the mobile as though it were a bomb as the two officers stood in his living room. He sat back down, woozy from lack of sleep and too much alcohol. He looked dishevelled and badly needed a shower.

DS Evans examined the phone with a frown, passing it to the young policewoman, who immediately placed it in an evidence bag. The officers declined the offer of drinks but sat down at Lewis's invitation, the omnipresent WPC Roberts perched now on the edge of the settee next to Evans, poised to make notes.

'We'll get the telecoms people to examine the contents more closely, but I'm afraid it appears that Catrin, if indeed this *was* her phone, was responsible for the distressing messages received by Lowri Morris.' He looked at Lewis strangely. 'Mr Bevan, have you any idea why she would have done such a thing?'

Lewis felt uncomfortable. He was nursing another

275

glass of brandy, his fingers constantly tapping the sides. He knocked it back in one and dropped his eyes.

His words were slightly slurred. 'I think – well, I *know*, she was jealous. She'd got it into her head that there was something going on with me and Lowri.'

Evans narrowed his eyes. 'And was – *is* there?'

'Hmm? Fuck, no. Sorry – sorry. Didn't mean to swear.' He got up and began to pace, swaying a little, Catrin's jibes from the other afternoon ringing in his ears. 'She's a lovely girl but . . . no.'

'You seem a bit defensive, Mr Bevan. Have I spoken out of turn?'

Anger flashed in Lewis's eyes. 'Good God, man. My ex-girlfriend has just been killed. I feel like shit that we parted on such bad terms. How d'you expect me to behave?'

'But we have it on your own admission that your relationship had run its course. Surely that must be something of a relief for you?'

'For fuck's sake – I may not have wanted us to be together any more but I sure as hell didn't want to see her dead.' He sank back into the chair and buried his head in his hands. 'This whole phone thing's as much of a mystery to me as it is to you. Christ knows what was in Catrin's head. You'd do well to try and find this "S.D." bugger who's in there.' His hand flapped towards the bag resting on the seat next to WPC Roberts.

'We'll do our utmost to track this person. In the meantime, I suggest you try to get some sleep. And please don't think of leaving the area for the foreseeable future. We may need to question you further.'

'Leave the area? Hardly. I'm going nowhere until you find the bastard that did this.'

Evans rose from his chair and gestured to the WPC with a tip of his head to follow suit. He paused, turning back to Lewis.

'I appreciate this may be a sensitive question, but did you and Catrin have intercourse yesterday? I mean, you *were* still cohabiting.'

'*What?* No! I've told you, we'd split up.'

'That's what I thought.' Evans shot a look at WPC Roberts and nodded, his eyebrows raising a fraction. 'We'll see ourselves out. Do try to get some rest – it may help you to think more clearly.'

*

Once again, the telecoms team drew a blank with the contact number for the elusive 'S.D.'. It was yet another unregistered mobile. Neither Brenda, Catrin's distraught parents or her brother, or indeed any of those closest to her, could think of anyone with whom she associated with those particular initials. The assumption was that it must be some kind of nickname, or pseudonym.

In other words, a needle in a haystack.

CHAPTER TWENTY-TWO

The Past, 1992

After two years backpacking round Europe and 'finding himself', Lewis had realised that he felt a deep longing to go home; a yearning for the place of his birth and his ancestors. *Hiraeth* – that's what his mam had always called it. He felt ready to settle, maybe find a girl and raise a family. But that would mean getting a steady job and saving hard. It had been fine as a young single man, living hand to mouth, but he couldn't expect anyone to see him as a viable prospect unless he could at least put a roof over their heads and food on the table.

From the outset, Lewis had known deep down the position at Ysbyty Gadlys wasn't for him. He was competent and conscientious, and did everything required of him, but seeing all those poor people in such a wretched state, day in, day out, was affecting him mentally. After only a couple of weeks, he knew he must definitely look for work elsewhere and move on. He was a young, fit man and there were plenty of things he could easily turn his hand to. The salary was decent, though, and he just wanted to save a few quid first.

He called in to Ty Coed Pinwydd on his way home from a particularly arduous shift one evening. He didn't visit often, but had made the effort to stay in touch with Awel and Elis, who had always been kind to him. Awel would ring from time to time to see how he was getting on and seemed pleased he had found a steady job. Their mutual dislike of Iolo Morgan had created an uneasy sort of bond between them.

Awel had already mentioned his new position at the psychiatric hospital to Gwyn, who sat him down in her kitchen and confided in him about a distant cousin of hers, Cyw. He was taken aback to learn that she was a patient. Ironic that the woman had actually been sectioned for attacking Iolo Morgan. Good on her, whatever had provoked it. The prick deserved everything he'd got. Just a crying shame that she'd been locked up for it.

Lewis liked Gwyn. He had met her a few times over the years, when visiting Awel and Elis, and found her slightly eccentric but straightforward and kind. After his mam died, he had spent much of the latter part of his childhood on the mainland living with his auntie, but always wanted to return to Anglesey eventually. Now that he had found regular work, he would soon be able to afford to rent a flat or small cottage in or near Llanbadrig. He had such fond memories of the place as a small boy, before his father passed away. The only fly in the ointment was Iolo Morgan, but he was easily avoided unless you frequented the local drinking den day and night. Lewis had better things to do than to spend his days getting pissed. It was the lifestyle favoured by losers – and he didn't intend to allow himself to get dragged down into such an existence. Which was just as well, since the very sight of his stepfather was enough to raise Lewis's blood pressure.

The daily commute to and from Caernarfon was proving a strain, and Lewis was delighted when, seemingly out of nowhere, Gwyn offered him temporary accommodation at Ty Coed Pinwydd.

'Just until you've saved up your deposit for somewhere to live,' she had told him. 'It'll make life a bit easier for you.' She paused, studying his face for a moment. 'I'll be straight with you, Lewis. The thing is, I'm hoping you'll do me a favour in return. I'd like you to do a bit of snooping for me – see how things *really* are in that place.'

'Oh?' Lewis sat back with interest. He glanced at Awel, seated at the opposite end of the table and avoiding his gaze as Gwyn handed him a mug of tea.

'If the girl's well looked after, then that's one thing. But I've heard stories. Oh, everything seems fine when I visit, but we're always supervised and in a day room, plus I can only go a couple of times a month. Cyw can be, well, strange at the best of times and she's heavily medicated, too. It's difficult to know exactly – well, you know what I mean. If you could just see how they're treating her, I'd be very grateful.'

He had listened in stunned silence as she told him all

280

about Cyw's sad history; explained her state of mind, how she was a simple soul who had acted completely out of character. Yes, there had been the odd occasion when she'd had outbursts expressing her frustration, which, given her circumstances, were entirely forgivable; but her rage was always directed at herself or inanimate objects. She would scream and tug angrily at her own hair, or throw something across the room. A sedative administered from time to time by Dr Price always seemed to settle her back down, and normality would resume for weeks. No one knew what Morgan could have done to upset her in such a way. In spite of her age, Cyw was still childlike and naïve. She needed love and understanding, not imprisonment.

It took little persuasion for Lewis to agree to report back. His role as janitor meant he could move freely around the hospital without arousing suspicion, while going about his daily duties. But what he saw when he began to delve deeper disturbed him. The facility was hopelessly understaffed, and adult patients of every age and gender were often herded into one large room, drugged to the eyeballs to keep them placid and easy to control. Many of them sat around in the old armchairs provided, rocking and twiddling their thumbs and staring into space. Others shuffled aimlessly through the corridors like the undead. The sleeping quarters were more like prison cells, with bars on the windows and steel-framed beds, offering no home comforts. And then there was the overpowering smell: the industrial-strength pine disinfectant that had to be slopped around daily to mask the stench of incontinence and unwashed bodies. Bathing seemed to be reserved for when a patient was due to receive visitors. Food was unappetising and often served lukewarm, since mealtimes were chaotic owing to poor logistics and general lack of organisation. The whole set-up was appalling.

Gwyn was distraught to learn what Lewis was witnessing.

'We've got to get her out of there,' she told Lewis and Awel, as they sat in the kitchen one August evening. 'I can't believe this is how she's been treated all these years. It's all wrong, punishing her like that for one ill-judged outburst. She isn't a danger to society. There's no malice in her.' She shook her head, angry tears flooding her eyes. 'We need a plan.'

CHAPTER TWENTY-THREE

Present Day

I couldn't bring myself to tell Awel the news DS Evans had given me about Beca. Not yet; not until everything was properly confirmed. It felt like a wild assumption – and a betrayal of my dad, to assume he could have got the teenage Rhian pregnant. Everything was going round and round in my mind; I tried to rationalise – maybe it could have been his brother, Dafydd? He was younger, after all. Maybe that was why he'd run off to Canada, never to return. It was feasible. I didn't have enough knowledge about DNA to know whether brothers were so closely related that one's genetic code could be mistaken for another.

Awel broke the news to me about Catrin that evening, as we sat in the small sitting room after tea. I couldn't believe it. Yet another horrible shock. For a remote, supposedly peaceful rural area, things were becoming disturbingly dark. I was sick with worry, knowing my little girl was still out there, with a killer at large.

'Poor Lewis. How is he?'

'In a bad way. Feeling guilty that he'd asked her to move out not so long ago. It's eating away at him.'

'D'you think we should go and see him?'

'Maybe not just yet. He'll come here when he wants company. I got the feeling he needed to be on his own.'

I was beginning to feel much better physically – still weakened, although managing to eat a little, and my head didn't feel quite so much as if it had been stuffed with cotton wool. But now that I was on the mend, my mental torment was heightened. It had been several days with no developments in the search for Ruby. My thoughts veered constantly to her welfare. Whether she was suffering; whether she could have met with a similar fate to Beca. It felt as though hope was fading and the gaping hole in my chest seemed to be expanding. The pain of not being able to hold her in my arms was deep and visceral, a terrible ache that made me want to curl into a ball and shut out the world. I had to keep telling myself that I would know if she were no longer alive; that I would *sense* it. It was the only thing keeping me sane.

Dr Rhodri Price had called earlier that afternoon, just to check how I was doing. I had been so unwell on the previous occasions he'd visited that I hadn't formed a proper impression of him, but he really did seem nice – not in the slightest bit like his father and very approachable.

I wondered if he knew anything about DNA. Not wanting to reveal what DS Evans had told me, I casually mentioned Beca Bennion, how sad it all was, then dived in to ask if there was any way DNA evidence could be wrong.

'No, everyone's DNA is unique. It's like a genetic fingerprint. I mean, of course, it doesn't necessarily mean someone's guilty of something: not without other supporting evidence. But if their DNA is found at a crime scene, it means they've almost definitely been there at some point – or at least, something belonging to them has.'

He looked at me curiously. 'Why d'you ask? Did you think it might have been a case of mistaken identity – with Beca, I mean?'

'No, no. I was just thinking about it all and wondered – could brothers be mistaken for each other – I mean, would their DNA be almost identical?'

He shook his head and smiled. 'No. Siblings still have their own individual genetic codes. Sure, they'd be recognised as being siblings, but every egg and sperm is unique, so they contain different combinations of their parents' DNA. Which explains variations in hair and eye colour, height, et cetera, in the same family. It's called genetic recombination.'

I must have looked blank, as he laughed. 'It's pretty straightforward, actually. I've always found it really interesting – I suppose that's the way my brain works. I was at med school with a guy who changed course and went on to do forensics. Fascinating stuff.'

I felt I couldn't probe any further without him

wondering what I was driving at, and left it at that. We chatted for a while before he rose to leave.

I saw him to the door. 'Thanks very much for calling.' I thought for a moment. 'Have you taken over from your father permanently, then? I mean, should we ask for you in future if we need a house call?'

The question appeared to have wrong-footed him for some reason and he stiffened.

'Just picking up the slack while he catches up on other stuff at present. The old man *is* taking more of a back seat these days, but I can't see him throwing in the towel completely. Ever.' He gave a hollow little laugh, then seemed to relax slightly. 'Glad to see how much better you are, anyway. You were in a pretty bad way there for a few days.'

I nodded weakly. I realised now just how ill I'd actually been – I should probably have taken to my bed much sooner. I'd obviously worried everyone, particularly Awel.

'Have you heard anything from the police? About your little girl?'

I felt a sob rise in my throat. All I could do was shake my head. The tears were there constantly, just brimming beneath the surface, and it needed little to encourage them.

His face fell, his eyes scanning mine earnestly. 'I'm so sorry. Easier said than done I know, especially with all this going on –' he waved a hand towards the woods, 'not to mention the awful shock about poor Catrin, but try to stay positive. Crime around here's actually very rare as a rule and the police seem to be throwing plenty of resources at it all. Hopefully you'll get some good news soon.'

I made him no answer. He meant well, I realised that; but how could anyone expect me to remain positive with everything that had been happening? I almost wished I was still in the earlier throes of the pleurisy, that I could retreat once more into delirium and the oblivion it had brought. Being lucid and fully aware of my situation was unbearable.

Rhodri gave me a watery smile and climbed into his car, raising a hand as he pulled away. I watched him go and went back into the house, leaning against the door for a moment as I considered our earlier conversation. I almost wished I hadn't asked.

There was no doubt about it, then. Beca Bennion and I shared the same father.

CHAPTER TWENTY-FOUR

Present Day

Awel and Elis eventually decided to go and see Lewis after he made a drunken phone call late that evening. He had been so upset, Awel said, that she thought he needed someone to check on him. I had wanted to go along, but Awel said it might be best if it was just the two of them – 'seeing as he's in such a state. He might not want you to see him like that.'

I waited in vain for their return, but felt increasingly weary and eventually decided to go to bed. Perhaps not surprisingly, sleep evaded me for much of the night. So much had happened since my arrival in Llanbadrig. Apart from the terrible anguish caused by Ruby's disappearance, the body of a dead child, apparently closely related to me, had been found in the woods. And now Catrin had been murdered. It was all going round in my head: were all these events connected? I was sick with worry, to think that a single perpetrator could have been responsible for each of these despicable acts. That my beautiful Ruby could be the next victim – or could already have been. The waiting; the not knowing. It was tearing me apart.

I was physically and mentally exhausted. I still didn't feel completely well after the worst bout of illness I had ever experienced, and eventually drifted off in spite of it all.

I woke with a jolt. Something had disturbed me. As my hand trailed limply from the side of the bed, I was startled to feel something cool and wet brushing against my palm. Rigid with fear, I looked down to see Mickey nuzzling me, his soulful brown eyes fixed on my face. I gave an exclamation of relief. As I tried to sit up, he trotted to the open doorway and looked back, as though wanting me to follow him.

I slid my feet into an old pair of slippers I had borrowed from Awel and went out onto the landing. Mickey was standing outside the locked door to the room from where I'd heard the harp music. He began to scratch at the panelled wood, pausing to see if I had joined him.

I pressed my ear to the door. It sounded as though something – or someone – was shuffling around on the other side. My heart quickened. I knocked lightly and listened again. The noise stopped abruptly, almost as though my tapping had disturbed somebody. Mickey resumed his scratching. He gave a sudden bark, his tail thrashing excitedly. I stroked his head lightly and shushed him, straining to hear any further evidence of movement.

There was a sudden squeak, as though a chair was being dragged along a hard surface or something similar. I knocked more loudly now, curiosity overriding my fear.

'Hello? Who's in there?'

There was a scuttling and what sounded like a door creaking. Then silence.

'Awel? Is that you?' No response.

I peered over the banister into the hall below and saw that Awel's coat and boots had gone from the stand. I went halfway down the stairs and could see through the fanlight above the front door that Elis's van was still missing from the driveway. They must have decided to stay with poor Lewis.

Cautiously, I retraced my steps and rejoined Mickey, who was still scrabbling, periodically leaping up at the door now in agitation. I knew I had to investigate. Steeling myself, I tried the handle. To my astonishment, it opened.

I found myself in total darkness. Groping along the wall, eventually I located the light switch, but even as I clicked it up and down, nothing happened. Maybe the bulb had blown. The opened door cast little light into the depths of the room, so I fumbled my way over to the window and pushed the heavy drapes aside, releasing a cloud of dust particles. The birds were just beginning to chirrup outside as the new day dawned. The window sill and panes were caked in grime and dead insects, with small puddles of condensation pooling around the edges of the rotting wooden frame. I spun round to see who or what had made the noise, but there appeared to be nobody but Mickey and me.

The room was huge; far bigger than the one in which Ruby and I had been sleeping. It was draughty and cold, the air heavy with the cloying smell of damp. An enormous black veined marble fireplace stood in the centre of the wall opposite the window. The wind whistled eerily down the chimney, making my heart flutter.

Several bulky items of furniture were covered in dust sheets, and pushed to the perimeter of the floor space. A large, heavily patterned blue and gold rug was spread across the middle of the room, its centre threadbare and faded. The floorboards visible around the edges looked robust enough, despite Auntie Gwyn's warnings of them being perilously unsafe. I couldn't understand what the room could possibly hold, that the need was felt to keep it permanently locked and unused. It made no sense.

Carefully, I began to peel back the dust sheets to see what they concealed. An old chaise longue, upholstered in worn royal-blue velvet. An ornate roll-top Victorian bureau, its mahogany wood edged in gilt. An old plug-in electric fire. A heavy, carved oak chest.

At the far end of the room was a battered-looking piano, its lid lifted as if waiting for the pianist's fingers to depress the keys. It felt somehow sinister.

Turning, I saw Mickey bounding suddenly towards the wall behind me. A bookshelf, crammed with ancient Welsh literature, stretched from floor to ceiling in the chimney breast to the right of the fireplace. The dog jumped up on his back feet and rested his paws on one of the dusty shelves, panting excitedly.

'Come on, fella.' I just wanted to get out of there and hurried back towards the door. Mickey was stubbornly taking no notice, his claws scraping insistently at the shelving as though trying to dig a hole.

'Come *here*.' I tried to sound authoritative, but it had no effect. As I turned to push the door wide in the hope that he would follow, I caught my breath. The key was jutting from the lock. *On the inside*.

I felt frighteningly vulnerable.

'*Mickey!* Let's go.' The dog was ignoring me completely and had begun to whine. I marched across to take him by the collar but, in my haste, somehow lost my footing on the slippery rug and toppled towards him. I reached out to save myself, grabbing for the shelves, which gave a slow, ominous creak.

Holding on for dear life, I realised in horror that they were receding. Mickey yelped, as inadvertently I stepped on his paw, and both of us fell forward into what appeared to be a deep cupboard. The shelves stopped moving and I sat on the floor, bewildered as to what had just happened. I could see now that at one side of the shelving were three substantial hinges. The pressure must have triggered some unseen mechanism.

The bookshelves concealed another wooden door, filthy and thick with cobwebs. I caught my breath. It seemed, for want of a better word, like some sort of portal. Cautiously, I took hold of the tarnished brass handle, which when twisted revealed a further large, and oddly windowless, room. Bizarrely, the doorway, which I assumed would originally have led out of it onto the landing, was bricked up. The light was dim but, from what I could see, there was evidence of recent habitation: a double bed made up and a wardrobe, chest of drawers and dressing table, all laid out like regular bedroom furniture rather than the obvious dumping ground of the previous room. And tucked into one corner, something tall and angular, covered with yet another dust sheet. Even before removing it, the tinkling note elicited by merely touching the fabric told me what I would find.

Auntie Gwyn's Nain's old harp.

And there was that smell again, but much more pronounced: the old, musky perfume I had noticed with no obvious source.

I backed away, almost knocking over a flimsy metal music stand, the crinkling yellow pages of the book it held opened to reveal the words, '*Llwyn Onn*'. I couldn't read the notes, but immediately recognised the title as that of an old Welsh folk song, known by another name in English.

'The Ash Grove'. My whole body turned cold. I could just discern an archway at the far end of the room. Picking my way carefully across the floor in case there actually *were* any damaged floorboards, I peered into the gloom beyond the archway. There was a stone passage, with steps winding in an upwards direction. It was impossible to tell how long it was, but as my eyes grew accustomed to the gloom, I could just discern a fragment of light at the end. My racing pulse filled my whole head. Breathlessly, I scrambled to my feet and grabbed Mickey's collar before he could go tearing off ahead of me into the unknown.

CHAPTER TWENTY-FIVE

The Girl's Story

The girl awoke to the sound of muffled voices. She had no concept of how much time had elapsed and was stiff with cold, curled up on the rickety bed. She hitched the blanket around her shoulders, her eyes scanning the space, but found she was alone. What sounded like someone talking seemed to be seeping through the wall. Baffled, she tried to orientate herself. The curtain hanging across the wall had been disturbed, as though it had been flung aside and carelessly drawn once more. The child pulled herself to her feet and padded across the floor. Cautiously, she peeled back the drape slightly, wondering what purpose it served.

There was another door. Heavy and studded, with a circular iron handle. The girl twisted it and the door creaked open a fraction. Yet more stairs led, upwards this time, from the doorway. She placed a tentative foot on the bottom step and looked up to see a thin rectangle of light. Dropping the blanket now, she tiptoed up the staircase, finally reaching the light source at the top. She could feel her heart, pounding like a bass drum inside her chest. Beyond the door, the voices became clearer. At once she recognised the quick, erratic voice of the strange woman, gabbling to someone else in Welsh. And then to her surprise, the response: calm and measured; a voice she recognised all too well. But although she couldn't understand what was being said, something about the responding tone stopped the girl in her tracks – and from making her presence felt.

Trembling with fear, she crept back down the stairs and, as quietly as she could, pulled the door closed behind her. Her mind began to fly, her eyes darting in panic around the forbidding cellar room.

Where *was* she? And what on earth was going on?

CHAPTER TWENTY-SIX

The Past, 1982

'So, this is the brat, is it?' The unwashed bulk of Iolo Morgan filled the doorway of the veranda, his decrepit van parked in the turning circle before Ty Coed Pinwydd. The words '*FRESH FISH*' peeling in black paint from the off-white sides belied the contents. No one who knew anything about the mobile fishmonger and his wares would risk life and limb by eating anything he sold.

Awel raised a hand to shield her eyes from the glare of the morning sun. Morgan sparked a match off the step and lit his cigarette, deliberately puffing straight towards Awel, who began to cough.

'Do you mind?' Scooping up the startled Lowri, she ushered her into the house, along with the doll that she had been playing with. 'Go and find Elis,' she told her. 'He'll make you a drink.'

Turning back to her father, she stood with folded arms, her cheeks taut. 'Is there anything you actually want? Or have you just come to be a nuisance as usual?'

He stood, chest puffed out, with an infuriating smirk painted across his face. 'My new bride and her boy will be moving in after the nuptials next weekend. That should give you ample warning to sort out where you and that gormless lump will be living. Can't say fairer than that.'

Awel's mouth fell open. She clasped her throat. 'Are you saying we'll be homeless?'

'Surely you didn't think you could carry on living there too? There simply isn't room. Anyway, high time the pair of you stood on your own two feet. You've sponged off me for long enough.'

'*Sponged*?' Awel almost spat the word. 'Waited hand and foot and provided for you for as long as I can remember. You worked my mother into an early grave. I hope that poor woman knows what she's letting herself in for.'

'She's gaining a husband, and a father for her son. What more could she ask for?'

'And no doubt you're gaining a housekeeper and a slice of her widow's pension.'

He sneered but didn't acknowledge this retort. 'Anyway, you've had notice now. Plenty of time to make arrangements.'

Taking a final deep drag on his cigarette, he cast it down and ground it out with the sole of his boot before returning to the van, leaving a cloud of noxious fumes in his wake as he pulled away. Awel stared after him in disbelief.

Gwyn appeared from the hallway in time to see Morgan disappearing from view. She pulled a face. Seeing Awel's obvious distress, she gently placed a hand on her arm.

'Are you okay? What did *he* want?'

'He's throwing us out. The bastard's actually throwing us out.' Awel turned to her, her lip trembling. 'But where will we go?'

Gwyn rolled her eyes, spreading her hands towards the house. 'Don't be daft, girl. You'll come here, of course. We're family. Get that brother of yours to take you to collect your stuff. You can both move in today.'

Lowri reappeared, beaker of juice in one hand, her doll tucked under the other arm. She beamed up at her aunt, whose face broke into a broad grin.

'And how are you this morning, *chica bach*?' Gwyn lifted the squealing child high into the air, swinging her round. 'Awel and Elis are coming to live with us. Won't that be nice!' She turned back to the gaping Awel and winked.

Awel looked dubious. 'But what about the others – won't they mind?'

Gwyn waved a dismissive hand. 'They have no say on who lives with me – gave up any rights to the place long ago. God knows they've had plenty of opportunities to step up and lend a hand. Dafydd is a waste of space. And the only reason Aron ever comes is to offload you-know-who.'

Awel glanced at the giggling Lowri. 'How's it all going?'

Gwyn grimaced. She lowered the little girl to the

ground and tickled her chin. 'Shall we play hide and seek? You go and hide, and I'll count to twenty.'

Lowri scuttled off excitedly, disappearing into the house. Gwyn sighed. 'Not so well at the moment. I'm hoping Alison will come round. Poor little soul must be pretty confused.'

'Children adapt. She's young enough. It'll all soon be a distant memory. And you're the constant. At least she'll always have you.'

Gwyn's face clouded. 'I do hope so. I really do.'

Awel gave her hand a squeeze. 'You've made the best of a bad situation. At least she'll be brought up by people who . . .'

Gwyn shook her head. 'I still wonder whether we made the right decision. But what's done is done. Time alone will tell.'

Awel paused. 'Have the hospital been in touch?'

'No. I've phoned a few times but they're quite guarded about what they'll tell me. It's early days – I suppose they're just monitoring things for now. Hopefully, given time and the right medication, her condition will improve.'

Awel glanced towards the road with distaste, as if the presence of her father had left an unpleasant odour. 'She'd have done us all a favour if she'd followed through.'

'Well, that's as may be, but we mustn't think like that. At least on top of everything else she hasn't been branded a murderer.' Gwyn exhaled deeply. 'I wouldn't want that stigma attached to Lowri.'

Awel squeezed her hand. 'The child never needs to know – about any of it. Least said, soonest mended.'

Their eyes locked for a moment, an unspoken pact.

A cry from within told them Lowri was waiting to be found. Gwyn smiled resignedly.

'Coming, ready or not!'

CHAPTER TWENTY-SEVEN

The Girl's Story

When the woman reappeared several minutes later, she seemed much brighter.

'We can go upstairs now,' she told the girl, 'and have a proper dinner.'

Apprehensively, the child followed her, past the curtain which was now pushed back, and they ascended the stairs she had discovered earlier. Beyond the studded door was yet another stone passageway, leading upwards but twisting and turning like a labyrinth. Although she had no real sense of where they were, the girl felt that it was far from the heart of the building. She had seen a film once about an old house with a secret tunnel and thought how exciting it would be to discover one. The frightening reality was not at all what she had imagined.

301

At the very top, they came to a latched door. The child sniffed. It was the smell of cooking. As the woman led the way into the room, the girl was amazed to see a small table set with two steaming plates of macaroni cheese, a jug of fruit squash and two tumblers. It was almost as though some kindly elf had left it for them.

'Dig in!' the woman instructed. The girl didn't need to be told twice. Hunger had nullified any earlier caution; she pulled up one of the little folding stools next to the table and began to shovel the food into her mouth.

'Not too quick! My mam always said you have to chew your food properly, or you'll get belly ache.'

As she ate, the girl glanced around, taking in her surroundings. It looked as though they were in the loft space. The room was actually quite warm and cosy, with a settee and small bed. Everything was lit by the soft glow of a lamp sitting low in one corner. A far cry from the dingy, cold cellar.

'*Ti'n licio hwn?*'

'Pardon?'

'Do you like it?'

'It's really nice. Thank you,' the girl added. She took a swig of squash. 'Did you make it?'

The woman scoffed. 'Me? *Nac oes*, I don't cook.'

'Oh.' The girl thought for a moment and put down her spoon. She looked suddenly hopeful. 'I just remembered – there aren't any nuts in this, are there?'

'What was that?'

'I'm allergic to some things. Nuts, especially.'

The woman's brow creased into a frown. She put down her spoon, too. 'What's lurjic?'

'*All*ergic. If I eat some foods, they can make me ill – I swell up and come out in a horrible rash.'

The woman's eyes widened.

Buoyed up by this reaction, the child went on. 'It happens to lots of people. A girl in my class is allergic to eggs. They make her throw up straight away. Sometimes it's hard to breathe – my mum says it can be really dangerous.'

'Ah. *Alergaidd*.' She nodded. 'No, I don't think there are nuts in it, anyway. Just pasta and cheese sauce. They don't put nuts in that, do they?'

The girl considered for a moment. She'd started to eat and nothing appeared to have happened to her so far. When the thought occurred, she'd even half hoped that she *might* have a reaction – maybe the woman would have been forced to seek medical help for her. Or maybe she had no intention of doing anything of the sort. Maybe she'd just let her grow old and die in there and no one would ever know what had happened to her. She might never see daylight again.

The child's face fell and her chin began to tremble. The woman cocked her head to one side and stared at her for a moment, then broke into a grin. She seemed to have read her thoughts.

'Don't worry. It's all right. You'll see your mammy again soon.' She patted the girl absently on the head. 'You have lovely hair, you know. Mine was lovely too, once.'

The child tried to smile back. 'Will you at least tell me your name?'

The woman sat back, seeming to consider this request for a moment. Eventually she nodded. 'Cyw. Everyone calls me Cyw.'

CHAPTER TWENTY-EIGHT

Present Day

Seeming to sense that he should be quiet, Mickey relaxed and allowed me to hold onto him. We inched our way along the incline of the stone paved passage. The walls were of cold, bare brick, with chunks of mortar missing in places. The air smelled dank and earthy, like that in an ancient crypt, undisturbed for centuries. I was increasingly fearful of what we might find, but felt compelled to continue. My whole body was rigid with fear, my steps small and faltering. It was like entering the depths of some macabre ghost train tunnel, huge cobwebs trailing before us, and at every turn I was half expecting an enormous spider to drop onto my head or some cartoon phantom to leap out and laugh maniacally. As the light grew slightly brighter, I could see that at the end were several wooden stairs rising to a door.

I moved as quietly as my wheezing breath would allow, and climbed the rickety staircase, wondering what on earth lay beyond. Thank God for Mickey. I would never have dared venture up there on my own.

As we reached the top, I paused to listen. There was evidence of movement, as though feet or fingers were tapping rhythmically against something. I stood rooted to the spot, my ear pressed to the door. I'd come this far; I had to enter. I could hear faint humming, a high-pitched rendition of the same mournful tune that seemed to be following me everywhere. Fear gripped my chest as the tingle of gooseflesh rose on my arms.

Bracing myself for a confrontation of some sort, I gripped the dog's collar so tightly its buckle dug into my palm.

But then an extraordinary thing happened. The voice broke into song; a happier, more upbeat melody. Mickey, cooperative until this point, started to pull against me, giving small, eager yelps. I recognised the refrain – 'Touch the Sky', from the Disney animation *Brave* – instantly. But more important was the small, sweet voice that was singing it out for all it was worth.

I felt my heart soar.

With fumbling, uncoordinated fingers, I lifted the latch. Unable to contain himself any longer, Mickey wriggled from my grasp, tail thrashing wildly, his whole body swaying from side to side with the movement. He yipped excitedly as he covered her face with wet doggy kisses.

I felt suspended in the moment, an onlooker; afraid to believe what I was seeing, in case it was a cruel trick of the light, an optical illusion. But as that captivating smile lit her face, I was satisfied; suddenly euphoric that what I was seeing was real. The nightmare was over.

I fell to my knees, unsure whether to laugh or cry as I pulled my daughter towards me.

'Mummy! I knew you'd come!'

CHAPTER TWENTY-NINE

We were at one end of a large attic room; no window or skylight, but reasonably well-lit by a pink-shaded brass lamp, set on a small table covered with an old-fashioned lace doily. The electric heater was throwing out adequate heat; attempts to make the space feel homely were demonstrated by the miniature watercolour prints hanging on the rafters and a flowery pink rug spread out on the floor. The small settee, on which Ruby had obviously been sleeping, was covered with a patchwork quilt, and an old eiderdown covered the camp bed pushed against the opposite wall. A partially completed jigsaw, depicting an assortment of cats, was laid out on the wooden floorboards next to the rug. On a small, low bookshelf by the wall was a pack of cards and a battered old box containing several board games – draughts, snakes and ladders, Nine Men's Morris. A colouring book and felt-tip pens sat beside a small pile of books. I noticed the ancient copy of

Johanna Spyri's *Heidi* that I remembered Auntie Gwyn reading to me as a child.

Cautiously, I opened a narrow door in the corner to find a basic-looking toilet and handbasin squeezed into a space about three feet square. How could I never have known about this place?

I could hardly take it all in. Everything poured out in a rush: she'd had to hide, she said; she'd been warned that there was a bad man that hurt little girls; she had to stay safe. She seemed confused and a little jumpy, constantly looking round as if expecting someone to appear at any moment.

'Who brought you here, sweetheart? Did they – did anybody hurt you?' My gut twisted in anger and revulsion at the thought.

She shook her head, slowly and deliberately. 'No. Cyw's a bit funny but she's nice really. I don't think she meant to scare me.'

'Who's Cyw?' My mind was racing.

'She's the lady who brought me here. I think she's friends with Awel – she said Awel made our lunch.'

An unpleasantly cold sensation snaked its way from my feet to my chest.

'Awel? Are you quite sure?'

'Yes. I think . . . I think I heard them talking the other day. At least, I think it was the other day. We had macaroni cheese. We've had soup today – it was nice. But I haven't had much else – I'm really hungry again now.'

My whole body tensed with rage as I tried to process what she was telling me.

'Where is this . . . this Cyw woman?'

Ruby frowned. 'I don't know. She went out in a rush just a few minutes ago. She goes out quite a bit, but I never know where to. She must go outside, because sometimes her shoes are muddy when she comes back. I think it was her I saw waving at the window and in the garden – you know, when we first got here. She might've just gone to get our supper this time, I suppose.'

'Sweetheart, it's early morning!'

'Is it? Oh. I didn't know. It's always dark in here and there's no clock. What day is it?'

I took a deep, calming breath. Despite my anger and confusion, I was actually having a conversation with my daughter – something I'd feared might never happen again. I wanted to pinch myself.

'It's the most wonderful Wednesday. One I'm never going to forget.'

I squeezed her to me, hardly daring to believe she was real and not just a figment of my imagination. She wrapped her arms round my neck.

'I'm so glad you came, Mummy. Did you find Doli glwt? Cyw was a bit cross 'cos I dropped her, but I thought afterwards, it might be a clue for you. You know, like in Hansel and Gretel? I wished and wished I could see you again, and now I have! Wishes can come true, can't they?'

'Yes, my darling, I really believe they can. Come on; shall we go and find you something to eat?'

*

After wolfing down four slices of beans on toast, Ruby began to tell me a little of what the woman, Cyw, had

309

said and how she had come to leave the house with her in the first place. On her way back from the bathroom at the wake, Ruby had gone into the kitchen to see Pwtyn, where she was startled to find Cyw. The woman had seemed distressed, saying her little dog was missing, and Ruby felt sorry for her.

But much later, after the initial excuse about wanting help to look for the lost dog, she had eventually admitted the real reason she wanted to get Ruby away from the house. Awel had told Cyw that there was a wicked man at the funeral – Cyw wasn't sure who he was, she'd told Ruby, but she knew it must be true. There was a man out there who hurt little girls: after all, young Beca Bennion had vanished, never to be seen again. *Someone* had to be responsible – and Awel *was* very wise. Cyw always listened to her.

Awel was extremely concerned for Ruby's safety, Cyw had said, and thought the child might be safer away from the house. She'd suggested perhaps Cyw could make up a story to persuade Ruby to accompany her to the caravan site, where she often liked to go, apparently. Cyw explained then that they needed to hide until the bad man had gone and the coast was clear. But as the days passed, Cyw became increasingly jumbled and still kept talking about Ruby being in danger, even though they had returned to the house and there had been no news of the so-called bad man since. Ruby had pleaded with her, but she seemed reluctant to release her in case he returned.

The more Ruby told me, the more I thought the woman sounded completely unhinged and probably needed help.

Rage started to build within me, but in the main the anger was not directed at Cyw. If everything she had told Ruby was true, Awel had been the main instigator of all this. And at that moment I wanted to strangle her with my bare hands.

CHAPTER THIRTY

Curled around the exhausted Ruby, the covers wrapped tightly around both of us, and Mickey stretched out like a draught excluder across the bedroom door, I slept like the dead for several hours. It was as though the relief of finding my daughter safe and well had drained me of every last remnant of energy. After the initial shock had worn off, and the tears of relief that, once started, I thought would never stop, had dried, I actually felt able to smile. I had my baby back. I offered up a silent prayer of thanks to anyone who might be listening. It felt like emerging from the depths of a dark, cold cave into the embrace of the warm sun. My nightmare was over.

There had been loud exclamations of what I now knew to be feigned relief and delight from Awel when she and Elis finally returned from Lewis's house later that afternoon. They had both stayed with him overnight, and it was probably just as well, as it had given me time to calm down a little. I hadn't called the police – yet. I wanted to wait until Ruby was safely out of the way before confronting Awel with what Ruby had told me. But my stony expression must have told her that I knew. I sat watching her, simmering with anger as I thought of what she had put Ruby and me through. She avoided meeting my eyes as she moved round the kitchen, preparing food and constantly telling Ruby how pleased she was to see her again. Ruby appeared to have just accepted everything and asked no questions. Finding Mickey had come to stay seemed to have made everything right in her eyes, and her face was lit with a constant grin. I had tried several times to ring Nina, but could get no reply. Maybe she was at the hospital with Ronnie – the signal was notoriously bad there. I left a brief message but was desperate to tell her the good news – and all the inconceivable details – in person. I knew it would be a massive relief to her, but wondered what she would think when she learned that Awel had been behind it all. Knowing Nina, I could already guess.

Apparently unscathed by her bizarre experience, but ravenous as ever, Ruby had eaten like a horse once more, devouring the huge plate of spaghetti Bolognese placed in front of her by Awel, followed by a slab of chocolate cake. I couldn't take my eyes off her. I wanted to pinch myself, hardly daring to believe that I had her back, safe and well but in need of a good bath and a change of clothes. Her hair looked like a bird's nest and her finger-nails were encrusted with grime. It occurred to me that she probably wouldn't have been able to clean her teeth, either.

But all this was trivia. Nothing else mattered other

than her being here; her solid, lively little presence. And above all, unhurt.

But with the dawning of the next day, the minute I opened my eyes, the anger resurged. How long would Awel have allowed this to go on for if Mickey hadn't led me to Ruby? I realised that she had been in no physical danger; but I'd been to hell and back. How could Awel have done that to me? And what really cut me to the quick was that Elis must have known, too. Did they both hate me so much that they wanted to see me suffer? But why? What had I done that could possibly have deserved such a spiteful act of vengeance? For that was what it felt like.

Of course, the police would have to be informed. There was no question of that – they had wasted enough time and resources searching for Ruby, and although none of this was my fault, I felt guilty. The only good thing, if you could call it that, that had come out of it all was discovering poor Beca Bennion, though what had actually happened to her was still a total mystery. I needed to know for certain if we did share a father, and in what way her death – and life – was connected to me. I suspected that, as a historical event, this investigation would be put on the backburner until Catrin's killer was found, which being a recent occurrence was the more pressing. What an horrendous couple of weeks it had been. At least the siege in Amlwch had been resolved without casualties.

But before I rang DS Evans, I wanted to have it out with Awel. We had sat in silence for the most part, while Ruby ate and chatted, none of her youthful spirit crushed.

For that I was incredibly grateful. Awel had been artificially bright, busying herself with the meal, focusing her attention on Ruby and making small talk. Although furious, I was too tired and emotional to begin interrogating her, or to speak to the police. I just wanted to hold my little girl and shut out everything else. Ruby was all that mattered.

I lay, cradling the still sleeping Ruby, wide awake now as grey morning light began to seep through the curtains, staring skyward as the hypocrisy of it all gnawed away at me. How could Awel have fussed round my daughter as though none of this had anything to do with her? There were so many questions I needed to ask. And I needed to go right back to the start.

I decided there was no time like the present. Satisfied that Ruby was in no danger under Mickey's watchful eye, and taking care not to disturb her, I slid from the bed. Downstairs, I found Awel standing in the small sitting room, staring out of the window. The sky was bleak and heavy with scudding dirty-white clouds, the trees swaying and dipping in the wind. She flinched slightly as I entered but didn't look round.

'I need some answers, Awel.' I felt the quaver in my voice. I sat on the small settee and watched the back of her head, held rigidly upright. I suppressed the urge to grip her by the shoulders and shake her until her false teeth rattled. My hands remained at my sides, curled into angry fists.

Slowly she turned, a strange look on her face as her eyes met mine briefly. She looked away again sharply and remained silent for a few moments. I could see her reflection in the window, staring vacantly straight ahead. When she eventually began to speak, her voice was hoarse.

'We kept this business going, Elis and I. Gwyn had been unwell for some time – she wasn't capable any more, either physically or mentally. Things were going from bad to worse and we worked our fingers to the bone to make sure the company didn't fold altogether. I was devastated when we lost her. And then, after years of pretending none of us existed, *you* turn up – and just like *that*,' she clicked her fingers, baring her teeth, 'I find out, all along, she'd had no intention of rewarding our loyalty. Not properly. It was clear I was just the old retainer, kept on out of a sense of duty; good enough to run the house and keep the business afloat, but never worthy of owning either. It felt like a monumental slap in the face.' She exhaled deeply, twisting her fingers together. She turned now to face me full on, her anguish palpable.

'But what on earth did you hope to achieve by taking Ruby – or at least, getting this . . . this Cyw woman to do your dirty work? Who the hell is she, anyway?'

Awel dropped her gaze, ignoring my last question. 'I just thought, I don't know, that if Ruby vanished for a while, it would make you reconsider staying on here. I mean, why on earth would you want to stay when something so awful had happened? I wanted to put the wind up you.' Her cheeks flushed slightly. 'It sounds ridiculously petty now. But if I'm totally honest, more than anything, I wanted to see you suffer.'

I was incredulous. 'So basically, you wanted to frighten

me away; but not before you'd put me through the wringer – is that what you're saying?'

She couldn't look me in the eye. I watched as she squirmed visibly, her head turned once more towards the window.

'I knew you'd make the connection with Beca's disappearance and it would make you think the worst. I had no idea then, of course, that the police would actually find Beca. I felt as if I'd dug myself into a proper hole. I was scared – it had all become really awkward. The time just didn't seem right to return Ruby to you. I was trying to reason it all through. I'd thought . . . I'd thought as soon as Ruby reappeared, that you'd take her and run and never come back. Leave us to carry on as we had before and not have you to answer to.'

She sighed. 'But the longer Cyw had her, the harder it got to end the situation. I'd never intended things to carry on as long as they did. Everything just spiralled. I hadn't thought it through properly; I realised that pretty quickly. But it was too late. I'd been *so* angry. So stunned by the will, after everything Elis and I have done here over the years. And we loved Gwyn. *I* loved her.' Her voice cracked with emotion. Arms crossed over her chest, she rubbed her shoulders and stared skyward. 'That was the worst of it, realising she hadn't thought as much of us as we did of her.'

I could see the hurt in her eyes, but struggled to muster any sympathy for her. Awel's whole existence revolved around the house and the business; I knew that. Apart from Elis, she really had nothing else to live for – in the same way that all I had was Ruby. It must have felt as though Auntie Gwyn hadn't considered her feelings or her future at all. But that was no excuse for what she had done.

'I'd never have asked you to leave; surely you know that? We could've all lived here together and worked things out between us. That can never happen now. You do realise I'll have to go to the police, don't you? They've wasted time and resources on a bloody wild goose chase. What the hell am I going to say to them?'

'You won't be going to the police.' Her voice was quiet and measured.

'Of course I will!' I threw up my hands in exasperation. 'They're going to want answers – I can't just call them and say, oh, it's all fine now, Ruby's come home and we don't need your help any more. I don't think that's going to wash somehow, do you?'

Her face was stony. 'You won't be going to the police because it will open a whole can of worms – that, believe me, if I tell you, you're going to want left shut.'

'Is this to do with Beca Bennion? Because I already know. DS Evans told me.'

Her brow creased into a quizzical frown, but she gave no response. I was livid now.

'I'm going to need a fucking good reason *not* to tell them exactly what you've done – all of you! I've nearly had a nervous breakdown over this and it's all because of your stupidity – and sheer malice, as far as I can tell. It's . . . it's unforgivable.'

I looked up to see Elis standing in the doorway, his face lined with pain. He balled his hand into a fist and rubbed it across his chest.

I'm so, so sorry.

But why? Why would you do such a thing? I don't understand. I swiped at my eyes as hot tears coursed down my cheeks. I had no other close family – I'd always loved Elis, felt I could rely on him. And now I didn't even have him any more. It was just Ruby and me against the world once again.

Come with me. He beckoned, then turned and went back out into the hall. Without looking at Awel, I followed him; through the hallway and past the kitchen, into the chill of the dingy passage that led beyond the preparation room. As the corridor narrowed, we reached a heavy wooden door. Elis inserted a key and it creaked open.

I peered apprehensively into the gap, suddenly fearful. I stopped abruptly. After all that had happened, could I even trust Elis?

I placed a hand on his shoulder and he turned to look at me. I shook my head vigorously.

Where are we going?

He made no response, but simply beckoned again. His eyes were pleading, almost desperate.

He pressed the fingertips of one hand to his chin and dropped them away from his body. *Please.*

And then: *I beg you.*

Hesitantly, I followed. There were uneven steps winding down towards another door. I held onto the rope banister attached to the wall, and picked my way gingerly downwards behind Elis, screwing up my eyes in an attempt to see what lay at the bottom. The air smelled stagnant and fetid, reminding me of the dungeon in an ancient castle I had visited once.

319

At the foot, we reached another door. Elis glanced at me solemnly, and then turned the key in its lock. He ducked beneath the frame and flicked on the light. We were in a dank, dark cellar; a part of the house I had never seen before.

I don't know who screamed first: me or the wild-haired, deranged-looking creature we had walked in on. I sprang back in fright as it rose from a makeshift bed pushed against one wall, arms flailing.

Forgetting myself, I yelled at Elis, hiding behind him for protection as the individual lunged towards me.

'Who *is* that? What the hell's going on?'

I could see now that we had disturbed an elderly-looking woman. Elis reached out both hands and grabbed her by the wrists. He looked into her crazed eyes and shook his head firmly.

'*Nac oes!*' he said sharply, the first time I had heard him utter a word in years. The sound was guttural, his consonants blurred. '*Ffrind.*'

She seemed to relax a little and sat back down, eyeing me suspiciously.

'*Pwy di hwna?*' she asked.

Elis looked from me to the woman and I could see tears brimming in his eyes. His voice came out as a strange croak.

'This is Lowri.'

CHAPTER THIRTY-ONE

The Past, 1992

They had got their heads together. Gwyn was due to visit Cyw the following Tuesday. Lewis would unlock her room and let Gwyn into the building after dark. He would then drive them to a place of safety – his aunt, who lived alone on the mainland, would probably be able to put Cyw up for a while. Knowing that the police would be alerted immediately, once the hospital realised the woman was missing, Gwyn suggested that they could make it look as though she had drowned. They would deposit Cyw's hospital nightdress and some of her other belongings on the coastal path at Llanbadrig. Wearing a wig, Awel would take a bus from Llannerch-y-medd, the nearest village to the hospital, to Llanbadrig, dressed in Cyw's distinctive multi-coloured jumper and red jacket, so that the authorities would think she had been sighted.

'They'll assume she's fallen to her death. No one is going to bother looking for her in those waters. Even if she has to be kept under lock and key forever more, it'll be a thousand times better than the existence she's having to endure in there. It's inhuman.'

Everything had gone according to plan. Sleepily, Cyw had accompanied Gwyn like a lamb and even climbed into Lewis's van without question. She'd seemed dazed and a little muddled, but obviously trusted her cousin implicitly. Lewis felt desperately sorry for the woman. She had an oddly childlike quality, and quirky, almost avian mannerisms that would undoubtedly draw attention to her in public. Lack of personal care and her time in the hospital had ruined her looks. But beneath the ravaged exterior, it was plain she had once been quite beautiful. So sad that illness had left only the broken shell of the lovely young girl she had once been. Lewis had learned from Gwyn that Elis had long held a torch for her as a boy and that he'd always been very protective of her. If anything, their shared misfortune had strengthened their bond, although there could never be any question of romance. What tragic irony that both of their lives had been devastated by the same disease. Elis had protested but, because of their closeness, Gwyn persuaded him that it would be better to stay away until Cyw was at a safe distance from the hospital, knowing that his presence might excite her and hence jeopardise the operation. If all went smoothly, there would be ample opportunity for a joyful reunion later on.

Just as Gwyn had predicted, passengers from the bus

Awel had caught came forward to report seeing a woman fitting Cyw's description on her way to Llanbadrig. After the discovery of the clothes left on the cliffs by the church, the hunt for the missing patient was eventually called off. Since Gwyn and her siblings were Cyw's closest living relatives, the initial search had been focused on Ty Coed Pinwydd, which meant that she had to be whisked away to stay with Lewis's aunt in Caernarfon until the dust had settled. Plus there was still the ongoing search for poor Beca Bennion, and everyone, police and public alike, seemed to be on high alert. Anything unusual would have been picked up on pretty quickly.

Lewis's aunt was more than willing to help, given the way in which her own poor sister had suffered at the hands of the contemptible Iolo Morgan. Lewis found work as a groundsman at a smart hotel in Trearddur Bay, and handed in his notice at the hospital. It was as though an enormous weight had been lifted from him. Now renting a tiny cottage just outside Llanbadrig, he visited Cyw every weekend and found she was adapting well to her new environment. She was a simple soul and questioned nothing – she was completely accepting of her new circumstances, as though it was all perfectly normal.

Gwyn had approached the local coroner, a man she had come to know well over the years, to request permission from the justice secretary to hold an inquest, which was required in the absence of a body, citing the need for the family to grieve properly and move on. Several months later, an open verdict was returned and a death certificate finally issued. Everyone in the house was able to breathe a metaphorical sigh of relief. They had effectively got away with it.

*

It soon became the norm. Cyw was brought to live in Ty Coed Pinwydd, apparently malleable and content to be steered in whichever way Gwyn chose to guide her. She appeared happy enough confined to the house. She would wander from room to room in her own little world, usually clutching an old rag doll she'd been given as a child, from which she had latterly become inseparable. Great care was always taken if any visitors or clients called to the house, and she would think it a wonderful game to hide in the cellar, or one of the larger bedrooms, which was kept permanently locked and reserved for her use. Gwyn had coaxed her into having her wild hair cropped and dyed dark brown, so that in the unlikely event of anyone spotting her, there would be no suspicion aroused and she could just be explained as 'a distant relative who was visiting'. A routine had been established, and keeping her concealed had become an accepted part of daily life for everyone in the house.

When the weather was fine, she was able to go out into the secluded high-walled rectangle of garden at the back of the main building, where Elis cultivated his vegetables and kept his tool shed. Here she would sit happily on the lawn, safely enclosed from the cliffs beyond, making daisy chains and singing to herself under the watchful eye of Elis, who was delighted to have her home. It was as though a great weight had been lifted from his shoulders: seeing Cyw in the hospital had tormented him. He had always wondered why she'd reacted to Iolo Morgan in the way she had, and it troubled him. After all, she'd encountered Morgan on several previous occasions and seemed fairly indifferent to him. Maybe a random thought had just come to her out of the blue and she had seen red. But she never spoke of it, never offered any kind of explanation, even at the time – Elis had tried to ask her once but she just stared at him blankly, then touched his face gently and laughed. He couldn't be sure she actually remembered what she had done or why. Cyw was a closed book. Trying to probe her would have just caused her distress, and that was the last thing he wanted.

Lewis, too, grew fond of Cyw and would bring her small gifts as one might for a child – comics, colouring books and pens, bars of chocolate. He knew with conviction that they'd done the right thing by bringing her back to Ty Coed Pinwydd. There was no question of her being a danger to anyone.

It was only after a year that Lewis heard the first mention of the little girl. Walking into the kitchen one afternoon, he inadvertently interrupted a conversation between Gwyn and Awel about Gwyn's brother, Aron. He knew that there had been a major falling-out between them, but wasn't sure what had been at the heart of it.

'I miss her so much, but he refuses point-blank. Says it'll disrupt Lowri and he's not prepared to let Cyw see her. Plus, I think he's concerned Alison will reject the poor child totally if Cyw's back on the scene.'

'*Pwy sy'n* Lowri?'

Lewis looked questioningly from Gwyn to Awel. They

exchanged uncomfortable glances, Awel's permanently pallid cheeks flushing unwontedly.

Elis came in, having been called out to collect an elderly man who had passed away in the village. Realising something was afoot, he turned to Awel apprehensively.

What's going on? he signed.

Everyone stood for a moment as though frozen in time.

'Sit down, Lewis,' Gwyn instructed eventually. Lewis's eyes travelled warily from Gwyn to Awel and back. He pulled up a chair and waited expectantly.

Gwyn sat opposite him at the table looking almost apologetic, twisting her fingers awkwardly as if unsure what she should say. She exhaled deeply as she took the plunge.

He was almost one of the family now. He had a right to know.

CHAPTER THIRTY-TWO

Present Day

The strange woman gazed at me in stunned disbelief. *'Paid â dweud celwddau!'*

She rose and stepped forward slowly, looking me up and down like some sort of specimen. My fear gave way to anger as she stretched out a wizened hand and I withdrew sharply.

'Don't touch me!'

She looked startled and backed away. Even above the dampness of the cellar, I could smell her now; that same musky fragrance that seemed to have been following me for days.

What's going on here? Who is she, Elis? I signed. The woman's movements were jerky and rapid, putting me on edge. I was on pins, expecting her to lunge at me again. This uncomfortable stand-off could have been no more than a few seconds, but looking back now it felt as though time had stood still.

Elis's eyes met mine, his expression earnest; almost pleading. He was clearly struggling with what he had to tell me. I had the feeling I was in for some sort of bomb-shell.

This is Cwy. That's what we always call her, anyway. He exhaled deeply, one hand reaching towards the woman now as though pre-empting some sort of reaction from her. He spoke rather than signed the words in his deep, faltering voice.

'She's . . . she's Gwyn's sister, Carys.'

I couldn't take it in. I stood staring at her and the harder I looked, beyond the lined skin, the softened jawline and wide, anguished eyes, the more the resemblance became apparent. Elis hesitated as he glanced from the dishevelled creature and back to me.

Lowri, she's your mammy.

CHAPTER THIRTY-THREE

The Past, 1993

Lewis could hardly believe what he had been told. The circumstances were shocking. No one seemed to know for certain who had fathered the little girl, but with the way that Cyw had reacted to the man, everything seemed to point to Iolo Morgan. Both Gwyn and Awel were convinced of it – but they had kept their suspicions from Elis, worried that he might take matters into his own hands. He was in blissful ignorance of the whispers within the community and they were happy to keep it that way. They had agreed between them to attribute the pregnancy to one of several itinerant casual workers who had worked for the business briefly, then moved on. It seemed the most sensible thing to do.

There was no way in the world that a simple soul like Cyw would have given herself to anyone willingly, much less a middle-aged, unkempt brute like Morgan. But proving rape, when nothing had been suspected until her pregnancy became evident months later, would have been near impossible, since Cyw seemed to have blocked it all from her memory. She had withdrawn into herself and didn't speak for weeks after the assault. Because she could be such a strange character, no one had been overly concerned initially. It was only when the pregnancy came to light that the family suspected she had been suffering some sort of post-traumatic stress.

Even if she *had* been able to express what had happened to her and who had done it, she would probably have been considered an unreliable witness. Attempting to identify the father through the baby's DNA wouldn't necessarily provide sufficient proof that Morgan had violated her. For someone to take advantage of a young woman as vulnerable and innocent as Cyw made them a twisted monster in Lewis's eyes. He felt sick to his stomach.

'I'll kill him,' he growled, anger turning his cheeks red, his fists tightened into pugilistic balls.

'You will *not*,' said Gwyn quietly. 'Why d'you think we didn't tell Elis? That man has already taken too much from too many people. He isn't going to rob you of your liberty as well. He'll get his comeuppance one day, you can be sure of that. No one can behave the way he has all his life without getting their just deserts eventually.'

Lewis said nothing. He thought of how Morgan had reduced his poor, timid mother to a wreck, the nights spent listening to the unbearable sound of her sobbing and pleading with the swine not to do this or that; how he had belittled and humiliated Lewis himself in front of anyone and everyone when he was only a child. The pitying looks from people in the community whenever he was sent on errands, or left waiting for hours outside one pub or another like a neglected dog those miserable few months after his mother's death, while Morgan drank himself into a stupor. He could feel it in everyone's eyes: *that poor boy*. The man had pissed most of Lewis's inheritance up the wall and thrown Awel and Elis out of their home. And now *this*.

Lewis had been saddened to hear Lowri's story. She was only two years old when her mother had been, to all intents and purposes, incarcerated, following her attack on Iolo Morgan. There had been no proposal for a review any time soon: as the assault had been ostensibly motiveless, she was deemed a danger to herself and others, and the recommendation had been that she should remain at Ysbyty Gadlys indefinitely.

While without question Cyw adored her daughter, she could never have taken care of her without help. It would have been like expecting a child to raise Lowri. Gwyn wouldn't have dreamed of putting the little girl into care. But when Cyw was locked up, the whole situation had changed. After much soul-searching, Gwyn had come to the conclusion that her brother Aron and his wife, Alison, would be the best people to bring Lowri up. They had been unable to have a baby of their own and were younger and fitter than Gwyn herself. It wasn't a decision she had taken lightly, and she had spent many a sleepless night mulling it over. But ultimately it seemed like the right thing to do: to send the little girl to live with people who could give her a decent life in a regular family environment. Of course, Lowri could come to visit often – she would always be welcome at Ty Coed Pinwydd. But since her birth mother would no longer be living there, it had seemed only fair to give the child the opportunity of a stable upbringing. Even if it had broken Gwyn's heart to see her go.

The return of Cyw ten years down the line had thrown everything into turmoil. Lewis could see the situation from both sides: Aron and Alison had raised Lowri as their own and would undoubtedly feel sidelined, plus reintroducing the girl to her natural mother when she had no knowledge or even memory of Cyw's existence might confuse her. Gwyn had been adamant that Lowri was old enough now to understand and to meet Cyw, who equally had every right to get to know her own daughter once more.

But Aron was having none of it and, after an acrimonious parting, all communication between them had ceased. Gwyn had pleaded with him to change his mind, but he had stubbornly stopped answering her calls and letters. Aron had claimed that, although he'd always put Alison first, he had come to care deeply for Lowri; even though Alison had never been fully able to accept her, the girl was his flesh and blood and he worried about her welfare. Cyw could no more help what had happened to her than if she had been a child, he knew that; but he believed that introducing Cyw and revealing her true identity could be harmful to Lowri, especially on the cusp of puberty. It wasn't a risk he was prepared to take.

His actions were carried out, on the face of things, with the best of intentions. But on the flip side, here was a child unwittingly deprived of contact with her mother and probably no memory of her. It was all quite tragic.

Iolo Morgan was a vile, despicable human being who had ruined so many lives through his callous, self-centred behaviour, breezing through his own existence without a thought for the consequences of his actions or a care in the world. None of this would have happened if it wasn't for him.

Something had to be done about the bastard. He needed to be taught a lesson.

And Lewis intended to make sure it was one he would never forget.

*

Iolo Morgan staggered from the Harbour Hotel in Cemaes Bay, full of ale and the buzz from the tantalising knowledge he had recently acquired. Who'd have thought it? He smiled to himself with the idea of what he could do with this nugget of information; how very useful it could be to him. He would bide his time for now; observe until he had something more concrete. But even this would be something he could use to his advantage. It could make him a very rich man indeed.

He began a covert surveillance campaign over the next fortnight; his van was too conspicuous, so he used his dead wife's old car that had been rusting in the garage the last few years. He took photographs, made notes of dates and times. A portfolio of irrefutable proof. Ha!

Tomorrow he would present what he knew, put forward his proposal and wait for the reaction. It would be an offer too good to refuse.

CHAPTER THIRTY-FOUR

The Past, 1993

As though purged of its rage, the sea meekly lapped the rocks as the sun rose gradually against the hazy violet of the horizon, the dawn full of promise after the unforgiving deluge of the previous night. The wide ridge of seaweed spanning the sand was slowly being reclaimed by the incoming tide. Large, brightly coloured buoys meandered to the surface, bobbing with the flotsam and jetsam waiting to be carried to the extremes of the bay. Eager beachcombers would soon descend onto the sands, hoping for finds of ambergris or other treasures brought in by the waves. A storm at sea always yielded something of interest.

At the far periphery of the deserted bay, a man lay supine, expressionless; glassy, bloodshot eyes staring fixedly skyward. His hair appeared darker than it was in reality, fanned out behind him and billowing slightly in the shallow rock pool which was becoming increasingly discoloured by the seepage from his skull. The once pugnacious jaw lay slack and lopsided, water sluicing through the opened mouth. The limbs, at odds with the angle of the torso, would no doubt have been shattered as he landed. The right arm trailed downwards, its bloated, bloodied fingers limply caressing the water as it inched ever closer to the shoulder. A curious gull alighted briefly behind the rock supporting the head and plucked with some force at the eye socket as though trying to extract a clam from a shell, then took to the sky once more in disappointment, its mournful shrieks penetrating the silence. One by one, others stirred and responded, leaving the crannies of the cliff face to swoop and soar high above the water. Soon the air was filled with their cries, fracturing the peace of the sunrise.

A hooded figure watched with some satisfaction from the cliff path as the tide crept stealthily over the body. Soon the sea would reclaim it and the man would be gone forever, washed away with the putrid stench of his wares and devoured by the marine life that circled the bay. A sea change: wasn't that how Shakespeare had described it? Soon he would become something unrecognisable, no more than decaying meat; food for the fish that had lined his own pockets for so many years. *Full fathom five* . . . the words seemed appropriate now. A fitting end for one who had made his living from these waters. An ocean grave.

Taking gulps of salt and ozone, the figure waited patiently until the body had finally slipped beneath the surface, disappearing as though it had never been there at all. Now for the slow, gruelling ascent back to the little church high on the headland. But despite the trauma and exertions of the previous night, today the climb was to be relished. Today things were resolved and the world had become a brighter place once more.

The face partially shrouded by the hood wore the trace of a smile as the heat of the rising sun grew ever warmer against its back.

It was going to be a glorious morning.

*

It was the landlady from the Harbour Hotel who first remarked on Iolo Morgan's absence. Not that his presence was missed, but very much expected. He lived alone and, while he didn't have any real friends, could be relied upon to put in a nightly appearance, to down several pints and chat and brag to some of the older die-hard regulars. He had last been seen four days earlier, when he had shambled out as usual into the dark at closing time.

Awel had received a visit from two police officers on the sixth day, when a neighbour had reported Morgan's van hadn't left the yard outside his home. She still had a key to the house, so accompanied them to unlock the door. They covered their mouths and noses as the smell of rotting food hit them the instant they walked in. The gas fire was burning in the living room and the house felt like an oven. Flies buzzed round a half-eaten plate of fish and chips left on the kitchen table, dirty crockery piled in the sink.

It was like the *Mary Celeste*. The television had been left on as though its viewer had just left the room. Awel and the officers went through the whole house, even the cupboards, but there was no sign of Morgan.

There would never be any sign again.

CHAPTER THIRTY-FIVE

Present Day

I sat in the kitchen like a zombie, clutching my mobile. I'd intended to call DS Evans, but couldn't bring myself to dial his number. Where would I even begin? I was shell-shocked, barely aware of my surroundings. I couldn't take my eyes off Carys, who, unless she was an accomplished actress, appeared remarkably unperturbed now by my presence. I could see traces of myself in her, and of Ruby, too. There was a familiarity about her frame, her bone structure; her small, quick hands. I had been horrified at first to see how malformed they were. Elis had warned me not to stare as Carys hated it, but I felt almost compelled to. It broke my heart to think what she had been through.

Though she had scoffed initially, Carys seemed nonplussed now by the news that I was her long-lost daughter and as accepting as if I was just someone who had come to read the electricity meter. She had deposited herself gracelessly onto Auntie Gwyn's old chair, her oversized dress hanging like a hammock between her legs, happily eating buttered toast and jam from a plate on her lap and slurping noisily on a mug of tea. She looked over once or twice and gave me a slightly vacant smile. Her face, jam aside, I noted, would have benefited from a good scrub with a flannel and hot soapy water. She looked like an ageing street urchin.

Elis, clearly keen to make himself scarce, had taken Ruby for a walk with Mickey while Awel seized the opportunity to explain the whole bizarre, unpalatable situation to me. My mind was whirring with everything I'd learned. But it was all starting to fall into place.

I couldn't begin to think of Carys as my mother. The very idea seemed absurd. She would always be my father's long-lost sister to me: not even an aunt, as such. In my mind she would forever be the young girl I had always believed her to be, lost to her family in the most tragic of circumstances. To have thought someone dead my whole life, only to find them very much alive and secreted under my own roof, then on top of it all to learn that I was her daughter, was unfathomable. I didn't know how to feel; what to think. My head was spinning with it all.

She was a poor soul; the damage done to her young, vulnerable brain by the virus had left her trapped forever in the naivety of youth, her body permanently mutilated by the resultant septicaemia. The strange, bird-like mannerisms she had acquired had earned her the nickname Cwy, meaning 'chick', from her siblings, and it had stuck.

Fate had dealt her more than her fair share of cruel blows. Her titian locks had faded to the colour of sand, patchy traces of the brown dye used to disguise her still clinging to the tips. Though she had the mentality of a child, she now had the face and physique of a woman approaching old age. It was tragic. I wanted to care for her, but knew I could never love her as a daughter should love their mother. The thought was totally alien to me. Auntie Gwyn had faked her death and brought her back to Ty Coed Pinwydd to spare her a life of undeserved misery in Ysbyty Gadlys. Carys was, after all, her little sister. And Ty Coed Pinwydd was her home.

It explained so much about the people I had always believed to be my parents. I understood now that there had been some agreement with Auntie Gwyn, who had obviously acted in my best interest; or so she thought. She must have believed that, as a childless couple, they would love and cherish me as they would a child they had brought into the world themselves. But they simply couldn't show me parental love that they didn't feel, through no fault of their own.

To his credit, my dad had tried; and I suppose we *were* closely related, even if I wasn't his real daughter. But sadly, the woman I'd always thought of as my mother could never bond with me. Knowing what I did now, it all made perfect sense. Alison had been unable to have a child of her own, and it sounded as though she had been almost coerced into taking me on. Maybe my dad believed that it was killing two birds with one stone:

providing me, his own flesh and blood, with a home, and her with a child to plug the gap in her life. But rather than growing to care for me, it seemed that the older I became, the more she resented my presence. Apparently, she had been desperate to have a baby and became deeply depressed for some years when she discovered she had a medical issue that prevented it. Rather than filling a void, maybe I was simply a constant reminder of that fact; that she felt she'd been forced to accept a consolation prize.

No one can be made to love another person, even a child, whatever the circumstances. I had wanted for nothing, and maybe they thought that in providing for me they were doing their best. But material goods are no substitute for nurture and affection. Every little girl or boy needs to feel loved.

I don't doubt that my dad was genuinely fond of me in his way, but Alison was the love of his life and his priority. Although a little reluctantly on occasions, in an argument, he had always sided with her eventually to keep the peace. Her behaviour was often irrational, as though she was almost on the edge. Perhaps he thought she might have a breakdown – or walk out on us – on *him* – if he seemed to be standing in my corner. After all, one day I would grow up and leave, and then where would he be? I would always take second place.

It made me realise even more, if that were possible, how very precious Ruby was to me. I was beyond grateful that she was safely back and apparently unscathed by her ordeal. Awel was insistent that Carys would never have harmed her, and I had to believe that. The thought that something terrible could have happened to her, even if it wasn't Carys's intention, made me feel physically sick. But despite Awel's pleas, and although torn, I still felt deep down that Carys ought to be turned over to the authorities.

Since Auntie Gwyn's health had begun to fail some months before her death, Awel explained that Carys had become less manageable – less cooperative. Her outbursts of frustration had become more frequent and her behaviour increasingly erratic. She wouldn't let Awel brush her hair and refused point-blank to clean her teeth, something Auntie Gwyn had always overseen. She was even resistant to changing her clothes. Everything had become very much a battle of wills between them. I felt that the onus should probably fall on me to care for her now and wasn't sure I could cope with it all. Plus, if she fell ill and needed medical care, how would we explain her presence at the house? There was so much to consider.

*

'What will happen to Cwy now, Mummy?'

Ruby's quavering voice startled me. I'd been so deep in thought that I hadn't heard them come in. I turned to look at her standing in the kitchen doorway, Elis hovering anxiously behind her, and saw tears glistening in her eyes. Maybe Elis had been explaining about Carys to her. But from her expression and the way she was looking at us both, she had clearly overheard some of my conversation with Awel – how much, I wasn't sure. Her distress was palpable and it made me feel terrible.

'Come here, you.' I pulled her to me, kissing the crown of her head. Her lower lip began to wobble.

My heart sank. 'I was just saying to Awel, I think we ought to take her back to the hospital, sweetheart. They'll probably check her over, make sure she's okay. She needs help and proper care from people who understand her . . . condition.'

'But couldn't *we* help her? This is her home, after all.' She pulled back, looking at me almost accusingly.

Here was I, trying to explain the situation to my daughter as best I could. But even as I said the words, doubt was creeping in.

'It *was* her home, a long time ago. But her family as she knew it is long gone. Look, she'll be much better where the doctors can keep an eye on her, somewhere they can make sure she doesn't wander off and come to any harm. Carys – Cyw – is still like a little girl in her head – she has no real idea of danger. She wouldn't be safe going out anywhere alone.'

'But she managed to look after me – sort of. I think I'd miss her if she had to go. She was actually quite nice really.' She looked wistfully at Carys, sitting oblivious to it all by the range, fussing Mickey and chuckling with all the innocent delight of a child at Christmas.

I wondered now what Ruby and this curious, childlike woman had shared. All the time I had been out of my mind with worry, my daughter had been safe, and, being separated from me aside, probably having something of an adventure. I felt suddenly guilty that I was contemplating sending Carys away again. Whatever she may have been, and as bizarre as it seemed to me, she was

343

still my mother. I realised that she had never meant to cause anyone distress, least of all Ruby. She clearly did what she did with the best of intentions, under Awel's persuasion. From her innocent perspective, she had just been trying to protect a little girl from harm.

I felt my throat tighten. I had begun to question whether I was being selfish, sending Carys back to the potentially soulless existence she had endured in Ysbyty Gadlys; even if things had improved drastically, it was still hardly the ideal environment for her. She wasn't insane; just damaged. And with the stories I'd heard about the disgusting Iolo Morgan, I could understand why she'd reacted to him in the way she had. The very thought of him made my skin crawl. Auntie Gwyn had risked everything to get her out of the hospital, and I could be undoing all her efforts with one ill-judged phone call. I put down my mobile.

'Okay. I won't call the police or the hospital – not just yet, anyway.'

'So you're really going to think about letting Cyw stay and live with us then, Mummy?' Ruby looked up at me, her eyes bright and hopeful.

I cupped her face in my hands. 'I have to think it all through. But I promise I'll try to do the best thing for her. For all of us.'

'Cris, croes tân poeth?'

'Hmm?'

'That's what Cwy said to me once. It means *cross your heart*.'

I needed time alone, to clear my head and think about my dilemma and the possible implications of not turning Carys over to the authorities.

Satisfied that Ruby was in no further danger with Mickey now pinned to her side, I left her in the care of Elis and wandered from the house, still dazed and confused. Almost on autopilot, I found myself walking up to the church. The late morning air felt damp and cool, and a light mist hovered over the turf as I approached. I passed under the stone archway, pausing to look at Auntie Gwyn's grave. I was at odds with my emotions, angry in one way that she had kept so much from me. But knowing her as I did, I realised that she would have only done what she thought was in my best interests. She was of a different, less open generation; one that thought it preferable to sweep secrets under the carpet. To let sleeping dogs lie. Maybe she thought if I discovered I'd been born as the result of a rape, it would have blighted my existence growing up. She may well have been right – perhaps I was better equipped to cope with such knowledge as an adult. But it was the realisation that my parents, as I'd always thought of them, were not my parents at all, which had really thrown me into turmoil. The reality seemed far worse, even, than the idea of the man who had raised me having secretly fathered a child with a teen-ager. That my natural mother was as much of a child in her head as Ruby – and my real father a monster. It all made me question myself – almost as though my whole life, my very existence, was a lie. There had been so many earth-shattering revelations that my head began to hurt.

Awel had blurted everything out. Now that I knew about Carys and the true nature of our genetic connection, I suppose there was no longer any reason to hold back. I wasn't sure how much more I could digest in one day. It had felt like one punch to the gut after another.

'My – our – father assaulted me once.' The admission was clearly difficult for her, as if saying it aloud made it all the more real. She had seemed to shrink somehow, her voice becoming distant as she relived her nightmare. 'I was nineteen – still living in the family home, of course; before Elis and I moved to Ty Coed Pinwydd.'

Her eyes travelled unseeingly to Auntie Gwyn's empty chair. 'He had come home blind drunk. Nothing new in that, but on this occasion, he came into my room. I was sleeping – felt someone's hands on me. Can you *imagine* . . .' She shook her head in blatant revulsion, took a deep, juddering breath. Her hand gravitated to her throat defensively. 'It only happened that once. I never told a soul, not even Gwyn, the full extent of what he'd tried to do. I managed to fight him off, kicked him where it hurt. But before he passed out on the floor, he punched me in the face.' She pointed to her mouth, her face lined with pain. 'Hence the false teeth. I couldn't hide what had happened there, could I? Not nice having to wear these before your twentieth birthday, I can tell you. And do you know what he said? *No man will ever want you now*. And he laughed. He actually *laughed* at me. The bastard. The filthy rotten *bastard*.'

I couldn't – no, didn't want to – believe that the man who was my real father had been such a lowlife. It made me feel nauseous to think of it; to know that I was related by blood to someone capable of anything so repulsive. My stomach lurched as I thought now of little Beca, her life cut short and, it would appear, at the hands of the same man who had taken advantage of her young, guileless mother. I thought too of Lewis, and the years of sheer misery he must have endured at the hands of his stepfather, and what his poor, downtrodden mother's existence must have been like for her to have taken her own life. Of how callously and disgracefully Morgan had treated Awel and Elis, his own children.

My half-sister and brother. I couldn't get my head round the idea at all. At what point had Awel and Auntie Gwyn begun to suspect that Morgan was my father? Was that why Awel had seemed so hostile towards me as a child? There was so much more that I wanted – *needed* – to know. From believing myself an only child all my life, I'd discovered that I actually had three half-siblings, one of whom I would never have the chance to know. Maybe there were more out there – who knew? My whole identity had been built on fabrication; that much I now understood. But the discovery about Iolo Morgan had left me reeling.

And what had become of him? No remains had ever been found and yet he must be dead. He would surely never have just walked out on his life and taken nothing with him. Maybe Awel was right – that he had drunkenly fallen into the sea or the reservoir. I just wished that a body had actually been discovered. Even though I knew in my heart that he was unlikely to reappear and posed no threat, it would have put my mind at ease. The spectre of him would forever now be lurking in the background, waiting to catch me unawares. It was a deeply unsettling thought.

Awel had been excruciatingly candid about everything – and deeply apologetic. It was clear that she bitterly regretted now what had happened. I could, to some extent, understand, if not condone, her behaviour. I truly believed she needed psychotherapy or, at the very least, counselling.

Enraged and profoundly hurt by the contents of the will as she was, I had become the focus for her anger. In the heat of the moment, she had been determined to teach me a lesson. She must have been a simmering mass of anger and resentment her whole adult life, and what she saw as a cruel snub from Auntie Gwyn was just the final straw.

Awel admitted to actively encouraging Carys to take Ruby without really thinking of the consequences. Things had just escalated, and by the time the police were involved, particularly after the discovery of Beca Bennion, it had seemed too late to undo what had been done.

I stood staring out to sea. There was a pod of four or five harbour porpoises dipping in and out of the gently rolling waves, guillemots flew to and from the crag, feeding their young; terns coasted lazily on the air currents with outstretched wings. Evidence of nature at one with the most peaceful place on earth – and yet here was I, struggling with inner conflict and my conscience. If I'd been religious, I might have prayed for spiritual guidance. I could certainly have done with advice from somewhere.

'Hello.'

A voice from behind shook me abruptly from my reverie. With everything else going round my head, I had almost forgotten that this was the same place Catrin's body had been discovered only days earlier.

My heart racing, I whipped round to find Lewis standing on the path. I clapped a hand to my chest, exhaling with relief. He looked as though he hadn't slept for a week; bedhead hair, his clothes rumpled, several days' stubble sprouting from his chin. His eyes were sunken and his normally healthy complexion pale. He offered me a tentative smile, searching my face for a reaction. I straightened, collecting my thoughts.

'Christ, you frightened the life out of me.'

'Sorry.' He looked uneasy. 'I went to the house, but Elis said you'd gone for a walk. Took a lucky guess.' His eyes lingered on the grave. 'Can we talk?'

'I thought we already were . . .'

'No, you know. I mean *properly* talk. I feel like I've got some explaining to do.'

Maybe I should have, but I felt no animosity towards him. He looked as though he'd been through the mill, and I was sure that what had happened to Catrin must have devastated him, even if he no longer loved her. 'I don't know if I can cope with any more revelations just now. But as long as you're not going to hit me with another bombshell, then sure.'

'We could go and sit in the church.'

I looked up at the building. It was cold and draughty, and I suddenly needed warmth and comfort. 'Could we go to your place instead?'

Lewis pulled a face. 'It's a bit of a mess at the moment.'

'I think I can cope.'

He had left his van in the little car park, a stone's throw from the entrance. We drove the short distance back to his cottage in relative silence. I wasn't sure what to say to him and his body language was self-conscious and awkward. He badly needed to wash and the fumes of last night's alcohol were overpowering. I wondered if he should actually be driving. I opened the window and relished the intake of clean air.

As we climbed from the van, two journalists, a man and a woman, appeared as if from nowhere and approached Lewis's cottage, their cameras clicking. It seemed the news of Ruby's disappearance had been knocked from the top slot.

'Mr Bevan – can you spare us a few minutes?'

'Mr Bevan – is it true that you and Catrin were no longer an item?'

We ignored them and marched swiftly to the door.

'Sodding pains. I know they've got a job to do, but you'd think they'd give me a break.'

'Tell me about it. They've been outside our door for days.'

Lewis gave me a lukewarm smile and flushed slightly. As we entered, he showed me into the living room, whisking the curtains across to avoid the prying eyes of the press and hastily scooping up several empty beer cans from the floor. 'Have a seat. I'll stick the kettle on.'

The space smelled stale, as though the aftermath of a series of wild parties needed to be scrubbed away. Recent copies of several local newspapers were strewn across the floor, their front covers emblazoned with various sensational headlines about Catrin. '*MYSTERY DEATH OF BLONDE BEAUTY*' shouted one. '*POSSIBLE DRUGS CONNECTIONS TO LOCAL GIRL'S DEATH*' declared another.

Her pouting image stared out, making me shudder.

Still the elephant in the room loomed between us, as we sat opposite one another on the armchairs, nursing steaming mugs of coffee. I could stand it no longer.

'I was really sorry to hear about Catrin. God knows what you must be going through – it's just awful.'

He nodded, his eyes drifting to one of the newspapers on the ground. 'Thanks.'

'Has there been any news?'

He shook his head a fraction. 'The police seem to think there may be some drugs connection. Christ knows what she'd got herself into.' His face was a picture of misery, his voice strained. 'I can't get my head round it at all. It's eating me up. Makes it even harder that we parted on such bad terms.'

'Oh?'

He put down his mug, slopping some of the coffee onto the rug but seeming not to notice. His eyes locked on mine and I felt heat rising in my cheeks.

'She was jealous. Got it into her head that there was something between us.'

'*Us?*' I swallowed. 'But why would she . . .'

'It was just how she was. Oh, that was just the tip of the iceberg – things had been over for months. She was supposed to move out ages ago. It was one excuse after the other. And then a couple of days before she . . . well, she said she'd found somewhere and she'd soon be gone.

And I was so *glad*. But I never wanted anything bad to happen to her, I really didn't. I feel . . . I don't know how I feel. Like shit.'

He stared at the floor, shaking his head. I felt the urge to put my arms around him but resisted. He looked up at me suddenly and I saw that his eyes were glassy with tears.

'I didn't bring you here to talk about Catrin. I wanted to explain – you know, about Ruby. About what happened.'

I straightened in my seat. This was what I'd been waiting for. 'I'm listening.'

He looked earnest. 'I never agreed with Awel's plan – I wanted you to know that. Not that it makes any of it right. I owe you a massive apology. I hope you'll accept it,' he added, searching my face imploringly. 'But I felt I had no choice. She assured me it'd all be over very quickly, that she'd make Cyw give her back within twenty-four hours. And I knew that Cyw would never hurt Ruby.' He smiled wanly. 'She's a gentle soul. I'm sure you've realised that.'

'Well, yes,' I conceded. 'From what I've seen of her, she wouldn't hurt a fly.'

'Still, I know none of this makes it okay. It seems that Cyw took things into her own hands – going AWOL like she did to begin with, refusing to play ball. She didn't understand, of course, what was going on. Thought Ruby really was in some sort of danger. I don't think Awel banked on that. And then when the cops found Beca Bennion – well, everything went completely tits up. Right from the get-go, I kept telling Awel to come clean with you, before things went too far. But she started to panic. It was like she'd dug herself into a hole and she was burying Elis and me along with her.'

'You could have told me, or maybe tipped off the police anonymously.' The angry memory of what I'd been through came to the fore once again and I could feel the tremor in my voice. 'I've been through some crap in my time, but this has been the worst thing I've ever had to endure in my entire life. You could have put a stop to it, if you'd really wanted to.'

He burrowed his face into his palms for a moment, then pushed back his hair with both hands.

'I know, and I feel terrible about it. But all I could think was what would happen to Cyw – and how Catrin would probably spill the beans about us rescuing her and everything. It would all have been for nothing. And Awel kept reminding me of how much she'd helped me, and everything Gwyn had done for me, and then she'd left me the money, and . . . oh, my head was all over the fucking place. I couldn't see the wood for the trees.'

I nodded slowly. It was obvious that he felt desperately sorry for his part in it all and I couldn't hate him. In spite of everything, I couldn't deny that I was still strongly attracted to him and my feelings left me confused. I needed time to work it all out in my head.

I stood up. 'Look, I'd better get back. My daughter has only been home for five minutes and I want to spend some time with her. Maybe – maybe you could come over tomorrow, have a bite to eat with us or something. I've got a lot of thinking to do, but even after everything that's gone on, I still reckon Llanbadrig is probably a good place for a child to be brought up. I want what's best for Ruby, and my gut feeling is that we'll find it here.'

I thought for a moment. 'And I think I really ought to get to know my mother.'

Lewis dropped me right outside the door of Ty Coed Pinwydd, his mood seeming to have lifted a little.

'Lowri,' he called through the open window of the van, as I mounted the step. I turned to look back at him.

'Yes?'

His earnest blue eyes sought mine and, in spite of everything, I found my pulse quickening, the thrill of the moment catching me off guard.

'Thank you.'

*

The heavy knock on the door later that afternoon sounded ominous. Something in my stomach swung like a pendulum as I saw the flash of blue lights outside through the fanlight. My first thought as I answered it was that the police had come for Carys; that someone must have tipped them off. Or that they had learned somehow what had happened to Ruby. But DS Evans's grave expression and the number of officers accompanying him told me instantly that it was something far more serious.

I could not have been more shocked with the actual reason for their visit.

CHAPTER THIRTY-SIX

Present Day

Police cars stretched across the gateway to the house. A couple of male journalists who had been camped outside for much of the day were now sitting together in a dark blue SUV parked opposite the entrance, apparently comparing notes. Daylight had started to fade, and with it the small gathering of nosy locals on the road had eventually begun to disperse. A fine drizzle had been falling for the last hour or so, leaving the onlookers damp and somewhat dishevelled. The chill descending with the evening air had finally overridden their curiosity and had obviously been enough to finally send them scuttling for the refuge of their living rooms and central heating.

Illuminated by the porch light, two uniformed officers stood in conversation below the front step as members of the forensic team, dressed in white hooded boiler suits, came and went. We sat in silence in the kitchen. The atmosphere was tense; one of stunned disbelief on my part, Awel and Elis sheepish and contrite. As well as the stock cupboard in the mortuary, the entire contents of Awel's pantry and kitchen medical cabinet had been removed, everything bagged up to take back to the lab for analysis.

I'd thought Rhodri Price seemed such a nice man. I couldn't take it in. It was completely shocking to think he could have been capable of such a thing. I couldn't pretend I'd been keen on his father, but to think he had ended up in the way he had was abhorrent. I wondered what on earth had made Rhodri do it. He must have just flipped. It sounded as though he'd slipped up by discarding a receipt from the Tesco superstore in Holyhead into a wastepaper bin in the family home. Amongst the items bought were two costly bottles of whisky, one of which was found in Iwan Price's hotel room. The last four digits of Rhodri's payment card had betrayed him – plus, Iwan couldn't possibly have bought them himself on the date the receipt was printed, having been away at a conference in Powys apparently.

It was common knowledge that they didn't get along, but patricide took it to a whole new level. And the suspicion that this may all have had some connection to Catrin's murder was even more terrifying. Had he killed her, too? It just went to show how deceptive appearances could be.

I was convinced Awel would have had no part in something *that* despicable. I had to believe her when she told me, and then the police, that she'd given Rhodri the formaldehyde with no idea why he wanted it. She had been so frank about everything else, I saw no reason for her to lie any more.

*

The second she had heard the sound of car doors slamming, Carys had grabbed Ruby by the hand and steered her hurriedly from the kitchen and down the passageway, past the preparation room and towards the door which led ultimately to the hidden rooms; the secret labyrinth of corridors which effectively concealed a house within a house. It was clearly something she had done a thousand times before, and she seemed to treat it like a game, her eyes bright and almost gleeful. I knew I would have to come clean about what had happened to DS Evans, but was grateful to be bought a little extra time while I thought how I would explain my delay in reporting Ruby's safe return. But this latest development seemed to have trumped it all.

Awel's voice cut through the stillness, startling me from my thoughts.

'You aren't going to tell the police *everything*, are you?' She spoke in a low voice. I lifted my head to see her gazing at me across the table, in the caring way one might look at an anxious child. I must have looked like a rabbit caught in the headlights.

'I don't mean about *this* – I had no part in Iwan Price's demise, I swear it. But if they knew Cyw's true identity, it would undo everything Gwyn set out to do. And it would reveal the secret we've all fought so hard to keep all these years – not to mention damage Gwyn's reputation and that of the business.' She dropped her eyes and I could see they had filled with tears. 'Please – think about what I'm saying. I'm so sorry for everything you've been through. I was hurt and angry. Not that it's any excuse, but I hope you can try to understand.'

I had already made my decision. In spite of everything, I couldn't send Carys back to the psychiatric hospital with a clear conscience. It would be the ultimate betrayal; both of her and of what Auntie Gwyn had put herself, and the others, on the line to do. I understood how Elis and Lewis, although vehemently opposed to Awel's plan, had felt they had to go along with it all. Lewis had essentially been paid for his contribution and Awel had wasted no time in reminding him of the fact; Elis was wracked with guilt, wondering if things he'd told Cyw about how Iolo Morgan had treated him as a child had further fuelled her rage towards the man and caused her to attack him in the way she had. And equally he felt torn because of his loyalty to Awel, who had looked after him for most of his life. In truth, they had all been in it up to their necks.

At the end of the day, what they'd done was illegal, even if they *had* acted in the interest of Carys's welfare. They'd managed to keep her presence in the house concealed for all those years and, with the routine they'd established, I could see how it had obviously become easier to do so over time. There were no immediate neighbours; the rear garden was enclosed by a high wall which shielded it from the cliffs, so she could go outside safely without fear of being seen. With her short, dark hair, even if she *had* been glimpsed, they had a plausible explanation at the ready. As the years passed, they had become more relaxed about things. Everyone in the community believed Carys dead, and soon she would be a distant memory, except to those who had been closest to her.

Only since Auntie Gwyn had fallen ill and her subsequent death had things started to go awry. Losing her sister must have been deeply traumatic for poor Carys and rebelling as she had was the only way she could exert some sort of control over her own existence. Perhaps she was trying to express her feelings, a sorrow she didn't fully understand herself. I felt sure that as time passed, she would settle once again, become more amenable. She seemed to have bonded with Ruby – hopefully that would help things along.

I knew that if we all pulled together, we could make it work again; lay down ground rules about where Carys could wander and when. Maybe Ruby could persuade her to have her hair cut and dyed as she had in the past, if necessary. It seemed bizarre but, even though she was my mother, I was going to have to treat her as if she were a child, create some sort of order and structure for her. We could keep her safe and her existence secret. Between us, we could make it work.

I felt I had no option, other than to form an uneasy alliance with Awel; with them all. Try to forgive and put my nightmare behind me; to carry on with what Auntie Gwyn would have wanted me to do. To come to terms with the discomfiting truth of my parentage. To build a better, more secure future for my daughter.

I knew, however, that I would have to inform the police that Ruby had been returned to me, safe and unharmed. How on earth was I going to explain her miraculous reappearance? But something Awel had said when I first arrived had planted a seed: *what about my ex, Darren? Were we still in touch? Didn't he ever ask to see Ruby?*

I had never officially blocked his access to my daughter – there had been no need, since he'd shown no real interest in her for years. Supposing she'd called him to say she was miserable? Partially out of spite towards me, he had come to take her away without informing anyone, then relented when she became a nuisance and wanted to return to Ty Coed Pinwydd. It was plausible. I'd heard a rumour some months before that he had moved to Shropshire with his latest partner. It would have been easy enough for him to collect Ruby and then bring her back when it had all got too much for him. He wouldn't have committed any actual crime, even if he didn't come out of it in a good light – after all, he was still her stepfather. And he could deny it all he wanted – it would be my word against his, and there weren't many who'd be prepared to give him a glowing character reference.

It could have just been a stupid misunderstanding arising from an ongoing petty domestic dispute, as far as the police were concerned. They would probably be very pissed off, but I was fairly sure they wouldn't pursue the matter further.

I thought back to how Darren had behaved towards me, a relatively brief but totally miserable episode in my life I never wanted to revisit. I'd been incredibly foolish to be drawn in by him: something I realised too late and lived to bitterly regret. Worse was his blatant indifference towards Ruby – and the fact he couldn't even be bothered to inquire about her welfare when she'd been declared missing spoke volumes about the kind of man he really was.

The more I considered the idea of blaming Ruby's disappearance on my amoral ex, the more I thought it just might work. I had no qualms about using Darren, nor of making him the villain of the piece – as far as I was concerned, he owed me one. He had treated both Ruby and me appallingly. But I knew that I'd have to involve Ruby in the deception, and it didn't sit well with me. She was such an innocent little soul, and asking her to lie made me feel like a terrible mother. Although on this occasion, maybe the ends would justify the means.

I watched from the door as Awel climbed into the police car. She looked back anxiously over her shoulder as it pulled out of the driveway. I was confident she would soon be released.

I raised a hand and waved.

*

I'd thought long and hard about what I was going to say. Where to even start? So much had happened, it seemed like a flight of fantasy. If I hadn't lived through it all myself, I would never have believed it.

Picking up my phone, I dialled Nina's number once again. She was the one person I knew I owed the whole unadulterated truth, before she heard a distorted version from elsewhere.

Hearing the familiar warmth of her voice, I took a deep breath.

'Nina? You're never going to believe this . . .'

EPILOGUE

Present Day, 5th August 2014

Rhodri Price had zipped up his suitcase with a subdued sense of satisfaction – that justice had finally been done. It seemed appropriate somehow that Dr Iwan Price had ended his days in a hotel bedroom. How many of these had borne witness to his sleazy, illicit liaisons in the past, his wheedling and flattery of foolish, lonely middle-aged women, all for financial gain? And worse still, the ego trip he'd got from his manipulation and seduction of younger girls who wouldn't have looked at him twice, had it not been for his access to the recreational drugs they craved. Iwan had been a lecherous, amoral philanderer, had constantly belittled and humiliated Rhodri and his mother, but Rhodri had never wanted to believe *that* of him. Not really. Lowri's DNA test had confirmed his worst fears.

He had confronted Iwan in his suite after the medical conference in Powys. His father was already stupidly drunk on the free alcohol provided by the hosts, naked but for the hotel's complimentary towelling robe. Rhodri hadn't attended the gathering himself, making the excuse that he couldn't justify spending two nights away when he had patients who might need him, and that his father could feed back anything useful he had learned. Which was partially true: Rhodri was faithful to his vocation. Hopefully after all this, the surgery would be able to find a suitable replacement for them both quickly. There were several decent locums in the area; of that he was confident.

Maybe it was the drink, and the tell-tale remnants of white powder Iwan had recently inhaled from the coffee table; or perhaps it was a combination, of his excesses and the relief of confessing what he had done with no fear of recriminations. After all, Rhodri was his son. And he had come bearing a gift!

Iwan had been arrogant enough to assume that, in spite of the appalling way he'd treated him and his mother, Rhodri would never shop him to the police. He had completely underestimated the depth of his son's hatred for him. As the horror of it all spilled out, Rhodri knew with complete conviction what he needed to do, for everyone's sake. And for that of his own self-respect.

Carys Hughes Owen may have had the body of a woman, but she was well and truly trapped in the mind of a child. His father's actions had been unspeakable – a total breach of trust in view of his professional standing; despicable and inexcusable as a human being.

It was ironic that, in certain circles, rumours abounded

of Iolo Morgan fathering Carys's child. He'd made a useful scapegoat and it suited Iwan very well that it had diverted any suspicion from himself, if indeed there was any. And whether Morgan was aware of what people were saying or not, it would have been water off a duck's back to him – he cared little about public opinion. But the dim-witted fishmonger had noticed Iwan speaking to Rhian Bennion once or twice. The man hadn't thought too much about it at the time. Several years after she had died, however, when her young daughter disappeared, an overheard hushed conversation in the pub between two known local druggies had set him to thinking. He obviously intended to use what he had discovered to his financial advantage. But Iwan wasn't about to take it lying down. He agreed to meet Morgan under the shelter of the portico at Llanbadrig church, but failed to show up. After waiting for an hour in the dark, the man had emerged, cursing him. And Iwan was waiting with a sizeable lump of rock, that he brought crashing down on Morgan's unsuspecting head.

The man probably deserved what he had got; he was an inveterate bully and had brought misery to all those whose lives he had touched. But Morgan wore his heart on his sleeve – no one was in any doubt of what he was about, and he had never attempted to conceal his unsavoury nature. He lacked intelligence and probably genuinely had no idea just how morally reprehensible his behaviour was.

But Dr Iwan Price – now there was another story altogether. A pillar of the community. A man of moral fibre.

A wolf in sheep's clothing.

It was a shame: under different circumstances, Rhodri could have easily fallen for Lowri. At least nothing had ever developed between them. He shuddered at the thought of what might have been.

It was a clandestine discussion he'd had with his old friend from the forensics lab as they sat in the pub one evening that had set the alarm bells ringing.

'Keep it under your hat, but it looks as though the Bennion girl and that little Ruby Morris are closely related. We're awaiting Ruby's mother's swab to see if she and Beca shared the same father. Mind-boggling.'

It was. But something Rhodri's own mother had once said with venom, as she sat staring out of the window, seemed to click into place.

'Doctors – not all of them, but some without a doubt – bury their mistakes.' It had been cryptic: as though she knew something; something more than she was prepared to divulge. But he'd often wondered what she was implying and had had his own suspicions for years. And now he knew for sure.

He had toyed with the idea of writing to Lowri at a later date, maybe explaining everything that had happened. But what would be the point? She'd find out soon enough, anyway. The little girl was still missing – now there was another mystery. His father had denied any knowledge of her whereabouts, and since he'd admitted to – almost *boasted* about, in fact – everything else, he had no reason to doubt him. Poor Lowri. So much to contend with. He hoped fervently that her daughter would turn up – one positive to cancel out some of the shit pile that his father had created. It could be enough to send the woman to an early grave, otherwise.

The thought of poor, innocent Beca Bennion, striding out full of hope to meet the father she thought would fill a gap in her lonely little life, only to have it ended so cruelly and prematurely by the person she thought would be her protector: the writer of the carelessly scribbled incriminating note that her mother Rhian had squirrelled away, waiting to be discovered. That someone – much less his own father – could have impregnated a teenage girl, who had essentially provided sexual favours in return for a ready supply of methadone, filled Rhodri with revulsion.

Foolish, empty-headed Catrin – after their brief dalliance, thinking she could extort more money from Iwan with the threat of exposing him for what he really was. 'Sugar Daddy' – that was what she had always called him. Playful, but with more than a hint of contempt. Her greed had ultimately led to her downfall. Could she not see that he would never let her get away with it? The man had no conscience; his only aim was self-preservation.

Iwan had even laughed when he'd told Rhodri.

'Silly little tart. So much peroxide in her hair, it used to fall out everywhere,' he'd said scornfully. 'If the *heddlu* had been more on the ball, they'd have found her DNA all over my car.'

He seemed to have taken a perverse pleasure in disposing of her by the church – the intention had been to roll her off the cliffs, in the same way he had Iolo

367

Morgan. The appearance of a night jogger in the distance forced him to abandon her lifeless body. He'd seemed conceitedly confident that no one would ever make the connection with him. That his self-perceived superior intellect set him high on an untouchable pedestal.

Rhodri had left clues to Catrin's murder back at the house: Iwan's car keys, along with a lipstick-smeared tissue and empty condom wrapper he'd found under the passenger seat; bank statements showing large, unexplained cash withdrawals. It might take the police a little longer to unravel what had happened to Beca Bennion, but he was sure they would eventually piece everything together. Maybe other vulnerable girls who had been in his father's thrall would come forward too, now he was no longer on the scene. He had cast a shadow over the community for too long.

This was for the best all round. Rhodri glanced at the digital clock on the TV screen. Two hours until his departure. Time enough for him to have reached his destination before anyone realised what had happened. Even then, given the evidence of recreational drugs and the empty litre bottle of eighteen-year-old Glenmorangie (Rhodri had been careful to remove the one that had contained the formaldehyde, of course), they would probably assume initially that his heart had given out. With his father's apparent history of cardiac problems, they might not think there was anything suspicious – at least, not until they opened him up. He wondered just how pickled his innards would actually appear.

The truth was, in spite of his lifestyle, Iwan was a sickeningly healthy specimen – or at least, he appeared to be. Rhodri had managed to access his father's medical files electronically and knew how to tweak things. It had been easy enough to manipulate his records to add supporting evidence to the list of medication, should it be necessary: betablockers, statins, a GTN spray. Samples of which had all been left conveniently scattered around the room to be discovered with the corpse. Enough to buy him a little more time.

Taking one last look in the bathroom, he felt slightly queasy at the sight of the ageing naked body slumped over the edge of the bath, its head lolling forward. Already signs of rigor were starting to set in, purplish-red bruises pooling in the extremities, patchy areas of white where it met the side of the tub. He made a mental note to turn up the heating before leaving, to help things along a little.

He'd been oh so careful. Gloves, surgical mask, disposable hooded overalls; even if he'd been caught on CCTV anywhere in the hotel, he would have been unrecognisable in the hat and thick-lensed glasses, the padding beneath his clothes. The room was booked for another twenty-four hours. He would leave the DO NOT DISTURB sign on the hook, to ensure it wasn't prematurely discovered. He felt slightly guilty about the disconcerting sight that would greet the unfortunate maid. Hopefully she wouldn't be too traumatised.

The police would be sure to search Ty Coed Pinwydd first. His father had visited there often enough and Awel usually offered him tea, or even something stronger. As a GP, Rhodri himself had no use for formaldehyde, but naturally there would be an abundant supply in a funeral home. A post mortem would reveal just how much his father had ingested. It had been easy enough to get him to drink – slipped into a bottle of his favourite (and very expensive) single malt, ostensibly bought as a peace offering after their latest disagreement. Disgusting stuff – even the smell of whisky turned Rhodri's stomach. But worth every penny for his purposes. Fortuitous too, that Iwan's years of cocaine abuse had eroded his sense of smell. Rhodri remembered wincing when he'd read about the inevitable side-effects of drinking embalming fluid. The smallest vessels in the body, those in the eyes, would congeal, causing blindness. Excruciating pain and failure of all vital organs would follow. But the more he'd thought about it, the more he had convinced himself that it was no more than his father deserved.

Awel had handed it over quite readily, with no questions as to its intended purpose. She was of that generation who still regarded anyone in the medical profession with sometimes misguided deference. Of course, they would soon realise that Awel wasn't responsible. But it would all help to deflect the focus from himself – for a while, at least.

He had always wanted to work for Médecins Sans Frontières. The post in Afghanistan seemed almost heaven-sent. Dr Rhodri Price had become *le docteur* Rodell Priaulx. It hadn't been difficult to obtain a fake ID. It was amazing what could be purchased from the Dark Web. His French was fluent enough to be convincing after spending three years on the Côte d'Ivoire. He would grow a beard, shave his hair, lose weight. He could easily disappear into the woodwork.

Making a final sweep of the room, he took a deep breath, closing the door on his father and the past forever.

Tomorrow would see the dawn of a new day.

Tomorrow he would be a different man.

GLOSSARY OF WELSH TERMS

Addo – promise
Alergaidd – allergic
Bechod – shame/pity
Brysia – hurry up
Cariad – darling
Cawl – soup
Crempog – pancake
Cris, croes tân poeth – cross my heart . . .
Diolch yn fawr – thank you very much
Doli glwt – rag doll
Duw anwyl dad – good God
Ffrind – friend
Heddlu – police
Hiraeth – homesickness
Hogan – girl
Nac oes – no
Paid â dweud celwddau – don't tell lies
Panad – cup (of tea)

Pob lwc – good luck
Pwy di hwna – who's this?
Pwy sy'n – who is
Su'mae – how are you / how's it going
Ti'n licio hwn? – do you like that?
Twpsyn – idiot
Ty Coed Pinwydd – Pine Trees House
Wyt ti eisiau bwyd? – do you want food?
Ysbyty – hospital